# DRUMS

*by James Boyd*

**WITH PICTURES BY N. C. WYETH**

Charles Scribner's Sons     *New York*

Fic
Boy

TO KATHARINE—LAMONT—BOYD

In this book the main facts of history have been followed except in two cases: the *Bonhomme Richard* did not sail from Brest but from Lorient; the incident of the vagabond in Chapter XXXV did not occur in Brooks's Club but at another club in London.

J.B.

# ILLUSTRATIONS

## IN COLOR

## PEN DRAWINGS

ILLUSTRATION BY N. C. WYETH

FOR THE ORIGINAL TITLE-PAGE OF DRUMS

# DRUMS

· The Little River Country ·

## BY JAMES BOYD

### WITH PICTURES BY· N·C·WYETH

CHARLES SCRIBNER'S SONS
NEW YORK : LONDON

DRUMS

BOOK I

## CHAPTER I

A FIRE BLAZED in the deep, clay-plastered fireplace; logs of North Carolina pine dripped turpentine in the wave of flame and sent up scrolls of clotted smoke to join the night. The steady, golden light flooded the brick hearth, flooded broad, hand-dressed floor boards beyond, then softening, touched a wall of shaggy logs and gilded the barrel of a flintlock above a closed oak door. Against the ceiling it threw the shadow of a man who sat before it, a man rough-hewn, brown and rugged, so still, so like the room, that he might have been built there when it was built. His short coat and his kilt were brown, his square beard was brown, only the twinkle of silver buttons and a touch of white stock at the throat showed him to be above the common rank.

Outside, the rustle of the pines crept by in long, low waves which came from the Atlantic to the eastward and crossed the forests of the Province on tossing tops to die away against the mountains in the west. Through this

3

deep murmur of the pines the sound of a whistled tune drew nearer, stopped at the door. The hinges creaked; a straight, thin boy, tugging a bucket of water, came in. With his skirted linen hunting shirt blown forward by the wind, his long brown hair blown around his bright-colored face, he looked almost like a girl, or would have looked so, except for the impish set to his mouth. He closed the door behind him with a thrust of his moccasin and swung the wooden bucket under a table in the corner. He gave a manly and professional puff and wiped his hands on the sides of his leather breeches.

"There's the water, Dadder."

"Aye, son, I heard ye. How's the wind?"

"East. But I reckon it might fair. I saw a star."

"If it storms the morrow I'm feared your mother willna come home."

"She said she would."

A half smile just touched the man's broad beard.

"Aye, she did. But she was wearing the new camlet gown."

The boy revolved this saying. He stared in the fire, knitted his brows.

"Now, then, lad." His father was looking at him. The boy started from his thoughts and turned to the table. He must get to work. Work! If it only were real work instead of lessons fit only for girls. He rubbed his small, hard, calloused hands together and threw out his chest. Study was no work for a man of the Pine Forests. But his father's eye remained on him. His chest subsided. Taking a horn spelling book and a Latin grammar from a shelf, he stretched himself on his stomach before the fire and peered at the dim letters through the yellow glazed sheet. As he murmured them over to himself he heard his father fumble in his pocket for his pipe, strike his tinder-box, settle back in his chair with slow, measured puffs.

The wind had made him sleepy, his eyes blinked in the firelight; but each time the letters began to fade, another puff from the pipe brought him back. He winked rapidly and put his mind on the words, words meaningless and dead compared to the life of the pine forest in which he spent his days, the life of gray foxes, muskrats, deer, wolves, dark swamp rabbits—another puff—he must get on.

"I've done the row, Dadder." He handed up the book, then rose to his feet with smooth ease and brought from the shelf a goose quill, an ink-horn, a small box of sand and a sheet of paper. Seated cross-legged by the fire, he held the paper on a board.

"Ten times," his father said, "for every word wrong and twenty for 'impartiality,' for ye got that wrong last night." The Great Man cleared his throat. " 'Impartiality is an attribute of philosophers.' " The pen scratched, the head bent low, the hair hung around the brown flushed face. " 'Misfortune can not impair true virtue.' " A list of aphorisms followed, some from the book, some gravely composed in his father's profound, deliberate brain. The last was, " 'Monarchs assume infallibility.' " The boy wrote it out, sanded the paper and gave it to his father. It was passed back after an anxious pause.

"Ten 'infallibilities' wi' twa l's; and close your a's at the top. A gentleman is known by the perfection o' his hand."

He wrote the ten "infallibilities." His father scrutinized them.

"Now for the Latin: 'Balbus has built a long, white wall.' "

"Dadder, what does 'Monarchs assume infallibility' mean?"

His father made as if to read from the Latin grammar. But the boy could see him turning the question in his mind.

"It means that kings think they canna do a wrong—that whatever they do is right. Do ye think that's so?"

"I don't know. I reckon so. God makes kings, doesn't He?"

"Aye, and He unmakes them, too. And for the matter of that, who made you—what says your catechism?"

"God made me."

"And do ye say that you can do nae wrong?"

The boy grinned shyly.

"Oh, no," the man went on. "God made a' men and a' can do wrong, kings above the rest, perhaps, what wi' a' the opportunities for sinfulness that are given them." He rubbed his bare knees with stern gusto. "Kings can do wrong, never ye doubt—and I should know, for I've fought for one king and against the son of another."

"Was that Culloden?"

The pipe stopped puffing. There was a pause and a whisper like a sigh, "Aye—Culloden."

"I'd like mighty well to hear about Culloden, Dadder."

"No doubt. But though it is thirty years behind me now, the tale comes no easier. We fought the English and we were beaten—and butchered."

The boy subsided, abashed, and stared in the fire. He saw in the flames a vague turmoil of swords and shields and drifting smoke. If only his father could be moved to tell him the tale, perhaps the fray would take shape. As it was, the dim battle scene, too far removed in time and place to stand out vividly, dissolved before the sharper, more familiar pictures of high adventure and great deeds, which, ever since he could remember, had for his secret delectation, formed, beckoned, vanished among the blazing logs.

There in the steady embers a thin line of Indian fighters, lean mountain men, climbed in single file a cloud-wrapped Western range, at their head himself, a long Deckhard rifle across his fringed arm. Provisions gone, hope gone, still they climbed upward, Westward, following their leader's trail above the timber line.

They crested a rocky summit. Beyond the nestling cloudbanks at their feet stretched the sought-for land, forest and park and plain, bright rivers, rolling hills, slow-moving herds of elk and buffalo. His famished men lifted caps high on rifles and raised a wind-whipped cheer.

Crumbling softly down, a charred log burst in flame, glowed, slowly shifted till it took form. Black towers raised their heads, from the battlements flames waved like banners, a drawbridge crossed a moat below the buttressed wall, a road wound off among the hills.

It needed no more to call up the finest dream of all. The distant road was already astir with moving columns. Now they came nearer; light shone on lance and helmet, on plumes and gold caparisons. Now they were here, all the King's horses and all the King's men.

Waving a silver baton, the Drum Major marched before, the trumpets winked, blared out *ta-ra, ta-ra*. "With a tow and a row and a row, row, row of the British grenadiers!" they played. Red coats and white crossbelts came behind, then the knights peering grimly through closed visors, and the King, himself, in mighty beard, full-bottomed wig and crown.

The King waved his sceptre; they wheeled into line, just as they always did, and faced across the fields where now, just as always, the French lilies on great white flags were waving up the slope. Their great white horses tossed their manes. Drums were rumbling. In the dreadful moment the words his mother had taught him murmured in his ear:

"They now to fight are gone,
Armor on armor shone,
Drum now to drum did groan,
To hear was wonder."

Steadily the white French host breasted the slope; now it was nearly on them. This was the instant!

Yes! From the right a flying cloud of arrows dimmed the white ranks.

"Like a storm suddenly,
The English archery
Struck the French horses."

Another cloud—another! He saw the white horses rear and run, he saw the backs of the crouching bowmen, drawing their bows again.

"With Spanish yew so strong
Arrows a clothyard long,
That like to serpents stung,
Piercing the weather;
None from his fellow starts,
But playing manly parts,
And like true English hearts,
Stuck close together."

The white ranks wavered, broke; the English knights, the red coats, the archers were charging after them.

"Huzzah!" he whispered, "huzzah! huzzah!"

The picture faded. His breath was coming through his teeth, he closed his eyes till his heart stopped pounding, then gave a shiver and a sigh. Try as he would, he could never see himself in this, his favorite dream. England, where men were knightly, brave and splendidly apparelled, was a land not only distant but of unattainable magnificence. Yet was he not a gentleman born? He needed but a suit of armor or a uniform.

His father shifted; he, too, was gazing in the fire. "Culloden," he murmured; his eyes fixed afar, stared through the flames into the burning heart of the ancient tragedy. He was forgetful of all else, forgetful, thought Johnny with a glow of hope, of Balbus and his wall.

"Culloden."

"Yes, Dadder," he said.

His father's eyes were torn from the fire. Beneath their stooping brows, they focused on him.

"Balbus," he said, "has built a long white wall."

The boy was still wrestling with the scratching, sputtering quill, still snatching at the fleeting Latin words, when a broad hand descended, picked up the paper.

"Ye've one word right. That's Balbus. Fetch the sand-glass."

His father turned the sand-glass and set it on the arm of his chair. The ruddy grains trickled from the upper globe.

"An hour by this, I'll give ye tae learn your lesson. If that won't do it," his grim glance fell on his son, "we'll just have tae find another way."

# CHAPTER II

Drawing his head under the coverlet as the early sunlight fell across his face, young Johnny Fraser retreated, turtlewise, from the dull blaze which struck into his dreams, and took up a new position conforming to the hills and valleys of the old flock mattress. The manœuver was performed in his sleep, for by long practice he had learned to know the contours of his bed as well as the Royal Surveyor General knew the topography of the Province. Far from resenting them, he accepted them as implicitly as the Surveyor General accepted the Appalachians. Indeed, they had acquired sanctity; they had somehow become identified with the region of his dreams. They were the hills which he ranged in his sleep, shielding valleys of adventure, sloping to a beckoning sea.

But now discomfort penetrated the dim borderland to which he clung. His new position brought him into contact with a stretch of unwarmed blanket. He raised himself on an elbow, squinting with disgust. The sun

9

came through the wavy English glass of a low window beneath the eaves, it glinted on the patchwork quilt, and lay level, waist high, on the floor. Aloft, the cavernous roof still held the dregs of night where, here and there, the tip of a shingle-peg caught the light and twinkled like a morning star.

Watching his breath mount in the chill, he sat on his hands indecisively. Goose flesh rose on his bare chest and arms; the warmth of his bed was evaporating. "Eheu, by Zooks!" he murmured, not without some pride in his command of objurgation. Bent forward, he rubbed his cold, moist nose on his knee. He listened for his father in the next room: no sound. But in the lean-to kitchen below his window he heard Sophonsiba, the cook, pounding hominy in the mortar. The fire must be well started by now. He took a deep breath and made a dive for his leather breeches.

With his shirt in one hand and his moccasins in the other, he pattered down the stair. "By Zooks, Sofa," he said, "it's mighty frosty!"

Sophonsiba raised a black, leathery face and eyed him coldly.

"Mist' Johnneh, das no way to talk—'Zooks.' " She sniffed. " 'Zooks'—whaffo' you say dat 'zooks'?"

She ran a dark glance over the slim white body.

"Runnin' roun' necked an' cussin'—mm-m-m!"

Her long black hand stole down his arm.

"Why, baby, yo' froze!"

She gathered him to her and chafed the back of his neck with low exclamatory grunts, "M-m-M-M!—froze!" She beat an intricate tattoo on his spine.

He put on his shirt and moccasins. With a regretful glance at the fire, he squared himself for duty. Taking a pinch from the salt box, he went out the back door to the well. It was cold enough, but through the tall grave pines, through the earthly, frosted chill, through his linen shirt, and spare body, right into the centre of him flew the subtle warmth of the rising sun.

Beside the well-hood hung three frayed black-gum twigs on strings. He picked up the smallest and, salting the end, rubbed his teeth vigorously. Then he filled his mouth with water from a gourd and squirted it between his teeth for an incredible distance. He was half through the morning toilet.

He looked up to where a dejected mocking bird was rustling in a sycamore, then across the shimmering, hoar-frosted fields to the somber ring of pines. Cow bells sounded from the pasture by the branch; down in the new ground the four field-hands raised their melancholy chant; the mocking bird twittered disconsolately, a wild turkey-hen fluted from the distant wood. The world, he felt, was wonderful and sad; and he was hungry.

Filling a wooden basin from the bucket, he seized the lumpy ball of soap, lathered his face gingerly, plunged it in the water and groped for the towel. He had forgotten it. "Sofa!" he called, stumbling toward the house. "Sofa! towel!" The word was smothered by the towel itself in Sofa's hand descending on his face and rubbing it unceremoniously.

"Let me alone—I can dry my own face!"

"I 'spect; if somebody git you de towel."

He sat down, glowing, by the fire, his feet tucked back beneath his stool so that the heat would not draw the bear's grease from his moccasins. Sofa handed him a large piece of buttered corn cake and a pewter bowl of milk and hominy sprinkled with brown sugar.

He leaned back after the meal, licking his chops and breathing deep in repletion.

"Now, Mist' Johnneh, you paw say come to de pasture an' he'p fix de fence. De yearlins bust out last night."

He deigned no reply to the voice of authority, but after a pause he rose and moved with calculated negligence into the big room. The cold hearth, the horn-speller on the shelf, silently biding its time, checked his spirits; but as he put on his new coonskin cap with the ringed tail hanging down behind, just like a trapper's, he was re-established in his esteem. He marched out the oak door with long, stealthy strides, his eyes on the path, looking for tracks and signs as trappers do. Unfortunately nothing appeared but the three-pronged marks of the chickens, obliterated at vast and regular intervals by his father's broad boots.

He stopped at the road and looked back carefully at the house. On the frontier, he had heard, a man always looked back at a turning to make sure that he was not pursued by wild beasts or malevolent enemies.

But the old house, sturdy and square, evenly barred with gray logs and streaks of tawny clay, presented no enemy but Sophonsiba throwing the dishwater with a magnificent gesture at a shrieking bevy of hens.

On the road were many hoofprints of fur-traders' pack-horses, a few ruts of freighters' wagons, and at one side the big square tracks of a hound, probably old Grizzly Gray jogging beside his father. He went down the gentle hill to the bottom, he passed the three faint patches of charred embers where twice—and what memorable days they were—Indians had camped over-night on their journey from the mountains to see the Governor at New Bern. Beyond, the snake fence of the pasture began. The pines gave way to cypress and gum trees, close-locked in a dark tangle through whose shade he caught here and there the sheen of ice on a patch of standing water. Following the fence, he thought he saw faint footmarks in the frosted bunch-grass. The dead cane crackled, three shaggy little cows stared at him, motionless. So they had not all gotten out, then. But where was his father? He stopped and listened. At once the silent world was filled with noises, the twitter of a wren, a burst of distant music from the new ground, the "tlot-tlot" of a turkey in the swamp. Frowning, he keyed his sharp ears for the sound of work on the broken fence. Then, just as silence was about to fall, one of the little cows coughed. "You cows!" he shouted. "Git!" and hurled a stick at them. They scampered off like rabbits, waving kinked tails. He listened again; far down the swamp he heard the note of a hound, the voice of Grizzly Gray. "Huzzah!" he thought, "that's him." He hurried on.

The ground was firmer, the trees sparser. Grizzly Gray's voice, wistful, dubious, was right at hand. Ahead, in an opening, he saw the woolen back of his father's waistcoat moving slowly up and down among the broken rails.

Johnny approached with gusto. He had reached the goal by virtue of his woodcraft; many a boy would have taken half a day to find a father in a branch like this; he expanded.

His father half turned; the sight of that firm, omniscient face checked Johnny with a sickening thought. By Zooks, by Zooks, he had forgot his morning prayers. Still, let a good face be put upon the matter. He moved forward briskly, whistling "Barbara Allen."

"Good morning, Dadder."

The big stooped figure rose from the clutter of rails, the eyes looked at him under shaggy brows, benignly austere.

"Good morn, John. Are ye well?"

"Yes, Dadder. Will I bear a hand with——"

"Did ye scour your teeth?"

"Yes, Dadder, Sofa told me——"

"And soap well your ears?"

"Yes, Dadder."

All was lost, the crisis impended, he attempted no further diversion but stood, a lamb for the slaughter.

"And give thanks tae your Maker?"

Johnny's eyes fell to the level of his father's waist and fastened on a large bone button. It had a streak of brown in it—all the others were white, in fact all bone buttons whatsoever were white except this one—and how could a streak of brown get inside a bone?

"Eh, Johnny?"

"I—forgot."

The big head shook slowly, the strong face fell into lines of grief and catastrophe.

"My son, how often have I taught ye? How will ye gain a blessing from Jehovah if ye do not give Him thanks?"

"I—I don't know."

"Ye do not, nor does any man. God is not mocked, ye ken that well. Down on your knees and ask a pardon."

Johnny knelt in the broom-grass, his eyes shut, his hands clasped before his fiery face, while his mind mechanically addressed well-known formal phrases to the Incomprehensible Personage who stood above his father as his father above him, who even now from His mighty seat far beyond the wheeling turkey buzzards and drifting clouds was watching him.

"Amen," he said and opened his eyes. His father, the all-powerful, was kneeling beside him. He fidgeted in an anguish of embarrassment till like a bison the great man heaved up to his feet.

"Now, lad," the voice was kindly, "just ye catch hold of this rail."

Young Johnny warmed his hands, fresh-washed for supper, before the fire. Conscious of growing pangs at his mother's absence, he could not be sure just where they left off and where hunger, sharpened by a day's work on the fence, began. But his father had no notion of eating; he dried his brogues and greased them, his head bent to catch the sound of hoofbeats; he glanced often out the door. The brogues finished, he pulled on a pair of moccasins and sat down outside on the narrow porch, unmoved by the gathering chill. Johnny hugged the fire and stared through the window pane at the wavy outline of his father's back. It disturbed him to discover Omnipotence so agitated; it increased his hunger in a dreary way. He slipped into the kitchen, begged a slice of white side meat from Sophonsiba and bolted it secretively. The act, if discovered, would have been held a sacrilege. But once again before the fire, he saw that his father was still motionless on the porch.

The sand-muffled jog of horses sounded on the road. He was out the door. The red colt was trotting flippantly up the lane. His mother's blue riding cloak was flying out behind, her face was bright. Behind her, old Scipio's teeth and eyes gleamed through the dusk as he bumped along on Grampus.

"Huzzah, huzzah, huzzah!" he shouted as he ran. She waved a hand, the colt snorted. "Huzzah!" she called out like a boy.

She pulled up when he reached her, leaned down and kissed him; he felt her slim arm round his neck and the colt's muzzle nudging his shoulder.

"Where is your father?"

Yes, where was he? He had been forgotten. But there in front of the porch stood the big form, waiting, reserved as always, to receive her at the proper place.

He ran beside his mother up the lane. His father did not stir until she stopped. Then he raised a hand to dismount her.

"Well, ma'm, how is everything wi' you?"

She slipped from the saddle and grinned like a young urchin.

"My thanks for your courteous inquiry. I'm fine. Here, Scipio."

The Negro on the white-furred and ponderous Grampus had just come up. A fowling-piece lay across his pommel, an ancient hanger clanked in its scabbard beside his green surtout. He beamed on the assembly with the benevolence of a titulary Deity, then lowered himself gingerly to the ground. He folded the fowling-piece to his bosom and removed his cocked hat. Grampus seized the moment to pull free and move sedately toward the barn.

"Let him go," John Fraser said.

Scipio hastily advanced toward the colt, who rolled an eye at the fowling-piece and backed.

"Johnny, hold the colt. Scipio, give me that gun."

The Negro's difficulties dissolved—only his hat remained—he could focus on his speech. He thrust a crooked leg behind him and bowed halfway down to his knee buckles.

"Bless you, Masteh, it des does 'spirit me to see you an' young Mist' Johnneh looking so gran' and salubrious. Ah declah——"

"Well, Scipio, I am pleased that ye are come safe home and have taken care of your mistress."

"Yessuh, dasso. Anybody gwine hurt de young missis, 'Bam!' go de gun. 'Bam!' Yessuh."

He sighted along an imaginary musket. Squire Fraser took the colt's reins from Johnny and presented them gravely.

"Rub his back well, Scipio, d'ye mind."

Indoors his mother paused and glanced around her.

"How cheerful it seems! I had near forgot."

"Ah, lass, it's what we feared, Johnny and I."

The kitchen door opened and showed the gaunt Sophonsiba silhouetted against her fire.

"Sofa!" His mother went to her. The woman bent down, kissed her hand. His mother's free arm passed across the peaked shoulders and gathered the ponderous head to her for an instant. Sophonsiba slowly drew herself up, looked down on her with protecting reverence.

"Go fix yo'se'f, Missy. Supper ready."

Taking off her three-cornered hat, his mother ran quickly up the stairs. His father followed her.

Sofa pushed the table before the fire and set three split bottom chairs around it.

"Now, Mist' Johnneh, be sca'ce—sca'ce." She strode to and fro with the pewter dishes. Sitting back against the wall, he watched her vanish into the kitchen and listened with awe to the crash of spoons and crockery. He heard the back door open timidly and Scipio's hesitating step, then Sofa's voice: "Scipio, keep out o' mah track. Let somebody work dat *will* work. Wipe yo' brogans. Whar you get dat white-folks hat?"

His father and mother came down. They took their places at the table, the kitchen clatter subsided, their heads bowed in silent grace. Johnny kept his eyes shut and repeated to himself the prescribed words, "Almighty God, accept, I pray Thee——" Here seductive kitchen airs laden with the fat scent of chicken and fried yams engulfed him; his gills expanded in ungovernable reciprocation, he swallowed and kept on to the end. "Amen." He raised his eyes to Sofa's steaming platters. She placed them on the table with a noise-less rotary thrust, samp, chicken, pork, a dripping golden mound of yams, spoon-bread, and a stone bottle of porter in honor of the occasion.

"Well, ma'm, what news of the Province? Our Johnny would know if the lads of New Bern dinna write a fairer hand and read the building of Cæ-sar's bridge wi'out aid."

Johnny rose to the challenge.

"Maybe they've got book-learning, but I reckon they ain't a one could have trailed you in the big pasture this morning. Mother, I followed Dad-der's tracks——"

"Tut, lad, what did ye but follow the fence? 'Tis naught to boast of."

Johnny subsided, angry and abashed; he could never combat his father's pronouncements. Unassailable, they made him seem tiny and absurd—and yet had he not trailed his father and old Grizzly Gray?

His mother's slim hand slipped into his beneath the table.

"If sonny says he trailed you, Father, why then, sir, he did."

"Nae doubt, nae doubt," his father muttered, "but I'll not have him a boaster."

"No, John, but you'll not have him a liar, neither. And in the matter of boasting, do you yourself grant that there's aught to equal a Highland Scot, or that any Highland Scots are equal to the Frasers,—and where among the Frasers, sir, would you put yourself?"

"Not first," John Fraser said. "There's Simon."

She gave a quick ringing laugh. "And to think that the Moores of Cape Fear reckoned it a comedown when I married you!"

"Ye've come back full of repartee, it seems, and what else have ye learned, my lass?"

"Why, to make a negus and dance the quadrille, to frolick genteelly with the nobility. You should have seen me at the Governor's palace."

"What did ye there?"

"Oh, the Governor and his lady gave a rout in honor of the Assembly. He sat on a throne in a scarlet coat and never left it except to dance with me. Three French horns from Charleston for music; laces, brocades, rapiers, diamond knee-buckles, patches, pomatum, full-bottom wigs; Wylie Jones down from Halifax in his glass coach, gallanting me about till Uncle James forbade it lest the family name lose credit."

" 'Twas well of him. The Frasers have never been lightly talked of."

"Indeed, sir; but Uncle James was thinking of the Moores. And truth to tell, I felt pity for poor Wylie."

"Why should ye? I have seen him on occasion in his ruffles and peruke, a vain young fop."

"But I assure you he grows serious and interests himself in public affairs." John Fraser's beard bristled in a dry smile.

"Has government, then, taken tae dicing and cock-fights?"

"Well, sir, if they had, they would be better employed. As it is they are determined not to remit their silly tax on tea. I think those big-wigs in London must be a set of noddles, for all their stars and garters."

"So it's the tea again, is it? Weel, I'm no a friend tae the English, nor tae taxation neither, but I'm fair tae say that never in all my life have I heard such a howling and yowling as has shaken the Province from one end tae the other over that picayune little thrippence on the pound."

"Indeed, that's not the way they talk at New Bern. Some of the young men breathe fire."

"Aye, and so did I when I was young. The young men make war."

"And the old men provoke them. If the thrippence is picayune, why need those horrid ministers be stiff-necked? I'll warrant they meet their match in North Carolina. Mr. Jones, Mr. Battle, and Mr. Hewes of Edenton, Mr. Harnett of the Cape Fear District, are corresponding with Virginia and other colonies with a purpose to import no more tea from England, nor nothing else beside."

"Very noble of Mr. Jones," John Fraser grinned. "The rich will surrender their luxuries and the poor their necessities."

"Oh!" she burst out, "I've no patience with you. You prove matters. I feel them."

"Aweel," he observed comfortably, "we've the porter." He opened the bottle.

"Allow me, ma'm," he filled her mug and his own, "a drappy for the wee?" Johnny held out his small pewter cup. The brown drink flashed from the bottle-mouth, specks of froth and myriad light-flakes coasted down the stream. In the dull mug the porter swirled, curdled, and threw up a merry, winking foam. He buried his nose in the depths and lapped the bitterish, soothing pool.

They were finishing the meal.

"And what more of Wylie Jones?" his father asked.

"He came to Uncle James' next day to see the red colt."

John Fraser strove to veil the interest in his eye.

"Aye?"

"He wished to buy him."

"Did he now—for how much?"

"Oh, I did not ask. I said he was yours and I knew he was not for sale." He laid an impatient hand on the table.

"Hoots-toots! 'Tis true—but ye might have got his offer. Then we could have tauld the neighbors. It might have been fifty guineas; that would give them something tae wag about."

"Oh, yes, I see," she simulated contrition, then bright intelligence. "You, the Justice of the Peace, a leading Elder and the foremost freeholder in the township—and a Fraser to boot—aim to astonish the neighbors at the price of a horse."

"But can ye not on'erstand that it's one matter to be a foremost citizen and another tae own the best colt—another and, in the opinion of many erring, sinful men, a more important? But ye can not on'erstand, coming as ye do from the Cape Fear, where the horses are little and puny, and altogether inferior tae the horses of the Halifax district."

She was roused. "You may have better horses than we, but we have wild duck and alligators and——"

He rose from the table with a roar.

"Ho! And what figure would an alligator cut on Wylie Jones' race path?"

Sofa cleared the table and dropped a knot of lightwood on the fire. Beyond the closed kitchen door rose the soft murmur of Scipio recounting the glories of the journey. Grizzly Gray scratched outside and was let in, licking greasy chops in a deprecating manner. He advanced to the fire, flopped down noisily, and lay groaning in its heat.

Johnny squatted beside him, sedulously refraining from a glance to the shelf where the Latin grammar crouched in wait. His father, as always, read his thoughts.

"We might let the lessons be, son. Your mother and I will chat."

Here was privilege and dignity. He stretched full length on his back, his hands behind his head, and composed himself to follow their discourse. He was a man, tonight, admitted to the free fellowship of his elders; it behooved him then to take an interest in grave affairs. They talked of the farm, the price of tobacco, salt, slaves, pine deals; their voices droned, blurred into a steady hypnotic hum. He roused himself and shifted, only to sink again in a sea of drowsiness and porter.

# CHAPTER III

Sunday was always, at best, a day of silence, of faint melancholy. After the milking no further sounds of labor were heard. The work horses, nonplussed by unaccustomed leisure, drooped their heads over the paddock fence, the very fields appeared disconsolate, as though nature abhorred this vacuum in the life of toil.

Within the house, good clothes and solemn manner constrained them, their life was hushed and stiff. Only the Negro quarters held signs of merriment, halloos, chuckles, dense chimney smoke laden with smells of yams and pork fat.

This Sunday there was to be preaching; solemnity was multiplied. John Fraser's stock was higher, whiter, tighter. He ate his breakfast with sombre relish, not so much of the food itself as of the sustenance it gave him for devotions to come. Johnny's mother was subdued, submissive to the injunction of Sabbath observance which issued from his father or from God. On such days there was confusion of identity between the two.

THE FRASER FAMILY

*He was crammed, stiff and heated, into the old chaise between his parents*

Johnny himself wore broadcloth, well-brushed black yarn stockings, and a pair of cowhide shoes. Breakfast finished, he was crammed, stiff and heated, into the old chaise between his parents. His father slapped the reins on Grampus' broad white back. They creaked down the lane.

The log church was set back in a hardwood grove within sight of the straggling houses of Blue's Crossing. Gray dogwood leaves, bronze oak, and yellow maple leaves covered the ground. Among bare trees the first comers stood in huddled groups; horses nodded at a hitching rail.

Tying up Grampus, Johnny watched the groups break up, drift toward the Squire by twos and threes. The men shook hands, passed the time of day, the women had a blunt word for his mother, received her chat and laughter grimly, but moved off looking pleased. Here came the blacksmith's girls: they tossed defiant heads at Mr. Fraser, swinging their hips.

"Squire!" they said and flashed black eyes, unwarrantably at ease. Johnny felt excited and nervous. They sent him a broad look. He grinned sheepishly, just raised his hat and joined his father in a heat of angry shyness.

"Trouble is, Squire," the little blacksmith was saying, "these lads from the Eastern distric's all has the idea they must cut up rough as soon as they gets beyond tidewater."

"And where are they now, Markham?"

"At the barber's, sir. He's letting whatever little blood's left in 'em."

"Markham, ye should be ashamed, fighting as ye do. A man wi' three fine daughters like you."

The blacksmith cocked his greasy hat over his eye, shot his thin arms out of his sleeves and grinned.

"Well, sir, a man with three gals like those yonder had best keep fit to fight—both for 'em and with 'em."

His burly wife standing by Mr. Fraser gave a booming laugh and tramped off after her daughters, who had already drawn two youths from the hitching rail.

An old man with a dogwood cane and a cocked hat drawn over a red knit cap led a small boy in a red tippet and black glazed gaiters by the hand. It was Mr. Mountford, the storekeeper. Beneath that knit cap, Johnny knew, was nothing but a vast slick scar. Mr. Mountford had been scalped in an Indian raid years ago, scalped and left for dead. But, as he was fond of telling, he had not died. He never told, however, what he had seen when he came to. But everyone knew that Mr. Mountford's little son had been with him in the cabin. Since then he had been a trifle touched. He always had a young boy about him.

Now he wiped his blunt, blue nose with the knob of his dogwood cane.

" 'Day, Squire. Sarvint, ma'm."

"How are ye, Mr. Mountford. Ye know my Johnny here."

"Johnny; knew him well, quilled moccasins, coon-hat, a good boy. 'Bout the size of my own boy, he were." The flat voice trailed off, he looked at Johnny without recognition. "Sarvint, young sir. Come, son."

He moved away with the little, round-eyed youngster, poking his dogwood cane among the dead leaves.

The Merrillees' chaise drove up. Inside the hood Mrs. Merrillee's leathery, set face peered over the top of Sally Merrillee's gray eyes and brown flying hair. Mr. Merrillee, slender, gentle, in an old scratch wig, a bottle-green coat and darned silk stockings, drove in abstracted, hesitating fashion. Sally's brother Joe sat on the perch, his fat, surly face nearly hidden by the thin brown horse. Sally waited for Joe to tie up the horse, then clung to him with a revolting pretense of dependence on that bulletheaded youth. As if they didn't fight at home every day; with her usually on top. In brown silk bonnet and muskrat tippet, she was letting on to be the shy young lady. Her play-acting depressed Joe even more than it did Johnny. He came up to Johnny, dragging her moodily on his arm.

"How you?" he mumbled gloomily.

"Middling. How you, Sally?"

This formal inquiry appeared to relieve Joe of further responsibility. He dropped Sally's arm and moved off to where two equally sombre youths were deep in conference.

"My land, Johnny, I never can get used to you in your jemmy Sunday clothes."

"Shucks. I could wear these every day if I'd a mind."

She tilted her head disdainfully. "I dare you to say that so loud your Pa can hear."

"I could wear these—" he began in bold tones. His father, talking earnestly to Mrs. Merrillee, looked up. Johnny's voice trailed off. Sally buried her snub nose in her tippet with derisive chuckles.

Creaking and rolling, an ox-cart turned into the grove. The white oxen bowed imperturbably beneath the yokes, their melting eyes dreamed of another world, their cloven feet cut the leaves, their wrinkling dewlaps swung, the solid wooden wheels turned slowly. The wain above them burst with children, a shapeless mound of mufflers, mittens, caps, tippets, red noses, shining eyes. A tall, tough old farmer, a flopping wool hat on his head, an ox pole in his hand, towered in front.

"Howdy, Corneilison!" called an escort of the Markham girls, a pimpled and impudent youth. "Getting in your crop?"

The farmer halted his team with a tap of the pole.

"Well, son," he observed with crushing blandness, "it's a crop you'll never raise, nor even sow, neither."

The other men laughed, the girls blushed and giggled, Squire Fraser looked up, annoyed, not at the ribaldry, but at the mirth.

A hush fell; the preacher was in sight. He jogged awkwardly into the grove, a lank carcass of a man, a lank plaster of loose hair beneath his flat-crowned hat, his mud-splashed stockings swinging below his little island pony, his hands, blue and knuckled, jerking on the reins. He made an uncouth gesture of salutation, swung down, stamped his brogues.

John Fraser stepped forward to greet him.

"Here, Johnny," he called, "tie up Mr. Harbitt's horse."

As Johnny led the pony to a tree, Mr. Harbitt's dingy black coat was shut out by the crowding congregation. The tall figure of the preacher entered the church door, Squire Fraser and the other elders behind him. The women slowly followed; the older men came next; the boys still hung back near the horses, whispered, grinned.

Further delay would mean disgrace. Tucking his hat under his arm, Johnny went in.

On the right the women's bonnets, felt, straw, silk, fur, stretched in uneven rows. On the left, brown, grizzled, shaggy, close-cropped, with here and there a scratch wig or a rusty-ribboned queue, the men's uncovered heads rose from an expanse of sober linsey.

Johnny slid into a seat and stared decorously ahead. The last boys scuffled in. Squire Fraser turned and fixed them with his eye. Young Johnny's heart leaped with joy at the thought that he was not among them.

The preacher rose; he was so tall that he could not stand upright under the beam above the pulpit. His neck, in its slack kerchief, was bent, his beaked face, thrust forward. Hard-eyed, fiercely solemn, he brooded over them like a great, high-shouldered bird. His mouth opened with a click.

"We will ask the mercy of the Lord," the words were a grating whisper, "on our sinful lives."

The people bent forward.

"Almighty God, Jehovah, look down in pity on the wretched transgressors gathered here together. For not a one but has this day and every day sinned against Thy most holy law. Not a one but has in pride and foolishness, in vaingloriousness and self-will, despised the precepts of Thy holy word. Not a one——"

The balanced phrases rolled out in cadence, the voice rose like the beating of a tocsin. Transgression on transgression, sin on sin wheeled with measured tread into the sombre, endless line.

The moments passed, the catalogue of evil grew until in one final, rounded phrase it embraced all wickedness of the universe. Johnny raised his head stiffly. All other heads were still bowed, the prayer was going on.

"But stained and scarred as we are, O Lord, with sin and vileness, Thou canst cleanse us, Thou canst wash us whiter than snow. Thou who, when Adam broke Thy commandment——"

A list of instances of divine mercy to unworthy man now followed. Johnny's neck inside the tight stock had turned to creaking wood, his head was numb. And still the dismal chanting voice rang on. Now it was raised in petition, first that abstract virtues might be conferred, chastity, obedience, above all orthodoxy. Request became specific; more members for the church at large, this congregation especially, more virtue among officers of the law, a better tobacco crop, industrious slaves. At the end came petitions for local needs, that an ailing member of this church might be given back the use of her right limb, that the keeper of the tavern might be moved to suppress unseemly brawling, that the blacksmith,—here Johnny's mind revived,—might come to an understanding of divine wrath and give over his fighting ways.

At last the benediction and "Amen." Stunned by the booming voice, lulled by the cadence, frozen by the damp air, the congregation struggled back to the perpendicular.

The preacher opened the Book, hooked his long hands over the corners of the pulpit, and read. Swaying slowly from side to side, he intoned with sombre gusto the story of Ananias and Sapphira, his wife.

He cleared his corded throat, he blew his nose, thrust his bandana in his coat-tail pocket and launched on the sermon. The story was first retold with horrid embellishments. A general survey of the whole field of lying followed, lying by word, by deed, by look, by thought. The Liar's Progress was then depicted, a tragedy wherein the career of an imaginary wretch was traced from the first casual misstatement down to his lonely old age, as a pariah, a shunned man, down to his suicide and his eternal damnation amid detailed torments.

The sermon passed on to lies theological, doctrinary, dogmatic, to heresies and false prophets; Johnny's interest wandered, he felt cold, strained; he would give a half-crown for something to lean back on. Looking around him, he found small comfort. Frozen into rows of blue-faced images, the congregation stared owlishly ahead. Only a child or two showed weakness. A boy rubbed his thin legs together surreptitiously; another breathed softly on his knuckles, the chapped face of a little girl crinkled up, two tears fell in her lap.

And still the gong-like voice droned on. Johnny listened again, not to the words, but to the intonation, hoping that each new crescendo would be the last. The voice became the booming of the sea whose mounting waves burst without hope or end over his shattered hulk. His mind fled from his aching frame, wandered curiously afar. His gaze trailed along the plastered logs, fled out the window beside the pulpit, paused a moment on a team of horses who dozed beneath two patchwork quilts, ran along their halter rope to an oak, up the oak, up to the wind-streaked sky through whose lanes and mottled cloud banks struggled a waxing and waning sun.

"——add His blessing to the preaching of His word. Amen." The end. Incredible. He fell forward stiffly for the closing prayer.

Outside, the people slapped themselves, chatted together, forgetful of their ordeal. A hardy race, they rallied instantly from the two-hour vigil on the backless benches.

The German chairmaker, a little spectacled dormouse, burrowed vigorously through the slow throng. "Vell, vell, vell," he murmured, "it makes cold veather. Yes? No? Dot's for me good business. De peoples sits much on chairs by fireside. Out busts de bottoms. No?"

He laughed, smiled, nodded. His wife and string of children, like a row of Dutch dolls, trailed behind him.

The preacher appeared among them. With the sermon behind him, he seemed a different man; his drawling voice was kindly, dry, his chat was racy, well salted with the knowledge of men. There was something in him of the farmer, and of the trapper; something, too, of the circuit judge.

"Howdy, Corneilison," he said. "Saw your brother last month at High Hill. The bears ate his young cotton in the spring, but the folks is well and making out good."

"No, ma'm, I didn't see her," he bent his head to a peaked little woman; "she was up the valley midwifing. But I heard tell of her. Her son's trapping on the Yadkin. They say he aims to go back over the mountains with this man Boone that's been there."

"Well, friend, how you? How's your lady? Better? No?" His wide mouth fell into lines of deep concern. "That's bad. I declare I'm sorry, brother." He dropped a hand on a bowed shoulder. "We can't do nothing but pray. You pray and I'll pray for you—both. I'll not forget."

The congregation slowly dissolved. On horse and afoot, they wound along the sandy tracks into the forest. Squire Fraser locked the church door and put the iron key in his pocket.

## CHAPTER IV

W E MIGHT just go down tae the Merrillees', Caroline," said John
Fraser after dinner. "I would chat wi' James upon what we talked of
for Johnny."

His mother's face fell.

"So soon? He's but a boy. I had thought another year or two."

"By then he'll be half a man and too old for proper schooling. Now, then,
lass, be of good heart, and we'll make our Johnny a gentleman in learning as
he is in birth."

Here was news, of huge but doubtful import. To go away—to see the
world—huzzah! But to go away to school—to be sent away for the purpose
of continuing interminably with Balbus and his wall, with Cæsar and his
bridge, and doubtless with many other classic structural enterprises of
which he was still ignorant.

"Will ye take a real schooling, lad? I've no time tae teach ye."

"I—I don't know, Dadder. I'm afeared I'm no scholar."

"Hoots-toots, we'll no make ye a dominie. But ye must have the learning due ye. The country needs such men." He paused and gazed out the window with judicial and comprehensive eye. "Look around ye: tae the south the new Scots, poor, ignorant, down-trodden Highlanders wi'out a word of English in their mouths, let alone the Latin and the Greek; the best stock in the Province, I warrant, but kenning only Gaelic and cut off from a' the rest. Tae the west, the Moravians, peaceable and grand workers, but thinking only of crops and crafts, their slow minds shut in by their barnyard walls, of no more effect in the Province than so many cows. Then on the border the back-country men, quick and hardy, but so untaught that they can scarce make their mark tae a deed, men who lack reason and self-control and will one day pay the price. And a' through the Province ye will find the conceit of ignorance, the folly of small knowledge. Only on the seaboard do ye see any whose minds are trained tae drive through tae the truth. And what is the result, lad? Those men, a handful, govern a' the rest. We talk of liberty. Some fools declaim against British tyranny. But observe the working of practical affairs. The only liberty is knowledge, and ignorance is the only tyrant."

He laid a great hand kindly on Johnny's knee.

"My lad, I would give ye the freedom of the world—under God's providence. Ye see I talk to ye as though ye were a'ready grown. Tell Scipio tae bring the horses."

Wrapped in solemn thoughts and a somewhat uncomfortable grandeur, Johnny went in search of Scipio. The vision of his father planning for him, eager for him, almost pleading with him, shocked and frightened him. The Great Man had always handed down pronouncements. That was his function. The pronouncements were implicitly respected. That was Johnny's function. Now, however, his father was troubled over him, and not over his errors of the past but over his prospects in the future: the future—a strange source from which to draw trouble, or hope, or anything save secret pictures of high adventure. He himself must be more important than he had imagined. Inflated and magnificent, he marched toward the barn.

"Scipio, the horses!"

He turned on stately heel, and stalked rapidly away lest the dignity of the scene should collapse through some refractory act of Scipio's. But he did not escape hearing, "Man, oh, man, Mist' Johnneh, ef you ain't got de majesty, dominion, an' powah dis evenin'. Hooo!"

Would his mother come to the Merrillees' too? It was, of course, splendid to have her, with her laughter and quick understanding. But if she stayed home he would ride the red colt, while if she came he would bump ignobly behind his father on the flat furry back of Grampus. In such a situation the new coonskin cap, calculated to astound the young Merrillees, would simply lose its point. But to canter into their view on the colt with the ring-tail swinging behind——

Here came the horses, Gampus in his state of chronic somnolence, the colt feigning dismay at every stick in the road. Each had a man's saddle.

His father appeared with a Highland bonnet and huge hunting crop. Johnny prepared to mount the bay. But just then his mother came to the door.

"John, I reckon I'll go along."

"Fine; it'll do ye good to have a crack wi' Mrs. Merrillee. We'll put your saddle on."

"Never mind, I'm not too old," and with that she kilted up her homespun skirt and slipped into the saddle. The colt stood quiet, chucking his bit. Her small feet just touched the stirrups, her blue spun-yarn stockings showed to the knee.

"Tut-tut, lass, what will the Merrillees say?"

"I reckon they'll be mighty surprised to find your wife has legs."

Scipio clapped a hand to his mouth, explosive whistles leaked through his fingers. Johnny's father swung heavily up on the groaning Grampus and reached down a hand.

"Come, Johnny."

John seized the great paw, made a twisting leap and landed sitting on the broad gray quarters. He thrust his fingers inside his father's belt and peered disconsolately around the big brown short-jacket. They moved off lumberingly, the bright colt skipping on ahead. His heart was full of bitterness.

Ten minutes before he had been made to think himself a person of consequence, a man, almost; now, without a thought, the overlords had plunged
him back into infancy. It was not that they were hostile—indeed, there would
be some dignity for him in that—but that they were indifferent; they grati-
fied their passing whim as a matter of course, never considering how their
careless edict deprived him of the chance to appear in glory before the
young Merrillees.

Here Grampus, with cavernous intestinal rumblings, broke into a trot.
Coherent thought was no longer possible. He clung to his father angrily.

"By Zooks! What a cursed sow-belly horse!" he said to himself. He pictured with some satisfaction how surprised that impassive figure in front of
him would be to know that his son was no longer the youth he supposed but
a man of rough speech and daring oaths.

They dipped into the lowlands' evening chill and splashed through a
ford. He saw the streaked white sand and shadowy minnows between his
feet; a hoot-owl quavered from the wood, a rabbit scuttled in the dead cane.
But what were all these things to a man unjustly used?

They climbed the slope past little crooked scrub-oaks and heaps of old
slash from lumbered pines. The horses' feet clicked on gravel soil; they were
in a land of hardwood trees, red-gum, oak, elm and hickory, beneath which
stretched the broad unfenced pastures of James Merrillee. He heard the bay
colt coming back. Grampus stopped, his mother drew alongside.

"I reckon Johnny and I might better change. My skirts keep riding up
scandalously; so I'll not shame you before the world, John."

He slid to the ground, and took the colt's bridle. His mother put a hand
on his shoulder and jumped nimbly up behind his father. As he mounted,
the colt swung away—an old trick—he landed in the saddle. "Steady now,
you!" He was off in pursuit of Grampus's gray rump. Now he passed them
with a wave; the colt opened up his long canter, striding out from the
shoulder, driving easily and strongly from his loins. He topped the rise and
saw the line of cedars leading to the square house. Its hand-rived siding,
weathered silver gray, gave it an air of elegance; it was, in fact, the only
weather-boarded house he had ever seen. He leaned in the saddle and

swung the colt up the cedar-bordered lane. What luck! The two young Merrillees were playing near the box bushes by the door. He pulled up before them and, ignoring the four round eyes, said with studied ease, "Hi, how you all?"

The hitching rail was right before him but he could not resist, "Wher' can I tie my horse?"

The Merrillees found speech.

"Why, Johnny! Why, Johnny, did you come alone?"

"Oh, more or less; my paw and maw are down the road a piece on that old fat horse. I reckon they'll be here after so long a time."

He tied the colt up; preoccupied and businesslike, he loosened the girths and briefly considered giving the red flank a hearty slap, but something in the colt's eye dissuaded him.

"Why, Johnny, where'd you get the coon-hat?"

"Trapper sold it to me. A good many trappers come by our place."

Joe Merrillee glowered.

"What's a coon-hat? We got a live coon."

Johnny's gaze, fixed on the distance, showed no interest.

"Huh, what is there particular *about* this coon? Just a coon is nothing special."

A triumphant duet,

"He's a fisher-coon!"

"I seen lots of fisher-coons; lots of 'em."

"Where?" demanded Joe. This was a poser fortunately relieved by another less formidable attack from Sally Merrillee.

" 'Seen! I seen!' What kind of grammar do you all talk?"

He turned on her with weary contempt.

"Come on, let's see your old coon."

Peering through the slats of a box behind the smoke-house, Johnny made out a black, gnome-like face and lustrous fairy eyes. As he moved closer the little animal raised two pleading hands. He felt a most unmanly tug at his heart and drew back, red, unhappy, wildly angry.

"Johnny's scared!" they shouted. "He won't hurt you, Johnny!"

"Scared nothing! I'll buy him."

"What you want him for if you've seen so many of 'em?" asked Joe. Johnny did not reply. "Huh?" Joe demanded. Still he was silent.

The two stared at Johnny with incredulous suspicion.

"Oh, Johnny!" Sally cried. "Johnny aims to turn him loose! Johnny aims to turn him loose!" she chanted.

"Well, if I do," he lied stoutly, "it'd be to let old Grizzly Gray run him. That'd make a pretty race. Tell you what I'll do. I'll trade you my cap for this yer coon."

He flicked the ringed tail over his shoulder. Joe gazed at it with longing eyes; he was going to trade. It was all Johnny could do to look indifferently away. The fisher-coon rustled faintly in his straw. At the sound Johnny felt excited color mount to his face. Joe saw it.

"Not much," he said. "What kind of a trade is that, a dead coon for a live one?"

Johnny read irreparable defeat in Joe's stubborn and suspicious stare. But again the straw rustled, his heart jumped. He must try again.

"But, Joe, this is a sure enough cap. What good is your coon?"

"Why, to look at, of course."

"Well, you can look at this cap, can't you? And you can wear it too."

Despite his sophistry, however, Joe would not trade; he stood, taciturn and proprietary, by the coon's box, shook his head, walked off. Impotent, raging, miserable, Johnny followed. Sally stayed with the coon.

Grampus had long since been tied at the rail before the house, and now his father and mother came down with Mr. and Mrs. Merrillee. Mr. Merrillee led the way with graceful, ushering manner. His wife's drawn, brown face and meager figure were stark and harsh, her movements awkward and weary. Johnny dutifully jerked the front of his cap. Mr. Merrillee inclined his head graciously, his wife nodded impassively. "Johnny, how you?"

Mr. Merrillee tapped the slip-rails of the barnyard with the head of his ebony cane. Two colts came up through the dusk and nosed under the flaps of his pockets. He gave them a carrot.

"They have good shoulders, John."

"Aye, ye might race them next year."

"Perhaps, perhaps, but I care very little for racing."

"But, man, it's a sinful waste tae buy colts like these and not run them. Ye'll no get the Fearnought stock for nothing, I ken well."

"No, quite so, but I like to have them here," he glanced aside shyly, "to look at them." He snapped a finger. The colts cantered lightly away. "They are splendid."

"Aye, they are. But tae my mind they'd look finer yet running home first on the Edenton course wi' a hundred guineas back o' them."

Mrs. Merrillee spoke harshly, "James will never take a penny—not if it's offered him. He'd rather read his Greek books."

Her husband dropped his eyes uneasily.

"You were speaking of Johnny's schooling, sir. Shall I give you a letter to Doctor Clapton? It is true he is a rector of the English Church, but a most excellent scholar and liberal minded. And at Edenton Johnny will meet many of our principal persons."

"I'll thank ye. I've small fear for our Johnny's religious beliefs—he has been forewarned from birth against Episcopalian flummery."

Night was falling. They went back to the house. From the porch Johnny saw Mr. Merrillee light the candles and pour out a glass of brandy for his father, then sit down at a great mahogany desk and write. He heard his mother's voice, running on softly, and the sparse hard syllables of Mrs. Merrillee. The seal stamped on the wax. "Now this, sir," Mr. Merrillee said, "will command Mr. Clapton's most particular attention whenever you care to employ it." It was spoken with quiet elegance, yet to Johnny the words were pregnant with dark, shadowy forebodings, and the muffled echo of a doom.

The elders came out on the porch.

"Servant, ma'm," his father said, bowing stiffly to Mrs. Merrillee. "Good night tae ye, James."

Johnny sought his mother's face through the dusk. She read his inquiry; her voice, sad and tender, just reached him. "Yes, Johnny boy, you take the colt."

He tightened the girths, jerked the reins loose, threw them over the little pointed ears, vaulted for the saddle. The colt made a circling rear, the row of faces by the porch shot past, he dug in his heels. One soul-shaking leap and the colt stretched out gloriously down the lane. Far behind he heard his father's angry roar, "Steady him, there, you—steady him!"

## CHAPTER V

WAITING FOR dinner on the porch, Johnny watched the ground frost heave up icy fingers which crumpled in the warmth of the false spring. He heard the sound of a bell drifting from the westward on the lazy wind. Down the big road where it split the pines on the crest of the hill crept a rider, followed by a line of nodding packs and drooping horses' heads. A light-toned cow-bell jingled from the gray mare in the lead; two men walked beside the column, another rode behind. As they came down the grade the leader, who leaned back listlessly against the cantle, head on chest, straightened in the saddle, assumed a dashing manner and thumped his heels against his horse's ribs. The nag laid back an ear, then broke into a stumbling trot. Elbows out and hands held high above his paunch, the rider turned up the lane; his white fat face, pompous yet keen, searched the porch for an audience. Johnny ducked in the door.

"Dadder! Hyer's a pack-horse man."

His father went to the door. The stranger was still on his horse, inflating himself, expectantly. He raised his rusty cocked hat with a flourish and pressed it to the dingy stock ruffle which hung down on his chest.

"Yo' servant, suh; most obedient servant, I'm sure. And how do we fine ourselves today?"

"Well, I thank ye. This is Mister——?"

"Jenney, suh, Jenney. Mr. Jenney, that's me. Mr. Cassoway G. Jenney of South Carolina."

"Ye are far frae home."

The pack train had come up; the shaggy horses hung their heads and stared into vacancy through half-closed eyes; their tarpaulins, patched and dirty, sagged in the rawhide lashings. Down the lane two sallow Negroes with hickory staves leaned listlessly against the packs, while the other rider, lank and black-browed, eyed Mr. Jenney with steady malignity. His glance, far from arresting Mr. Jenney, seemed to give him a fresh access of cordiality.

"Why, bless my soul. I had nearabout forgot. Gentlemen," he turned to Johnny and his father oratorically, "pray let me acquaint you with my ve'y good friend, Mr. Arrocks, a heart of gold, gentlemen, I do assure you, a heart of gold. No man in my native country," his voice took on dignity, "South Carolina, gentlemen, but would deem it an honor, a mighty distinguished honor, to be known as Mr. Arrocks' frien'. Mr. Arrocks, this," he waved an arm of comradely protection toward Squire Fraser, "is my good frien', Misteh——" He bent an inquiring ear.

"Fraser."

"Fraseh, suh; Mr. Fraseh," he repeated with some impatience as if Mr. Arrocks had been dense in catching the name.

The Heart of Gold acknowledged both the encomium and the introduction by a parrot-like stare at Mr. Jenney. He slowly turned his head toward Mr. Fraser, jerked it shortly in answer to the other's bow, and at once relapsed into brooding hostility.

"And this is young Mr. Fraseh," Mr. Jenney's face lit with a happy inspiration, "if my memory does not betray me."

To Johnny, never introduced like a grown man before, the sensation was pleasant. He ducked his head and grinned with polite rigidity. As for Mr. Jenney, the packhorse man was uncontrollably enraptured by the social significance of the occasion, he waved an expansive hat at Squire Fraser, he preened.

"I do assure you, my good frien's, it gives me mo' pleasure than I can describe to bring you two gentlemen together."

He glanced rapturously from Mr. Arrocks' saturnine face to the face of John Fraser, now shrouded in a thousand veils of caution.

Johnny's father, however, was not one to omit the proprieties.

"Will ye step inside? Dinner is just ready."

"Now I declare," said Mr. Jenney, "if that ain't like you, Mr. Fraseh, suh! But, suh, you mistake me if you think Cassoway G. Jenney a man to impose on friendship's sacred obligations. No, suh; we thank you, bless yo' generous heart! Time presses, however, and we planned to content ourselves merely by paying our humble respects," he paused, eyeing John Fraser narrowly for signs of protest. "That, sir, was our only idea. But now what do I see, suh? I see a great-hearted North Carolinian whose hospitality will take no denial. And when one gentleman meets another—whether he be of North or South Carolina—frien'ship's just claims will ever be reco'nized. Hyer, groom take my horse."

In the big room his mother, having read the portents, was hurrying fresh supplies on the table. On entering her presence Mr. Jenney outdid himself. All that he had said before seemed curt and brusque compared to the luxuriant flowers of speech with which he festooned the occasion. In conclusion he elaborately regilded the Heart of Gold, who was lurking uneasily in a corner. The Heart of Gold stared morosely into space and gulped, disclosing an Adam's apple of unusual size and sharpness.

At the table Mr. Jenney assumed charge of the meal. His studied efforts to make John Fraser feel at home brought small response. Mr. Jenney gracefully dismissed him into silence with a word of friendly encouragement and devoted himself to cementing imaginary bonds between Johnny's mother and the reluctant Mr. Arrocks.

Johnny was astonished at these gallantries and, in spite of himself, impressed. They marked a man from a country more elegant than his own; in the plain, direct manners of the neighborhood there was nothing to match against them.

Mr. Jenney was speaking again.

"Have you all heard the news from the Back Country?" He did not pause for a reply. "A set of low-lived scoundrels have defied the sheriff of Alamance, chased out his Majesty's judges and written—such of them as could write—cursed doggerel across the page of the court record. Doggerel of a character, ma'm, that I shall never sully the ears of Virtue by repeating in your presence. I was in Hillsboro the day but one after the event. You can imagine, suh, how trying it was to a man of my character and sentiments to learn that persons of the lower orders had showed insults to his gracious Majesty." Mr. Jenney rolled his eyes to heaven. "Very sad—most cursedly sad."

John Fraser raised his broad, red face from his plate. "His Majesty has no need for your concern, I'm thinking. It was a mere tax-riot. The men are foolish, but loyal tae the Crown. More so than some wi' better understanding." He glanced at Johnny's mother. She flushed and made as if to speak, but Mr. Jenney again had the floor.

"As to that, suh, I did not make inquiries. For you must know, suh, that bound as the Jenneys are to the reigning house of Britain by peculiar and distinguished ties, the ve'y appearance of disloyalty drives me into a ungovernable, I may say a damnably dangerous passion." He glanced fiercely around the circle.

"Sae ye're kin tae Geordie?" said Mr. Fraser composedly.

"Not absolutely kin, suh. But the Jenneys hold their ancestral domain under a South Carolina grant from King George the Second."

"I've nae doubt it cost ye dear, then. Geordie's father was a great one tae count the pennies."

"Oh," Mrs. Fraser put in hastily, ignoring her husband's wink, "your plantation must be most elegant, Mr. Jenney. Do describe it, I pray."

The mounting choler, receding from Mr. Jenney's eye, left it dreamy and inspired. His gaze passed over Mr. Fraser's skeptic grin and Mr. Arrocks' bleak stare, dwelt on Johnny's upturned face and gathered him into its spell.

"Why, certainly, ma'm; as far as the human tongue can do so."

For Johnny the meal became a trance. He heard vaguely the steady munching of Mr. Arrocks and his father, but his mouth was open, his eyes were fixed on Mr. Jenney's, while terraces, pagodas, marble halls unrolled before them.

"It is impossible, ma'm, to depict the brilliance of the scene in those days, now, alas, no more, when the first families of the Province, the Governor and numerous distinguished visitors from England—where the famous Castle Jenney still attests the distinction of our family's parent stock—were lavishly entertained regardless of *expense*. It was hyer, in the Temple of Venus on the South Lawn, that Major Munkittrick of the Charleston Independent Company declared himself to Miss Susie Pellew; the grotto was the haunt of the learned Doctor Wolp of Wolp's Neck, the author of a mighty affecting poem, 'Reflections of a Medical Man on Beholding Wolp's Neck from the North West Branch of the Wateree,' its title was; and the sunken walk was the scene of the duel between Colonel Popple and General Brashay which terminated so happily fo' all concerned."

Waving the last piece of spoon-bread flamboyantly aloft, Mr. Jenney, long after the rest had finished, continued to depict the pomp and circumstance of life in South Carolina. Johnny's father broke the spell; heartlessly he rose from the table. Mr. Jenney bounded from his chair.

"My frien's, permit me to show you something of interest." He went to the door. "Servant, open that first pack."

The Negro unhitched the ropes and lowered the canvas bundle to the ground. Mr. Jenney stepped down and laid back the flaps, exposing a mound of rough-dressed pelts, brown, red, black, gray. He drew them out slowly one by one; the skins of bear, mink, deer, fox, beaver shone softly in the sun.

"Those are fine pelts," Johnny's father said.

"Ve'y truly said, suh," Mr. Jenney bowed, "but wher' do you reckon they came from, now?"

"Frae the Yadkin Valley, I suppose."

Mr. Jenney drove a fist deep into a shaggy bearskin.

"These pelts came from beyond the mountains, ev'y one!"

"But no one hunts beyond the mountains."

"Well, suh, the lad I got these of has done it and got safe back, and, gentlemen, Cassoway G. Jenney is the man who bought his pelts and paid a thumping price to boot—a cursedly thumping price!"

"Ah," said Squire Fraser gruffly. "And who did ye say was the lad that got these skins?"

Mr. Jenney's glance sharpened. "Oh, a poor young man, a young man admirable, no doubt, in his humble way, but in ve'y ordinary circumstances and I sadly fear a little touched"—he tapped his forehead. "Many of the trappers are."

"Poor lad," said Mrs. Fraser. "Who was he?"

"He was a character, ma'm, a positive character. By way of being pleasant, I said to him when he came to trade:

" 'Well, my lad, I hear you have seen a new country.'

" 'Why, no, sir,' he says, very deliberate; 'no, sir, not exactly.' And with that his eye lighted up in a manner most alarming. 'I've seen a new Empire, that's all.' And he began to talk of plains and rivers, of grass-lands, of elk and buffalo, and then, upon my soul, of farmlands and towns that were to be. Towns, did I say? The poor fellow talked of cities. He laid a huge hand on my arm—I assure you I was cursedly upset—and sought to persuade me to go back there with him. I spoke to him of our intended trade in hopes to restore him to his senses. But 'No,' he says, 'I don't want money, I want men.' And he continued to hold me and gaze into space. At length his eyes came back to the land of the living, to my infinite gratification. Then bless me, suh, if he didn't look at me with the coolest manner in the world. 'I want men,' he says, and then he shook his head and released me with a cursedly upsetting smile. I did not care to remind him how he should address me lest I should provoke a second seizure; and, as you see, his pelts were uncommon fine ones."

He laid out a beaver-skin.

"Although, my good frien's, I opened these hides only as a matter of interest and as one gentleman to another, on beholding a creature so gracious and charming"—here he bowed again to Mrs. Fraser—"I can not, as a man of sensibility, escape the conviction that this beaver-skin would become the lady and receive added lustre, either fo' a muff or fo' a tippet."

"I thank you, Mr. Jenney, but I already have both."

"Of co'se, of co'se, but this would be fo' special occasions. And in reco'nition of our frien'ship and, I trust, mutual esteem, I had planned to remove this beaver-skin from the realm of commerce and, in a word, with my gallant and cultivated friend's permission"—here he bowed to Johnny's father—"present it with my most distinguished compliments, at cost, ma'm; fourteen and sixpence."

He flourished his hat.

"I thank ye, mister," John Fraser spoke with quick decision. "Nae doubt ye mean well, but just as it happens we're no in need of skins."

Mr. Jenney drew back, affronted.

"Suh, in my native country, South Carolina, suh, wher' I praise God the social observances are both known and followed, it is not customary for one gentleman to decline the generous offer of another. Negro, roll up this pack!"

He clapped on his hat and mounted his horse, he made a stately salutation in which sorrow struggled with majesty, and moved slowly down the lane. The pack-train followed him while Mr. Arrocks waited to bring up the rear.

His mother watched the fat, angry back.

"John, I fear he takes it ill. But was not fourteen and six quite dear for a beaver?"

"Over-dear."

"I wonder what he really paid for it—we never found out the trapper's name."

A hoarse voice startled them.

"Eight shillings. Boone—D. Boone."

Mr. Arrocks surveyed them owlishly, gave an almost imperceptible jerk of his head, and trotted away.

# CHAPTER VI

S PRING CAME; the pines thrust brilliant new green spray above the sober
old green leaves, the last cones fell softly bouncing to the ground, slim
white candle blossoms reached up to the sun; below, the dogwood opened
in a silver mist, song-sparrows bustled and twittered in the thorns. Vixens,
heavy with cub, withdrew to the dark swamps. The first young rabbits
frolicked in the dusk. The vulture now hung interminably against the blue,
peering in vain for signs of death in a land where life was now renewed and
beauty born again.

It would not be long now before young Johnny Fraser went to Edenton to
start his schooling. The thought hovered over him like the vulture in the
sky. Only in the evenings was there escape. They were chilly enough for a
small fire in whose weaving flame he caught flashes of his secret dreams.
The vulture doom was then forgotten, the pictures of high adventure and
great deeds which ever since he could remember had been forming, dis-

solving, in his brain, came crowding to inspirit him, winked, glowed, dissolved among the embers.

The picture of the Indian fighters had been well enough for a boy, that of all the King's horses and all the King's men still held appeal. But now that he was going to the coast, to Edenton, where things were elegant and fine, almost like England, that dim and dazzling land across the sea, he recalled what his mother had told of the Governor's Assembly, what Mr. Jenney had told of the glories of South Carolina, and devised for himself another dream.

Powdered, pomaded, satin-waistcoated, he saw himself parade with easy grace down marble stairs. The modish throng below him ceased their chatter, looked up, murmured deferential surprise. "Who was this handsome, splendid, gorgeous youth?" they seemed to ask. He raised a ruffled sleeve from the balustrade. They fell silent. He searched their faces till he found his man—the swarthly dastard who had spoken lightly of Lady Bessie Montague—drawing his rapier, he beckoned sternly, then led the blanched and cringing figure to the duelling ground.

He glanced eagerly at his mother, seated by the hearth. Bending over a web of blue broadcloth, she cut, pinned, sewed a skirted coat for him, a coat of a fine young gentleman. Already she had picked the best calf-hide from the loft to make him leather breeches. But his father would not have her work the heavy palm-needle; it was not for a woman. So she cut the pattern and sent the hide by Scipio to Blue's Crossing, the nearest hamlet, to be stitched by the harness-maker. She had finished a dozen linen shirts and cambric stocks for him. The time would not be long.

It seemed queer to Johnny that, with such a crisis impending, Spring should proceed as usual. It did, however. Pea-vines sprouted in the new ground, cotton in the bottom land, corn fought the crab-grass on the hill. In the barn a new calf, wet and wobbly, stumbled to its feet; the red-eyed bull pawed dust clouds in the lane.

A freighter, bound up-country, stopped his creaking schooner-wagons to deliver a pair of hard shoes and a small cocked hat which his father had ordered for him. The breeches came back from the harness-maker, very tight. All was ready. But now that all was ready he found that he himself was not. The day of bright adventure was about to dawn. He should be greeting it with a cheer. Instead, a lump formed in his throat and slowly settled on his laboring chest. He was not frightened, he did not want to cry, but he wanted air and a trace of his old appetite.

The night before he was to leave he put on his new clothes and marched wretchedly before his father and mother in the evening firelight. His feet clumped woodenly, his body felt hot and encased, his neck was swaddled; the stiff hat gripped his thumping temples.

"Well, sir, and what's the news frae London?" his father said with a kindly grin.

"Don't make fun of him, John. He looks just like a sure-enough young gentleman. Johnny, you look just grand."

Sofa peered in through her door.

"M-m-m-*m-m*! Ain't dat de high-mighty buckra-man in de big buttons an' knee buckles an' de cock-up hat!"

"My shoes hurt." He sat down, angry at a life grown suddenly formidable and bleak; angry, too, at himself for raising an unhappy flush to his mother's face.

Late that night he heard a soft footfall in his room. The white eyes of Sofa grew slowly out of the dusk.

"Hush, Mist' Johnneh!" She laid a lean hand on the coverlet. "Hyer; take disyer." She dropped a string over his head. "Das a snake-skin bag and a toad-eye. Keep off de swamp fever and de hants. Wear dat, honey, an' you be safe."

She stood up and repeated unknown words, hushed but resonant, rhythmic as drum-beats and as potent. He felt his hair stir. Falling silent, she looked at him, then bent down and pressed his hand to her leathery face.

"My li'l white honey!" she murmured and slipped from the room.

His father came down for breakfast in buck breeches and a gray coat turned back with brown, a blue felt bonnet under his arm. His mother talked gaily through the meal, but Johnny caught a glance from her eyes that closed his throat and made him want to cry out like a cornered fox.

The horses were at the door, their saddle-bags stuffed full. His father slipped a pistol in the cowhide holster by Grampus' saddle-bow.

His mother drew him inside the door and thrust a heavy paper wad in his hand.

"Three sovereigns, dear, and promise to keep one by you to send me an express if you should be ailing. Promise!"

He nodded, speechless.

"My boy, my boy!" She flung her arms around him and ran up the little stair.

Scipio held his stirrup.

"De Lo'd take care you, Mist' Johnneh; an' ef anybody don't treat you right, des send fo' Scipio, dassall."

He gathered the reins and sent the colt along, leaning forward lest his father should see his face.

For an hour his father kept behind him on the road. They were in new country by then and John Fraser drew up alongside and began quietly to talk as one man to another; he pointed out the scattered houses, a new log church, the county line; he showed the scene of an old Indian fight and told of all that had been done since those early days; told of the farms, the roads, the produce, the militia. As they rode along, the Province was slowly unrolled by his father's exact and comprehensive mind.

At noon they pulled up in an abandoned field beside the road. They tied the horses to nibble spring grass among the tall brown broom-straw. They stretched out under young pines and ate their corn bread and bacon. Through the pine leaves slanted the tender, embracing warmth of earliest summer, beneath which he felt himself expand. He took off his hot, stiff coat and his hard shoes. Here he was, voyaging afar, seeing new sights and talking with his father maturely of public matters and high affairs. His dress, too; it was irksome, but was it not the badge of manhood and rank? Yes, by Zooks! A gentleman must dress the part. It was all very well to have lived as a boy of the Pine Forests. There was no disgrace in that. In fact, it gave him advantage over the Edenton boys, sheltered all their lives and sappy, without a doubt. But it was time he came into his own, and became a man, not so much of culture,—that might be tedious,—but of assured manner, of commanding presence, a man like Mr. Jenney, only more reliable. He drew a long breath.

A red flash caught his eye. A cardinal shot past, soared to a branch, and cocked a crested head. As Johnny watched it his spirits fled. Did that bird, bright and free, ever by chance fly westward as far as the old clay-plastered house now left so far behind?

"Come now, Johnny, lad."

He stuffed his hot feet into his shoes and tied his coat by thongs behind the saddle. He tightened the girth, raised the colt's reluctant head and mounted. They took the road again.

The land was changing now. The fields, far broader and clear of stumps, were of a dark gray loam. Lines of tattered field-hands hoed between the young rows of cotton and corn. A sallow white man watched them from a horse. A whip hung from the pommel. Among distant cedars he saw a painted house.

Now the swamps grew denser, choked with cane and drooping, matted vines. The air was warm and heavy, log bridges spanned the streams, ox-carts met them on the smooth broad road. Toward evening they passed a lady in a curricle, with a Negro postillion, scarlet liveried. John Fraser gravely raised his hat. She bowed with elegance. Johnny raised his hat, too, but cursed himself that he was in his shirt sleeves. He kicked the colt on the off side and made him play up. That was some compensation; the lady turned and looked back at him.

The road led down a long grade through small fields and apple orchards. At the foot a cluster of houses bordered it on either side; two were of brick and all had brick chimneys. The street widened at the lower end of the hamlet and showed a few stumpy masts and a black stream stretching across to a wooded shore. Beside the landing, a house, larger and more dishevelled than the rest, bore a swinging sign: "Bait for Man and Beast."

"Here we are. This is Slade's Ordinary, and very ordinary we'll find it, I'm 'feared, unless it's changed."

Three hounds scratched themselves, perfunctorily, in the dust around the door. Through the open windows came the drone of listless conversation and the smell of stale beer.

"Slade!" John Fraser shouted. "Slade!"

A pale, unshaven face appeared at a window. "Slade's drunk," it announced with detachment and faded from view.

His father dismounted with a rumble of disgust.

"We'll just take off our saddle-bags ourselves."

They untied the thongs and swung the heavy wallets to the ground. Johnny put on his coat. What next? The murmur of indifferent talk hummed on inside the tavern. The hounds subsided into the dust, the street was empty, not a leaf stirred in the oppressive air. He felt as though he and his father had been caught up out of the actual world into some lethal trance where nothing really existed, least of all himself.

Around the corner of the house shuffled an old Negro in a filthy great coat and bare feet.

He halted in order to quaver: "Ah'se a-comin', boss."

"Here, take these saddle-bags. And don't ye call me boss. I'll have no new-fangled cant."

"Yessuh, dasso."

"Tell Mistress Slade that Mr. Fraser of Little River desires a chamber for tonight."

"Yessuh, Mist' Frazee, suh. Ah fine de Mistiss ef Ah can. She tek care de Misteh. De gent'men have frolickin' time las' night, an' Mist' Slade, he ailin' fum too much 'toxication. Den Ah come back an' he'p you gent'men wid de hosses. You all find de boun'-boy in de ba'n."

They led the horses to the log stable behind the inn. A single brogan protruding from a heap of pine straw showed where the bound-boy slept. John Fraser pulled it as if it were a door-bell. A ruddy little Irish lad in cowhide breeches and a knitted waist-coat sat up in the mow. He stood up, pulled his forelock, and took the bridles.

"Now there's a grand young harse, young gintleman, if I may make so free. Faith, he's let down behind the way he could fly a Mayo bank and ditch like wan of God's own swallows."

John Fraser had looked about him.

"Boy, ye'll have tae just take the muck out o' these stalls before ye put a horse of mine intae them."

The bound-boy beamed on John Fraser with cordial approval.

"Now, there, sir, if your honor didn't just take the verry words out of me mouth. You're not the gintleman to put up wid anything but what is right and proper."

"Well, see ye do it, then."

In the yard, dejected fowls were pecking over heaps of trash; a pot of drooping trumpet flowers and a dingy line of washcloths festooned the back porch. On the sagging steps a cat mused cynically.

His father led the way to the front of the inn, and passed through the open door. Three idlers slouching around a table drank steadily, without gusto. They nodded to John Fraser, as though across a gulf, and turned again to their tankards.

The old Negro creaked down the stair.

"De saddle-bags in de chamber, gent'men; de mistiss say come up."

They followed him to a room beneath the eaves; flakes and patches of old whitewash covered the board walls, a field bed without a tester nearly filled the floor, its doubtful-looking pallet sagged on the loose cords. Above their heads each cross-beam showed a dark, smooth stain around the end where the rats maintained their immemorial runways.

The old Negro backed from the room. They heard his footsteps shuffle down the stairway. A fly buzzed against the ceiling, a chicken clucked in the yard. Across the narrow hall a bitter voice cried, "Tell the bloody——" "Hush!" said a woman; a door slammed shut.

His father, too, felt imprisoned in a trance. He moved about restlessly, mopped his face with a cambric handkerchief, stared out the window at the bedraggled hens.

"Johnny, this is no place for ye, nor me, neither. The country hereabout's a nest of radicals, rowdy scoundrels, wi'out respect for the word of God or the law of their King, let alone for the gentry and the better classes. I only fear ye'll see so much of them as will make ye think the world's no place for an honest man."

He gave Johnny an inquiring glance and paused. Johnny was at loss for a response. He did not like the inn, but he could hardly explain that young gentlemen adventurers were interested in the world less as a haven for the virtuous than as an uncharted sea for the daring.

"My lad, never ye put trust in a radical; I should have warned ye before. But as ye see, they are dirty, lawless and drunken. They would wreck the structure of the State tae dodge a penny tax or steal a gentleman's lace hat. And now we'd best order supper."

A few more patrons were in the smoky public room; colorless and formless, in clothes and visage, they slunk in their chairs and drank with abstraction yet with unremitting persistence. The first three had by now progressed one step further. Their attention to the bottle had brought its reward in the form of countless bitter grievances remembered. As Johnny and his father ate their stringy pork and half-cooked samp, the three companions narrated in broken accents, and simultaneously, the slights, impositions, frauds, insults, which had for unnumbered years rained inexorably on their devoted heads. Turned on John Fraser, their eyes, red, bleary, filled with unutterable things, like the eyes of old hounds, showed in their clouded depths a disposition to admit him to their councils as confidant and possible purveyor of further refreshment. Johnny's father rose hastily and sought the outside air.

Once in the dusk, they drifted over to the boat-landing. A few chance cargoes bulked black on the crazy wharf, the river slid by, dull steel in the evening mist, the further woods were melting into the dark, enfolding sky. Mosquitoes labored through the thick air; along the banks, frogs raised their staccato in unbearable reiteration. About them a dense, hostile night was closing down; they had no place to go but their dirty chamber in an inn where men, taciturn and inhuman, were drinking themselves into a state less human still. Yet Johnny could not keep awake; the hum of insects and the high-pitched grating of the frogs blended together and lulled his tired mind; he nodded.

"Ye'd best go tae bed. If I can find a boat, we'll leave the horses and go down the river early. Come."

Candles were lit in the inn. His father took one and led him upstairs to the chamber. From the saddle-bags he drew two heavy linen sheets, neatly folded, and spread them on the bed. A bucket of water had been placed by the door in recognition of their peculiar dignity. While Johnny was taking off his clothes his father fished from the wallet a small gourd containing a lump of soap, then sat heavily on the bed while Johnny washed and knelt down for his prayers, as near him as he could without suggesting undue dependence. The small naked body slid between the sheets.

"I'll just step out and see the boatmen. I'll no be long."

For an instant Johnny had the hideous fear that his father was about to pat him or make show of affection; but he merely nodded brusquely and left the room. The next moment Johnny was asleep.

In the night he was wakened by the crash of glass and a hoarse drunken chorus—

> "Fill up the bowl,
> Empty the butt,
> God save King George,
> The lousy scut!"

His father's figure bulked beside him; beyond it, the window showed a star or two. Wide-eyed and rigid, he listened to the words of profanation. They died away in a murmur, then he heard a shout, "Let be! I'll snap his eyeball strings!" and the sound of feet outside running in the dust. A scuffle followed and what seemed, first, like a man's high, hysterical laughter; but in a blinding flash he knew it for a scream of agony. A voice said, "You've done it now, by God! Get off him!" He heard the short, shuffling steps of men who carried a weight and the sighing moan of their burden. The hackles stood up on his back, his heart hung an instant, then tumbled slowly over.

A big hand slid into his. He clutched it with something like a sob.

## CHAPTER VII

"TIGHTEN YOUR belt, son, and we'll just wait till we're aboard tae eat our corn-bread for breakfast. I'll have nae more o' this sink-hole."

They carried their saddle-bags down to the public room, now empty, but heavy with the evil odors and with echoes, it seemed, of the evil sounds of night. For Johnny, empty of stomach, sick at heart, the life of high adventure had turned out a sinister illusion. It had led him so far only to a nest of drunken, bloody radicals and a tortured scream.

In the stable the bound-boy was dressing down Grampus with a twisted hay rope.

"Indade, sor, that was altogither a bad business last night——"

"Never mind that," said John Fraser shortly, "just ye listen tae me." He held out two pence.

"That's for ye. And ye see this," he showed a silver sixpence in his palm, "that's for ye when I'm come back, two days from now—if I find these horses as they should be."

51

"Bliss your honor's gen'rous heart——"

"Muck out the stalls, morn and evening, pick out their feet; four measures of oats is plenty while they're standing up, and a' the water they'll drink. I see ye know your duty—but have ye the will tae do it?"

Standing beside the colt, Johnny tickled his muzzle and let him pull on his finger with soft lips, delicate trembling lips which pulled on his heart as well. Why could a person not go adventuring without these moments of emptiness and long backward glances? He had not bargained for this; there had been no homesickness in his firelit dreams.

He heard the bound-boy in the next stall explaining the merits of Grampus to his father as though John Fraser had never seen the horse before.

"Now this harse—stand over, ould felley"—he slapped the monumental rump—"is put up to carry weight, sor. Thrue it is, he may take a bit of time to thravel from wan fence to the next, what with the age on him, but wance *at* his fence, sor, a stag-royal wud lepp no grander."

"Pick out his feet," his father said. "Come, Johnny."

Johnny pulled his finger from the colt's mouth and bumped his muzzle gently.

"Good luck, colt. Keep you he'th."

On their way to the landing his father said:

"Never fret for the colt. Ye'll be back home tae see him and the rest of us this autumn, if it costs me three pound."

They found their boat, a long, flat-bottomed skiff with a short mast, already loaded with casks of wheat and drums of cured tobacco. Beneath a canvas awning at the stern a little man leaned against the tiller, a little marmoset of a man whose gray chin whiskers were so stupendous, whose face and body so wizened, that he seemed to have exhausted all his vital force in the production of his majestic beard. An admiral's cocked hat sat jauntily on top of a red bandana, his waistcoat was extremely long and much too big, loose linen trousers were tucked into his sea-boots.

"Howdy, brother Fraser," he hailed with piping familiarity. "Come aboard. We aim to cast off while the breeze holds."

They stepped down on the small after deck.

"So this is the young bucko, eh?" His hand closed on Johnny's like a trap. "Well, sonny, my lad, I reckon you've never left dry land afore. Set down, boy, and you'll see how a ship is worked. She's only a river craft, to be sure, but I was a deep-water sailor thirty years and, big craft or small, shipshape is my name. Stand-by, there!" he shouted with startling vehemence.

A large black Negro in dungarees slowly unwound himself on the landing stage and stood erect, in a posture bashfully abject.

"Now, then, cast off!"

The Negro fumbled at the painter made fast to a worn snubbing post.

"And when I say, 'Cast off!' what do you say, black boy?"

The Negro threw a glance of sheepish appeal over his shoulder.

"Ah says, 'Ah—ah, suh!' " he muttered in a suffocated voice and threw the painter into the bows. He slipped on board amidships and shuffled forward to the mast, his bare feet softly slapping on the broad thwarts.

"Give a pull on the throat!"

"Ah—ah, suh!"

"Steady now; belay!"

The sun-rise breeze just filled the little sail. The boat swung her head out toward midstream and gathered way.

Over the side the dark water moved with the boat, aloft the breeze moved with the boat as well; they seemed to hang motionless in a calm. But when Johnny raised his head from the deep shadows and amber weeds below the keel, the landing-stage and huddle of houses were fading into the morning mist. Cypress swamps, sombre and foreboding, lined the shores on either hand. Once they saw the stilts of a flimsy landing-stage below a weathered house and a patch of sparse young corn. Two fishermen sat, hunched and motionless, in a dugout canoe; a gun spoke in the swamp with a muffled, bumping sound; three purple-headed ducks flew by; a blue crane rose through tangled branches, his trailing legs followed his strong labored flight.

Johnny's interest in this new land, this sinister, secretive land of rivers, shrank in the clutch of hunger. He fixed his eyes on his father and awaited a pause in his measured discourse to the captain.

John Fraser stopped; the captain spat emphatically over the stern. "Bung my eye," he said, "if that ain't so. I'm no landsman, squire, as you can see, but I've kep' my eyes about me for nearabout fifty year, an' what I say is this: Things is going to the dogs, by crikes; an' always has gone to the dogs, an' always will go to the dogs." He spat again.

John Fraser paused, hardly satisfied by this synopsis of his remarks.

"Dadder, could I have a piece of corn bread?"

"Eh? Oh, bless my soul, son, I'd clean forgot ye. Tae be sure, ye may; fetch it from the wallet."

"No breakfast! Well, I'm a blue baboon! Here, boy!"

The Negro shuffled aft and stood gazing at his toes.

"Hand me that cherry tart from the cuddy."

Rummaging aimlessly in the cuddy beneath the deck on which they sat, the Negro first produced a fish net, a hurricane light, thole-pins, a formless lump which might have been soap or cheese, and then a deep cherry tart from which protruded a horn spoon. He shoved it diffidently toward them on the deck and started forward.

"Come back here and stow them ship's stores! I'm bound to keep this craft as smart as a British man-o'-war."

The Negro gathered the odds and ends in his arms and poured them back in the cuddy

"Now go to your station." The skipper pointed at the departing back. "Another month and that black boy'll be an able seaman. And all through my training. It's discipline that does it. If I had my strength, I'd tie him up and flog him every day," he sighed.

"Johnny, pass the captain the pie."

The captain waved a hand.

"After you, gentlemen. If you all was of the ship's company, it would be no more than sea-manners for the master to he'p himself first. But you being cabin passengers, it's the other way 'round. At sea, boy, there's a rule for everything and the less a man thinks and the more rules he knows the better off he is. That's the trouble with you landsmen; you're short of rules."

They ate the cherry tart in rotation, using the horn spoon. The captain accepted a piece of corn bread. He drew an endless blue bandana handkerchief from his hip pocket and swabbed his whiskers vigorously. From under the gunwale he produced a large, drooping pipe whose procelain bowl was profusely illustrated with figures of men in mustaches and bare knees drinking beer. He lit it and tapped the long bowl.

"This pipe's a mighty curious pipe, ain't it? Got it off'n a Dutcher at Frankfort in 'fifty-eight. Or was it 'fifty-seven? 'Fifty-seven—'fifty-eight—— Well, I declare!"

He sat down abstractedly on a keg beside the tiller and devoted himself to the solution of his pipe's chronology.

The sky grew bright and hot; the cypress-darkened banks were still the same. Their craft floated down the winding stream without change, without time. The sun smote the canvas awning, the captain's pipe-smoke drifted in their wake.

Squire Fraser produced a pigskin Testament from his pocket and settled down to read. The captain peered over his shoulder.

"Scripteh?"

"Aye."

"Never had time to follow Scripteh much, what with following the sea. But I respects a man that does. Scripteh," he added complacently, "is a mighty fine thing. There was a supercargo on the 'Brownwing'—or was it the 'Moorish Chief'—now let me see——

"My memory ain't what it was," he sighed; "not by a long sea-mile. Why, I used to be able to name every ship I'd sailed in, in proper order, and the day and year I'd signed on for each, name 'em backwards and forwards, I could, and often did, to entertain the boys."

Evidently there was more entertainment, Johnny reflected hazily, than he could readily fathom in this feat. There must be, for the captain was clearly a man of no ordinary parts. He was more like a figure of his dreams than anything yet encountered; there was adventure to him, to the old cocked hat, the red bandana, the sea-boots, the strange terms and oaths, the rough and ready discipline.

But now the excitement of the voyage wilted under the sun; the last air failed, the river was a breathless hedged-in lane down which they merely drifted. In the bows the Negro nodded between his knees. Johnny stretched himself on the deck and dozed.

Across a river now broad and straight and yellow, the sun, when he awoke, marked early afternoon. The chant of field-gangs stole over the water, from a clump of pines came the measured rasp of a sawpit and the coughing grunts of the Negro sawyers; the dock below it was piled with golden, dripping timbers; through the tree-trunks and flecked forest shade moved the dun backs of oxen, white plastered slave quarters stretched in a double row up a rise of ground. Barns showed beneath green oak-crowned terraces. It was clearly a country of great affairs, of riches. The pine woods slipping past, unveiled theatrically a stately, columned house, white, restful, proud yet gracious on its gentle eminence. By Zooks, it was a country of magnificence.

"See yon barge," his father said. Far down the river a speck appeared against the water. It looked like an insect crawling; a clipped bird flying; long legs or flapping wings rose and fell slowly on either side. Nearer it came; the silhouettes of oars rose all together, flashed together; now they could see the water gleam and shake from the swinging blades and the even-spaced pools whirl downstream in the barge's wake. She was painted brilliant blue and each black rower wore a brilliant blue short coat, and, bending forward, winked brass buttons in the light. A gentleman reclined on crimson cushions in the cockpit; he turned his head to the Negro boatswain standing above him. "Ease off!" the boatswain shouted in majestic tones. The oars ceased beating. Then moved gently, holding the barge against the current. The two boats drifted together.

The gentleman in a coat of orange-colored velvet and small-clothes of green satin raised a hat, crusted with gold lace, in easy salutation.

"Well, Mr. Fraser, sir, how do you? Captain, my compliments," he nodded to the captain as though bestowing a distinguished honor on him with indifference.

John Fraser just lifted the hat from his head and clapped it down again.

"Ah," the gentleman continued, "and this must be the young blood?" He

CAPTAIN FLOOD

*"Never had time to follow Scriptch much, what with following the sea. But I respects a man that does"*

favored Johnny with a glance of tolerant amusement, friendly enough but leaving the boy a feeling of impotent resentment.

The gentleman ignored the silence of the three with easy complaisance. "And how is your lady, sir?" he asked Mr. Fraser. "I had the honor of a minuet with her at his Excellency's rout, though I can hardly flatter myself that she recalls it." He smoothed the cascade of lace on his breast in a manner suggesting that he flattered himself very much indeed.

"I thank ye, she's well," John Fraser admitted grudgingly. "And you're bound up-river tae Halifax, nae doubt."

"Quite so. We had a main last night at Edenton against some Charleston birds—and won, for the honor of the Province." He waved a delicate hand toward a row of wicker coops in the bows. A cock's head, shiny black, the comb cropped close, was thrust up jauntily through an opening. The game bird rustled his wings against the wicker, threw back his head, and crowed.

"Aha! my beauty!" The gentleman's voice rang with the first sign of animation. "A pity you missed it, Squire."

"I've never seen a main in my life, young gentleman, and never will. It's sinfu' cruelty."

"Oh, my dear sir, did you know birds as I, you would think it cruel to deprive them of their highest pleasure."

The barge crew had backed water to keep alongside the riverboat, but the current now carried the larger craft downstream.

"Alas," murmured the gentleman, "the forces of Nature seem to part us; we can only bow to God's will." He smiled at the stern face of John Fraser with polished impudence and raised his hat. "My humble duty to Mistress Fraser. Servant, gentlemen. Bo'sun, give way!"

The oars poised together, a rower struck a plaintive note, they fell and rose again, the crew took up the chorus, the barge gathered way.

Johnny followed the bit of pageantry till its rhythmic flashes and unending mournful chanty were lost around a bend. His father was still at his side.

"There's the power of wealth and idleness, my lad, tae make a man a fop, a laced and scented ne'er-do-weel. Ye know him, of course?"

"How, Dadder?"

"Ye could guess. It's Wylie Jones of Halifax. Be warned against him. I would have ye acquainted wi' gentlemen, tae be sure, but wi' modest, sober, quiet gentlemen, not roysterers and randy-dandy young bucks. Beware of any man that cock-fights—no good can come o' him."

This youthful magnifico in his stately gondola was evidently a dangerous man, and, what with his cool assurance and smiling patronage, he was certainly an exasperating one. Yet Johnny, looking down at his honest home-made coat and breeches, could not ignore the notion, traitorous both to his father and his own self-respect, that he would like to cut a figure like Wylie Jones.

The river opened out, broad tilled fields and frequent houses crowned the banks, the banks themselves receded imperceptibly until it dawned on Johnny Fraser that they were in the river no longer, that this at last was Albemarle Sound.

"Dadder," he said, "may I go up in front?"

"For'ard," the skipper corrected out of the corner of his mouth, his eye glued on a channel stake, "for'ard's the word an' don't forget it. At sea there's a word for everything."

Johnny ran along the counter, using one hand on the row of barrels. The Negro in the bows greeted him with a deprecating half-smile and silently placed a coil of rope for him to sit on. Johnny squatted beside him, with a feeling of friendliness.

The bay stretched out ahead; dingy sails of luggers moved sluggishly across it, a nearing channel stake looked like a distaff with its carded skein of wool; the wool, surprisingly, flew upward and a seagull cried like a lost child. The day was dying behind him, the southwest sunset breeze filled the sail, ropes creaked, thin foam curled under the bows; then beneath his thighs he felt the deck lift gently, strongly, in the first incredible foretaste of the ocean swell.

The riffling water turned rosy in the sunset, the dingy sails turned golden, the eastern sky reflected delicately the blazing fire in the west; below this eastern afterglow stretched a soft blue shore-line, ringing the bay; in its darkest recess the crowded, many-angled roofs of a city reflected planes of light; a slim white cupola reached up to the sun; against the delicate horizon stretched a fairy lattice, the masts and rigging of the ships. Deep-sea ships, full-rigged ships, men-o'-war, merchantmen, sneaking coasters, slavers, rum-boats, whalers.

The Negro beside him briefly waved a dangling hand. His voice was a deep, soft whisper.

"Eden'on. Das wher' we boun'."

# CHAPTER VIII

As THEY slipped along past rows of shadowy docks, Johnny read the names and home ports on the tall sterns: "Swiftsure—Norfolk," "General Gage—Boston," "Hector—Antigua," "Caroline—Charleston," "Good Intent—Basseterre," "Ste. Geneviève—Quebec." Their high sides, brown and black, their lofty, jutting poops, carved fancifully, brooded over the waters; the tall, dark ships rode the tide like dragons shifting in their sleep. It seemed rash folly for their own skiff to venture even among their sombre, long reflections.

It came, therefore, as a disillusion to find that these incredible monsters of the deep supported a commonplace domestic life. A careless hand emptied a bucket of slops from a galley porthole. Johnny half expected to hear Sofa's voice, and see the chickens scatter. At the rail of the "Good Intent" a sailor in a jersey and linen cap nodded to them with no sense of high adventure; they might as well be meeting him in a lane. And finally, aboard the "Ste. Geneviève," a cat, a small and undistinguished cat, was rubbing her back along the spindles of the quarter-rail.

Now the docks were smaller and crowded with the little coasting boats, the "Peggy," "Sally," "Molly," "Jenny," all of Edenton, moored side by side along the quay, fat, round, drowsily nudging, like sucking pigs at the sow.

Then came the rafts and river-boats, deep in the water, piled high with sheeted cargoes.

He felt the bows swing round, she came up in the wind. "Ease away on the peak!" the captain screamed. "Let her run!" The sail rustled down, they slid in toward a narrow brick wharf. The Negro put out a broad flat foot and fended her off, picked up a rope-end and swung up on the coping. Johnny scrambled after him; he stamped his feet on the moss-lined bricks; this was Edenton.

A coil of rope came curling up from the stern. "Make fast that hawser!" The coil lay at Johnny's feet. The gentleman adventurer in him leaped to action. He threw it around a tall cypress pile and tied it as he would a halter shank. The Negro watched him with secret but insupportable delight. Just then the captain's whiskers and eyes appeared on a level with the dock.

"God help you, youngster, if you ain't gone and tied my ship up like a yearling calf."

Johnny gazed at the knot in humble silence. The captain's tone changed.

"Never mind, Jackie, you're smart and handy and intend your duty—even if you don't know nothing. How old are you?"

"Thirteen."

The captain shook his whiskers from side to side in mournful reflection.

"Too bad; you'd 'a' made an A.B. and a rousin' good A.B., if you could 'a' started in when you was young."

John Fraser's head and shoulders appeared and the two saddle-bags were heaved up on the dock. He shook hands with the captain gravely and climbed a slimy wooden ladder. The captain reached up a hand to Johnny.

"Good luck. This yer's my reg'lar dock; come down and see me when I'm in port and I'll l'arn you a little of a seaman's duty. You'll never make a sailor now, but that's no reason to remain a ignerammis. Humble servant, gentlemen both."

They shouldered their saddle-bags and marched. The bricks felt hard beneath Johnny's feet, but his eyes were raised to the shadowy houses of the town. First came the cluttered wooden dockside buildings, sail lofts, rigging yards, a rope walk, shipchandler's sheds, now dark and silent at the close of day. Tarred fish nets spread their misty folds, a tawny canvas hung on a fence; the smells of molasses, of tar and rosin, and of fish scales, drifted up on the soft air.

A cobbled lane led them between low sheds to a broad dark street where live oaks cast their dusk on the roadway and the first candles shone from windows set back in little gardens. The house fronts showed dimly white as they passed by, dark figures moved along the path, a spinet tinkled faintly up the hill. Stumping beside his father in his unaccustomed shoes, Johnny felt that this new life, mysterious, complex and elusive, might be too much for him. The boat had been splendid, but then there had been no one but the captain, the Negro, didn't count. Here, however, were a thousand people, living close together, walking on bricks, playing spinets—— Night was falling; he wished for his mother.

Above a ship's lantern hung out over the path, a sign depicted a youth in a cap of ostrich plumes sounding a trumpet from which depended a crimson banner.

"This is Hornblower's Tavern," his father said, "and verra different frae Slade's we'll find it."

Through a generous open door they saw wax candles and the gleam of burnished pewter against dark panelling, and a damp sanded floor new swept in a curling pattern.

A fat little man in a skirt-like apron and canary-colored waistcoat bounced out of a green baize door.

"Well, upon my soul and everlasting honor if this is not Mr. Fraser of Little River! Mr. Fraser, pray how do you do, sir? Well, I trust, sir? I do indeed. And this is the young Mr. Fraser. Pleasure, sir, most distinguished pleasure!" He rubbed two fat and fiery red hands on his stomach and brought them to rest on his hips. His smooth, round, ruddy face beamed on them in deferential ecstacy.

"And now, gentlemen, at your service."

"A chamber for the night, if it please ye, Mr. Hornblower. And we'll need our supper directly."

"Why, *to* be sure; to be *sure*. Allow me."

He lifted the saddle-bags and led the way up a broad oak stair. Taking a candle from a sconce in the upper hall, he bowed and entered a bed-chamber. Other candles flared up, they followed him.

The room was papered in a pattern of roses, the bed canopy and the chair covers were of rose-colored chintz. A mahogany dresser bore two brass candlesticks and a large mirror; a small carron stove was filled for the summer with paper, fluted in an ingenious design; three oval rag rugs lay on the black-painted floor.

On a table stood a pitcher and basin, each bearing a large blue panorama of Chinese Temples, junks and high-arched bridges. Mr. Hornblower peered into the pitcher with all the solemnity of a high priest consulting an oracle. "Fresh water, gentlemen," he announced judicially; "and should you require anything, you have but to ring." He pointed to a crimson, tasseled bell-pull by the door. He bowed, beamed, stepped lightly and carefully out of the room.

They washed, put on new stocks and changed to their extra shoes. While his father combed his beard before the glass, Johnny went to the window and pulled back the mosquito curtain of fine lawn. Outside it was night now, but everywhere dim shapes of fences, walks, houses filled the view; everywhere voices sounded through the dark, heels clicked on pavement. He felt cramped, hemmed in by this close-built place, these busy murmurs. The feeling grew unbearable. Cramped? No, by Zooks, cornered, with his back to the sea. Why had he left the long, unbroken forests sighing at evening in long, unbroken whispers?

His father snuffed the candles out; together they went below stairs.

Two gentlemen in dark coats, seated at one of the tables, played at backgammon. The elder wore a neat scratch wig, while the dark hair of the younger was carelessly tied by a black ribbon. Both faces, grave and strong, were bent forward, intently, over their game.

"Good evening tae ye, Mister Hewes," his father said.

The two rose with deliberation, the elder, long-faced and humorous, held out his hand.

"Why, Squire Fraser, I am well pleased tew see you." His voice, though cordial, was nasal and jerky, his "r's" were rounded and long drawn out. "Squi-ur Fras-ur," he said, "you know Mister Teague Battle?"

Mr. Battle, loose-limbed and more negligent than Mr. Hewes, put a big bony hand in John Fraser's.

"How you, seh?" His manner was easy, large and cordial, yet stamped with unstudied dignity and tinged with a fundamental reserve.

"Well, I thank ye. And you?"

"Can't complain, seh."

"Mr. Battle, " said Mr. Hewes, "is like tew become our leading lawyer if he ever gets araound tew it."

"I aim," said Mr. Battle with a slow smile, "not to make the same mistake as Mr. Hewes. Mr. Hewes flies round his shipyard so fast that he's not had time to think since the fall of seventeen sixty-fo'." He laid a hand on Mr. Hewes' arm.

The suspicion of an affectionate grin touched Mr. Hewes' face. Then he saw Johnny.

"Hullo, is this the jewnior?"

"Aye. Johnny, your duty tae the gentlemen."

"Humble duty, seh," Johnny murmured shyly and thrust his small paw into the two strong hands.

"I declare," said Mr. Battle, "this hyer boy's a natural-born North Carolinian. Hyear him talk."

"His tongue might be," admitted John Fraser; "he got that frae his mither. But his heart's Scots, eh, lad?"

"Yes, seh, I reckon."

The strangers laughed and Johnny scuffed his new shoes together.

"Weel, gentlemen, continue wi' your play. We have not yet supped."

Johnny and his father sat down to a large herring at another table. The players threw their dice and moved the pieces silently. John Fraser divided the fish and the heel of a loaf with care. Both fell to.

As they finished, the gentlemen were closing up their board.

"Ninety-fo'," said Mr. Battle.

"Thurty-nine," said Mr. Hewes. "I owe you four and nine pence. Hornblower!"

The baize door sprung as if on wires.

"Yes, gentlemen."

"Change for a half-jo."

Mr. Hornblower lifted up a small hinged counter and disappeared into the bar. The bar window showed racks of dark bottles and the top of Mr. Hornblower's bald, clipped head. The clink of coins came from behind the counter and the sound of his solicitous voice.

"I am sorry you gentlemen were disturbed last evening—very unfortunate—most unfortunate—quite unusual in this establishment, as you gentlemen know. I assure you I did my best, but——"

"Why, Hornblower," said Mr. Hewes, "I thought you were pretty smart to get rid of them at all."

"Did ye have a row here, then?" asked Johnny's father.

Mr. Hornblower's face, apostolically solemn, appeared above the counter. "Oh, no, sir; we never have that. But some young gentlemen from South Carolina had brought their fighting-cocks from Charleston for a main. Young Sir Nathaniel Dukinfield was the principal here and Mr. Wylie Jones came down the river from Halifax with birds."

"Aye, we passed him."

"Well, sir, it is evident that during the main, all became somewhat disguised with liquor. And afterward they had the unhappy notion to come here for further entertainment. They interrupted Mr. Hewes' backgammon game most inconsiderately, and when I remonstrated there was talk of—er —spinning me on my head."

"Accompanied by oaths and mighty provocative gestures," said Mr. Battle solemnly.

"Yes, Indeed. It was distressing. They finally left, however, roaring about and employing most uncivil language, and I must say I was unspeakably relieved." He raised a corner of his apron and mopped his glistening brow.

The gentlemen settled their score, pushed back their chairs and lit long clay pipes. They inquired of John Fraser for news of the Back Country and told him in turn the happenings of the coast, ships cleared, cargoes lost, hulls launched off the stocks, smugglers taken. Johnny listened hopefully, but in their talk all high adventure fell lamely to the level of shillings and pence, of accounts cast up, of rates of exchange and interest. His interest waned.

"Blood!"

He roused with a start. It was Mr. Battle speaking.

"Blood," he said, "they's plenty in this province who ain't afraid of it. We import no tea and we pay no tax, as you know, seh. But we're not short of lively spirited fellows who don't mind running a cargo in after dark."

"Aye," said John Fraser, "when profits and patriotism gae hand in hand, ye'll find many loyal tae the cause." His voice turned earnest. "But go slow, my friend, I beg of ye. His Majesty's government is tardy, but one day they'll put down these smugglers and the non-importers and belike the men that are behind them." He looked significantly at Mr. Battle and at Mr. Hewes.

"Why, Squire," said Mr. Hewes, "that's just abaout what we calculate."

"Well, then, my friend, ye are farther gone in folly than I guessed. Dae ye really know what ye are about and what it will lead to?"

Mr. Battle's light blue eyes shone bright and hard as frozen seas, his voice drawled more than ever. "We know we're right." His face broke into a careless, self-reliant smile. "And as to blood," he said, "why should that fret us?"

Hanging a long arm over the back of his chair, he swung it slowly and plunged in thought. His face turned grave, the corners of his large, bold, humorous mouth drooped into stern sad lines.

"Not that we look fo' trouble," he murmured. "Only justice."

He mused again. "Though it may amount to the same thing in the end. It must, I reckon—unless the English change their notions."

His swinging hand dropped swiftly, noiselessly to the table.

"We're building a country of our own. We're not the men to be treated as retainers."

He pulled a tankard toward him.

"Blood." He was smiling again. "The world is old and they's been blood shed befo'."

He turned his keen, daring eyes on each, he bowed to each, and drank.

Feet stamped outside, a young man in top-boots, red whipcord breeches and a buckled hat strode in. His face, as it quickly swept the room, was keen and knowing like that of a precocious child. But the eyes were blood-shot, the complexion a sickly olive.

"How do, all?" he jerked a riding crop. "My God, my head!"

"Why, Nat," said Mr. Hewes, "your gills are green."

"Been through the mill. Last night. Charleston bucks. Pitted twenty birds. Negus and Sangaree. That wouldn't do. New England rum. Did do. Hornblower!"

"Coming, sir!" cried a faint and flustered voice. Mr. Hornblower thrust a cautious head around the corner of the door.

"Come out, Pussyface. Small beer and plenty of it! My God, my head!" The young man sank down mournfully on a chair.

"Very good, Sir Nathaniel,—perhaps some bitters as well, sir?"

"Bitters! Been drinkin' bitters all day. Holland gin, too. Canary. Hot punch. Everything." He sighed with the resignation of one who has left nothing undone.

Mr. Hornblower brought him a large pewter pot and a stoneware bottle, whose seal Sir Nathaniel scrutinized with morbid intensity. He filled the tankard, slouched back in his chair and devoted himself to the methodical absorption of small beer.

"Small beer!" he muttered from time to time, blowing heavily out of the corners of his mouth. "Gad's teeth, small beer!"

For Johnny the figure of the young man, so shattered, so wild-eyed, held the fascination of a gay buck, the pathos of a shipwrecked sailor and the terror of a potential maniac. Surely something should be done about it; the watch should be turned out, a doctor should be called; at least the rest of them ought cautiously to steal from the tap-room. But to his amazement his father and the two gentlemen took up their talk as calmly as if a man in Sir Nat's peculiar state of health was the most natural phenomenon in the world. He himself could not keep his eyes off the dejected yet exciting figure.

Sir Nathaniel consumed small beer in measured gulps; he screwed up his eyes and gingerly shook his head; consumed more beer. He paused and fixed on John Fraser a glance, intent and brooding. Johnny felt that his father should be warned. But Mr. Hewes, looking up just then observed casually, "Nat, you know Mr. Fraser of Little River, do you not?"

The young man rose, crossed the floor, steadily enough, but with undue concentration, and bowed.

"Don't rec'lect. Never remember faces. Remember horses. See him on a horse, know him." He bowed again, "Pleasure!" and sat down abruptly at their table.

His father merely bowed and resumed his talk with the others. Johnny drew himself close.

Sir Nathaniel now cast backward glances at the pot of small beer which he had left; he seemed to be calculating its distance from himself and studying the topography of the intervening floor. He blew again from the corner of his mouth, squinted and shook his head.

"Hornblower!"

"Yes, sir."

"My beer."

The beer was brought him. He settled himself to renew his operations when his wandering gaze fell on Johnny.

"Hullo, bantam."

"How are you, seh?" Johnny whispered.

"Have a nightcap?"

"No, thank you, seh."

For some moments Sir Nathaniel seemed to view this answer as destroying all possibility of social intercourse. Then he leaned solemnly toward

Johnny and pointed a finger at Mr. Battle and Mr. Hewes as if they were a pair of wax-works.

"Teague and Plain Clothes," he said, in loud explanatory tones. "Powerful minds—powerful. But"—he wagged his finger under Johnny's nose—"don't know life. No blood-horses. No game-birds. Can't shoot. Can't ride. Can't drink. Too bad."

He leaned back in his chair, reflected for a moment, then turned on Johnny an engaging, uncertain smile and childlike eyes.

"Not clever myself. But lend you a horse—any time. Come see me."

He finished his beer in silence and rose. "Servant, gentlemen," he said. "Dull company." Clapping his hat down over his eyes, he marched quite steadily from the room.

They heard his voice, "Stand now, Peregrine!" and the hoofbeats of his horse trotting out of town.

The three men exchanged glances.

"The young feller won't last long," said Mr. Hewes.

"I've warned my son against such as him," said Johnny's father.

"And yet I reckon he has the best heart in the province," said Mr. Battle.

"What's a heart, sir?" asked John Fraser, not contentiously, but with the calm assurance of one who merely points out an axiom by means of a rhetorical question. "What's a heart, sir, wi'out character and a mind tae do the will o' God?" His glance, circling the group, fetched up on Johnny, for whose principal benefit the speech was made. His eye, resting on his son in benignant admonition, slowly widened with conscience-smitten surprise.

"Why, bless us," he exclaimed, "ye should be i' bed this long time! Say good night and tak' this candle."

Johnny stood up, holding the candle in his hand.

"Good night, Mr——"

"Battle," his father said.

"Good night, Mr——"

"Hewes."

"Good night, Dadder."

He made a stiff little bow to each.

"Good night, my lad," they said. He turned and climbed the broad stair.

To give himself assurance, he lit every candle in the elegant and formidable room. Undressed, he placed them all by the head of the bed, then slid beneath the covers and blew them all out with one tremendous puff.

The town-bred noises were dying in the lanes and houses; he heard infrequent footsteps, a casual door slammed to, a dog bayed, a girl laughed. Drowsy silence followed, silence through which came slowly drifting a murmur—distant, faint, like the murmur of the pines. He listened, comforted yet puzzled; then knew that what he heard was the vast, unceasing whisper of the sea.

## CHAPTER IX

THEY BREAKFASTED on bread and bohea tea in the twinkling taproom. His father read the last issue of the "Cape Fear Mercury" word by word. He was not the man to glance over things; he plodded solemnly through the notices of runaway slaves and indentured servants, of lost cattle, of black boys for sale. Johnny looked out the window by the table.

Workmen in woolen stockings and leather aprons were going down to the docks and yards. They moved leisurely by twos and threes, chewing tobacco, exchanging monosyllables and dry, hard-bitten grins among themselves. 'Prentice lads, meanly dressed, scurried along under their masters' tool-chests. A foreman, very respectable in a long plain coat, walked past with measured step. The bump of mallets, the grate of saws and the creak of pulleys came up from the waterside. Mr. Hewes, with an earnest face and a pace out of all proportion, it seemed to Johnny, to the importance of any earthly affairs, whisked down a lane. A mulatto girl with hips a-swing and

71

flat breasts softly moving under the calico, came, stepping smoothly, noiselessly. She threw a glance, deliberate, bold, yet ever-shifting, at the window
and passed on, tilting her head to her slow, weaving motion. Up from the
docks rolled a sailor with a white handkerchief bound under his small
round hat; he wore a rough round-coat and carried a dunnage-bag on his
shoulder. As he drew nearer Johnny saw, to his chagrin, that the man had
no earrings, no visible tattooing. And worse still, beneath the dunnage-bag
dangled a tiny flannel-covered cage from which came the flustered twitter
of a song sparrow. It was too much. Could ships and seamen never get away
from fireside flummery, from little pussy cats and birds in cages?

His father had drawn from his pocket Mr. Merrillee's letter of introduction wrapped in oiled silk. He studied the super-scripture and the seal, he
tapped it with his thick blunt finger, rose and put on his hat.

With the letter in his hand and Johnny beside him, he walked up the
shaded street toward the dark brick church, neat and squat, which stood
set back in a wide plot of green grass, magnolias and marble gravestones.
Beyond it stood the neat, squat rectory at the end of a brick path through
tuberoses. Johnny's father opened a low gate, walked up the path and lifted
a huge brass knocker. When it fell the little rectory seemed to rock to its
foundations. Inside there was a scuffling of slippered feet, a clicking of
crockery and a rustling of papers. A thin, gently serious little old man in a
flowered dressing-gown and iron spectacles opened the door and stood
blinking in an attitude of polite obfuscation.

"Yes, gentlemen, yes, yes, yes." His soft, babbling voice was cordial but
guarded, something between extreme civility to a stranger and temperate
recognition of a friend. He ventured no further remark, but stood there
blinking and vaguely smiling, content, apparently, that all three should
remain fixed and silent on the doorstep in perpetuity.

Mr. Fraser broke the spell; he held out the letter.

"Dr. Clapton, I believe. I bear a letter from Mr. Merrillee."

"Mr. Merrillee! Bless my soul, yes, yes!"

Dr. Clapton received the letter as if it were a royal commission, then
relapsed into a second benevolent trance. Lost in reflection, he appeared to
be framing a profound observation.

DOCTOR CLAPTON

*He ventured no further remark, but stood there blinking and vaguely smiling*

"Yes!" he said and flung back the door.

The room was like a cave which had been roughly hewn in the heart of a mountain of books. Books lined the walls, books paved the floor, at each small window a slit of sunlight climbed in painfully over high-piled books; books encrusted the chairs along whose edges Dr. Clapton had excavated narrow perches for himself; on the upper shelves, pendant fragments of torn bindings and scraps of manuscript gave the effect of the cave's very roof itself supporting stalactites of books.

"Dear me, one moment, gentlemen!" Girding up his dressing gown, Mr. Clapton set himself to clearing the books off the chairs and stacking them in odd corners.

"Can we lend ye a hand, Doctor?" asked John Fraser in a respectful voice.

"Oh, thank you, no! No, no." Dr. Clapton peered at them over an armful of books in alarm. "You see, I have a method.

"Yes, yes, a method," he murmured, lugging by successive loads of books and heaping them softly but indiscriminately in a large conical mound.

From the recesses of the second chair his labors brought up unexpectedly a slice of bread and an empty teacup.

"Ah," he said, "breakfast. I study early and breakfast late. It was found best by the Persian philosophers." While speaking, he absently placed the bread and cup on the chair he had already cleared and returned to work. When the second chair was empty he faced them, a little flushed, and waved a mildly triumphant hand. "Be seated, gentlemen, I pray." He burrowed a place for himself in the book-laden chair which remained and gazed on them with enormous concentration, looking quickly from one to the other in a manner which he conceived to be business-like and acute.

"And now, gentlemen. Yes?"

"The letter——" John Fraser said.

"Yes, the letter." Mr. Clapton's face fell into lines of distress and straining recollection. "To be sure, the letter. Of course, yes, dear me."

He felt in the pocket of his dressing-gown and threw a distracted look around the cavern.

"Never mind, sir, I beg," said Johnny's father hastily. "I can just tell ye what was in it."

Crossing one leg over the other, John Fraser carefully and slowly outlined his plans for Johnny's education. Mr. Clapton nodded almost continuously in high approval.

Johnny himself looked around the room. The shaggy leather bindings and dim gilt titles were broken only by the tops of the two windows, by a small grate, heaped with dead ashes, and by another door through which he caught glimpses of a barefooted Negro girl with a twig broom in one hand and a large piece of pork fat in the other. She peered in at him, tittered, made casual sweeping motions with the broom. "That servant," he thought to himself, "has been naturally spoiled." She vanished, trailing the broom behind her. He heard her hallooing to another Negro in the street, then the sound of endless Negro chat mixed with cackles and guffaws.

"Well, then," his father was saying, "we are agreed. Ten pounds, two beeves and a cag of cider each year, and we might just see his room before we go?"

"Yes, yes, indeed! Malley!" Listening for an answer, Mr. Clapton heard only the murmur of Malley's conversation across the back fence.

"Dear me," he said sadly, with the detachment of one who observes a natural phenomenon from afar, "my Negro girl, I fear, is idle. This way."

The chamber which he showed them under the eaves was plastered white and pleasant enough, but bare, hot and stuffy.

"Wi' the casements open, it will no do so badly," John Fraser said. "He'll want a rug, maybe, and mosquito curtains on the bed."

"To be sure, yes, yes. I shall order Malley to make curtains at once. And now, sir, will you not do me the honor to dine with me at three?"

"I'd like to real well, sir, but I have left my lady at home alone and must go up river this noon when the boat leaves."

"I am sorry indeed. But Johnny, of course, will come." He placed a timid, kindly hand on Johnny's arm. "I shall try to make things easy for him. And perhaps I can, yes, yes." He glanced from one to the other with appeal and yet with a certain shy confidence. "I am not perhaps a person of practical affairs. And yet there are corners of the heart, sir, which I understand better than abler men. Yes, yes," he smiled serenely, with a quaint and delicate beauty which did not seem ill fitting although it might rather have been the beauty of a woman. Johnny felt much embarrassed yet reassured. The plastered chamber looked less bleak.

As Johnny and his father went back down the street of live oaks to Hornblower's tavern, the ladies of Edenton were astir. They passed by in small chip hats and flowing callimanco gowns. The heads of some were hooded by capuchins against the dust. Some carried market baskets while Negro boys carried the baskets for others, for it was market day. Down the middle of the street swung tall, straight country Negroes balancing wooden trays of yams and cucumbers on their heads; an ox-cart laden with round-eyed calves creaked by. Beneath rude awnings in the distant market-place they caught the yellowish pink of dressed hogs, the white of flounders, and saw, beyond the knots of chattering heads, long ranks of vegetables and early flowers.

They went above stairs for Johnny's saddle-bags. To Johnny, the room, though elegant and strange enough, seemed almost like a home now that his father was to leave him. He had shared this room with his father, a man taciturn, exacting, apart, yet for some unfathomed reason, indispensable. He picked up his saddle-bags.

"It's a weight for ye, son; give it me."

His father threw the bags over his shoulder and led the way back to Dr. Clapton's. Dr. Clapton opened the door, courteously waved a hand with a book in it toward the attic room and left them to themselves.

They opened the saddle-bags on the bed and unpacked them. The shirts, the stocks, the spun yarn stockings, all made by his mother, were laid in a little wooden chest beneath the window. Johnny closed the lid on them and wished that he could close it as well on the dull misery that he drew from those neat rows. The fuzzy wooden tooth-brush went in the mug on the table, the bars of home-boiled soap beside it. On the shelf below they stacked his slender library, the horn speller, the Latin grammar, the arithmetic. His father drew the pigskin Testament from his coat and placed it on top of the others. They unfolded the linen sheets and spread them on the bed.

John Fraser smoothed a last wrinkle and stood up awkwardly. They faced each other in the little attic room.

"My son," he said, "I'll be leaving soon." His eye wandered to the floor in alarming embarrassment. He cleared his throat huskily. "When ye are grown," he said, "I want ye tae be a good man. And tae do that ye'll have tae be a good boy. There are no figs frae thistles. Say your prayers, lad, and keep your talk free frae oaths and badness. I know ye will unless it be through carelessness. For ye are a gentleman born." He mused gravely, struggling to break the ancient silent habit and speak his heart. "I've thought for ye, and dreamed for ye, and prayed for ye—and your good mother more than I. And, now that ye are to go alone i' the world, remember ye come o' honest blood and brave blood, and dinna be afeared o' any thing but sin."

He held out his hand, his face crimson from the ordeal, and gazed through the window till Johnny took it, clung to it. Then he passed an arm around the slender shoulders in one breathless, iron hug and cleared his throat abruptly.

"Come," he said, "we must go tae the wharf if I'm tae take that boat."

As they walked down the wharf to where the boat was moored the captain's whiskers popped up over the edge like a burst of spray.

"Howdy, gentlemen! Squire! Well, young fellow; come to see your old man safe aboard? Never you fear, my bucko, he can't come to no harm along with me. I'll see him off at Slade's myself, and tell you about it when I'm back hyer, come Thursday."

John Fraser gave Johnny a formal handshake and stepped down on the deck.

"Breeze right," said the captain. "Cast off, there, boy!"

"Ah—ah, suh."

The Negro, slowly emerging from a stack of cotton bales, proceeded to cast off with deliberation. Then, as the bows swung out, he landed easily on the little forward deck with a soft, padding sound.

The sail and after awning obscured his father till the boat was well out in the bay, and Johnny was glad. It would have been hard to stand there, helpless, and watch those features slowly fade. When at last his father could be seen he was but a figure who turned and looked at him, then held his right hand high in salutation, like an Indian.

The figure faded, then the boat, as well; the careless, gleaming water stretched between. He was alone.

He turned and stumbled down the quay. Through the mists a small blue-cloaked figure came to meet him. It was Dr. Clapton. Johnny felt him fall in beside him with pattering steps shorter than his own.

They reached the street. "I was passing by," Dr. Clapton murmured, "and thought that together we might walk back home. Home—that is what I hope you will call it, too. Yes, yes."

# CHAPTER X

IN THE book-cave next morning, Dr. Clapton stuck a finger to mark his place in the volume he read and gave Johnny a kindly though distracted smile. His spectacled eyes, wrested from the book with effort, still roamed through some distant field of thought. Laboriously Dr. Clapton brought them to a focus on Johnny and sat staring at him with benevolent but disturbing concentration. A light broke over his baffled face.

"Ah——" he said; "breakfast, of course. Malley."

To Johnny's astonishment, Malley immediately came in with a bowl of tea and a large plate of bread and butter for him. With practised hand she disengaged Mr. Clapton's empty cup from the surrounding books and carried it out to the kitchen.

Searching in vain for a place to put his bread and tea, Johnny finally camped out in a vacant space on the floor, though not without misgivings on the score of etiquette. Dr. Clapton, however, paid no notice until Johnny had finished; he then picked up the empty plate and bowl and tucked them away behind the books on a chair.

"Now," he said, "fetch down your school books and we shall see."

What Dr. Clapton saw by the end of the morning was this: that Johnny wrote a fair hand and spelled within reason, that he read the easier passages in Cæsar's Commentaries passably but with no pretensions to elegance; and that his efforts to write Latin were uniformly deplorable. In the realm of science he could add, subtract, divide and multiply infallibly if given ample time, but of fractions the less said the better.

"You must learn to cipher, Johnny. It is unfortunate that gentlemen's sons should employ their time in the commercial branches, and I should never subscribe to a young man's going a step beyond fractions and decimals, unless, of course, he were to enter his Majesty's navy, and even there I consider that the mathematics should be left as far as possible to the lower ranks. But with clerks and stewards what they are nowadays, a gentleman must know fractions if he would protect his affairs."

"Yes, seh. Dadder said I must learn fractions."

"I have no doubt. A knowledge of ciphering is commonly demanded by the parents of this Province." His eye wandered. "I have concluded," he murmured, "that ciphering is one of the unavoidable disadvantages of a new country. Yes."

Upon this remark Mr. Clapton reflected so long that Johnny at last put in a bashful, "Yes, seh."

"Oh—ah, now as to Latin exercises; that is more serious. When I was a Colleger at Eton the meanest scholar your age could do his fifty lines a day with never a false quantity."

Johnny wondered truculently how many squirrels these same young English scholars would bring back if sent into the woods with five bullets and five charges.

"But you have never heard of Eton, I suppose," Dr. Clapton was saying.

"Yes, seh, I did once. Didn't Mr. Wylie Jones get his schooling there?"

Mr. Clapton's face fell.

"Yes—in a sense, in a sense. But he was an Oppidan. They are not scholars as are the Collegers. In consequence, I am sorry to say, they are a much wilder set of fellows. Were you at Eton, I should wish you to be a Colleger. As it is we shall do our best here."

With that Johnny settled down to Mr. Clapton's gentle but none the less irksome routine. Each morning he did his rows of figures from the arithmetic, wrote out interminable conjugations, and plodded on through the Cæsar, parsing every word. In the afternoons he wandered disconsolately about the town, peeping in at the shipwrights' yards, looking shyly at other boys, while Mr. Clapton, in clerical bands and blue cloak, visited his parishioners or stopped in the main street to pass the time of day with the principal citizens of Edenton.

The next event to be awaited was the return of the captain with, perhaps, some message from his father. When Johnny reached the wharf on Thursday the river boat was already in. Three Negro roustabouts were leisurely rolling tar barrels out of her up to the dock.

A door slammed behind him. The captain, emerging from a little office, came swinging in maritime fashion down the quay.

"Hi, youngster! How you living?"

"Fine, thank you, Captain. How you?"

"Your old man stood the trip good." The captain tugged from his breeches pocket a crumpled letter. "Hyer's an express to tell you about it."

Johnny balanced the letter in his hand and stared at the small, fine superscription, "Master Johnny Fraser. Kindness of Captn. Flood." Turning it over, he looked at the stamp of his father's seal ring, three thistles, on the wax. That seal, that very seal had been stamped by his father's great square hand. How near that made him seem and yet how far. Only two nights ago his father's hand had rested on this paper. Now what inexorable nights and days divided them.

"Look it over, sonny," the captain was saying. "I'll be in the company's office making up the ship's invoices when you're done."

Johnny sat down on a bag of lint cotton and broke the seal. The letter was appallingly short:

> "Slade's Ordinary.
> "June 11, 1771.

"My dear Son:

"Having the Opportunity to send you a Letter under the Hand of Capt'n Flood I take Occasion to inform you that upon reaching this Place I found both the Horses in a most Satisfactory State, the Colt in especial. So much so indeed, that I hold that Scoundrelly Bound-boy under suspicion of a design to race the Colt against a Neighbour had I not returned to prevent him. As matters are you need have no further Uneasiness, for I sett out for Home tomorrow.

"Let me hear how you do, nor need you feel diffident to inform me of your Reasonable Wants though I would Caution you in advance that I can not undertake any Expense on your account until I have amply satisfied myself as to the Justice of your Requirements.

> "Your aff'nate Father
> "John Fraser."

This letter, the first he had ever received, he studiously deciphered three times, hoping to discover some closer and more intimate link than the stiff words seemed to afford. But his father, who had for a moment on the day he left Edenton appeared so warm and human, was once again the demigod; this precisely inscribed paper before Johnny's eyes was the Olympian's pronunciamento.

However, the colt was well. He clutched at that straw in his dark pool of loneliness. He would think of the shining red flanks, the springing black fetlocks, the muzzle, soft and questing delicately, the eye so mild and dove-like, so filled with latent fire.

Inside the company office, the captain, his hat on the back of his head, was sitting in profound dejection on a high stool at a high table. A goose-quill pen, protruding from his mouth, waggled to and fro forlornly as if a disconsolate fowl nested uneasily in the thicket of whiskers. The tiny room held nothing else except a vast quantity of bedraggled quill pens, heaps of papers, a block and tackle, a bundle of cypress shingles and innumerable ink spots.

The little captain spun round on the stool, tilted his hat over his eyes, withdrew the quill from his mouth and replaced it by a long twist of tobacco.

"Fo'teen barrels of tar," he mumbled, "at two shillings per barrel. Now what would you say that come to in a general way?"

"Twenty-eight shillings," Johnny answered thoughtfully. "One pound eight."

The captain brightened.

"Ah, my bucko, between us we'll work out our reckoning. You can't be far out, sonny. Look here."

He produced a scrawled and rumpled sheet of paper upon which among many ink smears he had set down this sum in huge figures:

$$
\begin{aligned}
2 \\
2 \\
2 \\
2 \\
2 \\
2 \\
2 \\
2 \\
2 \\
2 \\
2 \\
2 \\
2 \\
2 \\
\hline
30
\end{aligned}
$$

"Thirty I make it. Twenty-eight you make it. We can't be far wrong if we put it down twenty-nine."

He proceeded with labored breathings to make the entry in a colossal ledger.

"But, Captain," Johnny protested, "I know it's twenty-eight."

"And so it is, near about. You're just as close as I was, every bit. But two heads is better than one in a business like this. Because, between ourselves, the owners is partick'ler, mighty partick'ler."

"But it can't be twenty-nine, seh."

The captain, completing his entry with his small sharp nose almost touching the tip of his pen, straightened up.

"Now look here, young fellow, it's give and take in this world on land and sea. And when a man like me, forty year a deep-sea sailor, goes halfway to meet a young feller like you just commencing school, you ought to be grateful, youngster, that's what you ought to be, not ornery and contentious."

He punched the ledger with his thumb.

"Twenty-nine she's wrote and twenty-nine she stands. Now let's have a yarn about how you're coming on with the l'arning."

Johnny explained that he was doing sums and reading the third book of Cæsar. The captain listened with his head judicially on one side and his whiskers tilted over his shoulder.

"Bung me," he said at the end, "that's the stuff! Ciphering and Scripteh; a man don't need no more than that on sea or land, and I ought to know."

"Yes, seh." Johnny's tone was puzzled.

"Well," said the Captain heartily, "I reckon you'd like me to carry a letter back to the folks, eh?"

"Yes, seh."

"Well, then," the Captain directed a finger at Johnny's bosom, "write her out in a good round hand, like, and I'll send it on from Slade's by a freighter or a pack-horse man. Carriage not to be paid till delivery, eh, boy?" he winked. "Trust this old sea turtle," he spat. "Just trust him, that's all."

Back in his room in the rectory the flies buzzed, the heat rayed down on him from the sun-scorched roof, his hand stuck to the paper. Before he raised his flushed and puckered face from the table, the neighboring church bells struck once and again.

Around him on the floor lay many sheets, blotted and spoiled; on the desk were two more or less clean copies. The first and neatest letter was to his father.

"Edenton,
"15th June, 1771.

"Respected Sir:

"I take occasion of a Few Hours leisure to write you by Capt'n Flood. I am glad that you found the Colt in good Fix and that he was not raced but he would have beat the other Horse sure. In the matter of Expenses I will pay due Regeard to your Instructions I have no expenses as yet but I reckon I will. I study the great Part each day cyphering and Latin and Doctor Clapton has done me the Honour to compliment my spelling and my Diligance.

"Waiting your further Commands, sir, I remain

"Your humble obt. son

"John Fraser, Jun*r*.

"I send a Letter to my Mother also under this cover."

The second was scrawly and somehow in every way unsatisfactory.

"Honoured Madam;

"I am very well Doctor Clapton is a clever Friendly Man. I do my Studies every day I love you very much

"Your dutiful aff'nate son

"Johnny."

## CHAPTER XI

ON SUNDAY morning he attended the dark brick church. All of Edenton that mattered was there in broadcloth and bombazine, decorously sweltering under the noonday sun. They moved sedately along the magnolia shaded walk between the broad heraldic tombstones and through the shadowed archway, where they paused while the old pew-opener in white hair and black gown, shuffling up and down the carpeted brick aisle, opened the low little doors with their brass name-plates. Ranged in their mahogany box pews, they sat, waving fans of partridge wing and ivory, inclining velvet bonnets, caps of Irish lawn; smoothing down waistcoats, fluffing up stocks. The church was filled with the subdued flutter of conscious elegance whose extent was happily unbroken save around the fringes where, here and there, an artisan, a 'prentice lad, a homely housewife had been discreetly stowed away in the shadows underneath the gallery.

The gallery itself, in the centre of whose railing hung the Royal Arms, showed the black ranks of slaves, the women's heads bound in white handkerchiefs, the men peering solemnly over huge white stocks. House-slaves and body-servants, they knew well how to deport themselves and how to dress. Their chief concern in life was that no one, black or white, should mistake them for field-hands.

The rustle subsided, the organ, wonder of the province, opened its quavering, flutey note. As it reached its uncertain crescendo, Johnny from his front pew could see the head of the Negro at the organ-pump bobbing up and down phrenetically. The prelude ended in a whistling blast and Dr. Clapton, wearing his white lawn gown and embroidered stole, entered the chancel, knelt before the cross, his head half-hidden by his fur-tipped hood, and took his place at the reading desk, a great brass eagle.

With kneelings, risings, responses, chantings, the service droned along. For the sermon, Dr. Clapton mounted the high cedar pulpit with its sounding-board above, like a drooping morning glory, and proceeded for a few brief moments to ramble gently, aimlessly, away from the text. He seemed to be communing, in a desultory way, with himself. It was very different from the long, hard-headed preaching of the Presbyterian circuit riders back home. Dr. Clapton came to himself with a start.

"And now to God the Father——" he pronounced the formula and descended.

Outside, the congregation loitered, gathered in groups beneath the magnolias and the tulip trees. Ladies debated London fashions and the shortcomings of their slaves, little girls clung to their mothers' skirts and dug bashful heels in the turf before the audacious glances of little boys; body-servants relieved their masters of prayer-books and stood ready for the processional return home. Slightly withdrawn from the rest, Sir Nathaniel Dukinfield discussed the latest sporting intelligence with thin-lipped companions, while near the door, the principal citizens, Mr. Hewes, Mr. Battle, and the rest, heard news from other provinces, from England, and turned grave.

Next morning and every morning after that Johnny mulled over his lessons and, late each afternoon, went swimming in the tepid waters of the bay with the boys from the docksides. He did not form these unworthy associations without misgivings. They were, of course, beneath his dignity. But his peers, the elegant little boys he saw at church, lived far out on plantations and never appeared except on Sundays. It was too much to ask himself to decline all human intercourse because young sons of gentlemen were not available. And the dockside boys, unlike the boys of the back country, made no pretensions to equality. They recognized his status. Coarse-mouthed, hardy, they looked on his rank and learning with a sort of mocking admiration; behind his back they boasted of him to the members of the river gang. Not only was he regarded as a scholar and a gentleman, but his tough, slim body and his quick, easy way of handling it were viewed as a notable acquisition to the fighting strength of the dockside boys. Far from feeling lowered in his own esteem, Johnny drew increasing satisfaction from his position in their hierarchy.

One afternoon they found a neatly painted little sloop tied up to an iron ring at the end of their favorite landing-stage. Soon a dozen naked boys in loin clouts were turning back flips and hand-springs from her stern sheets. Bare feet thumped on the narrow varnished deck; thin, flying legs and arms were swallowed in a burst of spray; heads as sleek and darkly shining as young seals' bobbed up beneath the counter; the drowsy bay was filled with whoops and chattering.

Glancing up to the dock, a boy fell silent, grinned and nudged another. All followed his gaze. A fat, youthful face, pink with offended dignity, peered down at them. Squawking derisively and flapping elbows, the dockside boys dove overboard. Johnny was left alone by the tiller.

"I say, you!" the young elegant cried, shaking a pudgy ruffled fist, "get off my boat!"

"Who's a-hurtin' yo' boat?" Johnny squatted on his dripping haunches and grinned up like a monkey.

"You heard me, didn't you, boy?" the other went on in a tone of high command.

"Say 'please,' Mushface."

The other boys had left the water and gathered on the dock. At this indignity their gleaming, sunburned bodies shook with joy. "Mushface! Mushface!" they chorused. But Mushface was not to be drawn from his enemy. He climbed down the narrow ladder, exposing a wide expanse of light blue nankeen breeches. Reaching overboard, Johnny sent a double handful of water against the majestically descending posterior.

"Hurroo!" shouted a boy.

Nankeen Breeches cursed most fluently and come down puffing. He faced about and made a rush. Johnny dodged around the mast, ran up the ladder like a squirrel, and laughed.

"Dry yo' breeches, Mushface!"

The dockside boys raised a derisive cheer; Johnny walked away; the incident was closed.

He heard a heavy step behind him; Mushface, alarmingly purple, had gained the dock and, swinging his stout arms like flails, was coming on. Johnny brought up his fists. But the movement was mechanical; it was lifeless, without gusto. By Zooks, he did not want to fight! Mushface, slowly advancing, would soon be upon him, but the remaining instant was crowded with thoughts and pictures. In all his lonely life on Little River there had never been a fight, except, of course, the glorious, heroic action of his firelit dreams. But they were different—there was no sense in hitting at the fat, foolish face which lowered at him now. It would be inglorious, even low. For was not he himself, with his teasing monkey-shines, more than half to blame? But how explain? Mushface closed in. "Don't act the fool," said Johnny, "I was just carryin' on."

For answer Mushface swung at his head. Johnny ducked and backed away.

"Don't be a fool," he said. "I won't mess with yo' boat."

Mushface swung again. Johnny retreated, blocking with his fists the strong but aimless blows. What could he say to make this lumbering stupid understand? He caught a glimpse of the dockside gang, their mouths ajar in stupefaction. Their hero was on the run. Looking over his shoulder, he found only a yard left between him and the edge of the dock. Mushface still swung wildly at his head.

"If you want to quit," said Johnny, "quit now."

JOHNNY'S FIGHT WITH CHERRY

*"Quit now," he managed to whisper, "if you want to"*

He dropped his hands, but Mushface, drunk with victory, fetched him a clout on the jaw. A hot wave of frenzy closed Johnny's throat, but he kept his hands down.

"Quit now," he managed to whisper, "if you want to."

The other big fist struck him on the mouth; his lips turned numb; a mist of rage swept him; through it he saw only the fat boy's face; the rest was blackness—nothing but blackness and the fat boy's face.

When he came to himself four dockside boys were hanging to his arms and begging him to stop. Seated on Mushface, he held him by his ears and pounded his head in the dirt. Mushface's eyes were closed, his cheeks had gone gray.

Johnny stood up, trembling. There beside his clothes lay his hat. He groped for it and ran down on the shore. As he dipped up water he heard himself sob and saw tears falling into the bay.

The hatful of water brought Mushface to.

"Whyn't you quit when I said?" asked Johnny angrily. "Now what's your name?"

"Hal—Cherry—damn—you," said Mushface, tonelessly. He climbed painfully to his feet and walked away, his fat buttocks swinging in impotent defiance.

The dockside boys stared at Johnny with some admiration, but more wonder mixed with half-formed suspicions.

"Cricky!" he heard one mutter, "if he can battle like that, why don't he want to?"

Johnny wiped the dirt from his naked body in silence. Even in victory he was as much alone as if he had been beaten. The dockside boys were well enough, but they belonged to another world. And the only gentleman Johnny had so far encountered had just now left him with tears and curses.

Dressing disconsolately, he put his wet hat on his head and trudged mournfully up the street. He felt his cheek begin to swell and stiffen, his clothes clung to his wet body, his stock was all awry. Was there no back way by which he could gain the rectory? No young gentleman in his state could afford to parade himself before the town. But even as the thought struck him he felt that he was being scrutinized from the porch of Hornblower's Tavern. Looking up shamefacedly, he saw the precocious features, now quite pink and healthy, of Sir Nathaniel Dukinfield. Here was a problem. Did or could Sir Nathaniel recall their meeting? If he did not he would surely view a salutation from Johnny as an impertinence, an impertinence of which Johnny had small wish to be guilty, in his present condition of disarray. But if Sir Nat did recall it, to pass him by without a word would be a breach of etiquette unworthy of himself, a gentleman born, however temporarily besmeared with signs of dockside strife. Perhaps a distant greeting, a greeting not pointedly directed at Sir Nathaniel or anyone in particular, but casually bestowed on the environs at large, a mere vague raising of the hat, that might be the proper compromise. At this point, however, he saw from the corner of his eye that Sir Nathaniel's face lighted with something approaching recognition.

"Bantam! Come here."

Johnny raised his hat with dignity and crossed the street. Sir Nathaniel grinned at his well-mannered approach like a spectator at an amateur play.

"Thought I didn't know you, eh? Knew you by your half-boots. Back-country half-boots—no offense."

"No, seh, these ain't back-country boots; these boots came from Edenton."

"Wrong place, then. Go to Tappit. Proper English boots." He pointed to Johnny's clumsy high-low shoes with his riding-stick.

"Won't do."

He broke a twig from a vine on the porch, peeled it carefully with his thumb nail and stuck it between his teeth. Johnny was at loss to know if this procedure signified that the interview was closed. As he was about to leave, Sir Nathaniel drew the twig from his mouth and inspected it minutely.

"Fightin'?"

"Yes, seh."

"Who?"

"Cherry—said his name was."

Sir Nat shook his head judicially.

"Outside your weight—stone and a half. Who won?"

"Why, seh, I reckon I did."

"Ha! Good job. Nasty fat boy."

Sir Nathaniel bit off the end of the twig and imbibed it once more.

"Bitters?" he inquired.

"No, thank you, seh."

"Sangaree?"

"No, thank you, seh."

Sir Nathaniel, thus deadlocked, devoted himself to forming his lips as if to whistle and shooting the twig back and forth through this small aperture.

"Good God!" he said at last. "Ride?"

"Yes, seh, a little."

"Ought to ride more."

He stared moodily into space, weighted down by thoughts of the world's equestrian deficiencies.

"Today Thursday? Thought so. Come out Saturday. Half after three. Horses."

He flicked his crop toward his hat and entered the tavern.

Mr. Clapton, sitting opposite Johnny at a small table in the study, had just finished his two o'clock Saturday dinner of fresh pork, halibut and greens, and leaning back in gentle but deep-seated contentment, was now filling his church-warden pipe. His pink face puckered over the operation like a baby's over an engrossing toy. He struck his tinder, crossed a leg and gazed with vague benevolence at Johnny through the first cloud of smoke.

This was the moment to broach the subject.

"Mr. Clapton, seh," Johnny said, "I saw Sir Nathaniel Dukinfield the other day and he asked me to ride with him this afternoon. That would be all right, wouldn't it?"

"But I was not aware you knew Sir Nathaniel."

"Yes, seh, I met him when I was with Dadder at Mr. Hornblower's tavern."

Mr. Clapton's look was unexpectedly acute.

"But does he recall the meeting? And by the bye, it is not necessary to refer to Hornblower as Mr. Hornblower."

"Yes, seh, Sir Nathaniel knows me all right because the next time he saw me he asked me to ride."

"You should have told me sooner. Such matters deserve consideration."

"Yes, seh, I——"

"You thought your chance of success lay in a hasty decision. Your strategy is primitive."

His smile was mildly triumphant.

"I told you once before that I knew the human heart. Is it not strange that I can make so little use of my knowledge?" He drifted into reflections which apparently led further and further from Sir Nat's invitation. Anxiously scanning Mr. Clapton's face, Johnny waited; he put his school books away, he looked out the open window at the shining leaves of the magnolias in the churchyard, at the dusty leaves of the sycamores along the street; he looked up at the unbroken blue expanse of sky. Mr. Clapton cleared his throat; Johnny turned expectantly.

"I am often piqued," said Mr. Clapton, "by the reflection that although the success of men of practical affairs is something tangible and the failure of men of—er—impractical affairs, myself for instance, is something intangible, nevertheless it is far easier to assign causes for the failure of the one than for the success of the other."

He relapsed into thought again. It would soon be three.

"Yes, seh," Johnny said. "That's so. It looks like it was going to be a mighty nice afternoon."

"Eh?"

"A mighty nice afternoon, seh." He pointed out the door.

Mr. Clapton's eyes came to a focus.

"Ah, yes, yes. Now why do you say that?"

"We were talking about going to Sir Nathaniel's, seh."

"Why, of course, yes, yes!" Mr. Clapton exclaimed, "and you are seeking permission. Exactly!" He pondered. "I scarce know what to say. Riding is, I am told, an admirable exercise; although I myself have always found horses unsympathetical creatures; and this despite the fact that I have been for some years engaged on a work which in many respects has to do with horses. I think I have told you of it." He gathered himself with an effort. "But as to Sir Nathaniel; if only I could be sure that you would accept his virtues while rejecting, with all humility and tolerance, his defects! Sir

Nathaniel is fearless and candid to the point of rudeness; he is perfectly honorable and possesses at heart the sentiments of a gentleman. But he devotes his talents wholly to horses and game-cocks, both, according to Linnaeus, belonging to species of a lower order than dogs, elephants, or even rabbits, and, in my opinion, both less to be esteemed for their character than field mice and song-birds. Now the talents which Sir Nathaniel squanders may not be of the mind, indeed they are not, but they are none the less rare; he has cheerfulness and loyalty and he is, within the limits of his comprehensions, a fair and just young man except where the merits of horse-mastership are under comparison with those of other fields of human endeavor. He drinks much and, worse than that, he is contentious in his cups."

Mr. Clapton, who had bent forward at the close of this description, now leaned back and smiled. "There you have him. And I leave it to your sense whether you will take him or leave him."

To Johnny, trained by simple and undebatable rules of thumb, this question brought unpleasant responsibility. It was unfair; he even suspected Mr. Clapton of a design to dodge a tutor's natural functions and place him where the blame would be his alone should anything go wrong. If his father were here now, he would settle the business in short order; and how? Johnny's face fell. He could see his father's formidable negative. But he wanted to ride—Mr. Clapton was watching him with a smile—and, by Zooks, he would ride!

"I reckon I'll go, seh. I certainly love to ride."

To his surprise, Mr. Clapton showed no discomfiture. He searched for his place in a book, murmuring genially:

"Quite right, my boy, yes, yes. Take people or leave them, it makes no matter, as long as you take them or leave them for what they are."

The sandy road along which Johnny trudged ran north beside the Chowan river. He passed the last scattered frame houses of what he was learning to call the lower orders, and entered a belt of pine and cypress which ran down to the water's edge. Through the trunks to the left he saw the broad, slow-moving river shining blue beneath the cloudless sky. On the further bank lay green fields of bolling cotton and broad-leaved tobacco; a white ox, a mere dot, moved between rows of corn. A lumber raft drifted by, a line of washing hanging limp beside the deckhouse of rough boughs, a Negro leaning listlessly against the long sweep at the stern.

Around the turn was the white gate they had told him was Sir Nathaniel's. Johnny went through it and up a straggling drive among scattered hardwood trees. An apple orchard was fenced with sheep wattles, and in this rough pasture a ram, two pigs and a brown colt dozed out the long, hot afternoon. An ill-kept vegetable garden lay above the pasture. Along its upper hedge, the rambling double gallery of the house gleamed in the blazing light and threw a violet shadow on the white siding of the walls. As he crossed the burned and patchy lawn a fox-hound bitch trotted up with deprecating hospitality and thrust a wet muzzle into his palm. Here was something that seemed like home. He gave the high-domed head a hug and flapped the soft thin ears together. She followed him up on the porch, flopped down panting. As he looked for a knocker on the tall French doors, Sir Nathaniel's voice from inside hailed him.

"Bantam! Come in!"

The long high room was shaded by latticed blinds; a table was still strewn with the remains of dinner. At the farther end sat Sir Nathaniel in shirt sleeves and red plush slippers; a chair supported one foot, also his top boots and coat. He was deeply absorbed in reading.

"Seated, Bantam," he muttered to Johnny as the boy wound his way through the litter of windsor chairs and footstools, but he did not look up. He continued to run a stubby finger along the lines of print and form the words laboriously with his lips. Johnny searched for a seat; one chair, however, was occupied by a pair of freshly oiled gaiters and another by a terrier puppy. To fetch up a chair from a distance might disturb Sir Nathaniel, so he stood and wiped his hot face with his pocket handkerchief. Beyond Sir Nat the high mantel was hung with the brushes of a dozen foxes, the table in front of it was covered with hunting-crops, cutting-whips, spurs, hound-couples. Sir Nat threw the magazine on the table; its title was, "The Racing Calendar."

"Here's a go," he said. "Oh; seated." He brushed the puppy off the chair and tapped the racing calendar with his finger. "It says Diomed is backed to

win the Royal Plate at Newmarket." He eyed Johnny with intense solemnity. "But that's not the joke."

No, thought Johnny, it hardly could be.

"Race," Sir Nat went on, "was run in England in April. Haven't heard yet
how it came out. If Diomed won it means a hundred guineas to me. Here I
am, maybe a hundred guineas richer, and don't know it. Funny thing—
life." He stared moodily at the "Calendar."

"Did you back that horse, seh?" Johnny asked politely.

"No, but I've some of his blood. If he wins—big price for my colts.

"Question is," he said after reflection, "can Diomed stand an impost of
twelve stone?"

He relapsed again into silence.

"Ha!" he burst out with a short laugh, "here we are, arguing weights—
and the whole business decided months ago. Damned funny thing."

He opened the "Racing Calendar" and fumbled for his place. "This is
what it says." He proceeded to read in a loud voice, giving equal emphasis
to every word: " 'Late advices from the stable of Lord St. Leger are to the
effect that Diomed has been going sound some time since and that on
Thursday last he ran a trial seven furlongs in brilliant fashion under a light
boy.' All well and good," said Sir Nathaniel, "but can he carry twelve stone
at three miles? Eh, Bantam?"

"I certainly hope so, seh."

Sir Nat grinned his acknowledgments. "Good boy. And so do I."

He fished on the table for his boot-hooks, kicked his slippers under his
chair and pulled on his boots, tying his linen garters around his knee. "Don't
need spurs. Don't need whip. Come along."

He led the way out a French window on the opposite side of the room.

"Ever seen a house without front door? Idea of my own. People I don't
like come to see me—duns, prigs—sort of thing—go all 'round house looking for front door. Is no front door. Time they find out—I'm gone. Ha!"

The barn was unpainted and ramshackle. At Sir Nat's whistle, a Negro in
a pair of old Hessian boots and a meager undershirt crept out of the shade
and ducked his head.

"Yesso, Suh Nat. Whut you ride?"

"Nighthawk."

"An' de li'l' misto?"

"Peregrine."

The Negro rolled his eyes lugubriously toward Johnny.

"Hole up dat Pergreem's colt's haid, young gempmum, or you j'ine de birds," he whispered, and entered the dark, sweet-smelling cavern of the barn with a foreboding sigh.

When the colts were led out Sir Nat gave a professional pull at the girths.

"Leathers right?" he asked, pointing at the benevolent-looking bay Peregrine. "Right. Nip up."

The colt remained quiet, almost somnolent between Johnny's weak and expectant knees. Sir Nat stepped up to the brown horse and slipped into the saddle with incredible swiftness. Nighthawk stood straight up in air, the Negro fell backward into a pile of straw. "Steady," said Sir Nat composedly. Steady was well enough, but would the brown come over backward as he balanced there interminably? Johnny's thought, however, was cut short by the feel of the reins pouring hotly through his fingers. He felt the colt's back roach and saw his neck and shoulders disappear. He closed his knees and rose off the saddle just in time to take up the humping explosion that sent them both aloft. Sir Nat's voice seemed to come to him from afar, "Kick him, Bantam, kick him."

He drummed his heels and pulled up on the reins as Peregrine hit the ground. Then he was flying down the drive. "Hold him, Bantam, hold him," came the voice. He sat down in the saddle and put his shoulders into the pull. The colt came to a stand and looked around at Johnny in mild surprise.

Sir Nat's brown trotted up, shaking his bit and looking for trouble.

"Can't go to sleep," said Sir Nat. "He'll be all right now. Up this way—big woods. Fields all full of silly crops."

They jogged up the hill through small timber and came out above the house on a plateau of pine forest. Johnny turned his horse and felt the light evening breeze from the south. Beyond Sir Nathaniel's place he saw the river road, the cypress grove, the clustered roofs of Edenton, the masts and rigging and the hot, flat, shining waters of the Sound.

Sir Nat pulled a dogwood twig, stuck it in his mouth and stared at Johnny with curious interest.

"Looking at view? Don't go in for views myself. Come up, horse."

He jogged on, phlegmatically rotating the twig in his mouth as Nighthawk shied at invisible dangers. Johnny followed on and drew alongside him.

"Canter. Mind he don't bolt."

Boring and chafing, the horses opened up a long stride across the pine straw; branches and sun patches flicked by overhead, the southerly breeze was left behind, the warm wind of their riding was in their faces. As the ground slipped smoothly past, the horses settled, dropped their heads and took a light feel of the bit.

Sir Nat cocked the twig out of the corner of his mouth.

"Puts bottom in 'em," he said, "one more mile."

At the end of the ridge they came out in an abandoned field of broom. A covey of quail burst up like feathered bombshells under their feet.

"Mark over!" Sir Nat exclaimed, whatever that meant; he sighted over his finger at a bird. "Bang!" he said. "Missed him! Ha!"

It was just the way a boy would act, almost like a Negro. Cantering beside him, Johnny felt more comfortable and at ease.

Once again in the woods, they pulled up to a walk.

"Bring 'em back cool," Sir Nat observed, "or they'll break out." He turned to Johnny earnestly. "Never let horse gallop back to stable. Bad habit. Lots of people do." He shook his head.

As they came back to the end of the pine woods, Sir Nat withdrew the twig from his mouth. "Tell you something." He thrust the twig at Johnny to indicate that he was to be the subject. "Good seat; bad hands. No offense. Look. Turn 'em in so. Now make play with your wrists. Better." He glanced at the dropping sun. "Plenty of time—chaps coming to supper. You'll stay." He raised the twig in admonition. "Course you'll stay. See you home myself."

Up at the house the big table had been cleared and laid for five.

"Make self at home," said Sir Nathaniel. "Down in a minute." Johnny heard him climb the stair in an outer hall. The terrier puppy emerged, bristling, from under a bench, pounced fiercely at his shoe-tie and worried it. Johnny teased it with his finger; it pranced around him with menacing grimaces and flopping paws; tired of the game, it trotted up and clawed his knee. He lifted it to his lap, where, with a nestling movement and a sigh, it went to sleep. He sat there looking out the long windows at the fading day.

A shadowy bat flittered by after twilight insects. The tops of the pine trees slowly dissolved in the evening mist. Up from the river came the frogs' high, raucous monotone. The sights and sounds carried him to the twilights of his home. He felt suddenly tired, a little sad.

Thinking of Edenton, whose distant lights began to show, thinking of the life of high adventure so much less brilliant, so much more indifferent and complex than he had expected, he felt that he was futile, undistinguished and alone. He remembered how he used to climb to his mother's lap, and wished, in one of his queer flashes, that he could find a way, right then, to climb up into the brooding softness of the dusk.

## CHAPTER XII

CARRIAGE WHEELS sounded on the drive. Voices shouted, "Heyo, Natty!" A French window burst open and Wylie Jones, in flame-colored plush, stepped into the room. Johnny stood up in the dim light.

"Hello," said Mr. Jones. "Who have we here?" He came closer and stared quizzically into Johnny's face.

"Oh!" he said, "it's my young back-country friend. And how does your respected father, sir?" He gave an easy laugh, struck tinder, lit a candle.

"Gentlemen," he said to the two figures behind, "my honest friend, Master Fraser. This, young sir, is Mr. Heywood of Halifax, and this, Mr. Gerrould of Virginia."

The speech was made in a light, mocking tone, but Johnny could only mutter, "Servant, gentlemen," awkwardly enough and stand there, angry and ill at ease.

99

"Mr. Gerrould," Wylie Jones continued, "is the guest of the evening. And in order that he may gauge North Carolina hospitality, I propose that we treat him with the distinction to which every Virginian believes himself entitled. Perhaps I seem fantastical?"

He bowed ironically toward Mr. Gerrould.

"You seem to make a joke, sir," said Mr. Gerrould, a tall, solemnly aristocratic man in dark clothes, who now stepped into the candlelight, "though I can't say I understand it."

"Yes, Wylie," said Mr. Heywood, "don't be so clever. Jerry don't like it. Do you, Jerry?"

Mr. Heywood slipped out of the darkness up to Mr. Gerrould's side, his light eyes peered up at the tall Virginian, his scar mouth slid into an ingratiating smile.

"I am not accustomed to it," Mr. Gerrould replied severely.

"Hullo, lads," Sir Nat hailed them from the door. "What's row?"

"Ah! mine ancient!" cried Mr. Jones.

"Nonsense. Younger than you."

"A figure of speech, Natto. You know Mr. Gerrould."

"Respects."

Mr. Gerrould inclined, "An honor, sir."

"Hullo, Monks."

"How you, Nat?" said Mr. Heywood. "You've a new blue suit, I see— another remittance, eh?"

"No; tick; damn your impudence."

"Now, Natty, don't mind a joke." Mr. Heywood drew him aside and stood with him in the shadows, whispering.

A slatternly Negress lit the candles on the table. They sat down, Sir Nat at the head, Mr. Gerrould and Wylie Jones on his right, Johnny beside him on his left.

"Well, Nat," said Wylie, "are your birds ready?"

"Yes. Have only six, though, fit to be pitted."

"Never mind. Mr. Gerrould has brought two from Virginia. That makes a main."

So there was to be a cock fight, thought Johnny. He listened, thrilled and frightened, as all four men talked of weights, gaffs, betting odds and rules, while they ate their herring roe and cutlets and drank their sangaree.

Wylie Jones caught his eye.

"Our friend here seems all at sea in the world of sport."

"He's all right," said Nat stoutly, "rides like a Trojan."

"A Trojan? You damn with faint praise if I recall my Iliad. But, Natto," he rolled a golden half-jo on the table, "I'll lay you that you don't know what Trojan means."

Sir Nat clapped a coin from his pocket on top of the other.

"Taken." He shut his little eyes tight and recited, "Trojan—by Runway out of Quicksilver; ran third in the sweepstakes at Charleston in '61."

Mr. Jones arose and bowed with mock ceremony.

"Sir, the stake is yours."

"Not clever," observed Sir Nat complacently as he pocketed the money, "but can't be done easy, neither."

A bottle of claret was brought in with the syllabubs.

"No toasts," said Nat, "nuisance."

"Plenty of claret, though, I hope," said Mr. Heywood, grinning around the circle for approbation.

"All you like," Nat responded briefly, "and more than you need."

"Toasts," observed Mr. Gerrould sententiously, "are becoming difficult in my country, now that 'The King!' seems to come under the head of political discussion."

"Damned shame," Sir Nathaniel said. "Those chaps ought to be shot."

"But, good heavens!" exclaimed Mr. Jones maliciously, "one cannot shoot Mr. Jefferson."

"Oh, he has not gone so far as that, Mr. Jones," Mr. Gerrould raised a deprecatory hand.

"But I daresay he would drink to Monsieur Rousseau with more good will. And why not?"

Sir Nat rose. "Don't talk nonsense, Wylie. Puttin' a mounseer ahead of the King. Back directly."

The three men drank their claret in silence, and Johnny, sipping cautiously at his glass, stole glances at them.

Wylie Jones, quick and graceful, toyed with a nut-pick and looked carelessly about him, apparently amused by all the company, particularly Mr. Gerrould, who ate nuts with great decorum and stared pompously into space. Mr. Heywood fixed his pale, hard glance on Johnny and licked a thin line of claret from his lips. Johnny gulped his wine and looked away.

Nat reappeared.

"Pit's ready," he announced.

Outside, horsemen moved up the dark road, lanterns came slowly swinging through the trees. The great door of the barn glowed with a light against which the silhouettes of men passed and repassed, stopped, gathered into knots.

They went down to the barn, giving careless acknowledgment to respectful greetings. Inside, lanterns hung from every beam; a board wall as high as a man's chest enclosed some twenty feet of space in the middle of the tamped, clay floor. With admiring grins the scattered, low-class crowd around it made way for the elegant party. A cock crowed from the hampers at the rear. In the far shadows the horses chumped and rustled or cast a shining and distracted eye on the unaccustomed throng.

Sir Nat's stable boy and Wylie Jones' Negro handler were bustling about the hampers. The birds were brought out for inspection one by one.

"Yesso, dis bird gwine fight, yesso."

"A natchel bo'n liver-cutter, das whut he is."

"Nossuh, he ain't got de roup; no, suh, he's fittin to fight a b'ar."

The gentlemen took each gleaming bird in their hands and poked his craw professionally; they felt his dubbed crest, flattened on the head, felt his leg muscles and his horny feet.

"Shall we commence?" said Wylie Jones.

"Right," said Nat. "Heywood is judge. Don't need stakeholder, do we?"

Mr. Gerrould swept the group with an important glance.

"Hardly, seh; we are all gentlemen here."

"Well, then, Wylie, match my young buff stagg against your youngest for ten guineas."

"Taken. That's my black Dominique. Heel your bird."

The curved steel gaffs, pointed sharp as needles, were laced around the yellow legs. Part of the crowd gathered to watch, the rest lined up at the pitside, whispering, betting, laughing, spitting fiercely.

"Are you ready, gentlemen?" asked Mr. Heywood. "Well, then, pit your birds."

Johnny stuck close to Sir Nat as they moved to the barrier; the Negro with the buff cock shuffled beside them. Wylie Jones and his handler appeared across the pit. The crowd closed in around them, peered over them, perched above them. On the right, by common consent, stretched a triple line of black faces and gleaming teeth.

The tense murmur died. "Go!" said Heywood's voice. The buff bird and the black dropped lightly in the pit. Slowly they moved together, their hocks coming up behind them in sharp high action, their bodies bent low, their heads swaying from side to side, as each searched the other's vitals with a beady eye. At the centre they paused imperceptibly, then rose together in a mist of wings. They bounded apart in air, and as they landed the buff cock backed away and slowly circled, crouching as before. A drop of blood fell from his beak. The crowd was silent.

The black followed up; they rose again and hung. Falling together, the buff turned over and pulled free. His gaff came away, bright red; a bright red trickle lined the black bird's neck. From the crowd rose a long, hoarse whisper of applause.

Now they closed in to fight, rising and falling in a shower of blood spurts and whirling feathers, now they broke again. The buff staggered aimlessly, one eye a blank and bloody hole. The black cock bided his time, but the other did not return. An oath like a grunt broke the stillness.

"Beat!" said a voice, "by Crikes!" and laughed.

"Sir Nat, " called Mr. Heywood, "do you pick up your bird?"

All eyes swung to the man by Johnny's side, eyes beseeching, mocking, angry, greedy, cruel.

Sir Nathaniel paused, his pink, childlike face distressed and paling. He shook his head.

"Very well," the umpire said. "Breast them."

The Negro handlers climbed into the pit. They placed the birds face to face in the centre and jumped away. Both cocks dove upward, in a haze of blows.

Now it was the black that swayed giddily; a thin dark stream pumped from his dripping neck, his beak was open in a hideous grimace of agony. The crowd raised a fierce cheer and fell silent. From the gaping beak came tiny hoarse pants, like a dying whisper.

The buff closed in again unsteadily; the black cock tried to meet him but fell under, went down beneath a shower of slow, driving blows, crumpled up, lay still. The crowd was shouting madly; they saw the buff cock mount the body and spread his wings. They listened. Raising his red wet beak, he gave one clarion crow, swayed giddily, dove forward, feebly kicking.

Johnny tore his burning eyes away; all around the pit he saw the leering faces, grinning in malignant triumph, lustful, wolfish, licking their chops for blood.

He backed blindly, frantically through the press of dirty bodies and the hot stench. Air—air!

A hand caught him under the arm and swung him free.

"Come on." Sir Nat was hurrying him through the cheering and applause.

They were under cover of the trees and the healing darkness. He dropped face down on the wet grass, and broke into noiseless sobbing.

Sir Nat was kneeling by him. He felt the stubby hand, light as a woman's, on his shoulder.

"Bantam. Old chap. I say, don't."

The hand was patting him as though he were a frightened puppy. Johnny had a dreadful feeling that poor Sir Nat was about to cry, too; he sat up, shamefaced. But Sir Nat rose, cleared his throat reasonantly.

"Come to the house. Glass of toddy. Drive you back." He glanced at the brightly lit and buzzing barn. "Let the handler finish the stinkin' show."

As they walked up the hill Sir Nat's hand again came beneath his arm.

"Good sort. Be friends, what? Good."

## CHAPTER XIII

INSIDE THE rectory, Dr. Clapton, with the flutterings of a gentle and distracted bird, settled himself in his sanctuary. Papers rustled, books shifted one against the other, closed softly; Dr. Clapton was preparing with busy indecision for an evening's writing on what he had from time to time referred to mysteriously as "The Work." "The Work," begun years before, consisted, so far, in a number of sheets of manuscript, written with exquisite care and then crossed neatly out. And now, in the dusk, Johnny could see him through the doorway revising what he had written the week before. His quill poised above each word in solemn progression, while Dr. Clapton considered that word's merits, then falling with the precision of a guillotine, delivered the fatal stroke.

But today the heat was insupportable. Dr. Clapton first tried absently to fan himself with odd folds of his dressing-gown. His pen hand stuck to the paper; a splash of ink fell from the quill; it was too much. He climbed

laboriously out of his ambuscade, produced a silk handkerchief, and proceeded to dust his face and neck, impersonally, as if he were a piece of not
particularly valuable statuary. He came to the door.

"Really," he said, "it is too warm to go on with The Work. Yes, yes."

He set a stool on the step and sat down with his back against the door
frame.

"But perhaps it is just as well—for I can take the occasion to tell you of
The Work itself; though no doubt I have done so many times already."

"No, seh. I never heard tell of it."

"No? I have not described The Work? The Work," he said, "is to be called
'The Sminthiad, or the Cosmopolis of Smiths.'"

He paused for his effect. Evidently satisfied by Johnny's stare of stupefaction, he went on:

"Perhaps I should first explain the inception of The Work. Many years
ago, in the course of my studies, I came to feel that the subject of smiths
and other workers in metal, historical, legendary and mythological, had
been seriously neglected. I cannot say that I have any particularity of interest in smiths nor any knowledge of the metal-working craft; indeed, I consider the latter to be the province of the masters of the various guilds,
estimable fellows, I have no doubt, rather than that of the learned professions. But in the collection of material on the historical side, I may say I
think that I have made some progress. I have now a very full assemblage of
notes on all the famous smiths—Tubal Cain, Appollo Smintheus, Vulcan,
Wayland Smith, Basil the Macedonian, and others who may be less familiar
to you."

He bowed slightly to Johnny as if to imply that, intimate as Johnny no
doubt was with Basil the Macedonian, there were other smiths slightly
more obscure. He cleared his throat.

"So far so good. But when it comes to the actual composition of the work,
I find my progress slow. It is, as the name implies, a poem. And I have
chosen the heroic couplet. Unfortunately I lack facility in the composition
of verses, and particularly, it would seem, in the composition of heroic
couplets. And in addition, the plan of The Work, an invention of my own,

and superior to any other plan of which I have knowledge, presents peculiar difficulties."

He gazed out toward the bay and wiped his troubled face.

"In most works of the kind," he continued, "it is customary to begin with earliest times and lead down to the present."

He shook his head.

"Nothing could be more unnatural. It should be obvious that the age which is most familiar to us is the age in which we live. The present, then, forms the point of departure, from which I lead the reader further and further into the past. The difficulty is, however, that with each addition to my knowledge of the smiths of recent times, a new introduction must be written.

"It is here that perhaps you might assist me."

Mr. Clapton could not miss Johnny's look of confusion and alarm.

"Oh," he hastened to explain, "I do not suggest your collaboration on the scholarly side. But," he turned his kindly, dim blue eyes on Johnny, "it is well known that persons of the back country are masters of practical affairs. If, then, you command any facts as to the trade of smithing, I beg that you will place them at my disposal."

Johnny picked up a pebble and stared at it with the intensity of a crystal-gazer. He was immeasurably out of his depth. And yet he must say something. Just this morning at church he had realized more vividly than ever before, that he was now of the company of the well-bred, the fashionable, and in this circle it was clear that when one gentleman was asked by another gentleman for assistance, that gentleman must try to render it. He searched the pebble desperately. But he saw only pictures of the smith at the settlement back home, the spare little man with thin, corded arms and a knack of using what weight he possessed to great advantage in work and in fighting. He saw him drinking his morning pint of rum, chewing green tobacco, saw him skid out of the shop, clinging to the hock of a frantic horse. The pictures were vivid enough, but what had they to do with a learned work?

He must speak.

"We've got a smith at home," he whispered, "that bet a fellow a gallon of rum he could throw his ten-pound hammer over a sycamore in front of the shop." He paused. Mr. Clapton nodded encouragement. "He did it, too. But it went plumb through a Dutchman's roof across the street and the smith had to give the Dutchman two gallons to keep out of court."

He looked at Mr. Clapton in crimson suspense. Would Mr. Clapton laugh at him?

Mr. Clapton considered the statement judicially.

"Interesting," he said; "yes, yes, most interesting. I shall make a memorandum. The incident, however, might strike a note of lightness, almost of frivolity, inappropriate to The Work. We must consider that." He brightened. "Unless it could be suggested that an event of this sort, occurring in earliest times, might bear some relation to the legend of the thunderbolts of Thor. Yes—yes. The implication is most interesting!"

He nodded gratefully and plunged into reflection. Absently he waved at the mosquitoes gathering in the dusk. They multiplied. He sighed and went in.

The front door knocker fell once, lightly but crisply.

"Bless me!" said Dr. Clapton, shutting his iron spectacles into his book and smoothing down his white lawn bands, "it's Captain Tennant."

He trotted to the door.

"Ah, Dominie!" said a somewhat truculent voice in elegant English accents. "My respects. May I enter?"

"Indeed, you may, Captain. Let me clear this chair of books."

A short, middle-aged gentleman, excessively erect, stepped smartly into the room. His plum-colored coat was turned back and frogged in the military fashion, he carried a malacca cane as if it were a club, his red, indignant face stared at the world over the top of his incredibly high, stiff, bristling stock like an angry landowner watching trespassers over a hedge.

Turning stiffly from the waist, the gentleman fixed his small red eyes on Johnny and blurted out, "This is Master Fraser!" in tones indignantly triumphant, as if he had detected Johnny's true identity beneath some outrageous and unbearable imposture.

"Yes, indeed, yes, yes," Dr. Clapton said. "Johnny, pay your respects to Captain Tennant, the Collector of the Port."

Johnny, who had risen when the Captain entered, now bowed as he had been taught. The Captain, bringing his hand to the salute against his immaculately powdered bag wig, inclined his rigid body half an inch.

"In another moment, Captain,"—Dr. Clapton's flurried voice, accompanied by the sound of softly tumbling books, came from the depths of the room,—"I shall have you a chair."

"Don't trouble yourself, sir, I beg. I am just come back from Norfolk to find a letter from this lad's father." He thrust a denouncing finger at the boy. "Proud to do a service to John Fraser," he went on, as if he would add, "and show me, egad, sir, the man who denies it!"

He drew a snuff-box from his embroidered waistcoat, dropped a few grains on his wrist, snuffed them furiously, snapped the lid, and stared about him in search of a contradiction.

"Proud," he said, "I have called to carry the young man back to my house for a cold joint and a glass of porter."

"Johnny would be most happy, I am sure," said Dr. Clapton. "Yes, yes. And Mr. Fraser sensibly affected by your delicate attention. Johnny, get your hat."

Scuttling along beside the rapid-marching captain, Johnny had flashes of leisurely inhabitants taking the evening air. The languid groups flew by him as if he were whirling through the town in the clutch of an impetuous genie. It took but a moment to shoot the length of the main street. Turning sharply up the hill, they came to a large square house standing dimly above the mist which hung along the waterside. The captain ascended the porch steps—one—two—three—like the manual of arms, swung back the lawn curtain at the open door, and with a gesture of command beckoned Johnny to precede him.

A long dark hall was lighted by a single candle. Johnny hesitated in the shadows. "Left!" the captain said, and propelled him through a high doorway. Two candelabra blazed on two round tables; fiddle-back chairs were ranged around the walls, two small sofas flanked the empty fireplace above which hung a portrait of a red-faced old gentleman in scarlet coat and full-bottomed wig.

"Eve!" said the captain, "Master Fraser!"

A young girl of Johnny's own age slowly raised her head above the end of the nearer sofa, gave her mob cap a pat and surveyed him critically. Her expression, while not quite unkind, was disturbingly competent and assured. Johnny felt conscious of his country leather breeches.

He made his bow; she rose with easy deliberation and dropped him a curtsey, holding up the hem of her dimity apron and flouncing out her print-cotton skirts. Something in her manner toward him reminded him of her father's manner toward Doctor Clapton just now. He must learn the knack of putting people where they belonged. But first he would need better breeches.

"Ah, Master Fraser," she was saying in her English way, "charmed, I do asshaw you."

"Servant, Miss Eve, ma'm."

"Pray be seated, sir. Deon't you find it warm? But no doubt you are quite accustomed to this dreadful climate."

"Why, yes, ma'm," Johnny said as he sat on the opposite sofa, "I reckon I am. It's about the only climate I ever was in."

"How veddy interesting!"

"Of co'se, ma'm, where I come from, they's big pine forests and the air is kind of lighter."

"Ah, indeed! But I deon't suppose it is like England quite, is it?"

"Well, now, ma'm, I couldn't say. I don't know about the weather in England."

"Fancy, Master Fraser has never been in England, Papa!"

The captain, who had drawn up a chair precisely between the two, cleared his throat.

"No doubt he will; he should do, by all means. Complete his education and meet polite society. I should give him cards to some of my clubs."

"Thank you, seh," said Johnny, "but I don't reckon my Dadder would stand the expense."

The silent amusement with which Eve heard this remark suggested to the crimson Johnny that he had said the wrong thing.

"Nonsense," the captain burst out, "nonsense! What's expense to do with a gentleman's education? A gentleman must be educated *as* a gentleman, that's plain, isn't it? Well, then, young man?"

He glared a challenge.

"No, sir, egad! A bit of schooling here is well enough, it will do no harm. I was tutored myself as a lad and was never the worse for it. And Clapton is a worthy fellow, an old Etonian and all that sort of thing. But can a gentleman receive the proper finish from a twelve month's tutoring at the hands of a parson in a small provincial living? No, sir, egad!"

He snapped open the lid of his snuff-box as if he were cocking a pistol, took snuff, and drawing a huge white silk handkerchief from his pocket, whipped his stock and waistcoat very hard and very rapidly. Folding the handkerchief with care, he rose.

"Shall we sup?" he demanded in a manner that expected no reply. He opened the double doors at the back of the room. A mahogany table bore a large piece of cold roast mutton, a plate of biscuit and three stone bottles of porter. He stood at attention beside the door and Johnny found that he stood in the same rigid pose on the other side as if they were two yeomen of the guard, while Eve passed into the dining-room and took her seat at the head of the table. The captain took the seat opposite and Johnny sat between. He was about to venture a remark when the captain rose and shut his little eyes tight. Johnny just had time to bow his head when the captain rapped out, "Benedictus benedicat," and sat down abruptly with enormous self-satisfaction. He tested the edge of the carving knife with his thumb and cut three remarkably thin slices of mutton. A large pewter mustard pot followed the mutton round the table. Johnny fell to on the mutton in a way that did him credit, considering that he had already supped at Dr. Clapton's modest early hour. Both Eve and her father ate with astonishing rapidity, cutting large pieces of mutton and ramming them home with vigor and precision. Evidently English table manners, Johnny reflected with some rise in self-esteem, were not those of the provinces. They finished long before him and Captain Tennant filled the glasses. The meat had made Johnny thirsty. He was about to plunge his nose unceremoniously into the cool, brown porter when the captain arrested him.

"One moment, young sir," he remarked severely; "we will observe the proprieties, if you please."

He rose again, his glass in his hand, and glanced at Johnny to indicate that he should rise also. Eve remained seated but raised her glass.

"The King!" The captain drank. "God bless him!" He glanced at Johnny again with meaning.

"God bless him, seh!" Johnny stammered in confusion.

"Young man," said the captain as they sat down again, "if you will take the advice of an older man, a former officer of his Majesty's service, a man who has seen the world, sir, you will make that toast a part of your daily practice. It is the duty of an English gentleman," he added; "a term which I take to include a Provincial of your birth and training. Of course the low-lived scoundrels who, I am sorry to say, compose the greater part of your numbers are not gentlemen and can have no pretensions to the name. But if I had my way,"—he thumped a fist on the table,—"those vulgar fellows and radical upstarts should be compelled by law to drink this toast for their own good."

Johnny thought uneasily of the roaring drunken toast he had heard at Slade's tavern. There was not much chance of compelling that murderous crew to do anything—for their own good or anybody else's.

"Mind you, sir," the captain went on, "I do not refer to you, sir, or your people, or to a half-dozen other genteel families in this province. I come from an old Kentish family which has never, I trust, been lacking in distinction and a nice discrimination. And when I meet a gentleman, whether in England or out of it, I believe I do not fail to accord him recognition."

He rose and stood, puffing in a sort of furious triumph, while Eve went back to the drawing-room. He then bowed Johnny before him in a manner so stately that the boy, marching through the high doorway, could almost hear respectful murmurs from the lower orders at the sight of his magnificence. It was true, he was not the captain's equal in rank, but was he not vastly above nearly everyone else in North Carolina?

Eve, too, appeared to think somewhat better of him; she smiled quite kindly and asked him how he liked Edenton.

"Why, ma'm," he said judicially, "it appears like a mighty fine town." But even this sounded, perhaps, too enthusiastic for a man of the world. "Yes, ma'm," he added, "it looks like a permanent settlement."

At this she laughed with vast amusement.

"Oh, la! You should see London if you think this village fine."

"Why, ma'm, I reckon I will some day. I aim to go to London later on. I've heard tell it was a nice place, a mighty nice place."

He said this with admirable indifference and reserve as indicating that naturally he should go to London, it was incumbent on every gentleman to go to London, but all in good time; he was no impetuous youth to be stampeded even by thoughts of London, admirable city, no doubt, though it was.

"Indeed, sir, I fancy you would be quite amazed by the sights there," she answered, somewhat piqued; "the great houses and St. Paul's and the hackney coaches and the powdered chairmen and the grand noblemen's carriages and the Park and Vauxhall. Papa, tell Master Fraser of London."

The captain looked up, incredulous, dumfounded by the absurdity of this suggestion.

"London," he said, fastening a bellicose eye on Johnny, "why, London —egad, young sir, is London and that's all there is to it." He reflected bitterly, "London! Haw!" His grim, blunt laugh, wrung from his apoplectic frame, blasted all other cities of the earth and all ninnies who dared suggest that anyone, least of all himself, should attempt a task so absurdly impossible as to describe London.

"Then in the evenings," Miss Eve went on serenely, "everyone goes to the play or to routs and drums; they drink negus and play écarté and loo—— Do you play loo, Mr. Fraser?"

"No, ma'm, I can't hardly say I do. But I expect I could."

"Oh, I'm sure you could do. Papa says Ameddicans are so clever."

"Of the better class, Miss," the captain broke in. "There is nothing clever about the lower orders, I give you my word, and there *is* something damned impertinent and ill-conditioned. Jove, sir, I don't know what we're coming to in this province. Here on the coast they know their place, and if they didn't, there are enough of our sort to teach it them. But in your back country they are quite out of hand. When I commanded a regiment of frontier militia a few years since, just after I had come out here, we were called out to handle an Indian Rising in the West. Well, sir, will you believe it, one evening we were about to be attacked and I was attempting to form those ignorant, untrained fellows up in proper order to receive a charge when I noticed some of them whispering together. In a moment one of them came up to me without so much as a salute. 'Brother,' he said—fancy!—'jest set down behind that log yonder.' I was about to place the rascal in arrest when, damme, if my entire command did not disappear from sight. An instant later I heard the Indians yelling and a bullet cut a twig over my head. I was obliged to seek cover. I lay behind a log, wondering what was to come next, when all through the wood I heard my men commence firing. Then the Indians apparently fired, too, and there was the greatest amount of shooting and shouting all about me, but I could make nothing of it whatever, as there was never a soul in sight. After a time the Indians withdrew and my men came up grinning and carrying a few wounded who were grinning as well. The whole affair was exasperating beyond words. Egad, I'd have given a thousand pounds to have had our old sergeant major there. As it was there was simply no way of telling whether we had beat the enemy or no. I never even saw one, except a few dead which we found behind trees. And then, if you please, sir, if the mutineers didn't have the impudence to give three huzzahs for me."

The captain was now striding up and down the room in an ecstasy of exasperation. He came to a halt before Johnny.

"Egad, sir, when I think of chaps like that I despair of this province. I do indeed."

He cocked the lid of his snuff-box, sniffed up a prodigious quantity, snorted.

Here was a military gentleman, Johnny thought, who knew things far beyond the ken of the back-country people, even of the Edentonians. He himself had attended militia musters at home and thought them quite fine at the time, but now he remembered how the farmer boys and hunters in buck and homespun lounged and yawned in their broken ranks, laughed, spat, passed the whole business off as an immense and somehow indecent joke. He could picture Captain Tennant, his clothes immaculate, his boots iridescently varnished, parading his smartly turned out company of British Fusileers, true soldiers every one. Small wonder the captain saw no hope for the loose-jointed, careless mountain boys.

What luck, thought Johnny, for him to be able to learn all this, to escape from the ignorance and self-content of the back country. It was a privilege to know such persons as the captain and Eve. He hoped they would ask him to call again. Perhaps he had best not stay too long now. He rose and bowed to Eve.

"My thanks, ma'm, for a most agreeable evening."

"Must you quit us so soon? You must come again, mustn't he, Papa? We shall teach you to play loo."

Johnny bowed and turned to the captain.

"My thanks, sir, for a most agree——"

"Nonsense, come again."

The captain ushered him out the door; he found his hat in the hall and walked back down the hill in the night. The streets were nearly empty. He strolled along slowly, asking himself what impression he had made at his first venture among persons of rank. Not bad, on the whole, not at all bad. And yet as he left the drawing-room he had felt an uncomfortable twinge between the shoulder-blades, as if Miss Eve were casting on his retreating back a glance of superior amusement.

## CHAPTER XIV

ONE DAY each week Captain Flood's river boat lay over at her dock in Edenton. Johnny Fraser looked forward to that afternoon with the captain who stood both for a link with home and with the still elusive life of high adventure. And in his own exasperated way the captain looked forward to it, too. Eagerly and indefatigably he explained the mysteries of ships. But it was in the tone of one who merely tries, too late, to save the fragments of a career which had long before been ruined by neglect. "Why, God love me!" he would say, "you'd 'a' knowed that years ago if you'd 'a' joined a ship as cabin-boy," his small stern eye would fix on Johnny, "like I advised."

To this Johnny once made bold to answer:

"But, Cap'n, you never saw me till last month."

"Correc', my bucko, but I advised it then, didn't I? And how in the blazes could I advise you before I seen you?"

"Yes, but it was too late then, seh; you said that yourself."

The captain bristled.

"Well, am I to blame for that—could I see you before I seen you?"

He polished the bowl of his pipe on his shining nose.

"Don't always be argying, son. It don't look good in a youngster and besides you ain't a match for an old man like me. Get in this yer skiff. I'll row you round the harbor and see if I can't learn you something."

They paddled into mid-channel; the little captain, hunched monkey-like over his oars, rowed with the short, round strokes of a wherryman. In the light of late afternoon, hot and hazy, the shipping, docks, landing-stages and the distant shore line all seemed not so much to rise from the slick, dead water, as to hover, motionless, above it. Unreal, intangible, and light as air, they hung in a breathless trance, held to earth only by their soft and ever so slightly wavering reflections. The smallest pebble, Johnny said to himself, thrown into those reflections, in shattering them would shatter the charm as well, so that all the waterfront, the quays, the ships would fly upward and away, and perhaps himself with them. Up and away—but where? By Zooks, he must be careful that no one in the world ever found out what ninny ideas sometimes came to him.

"See that ship moored off-shore in deep water? How's she rigged?"

"Ship rigged."

"Right. And what makes her wind at her anchor?"

"Why, I declare I don't know, Cap'n."

"Don't look at me. Look at the tide. Tide's turning—ship moored by the head winds. She's the 'Indian Queen,' from Providence. Ever hear of Rhode Island?"

"Yes, seh, I've seen that country in the atlas."

"The men are mighty good sailors there, but mean; all New England men are mean, likewise the people in Virginia and South Carolina; mean."

"What about Georgia, Captain?"

"Never been to Georgia," the captain rolled an angry eye as if in search of casual Georgians, "but bung me if I'd trust a one of 'em."

"Mr. Hewes is a Connecticut man and he's not mean."

"He *was* a Connecticut man, and why did he leave and come to the country of North Carolina? Why, because he wa'n't mean enough to get on in Connecticut. And by the same token that's why he gets on in this province. No, sir, I've been a sailor forty year and seen all climes and countries and peoples. And there ain't a one of 'em fit ship's company for North Carolina—although if you ask me the truth, half the folks here are a set of scoundrels."

Shipping his oars, the captain lit his pipe and smoked in the satisfaction of a man who has handled a large subject masterfully.

As they drifted toward the bigger docks, a high poop seemed slowly to peer around a clump of piles. "The Little Goosen," Johnny read on her counter, "New York."

"Now, how's she rigged?"

"Brig rigged, seh."

"And what cargo has she aboard?"

Johnny scanned the dock for a sight of casks or bales; he ran his eye around her free-board for the stains of black coal or red ore.

"Why, Captain, they ain't any way of telling that I can see."

"Heh!" the captain gave a dry smack of mirth. "She ain't got no cargo. Look at her water-line."

Sure enough, the water-line, a dingy, green-dabbled red, showed high in air; indeed, the whole craft, now that he noticed, seemed to teeter precariously on stilts, saved from capsizing only by her bow and stern hawsers made fast to the dock. Her hold was empty; still, the question had not been fair and the captain's triumphant titter grated. He fell angrily silent.

"Never mind, son. That was a trick. You were figuring what her cargo was. Well, what was it? Have another look."

Through a warehouse door at the end of the dock Johnny caught a glimpse of a shrouded form looming in the shades of the wide dark building. Long, ill-proportioned, it hung suspended by its short, broad, dreadful arms—like a grotesque and bestial criminal. He half felt countless of its fellows lurking in the deeper gloom. Then he laughed. "Dressed beef!"

"To be sure. The Staten Islanders send it down. And I carry it up the river; and the freighters carry it to the settlements. Many's the time you've seed it rolling by your window."

His window—he remembered how he had crept from his bed at daybreak and peered out beneath the dripping eaves to watch the trains of freighters' wagons creak by through the mist. He had wondered where the freight they carried came from, and longed to voyage to that strange and distant source. Now he was here at Edenton where it did come from. And all he wanted was to join his lot with those ghastly forms, hanging by their blunt and horrible hands, and journey again to the Pine Forest. Those beeves, though, would be carried as far as his father's house and away beyond, would be cut up, cooked and eaten long before he would see it again. It was a curious world.

The captain sighed. "That's about the only ships they is in harbor now. Well, let's see if you remember your small craft. Pick me out a whaleboat, and a pink, and a sloop and a snow. Yes, that's a whaleboat right enough, and a pink too, though a proper pink sets flatter on the water. How can you tell a snow without her sails is set? Why, she's got a extry heavy back stay to carry her trysail. Didn't I tell you? Well, I should o'." He looked at Johnny reproachfully.

They were slipping past the smaller docks and landing-stages, back to the captain's river-boat. The sun was dropping; they felt the first soft stir of the never failing evening breeze. At first it came, warm enough but delicately salted, subtly clean. As it freshened, however, a strange and sickening odor bore in on them, an odor human yet musky, an odor, faint yet pungent, of filth and decay. He followed the sinister taint up the wind. Half a mile out in the sound, moored in slack water opposite the river mouth, a low, black schooner, flying no flag, rode to her anchor, a lonely pariah in the waste of waters.

The captain was watching him. He puffed hard on his pipeful of shag, made a wry face and buried his nose in the cloud of smoke.

"Slaver," he said. "She just come in off the middle passage this morning. Phew! They ought to make her change her berth. She'll stink up the entire town."

They made their skiff fast to the landing-stage. The creeping odor still hung around them!

"We might just go up to Terrell's Ordinary for a glass, to wash the taste out of your mouth. I know your paw don't allow you no hard liquor, but a mug of small beer now would do no harm." A mug of small beer, thought Johnny, would do a heap of good.

They turned into a narrow alley behind the rigging yards. A polished hurricane light hung on a bracket beside Terrell's door, and above it, on a signboard, a full-rigged ship, her stays and running rigging most minutely depicted, rode an excessively bright blue sea.

Entering the darkened tap-room from the brilliant light, they could make out nothing. They heard the buzz of flies, the scrape of a mug on a table top. A voice, Terrell's, no doubt, said, "Service, Captain, and who's the young mate?"

Objects took shape, a chair was thrust into Johnny's hand. The proprietor could be dimly seen approaching them. He bent over the captain in an attitude of burly solicitation, resting both knuckles on the table. The darkness cleared away and Johnny, to his joy, saw that Mr. Terrell's stout and hairy arms, bare to the shoulder, were solid patterns of tattooing: a lady in draperies reclined on a lion, an elephant raised the Union Jack in his trunk, a brass cannon, mounted apparently on a cloud, was shooting an arrow into a huge, red heart.

The order was given, the arms were withdrawn and disappeared, proudly akimbo, into the bar. Johnny looked about.

The tap-room was empty except for one squat figure sitting squarely in its chair and drinking steadily, silently. The jaw, half turned toward him, was blue, the cheek a deathly greenish yellow. The gray lips twitched from time to time, the whole frame shuddered.

The man gulped his brandy, shifted, and raised a pair of yellow, sodden eyes.

"Haowdy, mates," he said in a nasal voice. "Haow be ye? Garnt's my name. Josiar Garnt, Nooport."

"What ship?" Captain Flood's voice was not convivial.

" 'The Merry Susan,' that's what she's named naow. Maybe you know her.

She was a Portugee, the 'Holy Heart of Jesus.' But my owners is God-fearing men and wun't stand any papish flub-dubbery, so they called her 'Merry Susan.' Though what in the nation there is merry about her beats me." He poured another drink and offered the bottle to Captain Flood.

"No, thanky. She's the black schooner in the Sound?"

"That's her. Yew've seen her, then?"

"Smelt her, too."

"Ha! Yew should have sniffed us in the tropics, friend. The wust ones has gone overboard since then."

Mr. Terrell brought Captain Flood his rum and sugar and Johnny his mug of small beer. The stranger took another gulp of brandy.

"I dun't seem to get warm. I took the fever in the Bight o' Benin along with all hands and I ain't shook it off. The crew has, except them the fever shook off instead, that's the cabin boy and two forecastle hands. But I still shiver, though I've took enough bark and brandy the last two months to burn my 'tween decks black."

"You ought to lay off the tropics for a whiles, Mister; the tropics and the Trade."

"I'd like to right good, and that's a fact. My luck's turned on me. Do what I may I can't change her." His yellow eyes searched the captain's face for sympathy.

"First the owners skimped refitting the ship; her pumps was bad; her kettles, which come out of a whaler, was too small and leaked, and on top of that they only left two foot six between the slave decks, though I held out till the end for three.

"Nevertheless, we got to the Gold Coast right enough, with our rum. But the blacks was all hiding in the bush, so I tried the Slave Coast. Negroes all at peace and I lost my bos'un and three men trying to start a war. Nothing left but the Ivory Coast, and there we found what might or might not be called a cargo, in a Levantine's barracoon. They was all Gaboons, which everyone knows don't ship good, and half of them was young boys and girls, at that. But my rum casks was starting leaks and I knew another rum-fellow from Boston was coming behind me, so I loaded up for the middle passage."

He drank.

"And a passage it was, friend, I can tell yew. They begun dying on me ten days out, and on account of the decks being built wrong we couldn't get at some of 'em to cut 'em out of the irons.

"Then they tried a mutiny while they was at exercise and I lost two more men. And on top of it all the trade-wind failed me, we lay becalmed, and the beggars started going blind. My first went blind, too, and I had to keep the crew well heeled with rum to hold 'em to their work. And all the time, me with the ague, standing a twenty-four hour trick each day."

The stranger's twanging voice was tearful. Captain Flood took a pull at his rum and sugar and grunted. He thrust his beard forward at the dim, jaundiced figure.

"I expect you're about cured of the Black Trade, eh?"

"Yes, and no. It's a hard life and no mistake. But generally, except when I run across a fellow in a friendly way, like naow, I dun't complain. There's money in it, I dun't mind telling yew. And as my owners always says, every slave that reaches the Indies or Ameriky alive is saved from the heathen and turned into a Christian, providing that the folks that buys them knows their duty."

Captain Flood bared his teeth sardonically.

"Well, even if they don't, Captain, you've done your part. There's that comfort, eh, Captain?"

The stranger's pale, fuddled eyes sought his uncertainly.

"Why, yes, I guess you could look at it that way," he answered without satisfaction.

"Heh!" Captain Flood barked his short laugh. "Come on, Johnny. Sarvint, Captain." He marched from the tap-room.

Outside he burst into a flow of language such as Johnny had never heard, and, indeed, whose very existence he could by no possibility have conceived.

"The lousy limejuicer!" he concluded. "The sweet-scented slave runner! Excuse my chat, but them pious Yankees naturally turns my bile. I don't set up for nothing extreh, I'd buy a slave as soon as the next man, and I'm weak on Scripteh. But all I say is, God tar and feather the Holy Josiahs that works the Trade. Now, son, you better make tracks for your supper. And you needn't say nothing about what you've heerd." He held out an embarrassed hand. "Bung me," he said. "I didn't aim to get you into this."

That night the wind shifted; the air was clean. But in his attic room Johnny caught snatches of a sorrowful, long-drawn chant, stealing softly up from the black waters where the black hulk lay, stealing around the houses, around the people, around him. As he lay there, listening, his hair stirred; for above the sombre, wordless hum-note he heard the ghostly treble of a child.

# CHAPTER XV

CAPTAIN TENNANT, wearing a green cotton jacket and his own hair, was sitting on his porch in the twilight. At the sound of Johnny's foot on the step he rose punctiliously and made him a sharp salutation with a copy of the London Magazine.

"Damn the weather!" His face, red and angry, turned from Johnny's toward the red and angry setting sun. "But good Gad, sir, what can one expect? As I tell Eve, one can't expect English weather. It's like everything else. One can't expect to be in England when one is not in England, can one? Ha!"

He sat down and pointed imperiously at a chair for Johnny. He ruffled the pages of the London Magazine.

"I suppose you take in the London Magazine? What! No? Good Gad—I mean to say, everyone takes in the London Magazine." He tapped the pages vindictively.

"Although the London Magazine is not what it was. No, sir, egad! When I was a young subaltern the London Magazine was a publication that every gentleman read and that every gentleman could read and should read. But now!"

He rolled the paper tight and beat it on his knee.

"By Jove, sir. I don't know what we're coming to! If you were to offer me a thousand pound this moment, I'm dashed if I could tell you what we're coming to. Not that I haven't an uncommon good notion, as a matter of fact —— Oh, here's Eve."

She stood framed in the white doorway; her dress was white, her cap was white; the white fanlight arched above her head. Smiling faintly, with her tongue just peeping between her teeth, she dropped him the new curtsey, her skirts swirling and billowing in an airy cone.

"Master Fraser," she rose, "isn't it warm? Horrid."

"Torrid!" said the captain. "Ha!"

"La, Papa, how can you be clever in this heat? Master Fraser, are you clever?"

"No, ma'm, not exactly."

"Come now, I'm sure you are. Do tell me an Ameddican joke. Papa says you go in for jokes here."

Johnny felt the pores of his forehead bursting with hot embarrassment. What a girl! She didn't seem to understand the way people felt about things. Asking a person to tell a joke! He was uncomfortable himself and embarrassed for her, too. He recalled a guest of his father's who had gone laughing and crashing through the woods on a turkey hunt. He had felt the same way then.

He looked down at the ground, grappling blindly for some faint recollection of a joke. Evasion never occurred to him. The thing was an ultimatum. He had been asked by a lady to tell a joke. Nothing, then, but to tell it. So firmly fixed was this one idea in his stunned mind that he could hardly believe his ears to hear her say:

"Don't you like my dimity? You should have spoken of it. Papa says men never notice. Has he told you of Hoddin? It's quite wonderful."

"No, ma'm, the Captain didn't tell."

"Hoddin is Papa's old soldier servant. He is come clear out from England to take care of the house. He is too delightful. I don't remember him, but he remembers me. Isn't that odd?"

She smiled again, again he saw the tip of her tongue, demure, faintly derisive.

"I reckon he came in on the 'Indian Queen.'"

"Now you see, you are clever."

"But she's the only British ship in port."

"—And modest. Are all Ameddicans modest?"

Now she was really laughing at him. She was a peculiar girl. Just when he thought she was stupid she seemed clever, and the other way 'round. But here the captain burst in.

"Modest!" He sniffed. "Why, damme, sir, I've never met one yet who didn't think himself the match of any Englishman alive."

Eve, looking at Johnny, seemed slightly impatient at her father's interruption. Johnny regretted it, as well. Her questions were alarming, dreadful, yet somehow pleasant. It was nice to be asked questions, even blundering, tactless questions, by a girl.

A steady tramp was heard in the hall, a strong little man, long-headed, bandy-legged, long-nosed, with a ruddy, humorous face and a queue so tight that it stuck out straight behind, stepped out the door, brought his heels methodically together, and his hands to his sides, squared his shoulders, expanded his chest and gazed impersonally into space.

"Supper 'is laid, sir." He ejaculated the words with subdued ferocity. He said "laid" as if it were "lyde." Johnny had never heard anyone talk that way before; he hoped the man, it must be Hoddin, would speak again. But Hoddin merely stood there, staring at nothing in his disconcerting way, as if none of them existed. And the captain marched by him and in the door as if Hoddin did not exist. It could not be Hoddin, an old servant who had come out from England to work for them. Or if it were, he and the captain must have had some bitter quarrel.

But the captain seemed quite cheerful as he waved them into the dining-room.

"And now, my boy," he said, "you shall have a proper steak and kidney pie."

At the last words of grace Hoddin, who had been left apparently fixed through eternity on the porch, appeared from the kitchen bearing a deep, brown-crusted dish.

Captain Tennant carved the cold pie with a flourish; Hoddin served it and vanished.

"Isn't he a perfect love?" Eve whispered. "It is so nice to have him. I never feel quite comfortable with your black people. They are so—black, don't you think?"

"Well, yes, ma'm; the good ones surely are. I don't trust these yer yellow Negroes," Johnny added sagely.

"Oh, but all of them—they talk so oddly and they laugh so much. And then they try to be friendly; it's really very awkward."

On familiar ground now, Johnny expanded and began to talk.

"They're friendly, all right—the good ones are. Why, some of the best friends I got are Negroes."

He felt important, authoritative.

"Slaves is all right," he went on, "if you know how to treat them."

He glanced loftily around and noticed with surprise that Eve and her father had fixed on him a look of incredulous alarm.

"But surely, sir," said the captain in the voice of one who would put Johnny in a better light in spite of himself, "surely, one would hardly choose a black boy for a friend, what?"

"Why, Captain," Johnny answered easily, "it's not exactly that way. You don't choose the slave. The slave chooses you."

The captain abandoned his philanthropic purpose.

"Egad, sir," he blurted, "I don't see how that improves matters."

Johnny had evidently lost caste by his explanation. But this time he felt no qualms. When it came to Negroes he knew what he was talking about and they did not. And if they couldn't understand what he told them it was their own fault. They might be English, he said to himself, but they didn't know everything.

It was dark when they finished. Hoddin closed the dining-room doors smartly behind them with the same impersonal stare. By Zooks, thought Johnny, there must have been a powerful fuss between the captain and him.

Captain Tennant lit his pipe.

"Capital chap, Hoddin," he observed. "Look at these boots. Properly varnished. I warrant you haven't seen a pair of boots dressed like that in all your life. Hoddin did 'em. It used to drive me nearly mad trying to get my boots done out here. I always say if you want to know if a man's a gentleman, look at his boots."

Johnny felt his own new boots, made new, according to Sir Nat's instructions, by Tappit, softly receding under his chair. They were good boots, but he remembered that they had received nothing but one casual wipe from Malley since they came.

The captain flicked his shining foot.

"Now Hoddin's here," he said. "So that's all right. By Jove," he mused with something almost like enthusiasm, "you simply can't beat Hoddin on boots. And besides, he saved my life once on the Coromandel Coast. Oh, by the way, I asked in Hewes and Battle for a glass of port. Hoddin!" he shouted wrathfully.

The door opened and Hoddin stood before them at attention.

"Yes, sir!" he rapped out.

"Port for——" he turned to Johnny. "Port for you, young Fraser?"

"No, thank you, seh."

"Port for three!"

"Very good, sir!"

They stood like duellists firing into each other at point-blank range. Bang —bang, bang! It was thrilling. When the smoke of their fusillade had cleared Hoddin was gone. Had that last terrific broadside, "Port for three!" laid him low? No, beyond the dining-room doors the steady tread passed to and fro. It stopped, glassware clinked delicately.

"They should be here now." The captain rose and looked out of each window in turn. He drew a large hunting-case watch from his fob pocket and studied it. "Should have been here ten minutes ago. Never saw people so casual as these provincial chaps. Quite likely they won't be here for an hour. It isn't decent, egad it isn't. I always say that an engagement is an engagement, and you can't have it any other way. Port will be warm, and serve 'em right." His face cleared, he rubbed his hands with grim relish at the thought of this hideous fatality.

However, the gentlemen now arrived. Captain Tennant went into the hall to greet them. Johnny heard Mr. Hewes' New England voice.

"Captain! Haow do?"

Then Mr. Battle's soft but rugged North Carolina accent.

"Captain, how you, seh?"

Mr. Hewes, in a sober linen suit, with his wig left off for summer, showing his sparse clipped hair, swept the room in a glance of genial shrewdness.

"Servant, miss," he said to Eve. For a younger man his tone was perhaps too assured, his brown eyes too sagacious and fatherly. Eve was not pleased. She inclined her head loftily after the London manner.

Mr. Battle followed, friendly, at ease, yet self-contained.

"Evening, Miss Eve."

Eve clearly put him down as plodding, worthy. She bowed with well-bred condescension as to one well enough in his way, but lacking the graces.

"Hewes, take this chair. Battle, sit here. Fraser, be seated."

The captain's military eye swept the company commandingly. He assigned each member to his post with all the exactitude and vigor he would have shown in carrying out a well-thought-out battle plan—or an ill-thought-out one.

"Captain and Miss Eve, ma'm. I hope you all find yo'selves well?" Unconscious of his homely, negligent attire, his crudely darned stockings, his tousled hair, Mr. Battle hung one long leg over the other knee, one long arm over the back of the chair, and gazed on the company with easy friendly courtesy behind which seemed to lurk, unstudied, awkward, a fundamental dignity which, looking through his light blue eyes, did not so much ignore polite formality as penetrate it.

The captain seized on this inquiry carnivorously. His eye, his whole face glowed with dull fury.

"Why, sir, egad, I was well enough until this afternoon. Quite well, egad. Then I saw this."

He brought his hand down on the table. The blow caused the cover of the London Magazine to fly up into view.

"Hello," said Mr. Hewes, "that's the old London. I can't believe the London has gotten under your skin, Captain."

There was a tenderness in his twang.

"The London Magazine, sir, is not what it was, damme, sir, it is not. Look at this."

He bent back the pages fiercely.

"A petition from the merchants and ratepayers of the City praying government to withdraw the tax in America on tea in order that their trade may be restored to its flourishing condition. The pusillanimous shop-keepers fear the effects of your scoundrelly non-importation agreement, or whatever magniloquent name it is you call that piece of low chicanery by. Where was I? Oh, they fear the effects—and what do they do? They pray the Parliament and the King to knuckle under. And why? So that they may fatten their precious money-bags at the expense of the British flag."

He peered malignantly at the paper.

"There's plenty of 'And your petitioners do most humbly pray' and all that sort of thing. But egad, sirs, that's what it all comes to. And to think it should appear in the London Magazine. Good God, what would my old governor have said?"

Mr. Battle swung his big, country boot from side to side in slow reflection.

"Does the Magazine endo'se the petition, then, seh?"

"Endorse it! Do you know what you say, sir? It merely prints it and denounces it, and I must say denounces it roundly. But in my young days, when the London Magazine was the London Magazine and no mistake, it would have denounced it without printing it."

Mr. Hewes turned his long shrewd face on the captain with a dry grin.

"Do I understand, Captain, that you are opposed to this petition?"

The captain's body and face swelled dangerously with speechless frenzy. His little blue china eyes stared at Mr. Hewes in rage and desperation.

"Evidently," said Mr. Hewes. Cool and easy, he picked up the Magazine and handed it to Mr. Battle. "Battle's a lawyer—we'll get a free opinion."

The pressure inside the captain was relieved by a long hiss. He took a breath.

"Opposed! Opposed! Hang it, sir, can't you understand English? Opposed is not the word. I abhor it, I spurn it!"

"And yet I've the notion the petitioners are within their rights. We'll soon know from Battle."

"Rights! Who gives a tuppence for their rights! I say they're a low-bred pack of scoundrels. And I've no doubt they have the right to be a low-bred pack of scoundrels!"

On receiving the Magazine, Mr. Battle had held it negligently in his free hand and plunged into a state of deep professional attention. He now emerged.

"The petition," he announced, "is perfectly legal. As legal as the tea tax against which it is aimed. Maybe mo' so."

"That, Teague," said Mr. Hewes, "is an *obiter dictum.*"

"It's damnable nonsense," said the captain, "and sedition to boot."

"As fo' sedition," Mr. Battle remarked, locking his big-knuckled fingers across his knee, "you are not familiar with the law, seh. And as fo' nonsense, you are not familiar with the tax."

"What! D'you mean to tell me that, after all England has done for her colonies, she can't lay thrippence a pound on tea!"

"Why," said Mr. Hewes, "what's she done?"

"Done! Hang me, sir, are you trying to make sport of me? In the first place, she founded them."

"No, England did not found them. Different Englishmen and others did. And when they increased England took them over. And when they prospered she taxed them. They have been created by the men who adventured out here and by their descendants, like Teague, here, who without help from the mother country has made himself what he is—the second best backgammon player in Edenton."

He smiled kindly at Mr. Battle and then at all the company, as though he would deflect the talk from its more acrid course. He seemed benign, unruffled yet cool, shrewd, alert, in this air charged with anger and lurking, deep antagonisms.

But matters had gone too far.

"I don't know what Mr. Battle is," said the captain, "and I don't care. But I know that neither he nor any other provincial could exist without the protection of Great Britain."

"It seems to me," said Mr. Battle, drawling more slowly than usual, "like I recall the British protection of the late war." His eye blazed with unexpected fire. "My friend, yo' British Generals killed mo' provincials than the French and Indians together."

The color slowly flowed together in Captain Tennant's face, till just beneath the china eyes two small fierce spots blazed in a white, astounded mask.

It was at this moment of danger that the dining-room door opened. All turned from the crisis toward it. Hoddin trod steadily in with the port. The slim decanter in whose rich red, gently moving pool nodded and shifted a ruddy prisoned shaft of light, the slender airy glasses, thin and clear as bubbles, ringing to the lightest touch with an echoing fairy sound, all shone and twinkled on them, delicate, graceful, gracious. They felt the spell of mellow ancient ceremonial. The captain checked his speech and rose, red but controlled. He unstopped the decanter, poured three drops in a glass and tasted them.

"Quite all right, Hoddin. You may bring glasses for Miss Eve and the young gentleman."

He turned to Johnny.

"You need only take a sip, sir."

"Thank you, seh, I reckon I'd like a regular glass like everybody else, please."

At this the rest laughed the nervous laugh of tension relaxed. The glasses came. The decanter moved slowly on its appointed round.

Captain Tennant, holding his glass shoulder high, stood before them. They stood up and raised theirs.

"The King!" he said.

## CHAPTER XVI

A RAW OCTOBER wind trundled leaden clouds across the sky, fretted the leaden waters of the bay, turned the world, which till now had worn a summer face, bleakly forbiding, moribund. Above the dead leaves drifting, rustling down the street, the sycamores raised white, naked limbs and shivered. The sap had ceased to run in them, in everything.

Johnny Fraser, standing in the study so sombrely freighted with dead languages, and the dead works of dead men, looking through the cold pane on the dying trees, felt that the sap had ceased to run in him. The warm, fertile spring when first he came to Edenton seemed years ago, the early homesickness, a twinge, compared to the chill desolation now borne in by the Autumn wind. Life in him was suspended. He felt like a dreary bird moulting, like a forlorn bear hibernating; he felt old and gray. The bright adventurer had run his course; one thing remained, to creep home, home to the sheltering forest, dark green, deeply whispering, home to the fuzzy cows, the colt, the Negro laughter, home to his father's big hands, his mother's swift, soft eyes. By Zooks, the thought was enough to make him cry.

A huge cocked hat moved through the stricken bushes by the gate. It seemed to rest directly on the turned-up collar of a rough seaman's coat, leaving only a space just large enough for Captain Flood's nose and eyes. His spry figure was lost in the toga-like folds of the great-coat which seemed to progress under its own power, his whiskers, inextricably buttoned into the collar, were reduced to a few eccentric wisps.

A letter from home—it must be that. Johnny was at the door.

"Howdy, son. Letter from the governor."

"Yes, seh, that's nice. Step in, Captain."

"God in the mountain! Look at them books."

"Yes, seh, they's a heap of books hyer."

"Well, I'm blamed! Now how would you account for all them books? Eh, son?"

During this talk the captain was conducting researches into the pockets of his coat. He brought nothing forth, but through the cloth his hand could be made out picking up various objects and dropping them again. But while Johnny was searching for an answer to the captain's question, the old man gave a whistle of satisfaction.

"Thar she blows!"

He pulled out the letter and handed it to Johnny. He turned his back and began a systematic and minute examination of the room.

Johnny broke the seal and read the letter.

"Little River,
"19th October, 1771.

"My dear Son;

"I send you herewith under Captain Flood's hand a Bill for Two Pounds sterling. This Sum is for the purpose of defraying any small Obligations which you may be under and for your Expense Money to Halifax. I would have you go up to Halifax with the Capt'n on his return Voyage as Mr. Wylie Jones has been apprised of your intended

Arrival and will offer you Accommodation for the Night. Mr. Jones'
proffer of hospitality is kindly intended and though I approve neither
of that Gentleman's Principles nor of his Mode of Living I prefer that
you shou'd break your Journey there rather than at Slade's Ordinary
which you wou'd otherwise be obliged to do. And I have confidence
that, forewarned as you have been against Pomp, Luxury, False Pride
and Gaming, you will resist Improper Influences and retain the Character which you have ever Enjoyed.

"I most particularly charge you not to quit Edenton before discharging all your Obligations. A False Gentility makes light of such matters,
as I am well aware, but I shou'd be sorry to think that such might ever
attach itself to the Character of my Son.

"A letter to Doctor Clapton will inform him of my intentions to have
you return home for a short stay. I trust that you will bear from him a
Favorable Account of your Industry and Demeanour.

"Your aff'nate Father

"John Fraser."

A letter from his mother lay inside.

"Johnny my dear;
"I have missed you sadly but now that you are to come home I
become quite Chearful once more. If you show this to Capt'n Flood he
will advance you what Sum you may need. I wou'd not have you
stinted. I send you my love, my dear son.

"Your devoted

"Mother."

"Huzzah! huzzah!" he shouted, "I'm going home!"
"To be sure you're agoing home. I knew that all along. Boat leaves at mid-
day tomorrow. I'll send my deck-hand up for your dunnage, at eleven."

The clouds had vanished in the night. When Johnny went outdoors a
warm sun was flooding through the chilly air. With his two pounds in his
pocket, he started his round of the commercial houses to whom he was
indebted. The transactions were not numerous nor involved. There were,

in fact, only two. He called at Minchin & Minchin's to settle his account for the summer. He threaded his way among barrels of wheat flour, whale oil, bread, biscuit, tar, turpentine, and rum, he stepped over cheddar cheeses, coils of rope, pulley blocks, kedge anchors, he ducked under strings of cured tobacco, onions, hame-straps, traces, and reached the high counter and wooden cage at the rear.

"Mr. Minchin," he called, "I'm come to pay my reckoning."

There was no response, but from the gloomy shadows behind the counter came the sound of a ledger flopping heavily on a desk, of leaves rustling and a pen scratching. The dry cracked voice of Mr. Minchin was raised in doleful intonation:

"Maple sugar candy, half a crown; liquorice root, two and nine pence; caoutchouc bands, three and a penny."

The last item brought a pang. He had bought the rubber for a catapult to be used in hunting birds and, if need be, to repel the river-front gang from the sacred domain of the docksides. But within a week the catapult— hickory fork, leaden slug, rubber bands and all—had gone overboard in an interesting attempt to shoot fish from a dinghy. In one brief tragic instant three and a penny had sunk beneath the wave.

"Total eight and four pence," the voice went on. A blue-knuckled hand was thrust out through a wooden cage, Johnny dropped a half-jo into it and waited for his change. He heard teeth clicking on his coin. The change came back without comment. The incident was closed. He felt empty, frustrated. The transaction, so businesslike and manly, involving no mean sum, had caused not the slightest tremor in the soulless machinery of Mr. Minchin's store. He might as well have dropped the money in the collection plate.

His other creditor was Mr. Hornblower. The tavern was deserted except for Mr. Hornblower himself, who sprinkled the sanded tap-room floor from a pewter ewer resting against his rotund green-baize apron, then swept it into a pattern of dashing, interwoven arcs.

Johnny watched him from the open door. Giving a last twirl to the broom, Mr. Hornblower looked up.

"Well, well, I do declare! Why, bless my soul, I do, indeed, declare! I had no idea, Master Fraser—you almost frightened me! And now, sir, your commands?"

"I'm come to pay my reckoning, Mr. Hornblower."

"Well, well, indeed! And very kind of you, I'm sure. Although as to that there is no necessity. No, indeed, young sir, your credit, and all that, you know. Quite unnecessary."

"Yes, but I'm going home today."

"Ah, now, really! You don't tell me. Splendid. But you will be missed, young sir. You have friends here. I can't help overhearing the gentlemen, you know. Thank you, sir."

Taking the coin in his clean ruddy hand, he consulted a mysterious hieroglyphic slate beside the bar.

"A mackerel six pence, plum tart four pence, small beer a penny; that was when you dined with Sir Nat, share and share alike.

"Herring a shilling, cold veal four pence, floating island thrippence, small beer four pence; that was when you dined with Doctor Clapton, the day his Negro wench was run over by Sir Nat's dog-cart. I recall you insisted on standing treat—most liberal of you, I thought at the time. It should have been Sir Nat.

"Best Jamaica rum nine pence, small beer tuppence. You passed the evening with Captain Flood, and I must say the captain demeaned himself with perfect propriety, though hardly of the same class, between ourselves, as the generality of my patrons."

The ruddy hand came forward, dropped the change into Johnny's left and shook his right with a firm, soft pressure.

"And now, young sir, a pleasant journey. My respects to your father. Come soon again. Your humble servant, sir."

Johnny walked out of the inn, somewhat of a personage. All his debts were paid and he was recognized by Mr. Hornblower as a young man of quality. His clothes were packed, an hour or so remained. It was too late to say good-bye to Sir Nat, but a farewell call on the Tennants might not be amiss. Kicking the dry leaves in shyness and uncertainty, he wandered down the street, turned up the hill. Then, with a last bold dash, he reached the Collector's door. He sounded the knocker. The door flew open instantly. Before him stood Hoddin, looking out over his head to the distant horizon of the bay.

"I've come to see Captain Tennant."

"The Keptin is gorn to New Bern for to see 'is Hexcellency the Guv'ner."

Beyond Hoddin, Johnny caught a flash of dimity in the dark hall.

"Well, then, I reckon I'd like to see Miss Tennant."

"Miss H'eve is not at 'ome, sir."

"Why, man, I just saw her there in the house."

"Miss H'eve is not at 'ome, sir," Hoddin repeated patiently.

Johnny heard a patter of feet up the stairs and a laugh. Eve's voice called down:

"Show Master Fraser in, Hoddin. I shall see him in a moment."

Hoddin, his glance more distant, more profoundly grieved than ever, swung back the door.

Waiting in the drawing-room, Johnny looked out the many-paned window at the Sound. The further shore, a stretch of green and yellow, was flecked by the shadow of a passing mackerel cloud, and though the day was nearly calm, the water in between glittered and broke into countless little waves as though still troubled by memories of last night's wind. Below him rose the tangle of shipping; through a rift in the line of house-roofs he could see the stumpy mast of Captain Flood's river-boat, the admirable, splendid, sainted boat that was soon to bear him home.

"Master Fraser, you pay calls early—but I am happy to see you."

Her white, short-sleeved dress had blue polka dots on it, a cluster of blue flowers bobbed archly from her mob-cap. He bowed elegantly.

"And I'm mighty pleased to see you, ma'm. That Englishman said you weren't home, but I saw you in the hall. I reckon he's not very smart."

For some reason she laughed.

"He has been trained that way. It is a custom." She looked at him warmly. "But to you I am always at home."

He felt his face burning with furious embarrassment and elation.

"I thank you, ma'm, I certainly do. I appreciate the compliment." He was elegance itself, and romance too. Perhaps a more practical note would be safer. "But how can you be at home if you don't know when I'm coming?"

Here to his irritation she laughed again.

"You are not at your lessons this morning?"

He was no better pleased at this. It was not the thing to talk of lessons to a young man of fashion. And she, in spite of her airs, was no older than himself.

"I'm going home," he said bluntly.

"Oh, dear, I'm so sorry! I had no idea!" She was really distressed. He softened, his heart expanded, grew strong, generous, touched with a tender and protecting pity. Life was hard on girls. They lived shut up, not knowing what was going on. Then suddenly a man, like himself, dropped in and told them offhand that he was leaving within the hour.

"I expect I won't be gone long. A month maybe." He could not resist saying a month, though it would more likely be only a fortnight.

"A month!" she cried; his heart pounded; he had touched her. "A month! Oh, la! that's no time at all. You will be back before we know it. I had thought you were leaving for good and had come to say good-bye."

She glanced at him archly, but he was angry and unmoved. If he came back in a fortnight now, he would look ridiculous.

"Well," he muttered obstinately, "a month's a month. And a man can say good-bye for a month, cant' he?"

Now she was contrite, but there was a veiled mischief in her glance that he did not like.

"Indeed he can, and a very delicate attention it is, I am sure."

She shot him a look so full of meaning that his knees turned to water, his terrified heart bumped in his gullet.

"Of course," the words stumbled, "it's no more than what I would do for any lady that had used me hospitably."

"Oh," she made an angry little face, "then I must say your manners are better than any we have found in this province."

"My manners ain't a patch on lots of manners in this country. I reckon you don't know the folks that has manners if you talk like that."

She froze.

"I know one person that has no manners at all."

By Zooks, it was impossible to argue with her. One minute she said he had good manners and the next she said he had none. She didn't know her own mind. He had an idea to walk majestically out of the house without a word. But he heard himself say:

"Look hyer, Eve, I didn't aim to start a fight. Honestly, I didn't."

"Who said there was a fight, sir? And who asked you to call me Eve?"

"Well, a argument, then. And I won't call you Eve if you don't choose."

"You may."

He glowed under her smile. Everything was all right again. For the moment. Now was the time to leave.

"I can't stay." He rose. "I've all my things to get ready; the boat leaves at mid-day. I only just could come for a minute." He held out his hand. "And I haven't called on any person else but you."

She took his hand and clung to it, raised soft, pleading eyes to his. Again his heart was pumping.

"And that's a fact," he muttered inadequately.

"Good-bye, Eve."

He reached his hat in a desperate burst and hurried down the hall.

"Good-bye, Johnny," he heard her call with what he hoped might perhaps have been a muffled sob.

Dr. Clapton, in his blue cloak, walked with him down to the dock; shuffling behind them, Captain Flood's deck-hand with the saddle-bags yokewise on his neck, answered the derisive salutations of Negro friends with soundless chuckles. A breeze was springing from the south, the air was warm and summery again. Homeward bound! The sunny world was soft and radiant, the graceful houses, the homely, cluttered dockside lofts and shanties basked in the light, the glorious blue bay ruffled and twinkled, the brown sail of the river-boat, half raised, swayed eagerly, bellied, spilled the wind, rustled in glad impatience.

The very hairs of Johnny's neck prickled with intolerable joy. Homeward bound—huzzah!

The captain, his hands behind his back, his whiskers blowing over his shoulder, paced the dock, tilted his nose to the breeze. He raised his big cocked hat to Doctor Clapton.

"On time," he said, "but only just. Come aboard, son; we can't waste our breeze."

Johnny dropped down to the deck; his saddle-bags fell with a muffled bump into the cockpit. Dr. Clapton, on the edge of the dock, gazed down at him benignly.

"You have been a good boy, John. Yes, yes. And I wish you a happy holiday. Oh, bless my soul, I had near forgot." He reached inside his cloak and brought out a letter. "This is to your father."

Johnny looked at the inscription, "Kindness of Master John Fraser," was written at the bottom. He swelled. Under his finger he felt the loose flap and turned the letter over.

"It ain't been sealed, seh." He tried not to show pride or reproach.

"Yes, yes; quite so, my boy. It is not customary for one gentleman to seal a letter when it is to be delivered by the hand of another. Letters are sealed only for servants, expresses and the like."

"That's right," Captain Flood broke in approvingly. "L'arn him to be a gentleman, Doctor. For God knows it's too late to l'arn him to be aught else. Negro, clear that bow hawser and stand by to cast off!" He turned back to Dr. Clapton. "If I had it to do over again, I often think I'd have went in and set up for a gentleman myself." He spat over the side regretfully.

Doctor Clapton looked on him kindly. "Why, Captain, you are trusted, respected and loved, what do you desire more? Many gentlemen would give everything for that."

"They wouldn't give up their gentility, excusin' my contradiction. No, sir; I never yet seen a man who set up to be a gentleman what would admit it was no go."

Dr. Clapton laughed.

"Bless me, sir, if you are not a Natural Philosopher."

"That's the name, more or less, I always had in the fo'c'sle," the captain answered complacently. "Of course they didn't call it that, but any little disputes about rum or dunnage was 'most always brought up to me.

"Well, sir!" he added briskly, making Dr. Clapton a salute. "Cast off, there, black boy!"

The boat swung very slowly, creaked against the piles.

"You are a good lad, John. I shall miss you. Yes, yes. Come back soon. I have great hopes of you."

He raised his ebony stick in a gentle, uncertain gesture of farewell. Then, as the slit of water opened between them, he broke into a smile which, like the sunlight, flooded over Johnny, enfolded him, and, warm, radiant, drove straight into the marrow of his bones.

## CHAPTER XVII

THEY PASSED Slade's dingy ordinary at dusk, the breeze still holding strong, and wound the narrowing stream beneath a crescent moon. Owls flittered soundlessly through tangled swamps, a bat wheeled overhead, they saw the dull embers of a logging camp.

The wind failed; they tied up to a cypress. Johnny and the captain slept under a pair of quilts beneath the deck awning. The Negro curled in the bows, his head between his knees.

At the first chill of dawn they woke. A mist hung over the stream. Nearby dim shapes of wild ducks left the water on dripping wings. The Negro unlashed a pole, thrust it against the bottom and threw his weight on it. The boat hung in the stream, gathered way; they moved silently ahead through the cold, wet haze. The Negro slipped forward along the counter, balancing the pole, plunged it in again, pressed his way slowly to the stern.

The captain lit a charcoal fire in an iron pot, boiled a pannikin of water and dropped in a handful of tea. He grinned at Johnny.

"They's been a row about this yer tea. I expect you heerd tell of it. A tax or something. And bung me if I don't think the province is right, what I understand of it. Anyhow, I like to see 'em stand up against England. It looks good. I'm for shutting down on tea. But what I says is, shut down on it in a general way, but a little tea never done no harm to no one. 'Specially on a chilly morning like this yer."

He passed Johnny a steaming cup. From the cuddy he fished out corn-cake and a pot of muscovado sugar, brown and wet. He sugared the tea from the blade of his case-knife. They ate their breakfast luxuriously, lying on the quilts, watching the Negro pole her up-stream. Now and then the captain touched the helm, kept her in slack water, close to the bank.

The mist rose, but still hung close above the water whose stretches, darkly green, moved sullenly beneath the canopy. From the distant shore, shrouded, invisible, almost forgotten, almost incredible, the muffled clip of axe-strokes struck them with a shock. The sound fell behind them, they crept along, ghosts in limbo again.

The sun, a blurred white lump, fought its way down to them; a struggling breeze caught up with them. The haze gave ground, split wide above their heads and trailed off in shattered fragments on the freshening airs; to right and left the cypress banks stood clear.

They hoisted sail and climbed on slowly through the endless forest. The Negro ate a hunk of salt pork, licked his chops and went to sleep again. The sun warmed up; a vapor rose from the dripping decks. Listless, they watched the unchanging swamps creep by.

By noon a few sparse corn-patches, littered with stumps and ringed, dead trees, appeared. Near a landing a lank woman carried a pine knot into a cabin, a lank hog heaved up from a mud bank with a grunt. Fishing like a heron from his log, a peak-shouldered man waved at them with a lifeless, drooping gesture. The cypress swamps closed in again.

Now came other fields, larger and stump-clear, and houses of dressed logs or sided; box-bushes, cedars, sycamores stood before the doors. Rounding a bend, they saw broad lawns, Negro quarters in a long, uneven row, a cedar-shaded family burying-ground. A great plantation house moved slowly by, white, tall and graceful as a passing ship.

A calash, showing a lady's bonnet above the turned-back hood, jogged down a road. And then—oh! joyful sound—an unseen pack of hounds opened with a burst of music from a side branch. "Hi, you—hi, hi!" Johnny shouted. He heard the hoarse note of the horn.

Captain Flood looked at him curiously. "What's the idea of this yer fox chase, son? I often hyear 'em. But what's the idea? You can't eat a fox, now can you?"

"Why, it's fun to see whether the fox fools the dogs or whether the dogs catch the fox. I reckon that's it."

"But if he fools 'em you don't get nothing. And if they catch him you don't get nothing. What can a man do with a fox?"

"Why, you can hang his hide on the barn door. I know a man has twenty of 'em right across in two rows."

"But bung me, you can hang anything on a barn door, can't you?"

A long pause followed. More great houses on the cleared banks, horses and oxen at fall plowing, and then a white village with a white steeple and a landing-stage.

"Halifax," said the captain, "and we're lucky to see it before tomorrow. There's no money," he observed morosely, "in warping up to these yer inland towns."

As they came up to the landing-stage a yellow chaise with red wheels came trotting down to the dock. A Negro in cockaded hat and scarlet coat, his elbows held magnificently high, pulled up the dun horse with a flourish and climbed down over the shaft.

"That's Wylie Jones' rig," Captain Flood remarked. "I reckon they seen us coming from the Grove."

The deck-hand swung up and made fast, the Negro driver, sleek and elderly, bowed low.

"Mist' Fraseh, seh? Yesso. Mist' Jone' present his compliments and ast' you to 'scuse his pus'nal absence. Yesso."

The deck-hand passed up Johnny's saddle-bags, ducked his head and grinned with silent rapture at the penny from Johnny's purse. Johnny turned to the captain.

"I forgot to ask you how much was the passage, Captain?"

"How much you got, bucko?"

"Eleven and a penny, seh."

"It won't do. No, sir. The tariff's nine, and that leaves you only two. Pay me next trip."

"Thank you, seh, but my Dadder wouldn't like that."

"I know, son, but what would your maw say if you was to go up to the Grove, with two bob in your breeches, eh?"

"But I won't have to pay anything there, will I?"

"Course not. But it don't look right. And when a man is going in for to be a gentleman, like you is, looks is the thing. Yes, sir."

"Dadder won't like it."

"That's so. I told you once before. But I'd a heap rather have your paw on my trail than I would your maw. A heap. Women is liable to be vindictive. Here." He took Johnny's purse in his hand.

"Now you've paid me, aint' you?"

He gave it back.

"And now I've loaned you a loan, as between man and man and the less said the better. So that's fixed. Good luck, son."

His wiry claw closed on Johnny's fingers in a quick shake.

"Thank you, seh; you're mighty generous."

The captain turned his furious whiskers on Johnny.

"Now, then, are you going to keep that rig a-standing all day?"

Perched in the chaise beside the Negro, he looked down on the horse's round, fat back, with its territs of polished brass. The territs twinkled, bobbed to the motion of the shafts. A row of neat houses passed, and a group of children, goggle-eyed.

"Hi, chilluns!" the Negro said with benevolent magnificence. They pulled their thumbs from their mouths.

"Heyo, Roskus!" they called.

Then they were on the country road between hedge-rows of wild plum and reddening sumac. The straw hats of a slave gang flopped to and fro among the brown stalks and white bolls of a cotton field.

"Whose slaves is those, Roskus?"

"They's my masteh's, Mist' Jone', suh. Fiel'-han's." He waved a complacent whip.

"We must be close to the great house, then."

"De Grove? Mah, no, suh! We's des come on de domain, das all we is. Fo' mile we got to travel. Come up yeh, Berry!"

The road turned back down the river up which Johnny had come. It lay inland among gentle hills, but now and then he could see the tops of the cypress swamps and a flash of water between dark foliage and gray boughs. Fawn-colored oxen, evenly spaced across a field, turned dark red furrows with the plows. They were the same he had seen from the boat. Low-headed, soft-eyed, they stumbled slowly through the deep soft ground in a moody trance. Negroes hanging back on the plough handles, shouted musically, touched the impassive sides with slim poles.

An overseer in white linen rode by. He raised his straw hat genially to Johnny, but with a hint of deference. Johnny saluted him, clinked the money in his pocket and whistled airily. He must show Roskus that he was accustomed to the respect of grown-up white men.

They turned in through a brick gateway, creaked softly up a hill beneath the boughs of elms. The first dead leaves of fall were floating down. A glint of white between the trunks, and they drew up at the columned portico. An elderly Negro in blue hobbled briskly down the brownstone steps.

"Welcome to de Grove, suh. Mist' Wyleh 'spect you inside de house. Mose!" A discreetly grinning black boy hurried up. "Carry de gentleman's equipage to Parnassius."

"What?" said Johnny.

"Ah give Mose his instructions, suh. 'Bout de bag."

"But what about Parnassus?"

"Das de name, suh. Ev'eh room got a name. Dey's Olympius, an' Illium, an' Delphy, an' all sech. Dis away, suh."

The hall was flagged with checkers of black and white stone. To the left he caught the glint of gilded chairs. A door opened on the right.

"Ah, there you are, young Fraser."

Wylie Jones, in sweat-stained riding-boots and a whipcord coat, came toward him. His hand was outstretched cordially enough, but in his voice and in his eye Johnny felt a touch of cool mockery. Accustomed to the homely, hearty greetings of the back country, he was chilled by this man who never disclosed his inner self—who seemed determined never to be impulsive, wholesouled, too much in earnest; in a word, never to be ridiculous, like everyone else.

"How do you do, seh?" Johnny said stiffly. "I hope your he'th is good."

The young man laughed.

"You are kind. I am well. But you have not dined, you must be famished."

"Yes, seh. I had some dinner on the boat."

"Well, then, a glass of sherry and a biscuit. Come to the dining-room."

He led the way through the white-panelled library from which he had come. There were as many books as at Dr. Clapton's and all well bound and neatly arranged. A globe of the world stood in one corner, a brass telescope on three legs in another.

"Mose," the young man said, "has your saddle-bags. He will lay out your things."

Lay out his things? What in the nation was the idea of that? He didn't want any valet messing with his fixings. That Mose was an impudent young servant, too; mightily pleased with himself, anyway.

The dining-room, panelled like the library, was a light green. Three windows of large-paned English glass, nearly filled the far end and gave a view of a broad, flat lawn around which ran a white-painted, oval fence. Johnny looked again; the lawn beside the fence was cupped and scarred. Hoofmarks. By Zooks, a race path! A race path under the dining-room windows! If you told the folks at home they wouldn't believe it.

The butler came through a swinging door.

"Burgwyn, a glass of Madeira for the gentleman. Or no, I don't quite like that last Madeira—a shade too sweet. Sherry will serve better, I think."

"Yes, suh, Mist' Wylie. De sherry is de mo' epicurious." He retreated elegantly through the pantry door.

"Burgwyn is invaluable to me. He keeps me up to the mark in decorum and polite usage, and enlarges my vocabulary."

Mr. Jones seemed to be laughing to himself. "You see, he possesses the advantage of me in having passed his youth, if Burgwyn ever had a youth, in Charleston. While I have been obliged to pick up what scraps of elegance I could from private tutors in England and from Eton College."

"Yes, seh. Doctor Clapton went to that school and he has a powerful learning."

"Ah, but the good doctor has a powerful mind. Burgwyn and I acquire only by imitation."

The decanter came in on a silver salver.

"Not any, thank you," said Mr. Jones. "I have just dined." He stuck out a boot. "I was hunting till near two o'clock."

"I reckon I heard your dogs when we were coming up the river. They were throwing their tongues, sure enough."

"Was that you who shouted? You have a good halloo. Yes, they were doing nicely on a cub. And now," he rose, "I must change and keep an appointment in the country. You will excuse me, I am sure. Mose is at your service and will show you about if you wish. Perhaps you might care to see the kennels and the stables. Oh, by the way, your people are to send for you tomorrow; or come for you. Naturally I hope for the latter, especially if it should mean a visit from your charming mother."

He waved a graceful hand.

"Supper at six. Till then, adieu!"

Johnny followed Burgwyn up the slippery marble stairs to his room. He had a glimpse of a gorgeous flowered pattern on the wall-paper, on the chintz of the curtains and on the chair-covers. Young Mose was storing the last of his meagre belongings in the huge depths of a mahogany high-boy.

"You Mose!" said Burgwyn, "Misteh Wyleh say to show de young gentlemans 'round de place dis evening." He went to the washstand. "Towels, hot water, an' incense soap, all de proper accoutrements, correct." He turned to Johnny.

"Mose, he wait in de hall when you ready, suh."

Bowing in unison, the two house Negroes withdrew.

Johnny looked about him. A fragile lace counterpane lay on the mahogany field-bed. Two steel engravings hung on the wall. He went to look at them, his shoes, the old ones, squeaking in the soft depths of the carpet. One was "Mr. Pope," a dapper, sheep-faced little man with thin silk-stockinged legs and a full bottom wig, sitting stiffly on the edge of a heavily upholstered chair. The other showed the face of Dr. Samuel Johnson, a red, angry, heavy-breathing man, like a huge Captain Tennant.

He stripped to the waist and scrubbed himself with hot water and the scented French soap. He put on fresh linen and tied back his hair with a fresh ribbon. Outside he heard a horse led to the door. He looked out to see Mr. Jones, wearing a different riding habit, canter down the lane.

He took off his shoes, to put on the best pair. But it was comfortable in stocking feet. The air was warm and drowsy in the shaded room, the bed looked grateful. Gingerly he removed the lace coverlet and stretched himself down.

He was more tired than he had thought. He lay relaxed and dreamy, listening to the sounds which drifted up the hill through the lifeless afternoon heat, to the deep-toned clink of blacksmiths' hammers, the rhythmic shriek of a carpenter's plane, to a loom rattling, a mill-wheel grumbling. They merged into a faint hypnotic buzz. He dozed.

A soft tapping on the door. What was it? Where was he? He opened his eyes. It was almost dark. Still, there was the flowered paper, the high-boy, the atmosphere of majesty.

"Hullo!" he called.

The suave, smug voice of Mose came through the slatted panels.

"Supper ready, young misto."

# CHAPTER XVIII

DRESSING NEXT morning, Johnny still felt somewhat oppressed by the heavy dinner of the night before and the heavy evening which had followed it. Two long hours in the room of gilded chairs and rosewood harpsichord, with Mr. Jones now reading from a full-morocco Horace, now discoursing like a gentleman in a play, had nearabout worn him down. But it was mighty magnificent, just the same.

Outside he heard a steady, dull, drumming sound. It reminded him of the cavalry on militia muster-days. Did Wylie Jones have an army, then, as well as everything else? He went to the window.

Around the brick corner of the house he could see part of the race-path. It was from there that the sound came. As he looked a long double line of hooded and sheeted horses jogged in sight. On each near horse perched a little Negro jockey who led an off horse beside him; at the head, the white trainer set the pace. The horses trotted lightly; beneath the clean yellow sheets their quarters were swinging free. They tossed their heads, pulled back, sidled, looked askance through the peep-holes of their hoods. The little Negroes admonished them in piping voices, tremulously implored them not to put them down. The long string disappeared, the delicate patter of small hoofs died away.

Dressing leisurely, he thought of the colt at home. Pshaw, that colt could most likely beat the natural tar out of any of these Wylie Jones horses, with all their fancy stables and clothing. And to think that he would see the colt tomorrow, maybe tonight! By Zooks! He dressed more rapidly.

Mr. Jones sat at the dining-room table behind a large silver teapot under which an oil lamp burned. He looked up absently from the letter in his hand.

"Good morning, young Fraser; you slept well? Good. Pray help yourself; tea, bread, and butter, and apricot preserve. If you wish anything, pull the bell for Burgwyn." He pointed to a bell-pull of orange satin and dropped his eyes to the letter.

Johnny felt deserted yet rather grateful. Clearly no one would keep track of the breakfast he ate. He looked at the fine white sugar in the fluted silver bowl, at the fine white bread on the gold-rimmed plate, at the apricots, a deep, sticky orange in the blue glass jar. He helped himself all around, as quietly as possible, and fell to. The tall stack of slices on the gold-rimmed plate sank to almost nothing, the bottom of the blue jar showed through the last thin film of apricot. His face was heated, his waistband cut him; he could do no more.

From time to time Wylie Jones broke the seals of other letters that lay in a pile before him. Now he finished the last.

"Have you any concern for politics?" he asked.

"Why, yes, seh, some. My father's the justice."

"Splendid!" said Mr. Jones politely, perhaps a shade too politely. "Then as the son of one functionary you will be interested to hear of another. A friend has written me to describe the new governor. You have not seen him, I suppose?"

"No, seh, I never have been to New Bern. My mother told me about the Palace, though."

"Quite so. I recall a delightful minuet with her there, or was it a pavanne? No matter. That was in the days of Governor Tryon, only last year, to be sure, but it now seems long since. He was really an admirable fellow."

Mr. Jones mused. His fine aristocratic young face was grave as though weighing nicely the departed governor's qualities. What a magnificent young man this was, thought Johnny, who could confer a word of well-considered approbation on the Governor himself.

"Tryon," Mr. Jones went on, "was, first of all, a man. He was also a gentleman. The office which he held is of course absurd. Man in the happy state of Nature knew no governors, least of all governors sent by authority outside the people. But Tryon made his position as little absurd as anyone well could." He nodded his approval.

"But now we have a certain Martin, sent to replace him. And I gather that this Martin fairly represents the British official class in these colonies." He smiled urbanely. "Though I should not care to prefer so serious a charge before I had given him every opportunity to clear himself."

He gathered up the letters.

"Have you ever considered the contribution of England to these colonies? She sends us her felons, her paupers as citizens, her discarded court favorites and superannuated placemen as rulers, and demands nothing but our taxes and our devotion in return. As to the unhappy paupers and felons, I say nothing. Neither are natural to man in his primeval state and many become excellent citizens in our happier society. My English friends look askance at us because we make these unfortunates into citizens. But I, for one, without possessing the slightest desire to associate with such persons, nevertheless rejoice in their improved condition. 'Which state,' I say, 'is the more admirable, that which makes its felons into citizens or that which makes its citizens into felons?'"

He looked about him triumphantly.

"By Jove, well put!" He clapped his hands and smiled satirically.

"Shall we go into the library? I must make a note."

Seated at the inlaid desk, he wrote out the sentence. "Citizens . . . felons .
. . felons . . . citizens," he murmured. He filed his letters away in a tall
cabinet above the desk, locked the cabinet door and put the key in his
pocket.

"My papers," he said, "contain nothing of which I am ashamed. But
British officials are capable of all errors, including that of mistaking philosophical thought for treason. Shall we have a look at the stables?"

The long white stable showed through the sycamores below the house.
Passing through the trees, they heard the switch of tails and the munching
of hay in the shaded depths of the loose boxes. Shining heads were thrust
out over half-doors, blinked at them in the sun, cupped their thin nostrils,
withdrew with a delicate arching motion.

On the far side, the stable loft overhung a line of boxes to form a pillared
arcade. From the end came the sounds of singing and whistling, the dull
bump of full buckets and the light clink of steel.

"The Negro boys will be cleaning the tack," said Mr. Jones. "You might
care to see how we manage our establishment." He led Johnny to a big,
brass-hinged door and swung it back.

In a room around whose long wall ran a gleam of innumerable bits, each
in its well-cleaned bridle, sober saddles each on its rack above, the little
Negro jockeys stopped work, ducked their heads, grinned; Roscius, the
coachman, in a striped canary waistcoat, pulled the wool on his forehead.

"Go on," said Mr. Jones.

Under his eye they redoubled their efforts, with hissing through the
teeth and theatrical flourishes. They soaped reins hung from ceiling hooks,
plunged bits in hot water, scoured them in the sand box, burnished them
with a chain. Dogged if these little Negroes didn't keep the stable cleaner
than most white folks kept a house.

"The horses are feeding and we will not disturb them. But the kennels
might interest you."

They walked across to a blue gate in a high board fence. Inside Johnny
heard the soft patter of hurrying pads.

"Stand back, all of you!" said Mr. Jones. They slipped through the gate
into a ring of moist, gently thrusting muzzles and feathered sterns, stiffly

curved and lightly waving. A single note, mournful, tender, chiming, rang in their ears.

"Hush, Dairymaid, good bitch!"

Wylie Jones pointed here and there in the mottled circle.

"That is Stormalong, my old American hound. He cannot run up as he used, but he still works out a cold line best of all. The two with rounded ears are English, Woodsman and Watchful, from Earl Spencer's kennels. They are like the English soldiers, brave and well trained and stupid. Watchful, good boy!" he patted the broad flat head. "You would have died like the rest with Braddock,—eh? You see yonder high white dome with the long ears? 'Voltaire,' that is; he was given me by the Duc de Montauban, whom I knew in Paris."

The hound, at the sound of his name, shouldered through the press; gravely placing his forepaws against Mr. Jones' waistcoat, he stood looking into his face in a manner affectionate, searching, yet reserved and cere- monious. Mr. Jones laughed. "Voltaire is privileged. His mate died on ship- board and he finds me the only one here to comprehend his nation." He patted the narrow peaked skull. "Ah, mon vieux, nous sommes bien en rapport, hein?" He turned to Johnny, "Voltaire is the most intelligent, the most truly civilized. If he has a fault, it is his aversion to combined action. The Americans come somewhere between him and my brave Britishers. They hunt together, more or less, when necessity compels, but each in his own way; they are unmanageable and will not learn except through misfor- tune. And yet I have great hopes of them.

"My fellow citizens!" he cried oratorically, "you break the rules and drive me distracted when I would put you on the line. But somehow, gentlemen, you seem to catch the fox."

With a dry smile he bowed himself and Johnny out of the kennel.

Further down the hill lay the cluster of shops from which the sounds of labor came. Here big Negroes in leather aprons plied the bellows and ham- mered out horseshoes and iron hinges; small Negroes in hemp aprons spun lumps of clay on potters' wheels; an old black man, all woolly beard and iron spectacles, soldered a patch in a copper kettle. In the carpenter shop four men, one white, tapping mallet on chisel, worked ox-yokes out of oaken slabs. A finished yoke, painted bright red, hung from a beam. Down by the branch where the mill-wheel clacked, the miller, brown, half-naked, yellow-powdered, leaned against his wide mill door. Over his shoulder came the steady, muffled grumble of the stones. Beyond the mill in a wooden shed Johnny heard the quick "tick-tack, tick-tack" of looms, and more distant, the giggle and chatter of Negro wenches drawing rations at the store.

It was a regular, sure-enough town, this place, a town all by itself, a private town. He felt tired and confused. This place of Wylie Jones' was high-tone, all right, but it was mighty complicated, too.

"You have seen enough, I take it," said Mr. Jones. "Let us return."

They walked up the gently sloping path to the big house. An old chaise reared its high back and hood before the door. Dusty, ill-kempt, it seemed to belong not only to a rank far beneath the polished elegance of The Grove, but even to a time more ancient, cruder. The gentle oscillation of the body on the strap-springs showed that someone was inside. A farmer, perhaps, to buy a pig. Then there was a glimpse of a blue cloak, of Grampus's ponderous white quarters between the shafts; his mother was leaning down toward him, laughing, stretching out her arms, winking back tears. He hurled himself over the high wheel.

Now he was on the ground again; her light, strong hand came down to rest on his shoulder. She jumped down from the bobbing chaise.

"Why, there is Mr. Jones," she said, and tucked a stray lock beneath her hood. "Indeed, sir, I had near forgot you." She dropped the faintest suggestion of a curtsey. Mr. Jones bowed low.

"A misfortune, ma'm, to which I am accustomed but not reconciled."

She smiled. "Very charming, sir, but spoken as though by the book."

Mr. Jones appeared perturbed. "You think I plagiarise?" He recovered his look of urbanity and even added a touch of polished impudence. "I assure you, ma'm, that in affairs of the heart I do not stoop to plagiarise even myself. But may I venture a remark which I cannot claim as my own?"

"Oh, do!" she cried, with maliciously feigned eagerness. "It may shine by contrast."

"Well, then—and fie upon you—will you please to step in for a glass of sherry?"

He handed Johnny's mother up the marble steps.

Johnny was conscious of a vague commotion near Grampus' head. Scipio, the reins in one hand, his hat in the other, was performing miracles of salutation. As Mr. Jones and Mrs. Fraser mounted the steps Scipio ceased his elaborate pantomime and scuttled up.

"Fo' de Lo'd, Mist' Johnneh, if dis ain't de day Ah'm waiting fo'. Man, O man! To see de young misto—hoo!" He raised his eyes to heaven. "Des look at him now. Struttin' hisse'f 'round wid de quality folks—slick-leather shoes on he feet!"

"How's everything at home?" Johnny asked abruptly. He looked secretively to see if anyone observed the unwelcome familiarity of Scipio's admiration.

"Oh, we makes out fo' to live along. Yo' paw keep his he'th, de colt fat as hide'll hold, Sofa raise de rumpus now an' 'en, but don' mean nothin'. Who's dis?"

Mose had appeared round the corner and stood looking at Scipio's ornate and tawdry finery with youthful condescension.

"That's Mose, my servant," said Johnny loftily.

"Lan' o' lan'! Is you got a servant, Mist' Johnneh?"

"Just while I'm here," Johnny admitted.

"Mose," Burgwyn's stately accents sounded from the porch, "is de young gentleman's temporarily servant. Of co'se he's de permanent servant of Mist' Wylie. But every white gentleman dat come to de Grove gets de loan of a personal servant enduring his visitation."

"Well, 'en, you Mose," said Scipio, by no means impressed. "Catch hol' dis ho'se."

Relieved of Grampus, he brushed off his faded and flapping coat with elegance. "Well, well," he mused judicially, "das very nice; to len' de gent' men a servant. Co'se in our domain, less'n de visiting gent'man bring his own, my masteh *give* him a servant. No, suh," he fixed a stern eye on Burgwyn, "dey ain't none of disyer borrowin' and len'in' wher' Ah belongs."

Johnny turned his face away.

"Scipio," he murmured, "you go 'long with Burgwyn. I expect he'll find you a snack before we start."

He ran up the steps to join his mother.

She was seated on a gold chair in the drawing-room, her cloak thrown back, her slim boyish figure in the green camlet gown outlined against its blue folds.

"But surely," Mr. Jones was saying, "you can stay to dine. We will fix the hour to your convenience."

Without replying, she reached out a hand to Johnny and drew him to a seat beside her.

"Thank you, sir," she said, "you are kind. But we must set out for home, Johnny and I." She smiled. "I lay last night ten miles from here with the Raes, so that we could make our journey back today. My husband expects us."

"Ah, that settles it. I shall importune no more. I tremble to think of disappointing Mr. Fraser's expectations."

"How I wish I could believe you. It would do you no harm to tremble for once in your life. You should marry. A clever girl might give some check to your assurance."

"But how difficult it is to find one so clever as that,"—he waved his hand toward Mrs. Fraser,—"who is unattached. Here is the sherry."

Johnny sipped away at his glass, stealing glances at his mother's face, only half hearing her chatter and gossip of the county families, but feeling with a vivid thrill the touch of her fingers beneath the blue cloak.

The sherry and biscuit finished, Mr. Jones dusted an infinitesimal crumb, rose with Mrs. Fraser, and handed her down the steps into the chaise. Hopping up beside her, Johnny saw that his saddle-bags were stowed beneath the seat. Zooks, he had near about forgot them! But here they were, packed and put away. High-tone. Where was that Scipio? Why couldn't he learn to do things like these servants at the Grove?

He tossed a sixpence negligently at Mose, which Mose accepted politely but without undue elation.

Scipio, wiping his mouth with the back of his hand, rounded a clump of lilac bushes at a deliberate pace, ducked his head to Mr. Jones, and mounted creakingly to the perch along the shaft.

"Good-bye, seh," Johnny said. "My thanks for your hospitality. Servant, seh."

To this well-turned speech Mr. Jones merely gave a nod, quite casual and inadequate.

"Good day, sir," Mrs. Fraser said, taking up on the reins. "And pray for modesty."

The wheels turned, Mr. Jones shot a mocking look.

"Even from Providence," he said, "one should not ask the impossible."

Toward evening they crested a rise in the land, a rise so gentle as to be almost imperceptible, yet, once gained, giving a wide expanse of western forest. The brown of oak leaves and the buff of maple was flecked with dark patches like cloud shadows, and further west was hemmed by a dark band stretched against the sky. These were the outposts of the pines.

They creaked down toward them, the chaise wheels parting and spilling the sand with a sifting sound. Now the crusted, brown-gray trunks were all around them, the wheels were muffled in a depth of needles; far above them, black, twisted branches and misty, spray-like tufts wove their pattern, familiar yet fantastic, against an opalescent sky. A breeze, up-springing, sent its deep-sea whisper through the lofty tracery. The ocean-tinted sky, the surf-sounding wind, the branches, strangely fanciful, gently nodding, like huge, unfathomed seaweeds, wove the texture, slight yet strong, of another world above him, a world from which he drew the deep-drowned contentment of a man sunk, of a ship foundered. He reached a hand to his mother's.

Grampus trotted, the light failed, Blue's Crossing, a scatter of houses, passed them by; they jogged on through the dark.

Here was the lane, the strong ancient house, and, before the lighted window, the strong ancient figure.

"Dadder!" he shouted. "Dadder, Dadder, Dadder!"

The chaise lurched to a stand, a big hand reached him through the night, an arm closed on him, swung him to the ground.

"Ah, lad—lad. And are ye well?"

After supper they sat by the fire. His mother's gusts of chatter died in contented silence. Then he remembered the letter from Doctor Clapton. He tugged it out, handed it to his father.

"The Doctor's report o' ye, eh?"

His father read, pursed his bearded lips as if to whistle, jutted forward his eyebrows. Johnny and his mother drew together, like two young, innocent prisoners appearing jointly before the bar. John Fraser folded the letter.

"The sense o' this is no unfavorable." He searched Johnny's face. "I'm feared ye may have been up tae your old hoodwinking practises."

"John, how can you talk so when here Johnny is come home pale as a haunt from too much study? Would you have him kill himself?"

"Tut; I've not observed him any paler than common—and if he were, a man can grow pale idling on the coast as well as working there."

"You never will admit there's good in him."

"Hoots, lass, can nothing satisfy you? I've said the letter was no unfavorable. What more would ye have? There's one thing," he hurried on to other ground, "there's one thing, though, that we mustna overlook. That's the Latin. What daunts ye wi' the Latin, boy?"

"I—I don't know, seh. What all did Mr. Clapton say?"

"Why, that despite the best endeavors of himself and you—which latter I doubt:"—he glanced firmly at Johnny's mother—"now, not a word, Caroline. I've taught the lad mysel' and I ken well that he'll scuttle and squirm awa' frae his Latin if ye give him an inch tae turn in. The Doctor says that despite endeavors and a' that, ye seem tae get no grip o' the matter."

"Yes, seh, that's a fact, I expect." Johnny curled his toes inside his shoes. "I can read Latin pretty good. He says that, don't he, Dadder?"

"Aye—tae some extent."

"But I can't write it—not to make sense. I declare I don't seem to get head nor tail *to* it."

He warmed to his subject, gained confidence, his toes uncurled, he planted his feet square on the floor.

"I've worked and I've slaved——"

"Now, lad, that'll do. I'll hear no nonsense. Ye've ducked and ye've dodged, ye've juked and ye've jerked; and ye've hoped for the best. But ye've never put in an honest hour's work at writing the Latin i' your life. I' the whole grand subject o' Latin prose, ye've not sae much as the first declension that ye can bite your teeth on. Now, Caroline," he raised a silencing hand, "I'm talking sober sense, and if ye've not the wit tae see it, ye'll just have tae listen the same as if ye had.

"Well, then, my lad, there's but one thing for ye. Ye'll have tae leave off your diddling and set yoursel' tae the task o' learning your book frae the first letter on. And twa hours a day it will need tae make up what ye have frittered awa'. I'll give ye a letter tae Doctor Clapton when ye leave."

His father looked at their downcast faces benignly. He smoked.

"Then," he said in a hearty, hopeful voice, "when ye have mastered your Latin prose, ye'll be ready tae learn Greek."

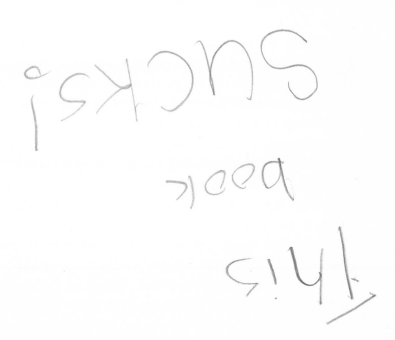

# CHAPTER XIX

CHILLED AND depressed, Johnny Fraser stood in the naked hardwood grove and watched the people coming slowly out of the log church. The preaching had been longer than ever; his back was contracted, aching, numb; his feet were dragging lumps of ice. The stream of drab humanity which trickled through the narrow door into the cold blue winter air seemed to spread for an instant, then freeze into rigid groups.

Underfoot, the shrivelled leaves lay unstirring in the still air; above, a pale, half-hearted sun showed a white ring through bleak clouds.

A dreary sun, a dreary world, he thought; a world where folks were awkward, crude, where life was stark and meager. Five months at Edenton had taught him something. Now that he had mingled with the elegant, the polished and correct, he saw the people of the pine forest as they were: their linsey coats and dresses, dull, shapeless, their manners and speech, well meant, no doubt, but uncouth. They not only lacked all grace themselves, but they suspected it in others. His return from Edenton, almost a full-fledged young gentleman, instead of striking them with suitable admiration, seemed to move them only to slightly contemptuous amusement.

"Squire's boy is back from schoolin'?" he had overheard Corneilison say. "Well, I reckon it won't hurt him none. He'll soon fergit it."

When first he had come home he had wanted to stay forever, but already he was beginning to look forward to the day he would go back to Edenton, where a gentleman was appreciated.

He wished that he could leave the dismal grove at once, instead of standing there, conspicuous in his city clothes and ill at ease, exposed to the congregation's neglect or clumsy familiarity. But he must, of course, wait for his father, and his father would, of course, linger and talk forever with Mr. Harbitt, the ungainly and ill-dressed circuit preacher, and, after that, would still wait on until the last back-countryman had departed before he locked up the church door.

Here came Joe Merrillee, and with him Sally in the same old bonnet and the worn beaver tippet. Johnny felt incapable of supporting such a meeting. What would he not give to escape this young girl's chatter and tedious humor? He pretended not to see them.

"Hello, Johnny," she piped from quite a distance.

They planted themselves in front of him as doggedly as if they guessed his thoughts.

"How you?" Joe muttered with a look of dismal satisfaction.

"Middling——" He corrected himself, "Quite all right. How you, Sally?"

"Why, Johnny, where you been? I thought you were coming home last week."

He brightened at the opening she afforded.

"Oh, I aimed to first, but then I stopped for a visit with Wylie Jones."

"I bet he was glad," Joe observed bleakly.

"Sour belly."

"Hush, Johnny."

"Well, what ails Joe? I ain't said anything to him."

"Joe was just funning. You get mad too easy."

She looked at him disapprovingly. She was more tiresome than he had remembered; he smothered a yawn.

"How's things out your way?"

" 'Bout the same."

"Coon got out," said Joe.

Johnny's heart leaped.

"That fisher coon? How come him to get out?"

"Prized open a slat one night."

"Did he now? Is that a fact?"

He read in Joe's face a hint of insight into his thoughts.

"Well, well," he added hastily, "that's too bad, I declare. You ought to have traded him for my hat."

"I'd rather have had that coon for a month," Joe said, "than your hat for a year."

"My land, Johnny," said Sally hastily, "you look mighty elegant."

He grunted. "These are my old shoes. My new ones are too good."

"I expect you're too good, too, after Wylie Jones and such."

"Can't a man say anything without being taken up?"

At this Joe, who had been eyeing them both morosely, emitted a short and perfectly mirthless laugh.

"Come on, Sal." He pulled Sally along to the hitching-rail. She said nothing further, but to Johnny's exasperation and immense surprise, she looked back at him with a glance intimate, warm, smiling, as if their meeting had been singularly cordial and full of meaning.

Mr. Harbitt's high-peaked shoulders appeared above the gray bonnets and wool hats. In slow progression, firm, unhurried, his big-knuckled hand closed on the worn blunt hands, the stiff worsted mittens of the congregation.

"Yes, sir! It's cold!" he said. "But that means good skins for the trappers, don't it?" He fished awkwardly in his coat-tails for his bandana, blew his large, sharp nose, gazed down at them with his grim kind smile.

"Them over-mountain skins gets the good prices now," a little mink-faced man observed dismally. "If I was young that's where I'd be."

"Maybe you're just as well off, brother," Mr. Harbitt said. "The most of the boys that went over with Boone ain't come back."

"Is that a fact?" the other replied more cheerfully. "Indians?"

"I reckon so. In the frontier settlements they said the Cherokee are making war talks again."

The people gathered around attracted, attentive, their eyes lighted with professional interest, with relish sharpened with the knowledge of their own safety.

"What's the trouble now, preacher?" said the mink-faced man.

"Same as usual, I reckon. Squatters on their land, then horse stealing, then ambushes. They's three, four of their chiefs heading down this way now. I saw their teepees up the valley. They're bound for New Bern to see the governor about their land."

The mink-faced man was scornful. "What kin the governor do? Does he reckon he kin set in his stone palace and keep them mountain boys and long hunters from trappin' wher' they please? Them Indians is squanderin' their time."

Mr. Mountford, the storekeeper, his knit cap pulled down over his old scalped head, the little round-eyed boy beside him, crowded into the circle.

"Indians?" His cracked voice was sharp. "Kill 'em. Come on, boy."

Pulling the little lad by the end of his red tippet, he shuffled down the hill.

Mr. Harbitt's eyes followed him. "I reckon I should not have mentioned about Indians in front of him. It's but a rumor anyway." He grinned at them, sardonic and not quite at ease. "A rumor carried by your preacher, you'll maybe say." He pulled out a dented silver watch. His knuckled hand snapped the cover shut. "And now, God bless you all."

"God bless you, preacher."

One by one they shook him warmly, briefly, stiffly by the hand.

As they jogged home in the chaise, Johnny's father turned and searched his face.

"Come, lad, what ails your spirits? Ye seemed tae take no pleasure i' the preaching."

"He's tired, John." His mother put in.

"Ye've been regular in your attendance on Sabbath worship, I take it."

"Yes, seh, I go to St. Paul's every Sunday."

"And what sort o' preaching dae ye hear?"

"Why, seh, Dr. Clapton preaches pretty good. Not very long. But there's a organ."

"Ah." His father's voice was grim. "A whistle-kirk. There'll be no preaching there."

Two evenings later Johnny Fraser saw a thread of smoke and three tufts of lodge-poles rising from the hollow down by the branch. That was where the Indians once or twice before had camped, and now again they had stolen in and set up their teepees without a sound and without, as Mrs. Fraser coldly remarked, a by-your-leave.

"A-weel," said Squire Fraser from the porch, drying his big square hands for supper. "We can afford them a one night camping ground. We've got a continent frae them. Ye might bid Sofa, though," he added reflectively, "tae shut up the hens."

Johnny Fraser was not thrilled by this barbaric visitation. Indeed he felt that this wandering Cherokee encampment added the final touch of savagery to a background already far too crude for a young gentleman of his pretensions. What would the Tennants say if they knew that his home, which he had tried to picture to them as a country gentleman's estate, was looked on as free camping ground by casual Indians? Yet he must have a look at them. He wandered down the lane, down the road till the weathered hides of the teepees showed beneath the shoulder of the hill. A bundled squaw hung over a tiny fire; a buck smoked on an elk-hide before a doorflap; a mangy lemon-colored cur with yellow eyes licked an impassive baby; three wretched skewbald ponies, loosely hobbled, grazed down towards the swamp. Into his nostrils came an odor, greasy, musky, acrid, a smell revolting, yet like the scene, subtly intriguing, disturbing, barbarous and strange. Half disgusted, half uneasy he turned back home.

Seated at the table in the corner, breathing laboriously, Squire Fraser had just finished the letter which Johnny was to carry back to Dr. Clapton. Ignorant of the finer points of etiquette, he sealed it firmly with his ring.

"Ye might snuff the candle out, son. There's light enough frae the fire. Caroline, ye shouldna grieve."

"Would you like to see me happy, then, with Johnny going back to Edenton?"

"Ye could be satisfied. We're paying out good money for his schooling."

"I know, I know. But he'll not be a boy for long now."

"Well, then, let's make a man o' him. Would ye keep him at your skirts?"

She twined her hands.

"I'm afeard of the times. There might be a war, they say."

"That's Wylie Jones. Well, my lass, what's tae trouble ye? There will always be braggarts everywhere. And when a' the rest are gone there will still be plenty in America."

They fell silent, listening to the wind.

A cold gust passed over them, twisted the flames; they turned. In the open doorway stood an old Indian wrapped in a red trade-blanket, his free arm raised stiffly in salutation.

"Greeting, white brother." The cracked voice, still touched with liquid music, brought hazy memories to Johnny. John Fraser rose.

"Long Thought, I give ye welcome."

The Indian closed the door.

"Peace to this house."

He opened his blanket; his pinched bare chest was painted ceremonial vermilion.

"Draw tae the fire."

He reached the fire in a stride, sank slowly to the floor, stretched his claw hands to the blaze.

"Caroline, will ye just bring Long Thought a plate of provender and a dram."

Without enthusiasm, Johnny's mother went into the kitchen.

"It's six year," his father continued, "since I've seen ye."

"Seven. I come from over the mountains now."

"Ah! And where are ye bound?"

"Here. I come to make council talk."

"Ah! Well, I'm real glad tae see ye."

"I come because in the old days, when my Cherokee people hunted these forests, my white brother was not as the other Long Knives. He was wise to give talk and to hear talk."

"Aye, between us we stopped a deal o' trouble. A few more like us and there'd have been no trouble at all."

"The wise are few."

Mrs. Fraser came in with the plate and cup. Reaching up his thin arms, Long Thought took them without acknowledgment. He drained the cup. His eye brightened. He demolished the heaped yams and mutton voraciously. From beneath his blanket he produced a pipe, its reed stem browned with use, the tip of a wolf's brush hanging from the black stone bowl.

"We smoke. Then will be time for council talk."

He glanced significantly at Mrs. Fraser. She flushed and flashed an angry look into the ancient, cryptic face.

"I'll go above stairs, John," she said.

"Vera well. And take Johnny."

"Let the young man hear the talk, that he may learn from the wisdom of the old men," a wintry smile just touched the Indian's face, "and from their folly."

He lit the pipe, passed it to John Fraser, who puffed gravely during many minutes, then gave it back.

The pipe was finished.

"And now, Long Thought, what is in my brother's mind?"

"As my white brother knows, we once hunted here. Now the Long Knives hold it. Then we hunted the mountains. Now the Long Knives hunt there. We are beyond the mountains, seeking peace. But still the Long Knives come and there is no peace. But many troubles. The young men would fight the Long Knives, but they know not how. The old men would save the people, but they know not how. And I who in old days led the people with wise talk am come to nothing."

He bowed his head.

"I lie drunken in the street of the bark houses. The children mock me. My horse is gone to buy rum. My beaded council dress is gone to buy rum. My power is gone, to buy rum. This is a hard talk to say."

He was silent.

"Why, my brother, I'm sorry indeed. Ye were never so in the old days."

"In old days I had hope and great dreams. I would save my people, make them brothers to the Long Knives."

His black hair fell about his toothless, bitter mouth.

"Hope went, then came the rum." He touched the cup. "Rum brings dreams."

"So now," he went on, "I am mocked. And yet when a new trouble now comes to my people and they will send chiefs to the governor who never hears, I say, 'I will pass back across the mountains to my white brother. Again we will make talk and I will bring new wisdom to my people.'"

"I'll do the best I can, my friend. But I'm no sae sure as I used tae be when we were younger."

"Nor I, brother."

"Well, then?"

"War-drums, drumming, drumming. At night I walk on the hills to hear what the Great Spirit says to me. But I only hear drums. All the earth, from the Father of Waters to the sea, is filled with drums—drums to Northward, in the Long House of the Six Nations, drums to Southward in Seminole lagoons, drums to Eastward in the Long Knives' stone towns. All night they drum."

"Ye think it means an Indian war?"

"I do not know, but in this drumming Long Knife drums against Long Knife, Indian against Indian."

A pause followed.

"Well, there has been talk of some trouble between the provincials and Britain. But it's talk, only just."

Long Thought shook his head wearily.

"My brother is wise. But he has not heard the drums. I am now an old man. I have not heard such drums before."

"Let us put it thus, then, brother. If ye are wrong, which God grant ye may be, then your troubles are naught. And if ye are right, what is it ye would ask?"

"I ask: When Long Knife fights Long Knife, what shall my people do?"

"They'll try tae bring ye intae it, I've nae doubt."

The Indian nodded.

"And if ye would know whether the rebels or the King would win, I think I can tell ye, having once been a rebel mysel'." He grinned.

"I would know," answered Long Thought simply, "what is best for my people."

"Aye, and I would tell ye, my friend. It's thus: If there's a war and ye are on the wrong side, ye'll be massacred, and if ye are on the right side, ye'll be neglected and forgotten, having made enemies o' the losers wi'out making friends of the winners. Both sides will try threats and bribes and promises. But just ye bide in your towns and when it's over they'll respect ye the more."

He checked himself.

"I talk as though there was tae be a war. But that was merely tae answer your question, my brother. There will be no war."

The Indian rose, went to the door. From the porch he beckoned. John Fraser joined him.

"What does my white brother hear?"

"I hear the wind."

Long Thought's old head craned forward intently beneath his huddled blanket.

"Listen—you hear?—Drums."

THE INDIAN LONGTHOUGHT

*"All night they drum, and never cease until the Sun, the Bloody Hunter, sets the hills on fire"*

BOOK II

# CHAPTER XX

IT WAS not a bad sort of young gentleman that John Fraser, Junior, Esquire, of Little River, inspected in the shaving-glass of Doctor Clapton's attic room. Not a bad sort at all. Three long years' schooling under the Doctor might or might not have improved his mind. But three years of polite intercourse with the first Provincial families of Edenton, not to mention several English gentry, had undoubtedly taught him where to order a coat and how to wear it. He smoothed back the bright blue lapels, and fluffed up his Irish cambric stock. What a guy he must have looked that first day, four years ago, when he landed in Edenton, a little snub-nosed boy in a home-made suit, trotting shyly beside his father. He studied his nose in the glass; it was still too blunt, it lacked the thin bridge and pinched nostrils of the English gentleman, of Captain Tennant, say. But on the other hand, his teeth were white, regular, sound, which seemed seldom the case with English gentlemen; his hair was so thick and darkly waving that he hardly regretted the London bag wig now resting on its wigblock for the summer; and his eyes, a blue, not light but brilliant, beneath their dark brown eyebrows, gave him a look which his father once grudgingly admitted reminded him of Bonny Prince Charlie. A cursed shame—that nose. With a proper nose he would be perfect.

And now, just as he was finishing his schooling, just as he was ready to take his place, and no mean place it would be, in the world, dashed if it didn't look as if the world itself were going to pot. Once when he was a youngster, two or three years ago, an old Cherokee had come to see his father and made a talk about hearing drums beat for war. He remembered being thrilled and scared at the time, but thrilled and scared as a boy is by a ghost story he does not believe. Since then, however, he had thought of that old Indian, against his will; the memory of that drum talk had been forced on him by events,—once by news of a King's ship scuttled and sunk by the Yankees at Providence,—once by the sight of ragged militia columns swinging through Edenton, called out for an Indian border war,—and more than once by the talk of Wylie Jones and his friends, by the sense of secret letters passing, of secret schemes. And not a week ago, wagon-trains had rumbled to the quay near Hornblower's and loaded a solid cargo of grain aboard a Boston packet, a free gift from the Province of North Carolina to the hungry Bostonians, blockaded by the British Navy until the Colony should knuckle under to the Crown. The crowd had cheered the very teamsters. That was the worst sign of all. One would think New Englanders were blood brothers. If every province would but mind its own business, the trouble would blow over; he would take his place as a young North Carolinian of family and culture. But some of the crowd who had gathered spoke of affairs in Boston with hot, astounding anger, and some, with dark foreboding.

He thought he heard a step on the stair and started hastily from the glass. It was only Malley sweeping below. The dinner hour would soon be here. The first arrivals would be coming into town for the race meeting tomorrow. Sir Nat would be at Hornblower's making up his betting-book and drinking, glass for glass, with half the Province. Johnny drew a varnished

chintz hat-box from under the bed and took out his new cocked hat, not
furry and fuzzy like the old, but short-haired, sleek and shiny. Standing
before the glass, he tried it at different angles. Ah, that was it! Nothing
rakish, but a touch of the knowing sportsman. With a final tap on its crown,
he descended the stair.

The broad, sandy street was already lined with chaises and riding-horses;
above their dust the mottled sycamores raised white branches and tender
pale spring leaves. Far off down the gentle slope, over the wagon-tops and
calash hoods, he could see the dark waters of the harbor and the bright
green waters of the shallow bay. Two high-wheeled farmers' ox-carts passed
him, then Wylie Jones' glass coach, rattling prodigiously, its lacquered
saffron panels well streaked with forty miles of country clay. The Negro
postillions raised their scarlet elbows proudly as they posted to the trot.
More rigs and riding-horses followed, turned off, tied up to hitching-rails or
the sycamores. That line of alien horses gave him comfort; a man was a fool
to fret over war and drum-beats when here was the flower of the Province
gathering for sport and conviviality just as they always had and always
would.

The taproom was crowded and bustling; broadcloth from Norfolk, Bath
and New Bern rubbed shoulders with home-spun from back settlements,
tasseled malacca canes hob-nobbed with homely ash plants; behind the bar
Hornblower's voice warbled, "Coming, sir, coming!" in a steady refrain. All
the faces at the tables or clustered about the sanded floor were strange, but
after the custom of the Province, there were many greetings for him, the
hearty, "Hawdy, brother, how you fixed?" the elegant, "Ah, so this is young
Fraser. Knew your respected father, sir!" An importunate hand clutched
his sleeve, "Say, son, have you any knowledge of this Peregrine horse of
Dukinfield's?"

"Why, yes, seh. I've rode him."

He was instantly surrounded, plied with questions, made the hero of a
moment.

"Yes, seh," he said, pulling out the ruffles of his sleeves. "I know everything about the horse."

"What's his chances?"

He looked around the circle with portentous solemnity.

"Gentlemen, he's bound to win, he's put up to win, he's got the heart to win. He's had slow gallops fo' a month; they breezed him twice last week. In all my life"—he paused in impressive reflection—"in all my life I've never seen a horse fitter to run."

"That's the way they always talk," a voice observed. "He may be a good little horse, but a good big horse'll beat him, and that's just exactly what Comus is. I saw him at Gerrould's place in Virginia last month."

"What, you've seen Comus!" they cried. They turned their backs on Johnny, hung on the speaker's words. He was once more alone. The prospect of becoming a mere hanger-on sent him from the tavern to while away the time till someone that he knew was there. The walk was well filled with the wives and daughters of the tap-room sportsmen; they fluttered into groups, chattered, rustled in and out of the houses and gardens behind the live-oaks and sycamores. All of Edenton was thrown open to them. Johnny did not know these ladies, but he raised his hat with a gentle melancholy which he believed fetching, especially as it was partly sincere. For the sight of them, particularly the young ones, reminded him of his misfortune. He had wanted, or half wanted, to invite Sally Merrillee to Edenton for the race meeting. She had struck him, the last few times they had met, as pretty, in a way. She was less tiresome, also, than she used to be, not so apt to attempt humor at his expense. But then her clothes, her manner, were countrified; as his guest she might imperil his standing. Hang the girl! Why couldn't she have some style about her, like Eve, for instance? He had asked himself this question so often, vacillated so long, that the invitation was never sent. It was just as well; he would take Eve. But by that time Eve was engaged, as she told him in a coldly airy manner, to go to the races with Master Cherry.

So he had been left without anyone; the other girls, mere casual girls, were out of the question.

He went over Sally's merits and defects again. And as always before, he found these merits and defects so nicely balanced that they might be said to produce a perfect equilibrium. Yet it was an equilibrium which lent no stability to his mind. The question, as far as the race meeting went, was academic. But he argued it as intently as though he still had to decide whether to invite her. In fact, he was so engrossed in re-casting the old accounts, so distressed at finding for the hundredth time that the totals were what he had always known them to be, that he was unconscious of his surroundings until he found that he was staring into the water from the stone dock, and heard a husky voice in his ear:

"What do ye look for down there below, young gentleman?"

The stranger, standing squarely, legs apart, was short and powerful. His shoulders, though not stooped, were so heavy that they gave the back of his shabby coat a pugnacious and bristling look like the back of a terrier. His swarthy face, smooth-shaven but blue jowled, had the bristling look of a terrier, too. Despite the lively eye, it was marked by age or hardship, one could not tell which. The stranger might be an elderly man, well preserved, or a young man not preserved at all.

"Why, seh," said Johnny in his best and most distant manner, "if you must know, I was thinking."

"Ye were looking for peace of mind, then," the stranger favored him with a hard grin. "Ye'll never find it in the sea." He laughed shortly, without relish, as at a joke profoundly good but more unpalatable.

To this Johnny had no reply, and for that matter he had no wish to prolong the conversation with a dingy stranger, unwarrantably free and easy, and uncomfortably grim. The man, however, continued to stand there with his feet braced, whistling a chanty between his set teeth and running a dour eye over the rigging of a Bristol brigantine. His hat, clapped tight down on his head, was the hat of a merchant officer—a merchant officer in decayed circumstances.

"I suppose you are off a merchantman," said Johnny coldly.

"No," said the stranger, and continued to whistle.

His rude manner by rights deserved a snub, but the figure, enigmatic, impudent and sour, held Johnny to the spot, and led him, against his will, to a further inquiry.

"What is your name, then, may I ask?"

"That," said the stranger, his eye still travelling over the rigging, "is the question." He gave a grating laugh, swung on his heel, and without so much as a glance at Johnny, marched off down the quay. Enraged and impotent, Johnny watched him till the bristling back and slightly bandy legs were lost among the dockside sheds.

As he walked back to Hornblower's, Johnny plunged into philosophical reflection. It was not pleasant for a man of his position, and dressed accordingly, to suffer the brusquerie of a seedy dockside loafer. Yet was not he himself to blame? A young gentleman of parts should not attempt intercourse with persons of lower walks of life. Let him stick to his peers. He hoped that Sir Nat would be at Hornblower's by this time; and from the sounds which now rolled down the street of live-oaks, Johnny felt sure that he would be. He heard laughter, a cheer, a redoubled din, and then, as he reached the steps, Sir Nat's voice, "Who-oop! Hornblower! Take gentlemen's orders."

"Yes, Sir Nat. Which gentleman, Sir?"

"Every gentleman."

A second laugh and cheer met Johnny as he stepped through the door.

Sir Nat was in the center of the floor, shaking a hundred hands, slapping a hundred backs, his pink face very pink, his round eyes very bright.

"Hello—hello, you chaps, how do—how do, sir—hello—hello! Oh, bless me—Bantam! Bantam, come here! Know these gentlemen? Young Fraser —Little River—gentleman sportsman—'cquainted."

It was nearly four by the time they sat down to dinner. They leaned close together on the crowded tables, chatting, listening amid the din with hands cupped behind ears, wagging earnest fingers beneath each other's noses. Hornblower, warm, glistening, distracted, marshalled his temporary waiters. Grinning with exquisite self-consciousness, the bashful town boys stumbled in with the trays and platters. Johnny, at Sir Nat's table, recognized among them one of the old dockside swimming gang and greeted him with nice discrimination, well-poised but friendly; there was even a hint of companionship; it was, however, of a companionship long past and not to be renewed. Unfortunately none of the diners, engrossed in gossip, tales and racing form, observed him.

"Right," Sir Nat was saying, "thirty pound to twenty, proc, against Peregrine for the match and ten pound, even, on first heat. Bantam, what's thirty pound proc. come to sterling?"

While Johnny figured the rate of exchange Sir Nat, breathing somewhat hard, made an illegible entry in a note-book with thin ivory leaves.

They fell to on their herring and lamb cutlets, they stood staunchly to their glasses; hard drinkers, hard eaters, hard talkers, they downed course after course and kept a steady hum of chat which mounted in volume with Mr. Hornblower's chalked-up score of rum and burgundy. Before they finished, night had fallen, candles were lit, then pipes; in the wavering light and drifting smoke the sportsmen, elegant, plain, keen, dull, ruddy, pale, clustered in close groups, slapped thighs, poked ribs, made noisy, ill-judged bets, settled to their Holland gin and water.

Mr. Hewes and Mr. Battle appeared through the smoke, and with nodded greetings, genial yet reserved, joined a group of sober back-countrymen deep in conference. Behind them, Captain Tennant, tapping his malacca stick sharply, marched up to Johnny's table, without a glance on either side, and took his place in their elegant circle.

"Where is Mr. Jones?" said Captain Tennant. "He was to have been of the party this evening—what?"

"Wylie's at Battle's," said Sir Nat, "readin' letters off the Bristol packet."

"They must be deuced pressing," Captain Tennant replied, "to prevent his keeping his engagement."

"Must be," said Sir Nat. "Wylie's all upset—stampin' about—bitin' fingernails. No sense to letters. Have box myself. Letters come—drop 'em in box"—he smiled triumphantly—"then—there they are!"

"I take it, Mr. Fraser," ventured a neat, mild little man from New Bern, with an air of making conversation, "that you are quite a sportsman."

"Why, yes, seh. I always have been mightily interested in sport; ever since I was a boy." Johnny raised his chin loftily above his stock. "A good horse," he said, "well let down in the hocks, well laid back in the shoulder, with plenty of girth and bone, an' plenty of blood behind him—and—" He paused. Zooks! What was the other thing? Oh, yes—"And a nice top-line—that, seh, is what naturally appeals to me."

"Oh—ah—yes, indeed," the little man replied, quite at sea.

These New Bern folks had no more notion of sport than a codfish.

"I aim to race a string of horses myself," Johnny continued, "a little later on. And as for fox-huntin'—if I had a sovereign for every day I've squandered fox-huntin', I reckon I'd be as well off as any man in the Province. Yes, seh, where I come from, my barn—my stable door is clean covered over with fox hides!"

At this point Sir Nat turned back to Johnny and cocked an eye. "Hark to Bantam!" he cried. "Bantam's in full cry!" He placed a finger along his ear. "Who-oop! tear 'im, puppy!" he cried.

The others laughed—the little man who had been listening, goggle-eyed, smiled uncertainly. A hot wave of embarrassment flooded Johnny's neck. He managed, however, to retain some semblance of good order in his retreat. He took a sip of toddy with deliberation.

"All right, Nat," he said stoutly; "come out to my place and see for yourself."

"Good lad!" said Sir Nat. "If you tell a lie, stick to it!"

"Sound advice, sir," said Captain Tennant. "Advice every gentleman should remember."

The talk rose to a steady whir; the white-aproned bus-boys hurried back and forth with dark bottles; a pipe-stem cracked, a glass crashed on the floor; in a corner the damp, gray face of a rustic-looking man fell on his chest, he sagged limply in his chair.

"Back-country fellow," said Sir Nat. "Can't hold liquor."

"A fellow ought not to drink," Johnny observed sagely, "that can't hold his liquor." He threw out his chest and squinted at his glass of toddy.

"Ought to learn to hold it," Sir Nat replied with uncompromising conviction. "Nonsense not holdin' liquor"—he blew out of the corner of his mouth —"nonsense!"

At a far table they raised a song, bending heads together, then throwing them back with a roar.

"Here's to the drink that makes us wink,
Rum puncheon!
A tinker's damn for any dram
But puncheon!
Oporto, claret, sangaree,
Let maids and striplings sip the three.
But rum's the liquor, so say we,
Rum puncheon!
Fa-la, fa-la, fa-lorum, horum, jorum,
Rum puncheon!"

The whole room joined in the refrain: "Rum puncheon!" The deep hoarse chant reverberated against walls and ceiling, filled the room, filled their glowing hearts; not a voice faltered, again they raised their chorus:

"While he may last, let each stand fast
By puncheon!
And when he's under we'll still, by thunder,
Drink puncheon!
We'll buzz the bottle while we sup,
We'll troll the bowl and fill the cup,
A toast, my hearties, bottoms up!
Rum puncheon!
Fa-la, fa-la, fa-lorum, horum, jorum,
Rum puncheon!"

As the last note died away, an orange-colored coat flashed in the doorway, the pale, smiling face of Wylie Jones swept them with commanding glance. His ruffled arm was raised theatrically for silence. Johnny suspected that Mr. Jones had waited outside for the dramatic moment.

"Gentlemen," he said in a low, ringing voice, "I regret to interrupt your merriment, but I have just received private advices by the Bristol packet which concern us all." He opened a letter. "I will not trouble you with full details," he tapped the sheet, "but my London correspondent, writing on March third, concludes as follows:

" 'This day the ministerial party brought in a measure to present a memorial to his Majesty, praying him to declare the American Colonies to be in a state of rebellion.' "

A pause, then a low murmur like a ground-swell, a murmur of voices, incredulous, fearful, defiant, angry, which gained volume, mounted to a roar.

Teague Battle was on his feet, his light blue eyes ablaze. "Well, sehs, it's come, I reckon."

"And if it has, sir," shouted Captain Tennant, pounding his stick on the floor, "egad, we shall soon see who has cause to regret it!"

The hum of voices broke out again. "Huzzah for Battle!" "Well said, Captain!" "Put him out!" "Who said 'put him out'?"

Sir Nat rose, swaying almost imperceptibly. At the sight of his pink, kindly, stupid face, the murmur died.

"Bravo, Sir Natto, my lad!" cried a voice. They grinned at him affectionately.

"Don't talk nonsense!" he said. "King won't listen to silly address. Parliament damn fools—have uncle there myself."

He sat down amid deafening cheers and laughter. They crowded round him, shaking hands, clinking glasses with him. "The King!" they said. "God bless him! The King! He'll see us righted. Curse the ministers! The King! The King!"

Johnny noticed, however, that Wylie Jones did not join the throng. He withdrew to the far table, talked in whispers to Mr. Battle and Mr. Hewes. The gathering took their chairs again, fresh bottles were brought on, they tried to raise another chorus. But they could not find again the elusive spirit of the evening, the spirit, shy and uncertain, which in moments rare and unforeseen descends on men, breaks down the barriers, bridges gulfs, gives them a glowing hour's contact and release. They drifted out by twos and threes to their lodgings in the town; their steps stumbled in the chambers overhead. Sir Nat and Johnny walked out to the hitching-rail.

"Confound Wylie!" said Sir Nat. "Tryin' to make feelin'. All nonsense." He leaned somewhat heavily on Johnny's arm and drew it toward him as though to make sure nothing had come or would come between them.

Under that kind, honest pressure Johnny sought for a word of response and cheer, but just then the last convivial murmur died; through night and silence whispered the rustle of the sea. Its sound, so like the pines', brought back the never-quite-forgotten picture of the ancient Indian craning into the darkness for the beat of drums. Speechless, he put an arm around Sir Nat.

"Good chap," Sir Nat said, satisfied. "Where's chaise?" He moved along a step. "Funny thing," he said. "Life. Here comes Wylie with piece of silly news just when I've dashed important news myself."

"Why, Nat," said Johnny, laughing, "has somebody left you a fortune?"

"Exactly," Sir Nat responded without the least surprise. He patted Johnny's arm. "Clever chap. Always said so. Maiden aunt—Bishopstortford—hopped twig two months ago—left me two thousand guineas."

"By Zooks! You can buy the best blood in the country now."

"No," Sir Nat replied. "Won't do. Runnin' to seed here. Know it myself—so do you. Here's a chance."

"What! You're not leaving, are you?"

"Must do, old chap. Here's a chance. Always wanted to be soldier. Buy a commission—Fifth Dragoon Guards—fellows I know." He paused uncertainly, awaiting Johnny's verdict.

But Johnny, with the muffled drums of the war-foreboding ocean in his ears and the touch of Sir Nat's hand on his arm, could only look at him and swallow.

"Ought to make a go. Cavalry." Sir Nat explained with shy appeal. "Don't need brains."

He seized Johnny's hand and shook it.

"You come too," he said. "Ride like a Trojan."

The Negro groom had unhitched his horse. Sir Nat climbed painfully into the chaise.

"Think it over," he said. "Nice for me. Come up, horse."

## CHAPTER XXI

I T WILL be quite useless," said Dr. Clapton after breakfast next morning, "to attempt our studies today. I notice that you are abstracted and prepossessed."

"Well, naturally, seh," said Johnny, "being a friend of Sir Nat's, I am interested how his Peregrine horse makes out."

"I offered no criticism, my boy—if I may still call you that—merely an observation on the state of society. The spectacle of a horse running is lively and inspiriting; although I myself prefer to behold it in a pasture where the act is spontaneous and to that extent more exhilarating. As to the relative speed of given horses, that is a problem which will be infallibly determined by the race itself. Speculation before the event is, therefore, idle."

"Well, seh," said Johnny, "what about the First Ode—'*Sunt quos curriculo pulverem Olympicum*'?"

"You are apt, my dear young friend, but note the context. Horace merely observed the phenomenon without endorsing it," he smiled gently, "as, in my humble way, do I." He turned suddenly grave. "However, I would have you enjoy yourself to the full. For I begin to fear that between violent men on this side of the water and foolish men on the other, our pleasures may soon be forfeit."

"Do you really think there will be trouble, seh?" asked Johnny, suddenly chilled and miserable. "When the news came last night the gentlemen seemed to think the King would take our part."

"Yes, yes. That is my hope, too. My hope, do I say? My firm belief. The King is the servant of God and must see that justice is done his subjects." He reflected tenderly. "The people of this Province are children—most lovable children—and, like children, they are unschooled, impassioned, but they are also bold, buoyant, eager to learn. I am sure that God will lead his Majesty to act the good parent to them." He looked out the window, over the roofs and chimneys, over the dust of the noisy gathering race-crowd, over the sleeping bay; his face, fallen into delicate lines of musing, was touched, as it had been the first day Johnny saw him, by a beauty like a woman's.

Unhappy, Johnny waited. Gazing at Dr. Clapton's face, delicate, transparent, luminous, he felt oppressed by a vague impending doom, he heard his laboring heart beat time to the sombre marching of events. Its drumming quickened: he must have air! He plunged from the room and almost ran down the street to Hornblower's.

The country neighbors and farmers were coming in. Inside the tavern a press of people seemed to bulge the very windows, and still others trickled slowly in the door, clawing and elbowing good-naturedly; trickled slowly out, smacking lips, cracking jokes. Johnny hurried round to the pantry window.

"Hornblower, a glass of spirits, for Gad's sake! I feel like I had a chill."

Mr. Hornblower's distracted face shot into view, stared at Johnny, almost without recognition. He passed out a glass of spirits automatically. "Coming, sir, coming!" he cried in despairing tones and plunged back into the roaring tap-room.

The fiery rum brought heat to Johnny's spine, a look around still further warmed him. Here in high-pitched, comic, friendly mood the pick of the Province crowded in for fellowship and sport. They swarmed the street and sidewalk, overflowed into gardens, on doorsteps. Their carrioles and chaises lined the footpath, their horses were tied to every tree.

They parted slowly as Sir Nat, perched high on a yellow dogcart, drove up to the tavern. His Negro boy took the horse's head. Sir Nat, holding whip and reins in his right hand, climbed down. He laid the whip across the seat; he looped the reins through the terrets; he removed his tan box-cloth coat with the grave preoccupation of a Royal Post driver. The crowd watched his careful ritual with good-natured grins.

"How's Peregrine?" they said.

"Fit."

"Huzzah! You've got to beat that Virginia horse!"

"Right. Oh, there's Gerrould now."

The tall, grave Virginian came through the crowd.

"Hullo, Gerrould. Missed you last night. Comus fit?"

"Ah, Dukinfield. My chaise broke down. Yes, sir, my horse is ready to run. How is Peregrine?"

"Fit. Thanks."

Mr. Gerrould glanced about him importantly and clasped Sir Nat's hand.

"Well, then, sir, may the best horse win!"

"Right," answered Sir Nat, overcome by the somewhat theatrical tableau. "Bitters? No? Well, then, let's get for'ard. You know young Fraser?"

"I think, sir, I recollect the pleasure."

"Come along, Bantam; should be at the course."

Dubiously eyeing the dappled March sky, Sir Nat put on his box-cloth coat, buttoned the large mother-of-pearl buttons, took up whip and reins and mounted. Taking the seat beside him, Johnny focused every faculty on the effort to appear at ease and by no means elated.

"Let go," said Sir Nat to the Negro. "Take care yourself!" He laid an accurate lash along the bright flank. The dog-cart shot ahead. The little Negro made a white-eyed dive for the tailgate, hoisted himself aboard, legs wildly dangling. All down the street the crowd scattered and raised a humorous cheer.

The tide of sportsmen was already setting strong for the race-course. They passed knots of workmen trudging along, handkerchiefs stuffed into stocks, smoking stolid pipes, 'prentice lads who whistled through their teeth and winked, pig-tailed seamen, for the most part drunk and bellowing. Farmers and small planters bumped along on trace-marked plough-horses. Barefoot Negroes moved smoothly single file, each with his ticket of leave pinned to his breast; they pulled caps, ducked heads, grinned. "Looky, Negro. Heah come de golden chariot!" A deep-toned giggle and a high "Hyah! hyah!" ran down the line. A country chaise, mud-spattered, bristled with home-made female finery and bold untutored country glances. Two gutter-snipes from town paddled doggedly through the dust, dragging a weeping sister and a reluctant cur. A straw-filled farmer's wagon gave them a row of ruddy, inarticulate grins.

Captain Tennant, rigid in a hired fly, turned a furious eye on them as they scraped his hub, recognized them, took their dust with an almost benign salute.

"Good luck, young gentlemen!" they heard him call.

"Good luck, Sir Nat!" said a couple of back-country sportsmen on nervous, raw-boned colts. "We're a-backin' you, boy!" The foot people turned at the rattle of hubs, nodded bonnets, raised cocked hats, sticks, high-crowned buckled hats, and smiled. "Good luck!" they called. "Good luck! You're bound to win. North Carolina wins! Huzzah!"

Ahead in a neat little trap with scarlet wheels, Johnny saw Eve Tennant's new green capuchin beside the stout back of Master Hal Cherry.

"Silly fat boy," said Sir Nat. "Give him the go-by, what?" He cut in around them dexterously.

"Confound you!" cried Master Hal, jerking the reins up under his chin. "Do you know what you're about?"

"Yes. How do, Miss Eve?"

"Sir Nat! Johnny!" She smiled at them and laughed at her escort's discomfiture.

Johnny raised his hat and grinned delightedly. She had never seemed so charming and friendly. The fat boy had never seemed so absurd. A sobering thought occurred to him: girls were peculiar, they would inveigle a man into taking them to a party and then be the first to laugh if someone made a monkey of him.

They overtook four handsomely dressed young Virginians in a travelling carriage. "Here comes a rather decent horse," remarked one loftily. Johnny's gorge rose. "Hello, Virginia!" he shouted. "Is that Comus?" He pointed to the fat old cob between their shafts. "No, sir," they answered, "but I reckon he'd win just as easy."

"I reckon he'd stand as good a chance!" He waved derisively.

Wylie Jones, lying back in his saffron-panelled glass coach called to his monkey Negro postillions and, with a wave of tolerant amusement, allowed them to pass.

Now the race-course was in sight. The first comers already outlined a long oval on the greening pasture-lands.

They found Peregrine under a light blanket in a clump of young pines. Sir Nat's old Negro, in a bright yellow waistcoat, his Hessian boots freshly shined, waddled distractedly to and fro, babbled conflicting orders to three Negro strappers.

"De hind leg, Amos, da's what Ah said. Sassfrass, bring me de water-bucket. Wher' de sponge? You yaller boy, chase off dem chilluns!"

The yellow boy reluctantly approached a ring of youngsters.

"Li'l' white boys, please to go on along. De ho'se despise to be looked at."

"Good horse, Peregrine," said Sir Nat, walking up.

Peregrine seemed not to hear. He chucked his long fine head and kept an apprehensive eye on the distant bustle and confusion.

"Peregrine!"

Now his sharp ears tilted, his pointed muzzle made a nervous thrust at Sir Nat's pocket. Sir Nat brought out a tiny slice of carrot. Peregrine's lips closed on it swiftly, delicately. He turned away and once more fixed his uneasy gaze on the course.

"Nervous," said Sir Nat. Don't bother him. Amos, leave his leg." He unfastened the halter shank and walked off, leading the bright horse, softly whistling "Rum Puncheon" in his ear. Johnny waited; now and again he could see the pair through the trees and hear Sir Nat's soothing, endless refrain. The three black strappers squatted on the pine straw, solemn as apes.

"Ain't he de man now?" said the old groom. "He des naturally rock dat ho'se to sleep."

Just beyond, Johnny could see the tall black figure of Mr. Gerrould and the scarlet blanket of his Comus. As he walked over, the white jockey stripped the blanket and started to rub the chestnut quarters.

"Stand over, you Comus!" he shouted, and struck him with the back of his hand. Comus stood over quickly enough, but the look in his eye was not agreeable.

"Ah, Mr. Fraser," said Mr. Gerrould. "We are quite ready. You have not seen this horse before?"

"No, seh. He's a sure 'nough fine-looking horse. I certainly like his looks," he added, with the mental reservation that he would like them better were Comus a little stronger in the gaskins and a little more honest in the eye.

Mr. Gerrould received his remark in complacent silence—there was nothing more to be said. Johnny moved off toward the race-course crowd, which now grew in a steady stream and raised an ever-mounting din to heaven. Carriages, wagons, carts and chaises lined the homestretch. Horses munched nose-bags at the hind wheels. The crowd buzzed to and fro, formed jams, broke up, flowed on again. Here two young country boys, stripped to the waist, swung wildly at each other in a shouting circle. Beyond, a man in a white box coat and a white paper hat stood on a chair intoning, "Five to three on Comus! Five to three on Comus!" in a beery voice. Beside him a pock-marked, ratty man sold tickets. Johnny fell over a sailor sleeping soundly with his hard leather hat clasped to his chest. He stopped, stood wondering how he could get him to his feet again. But the crowd, after tripping over the sailor, seemed to accept him as a feature of the local geography and flowed around him on either side. Johnny strolled on.

A dark foreigner in earrings and feathered cap led a dingy bear. The man's wife bent forward beneath a barrel organ, a bright silk handkerchief drawn down to her tired eyes. On top of the barrel organ a monkey shivered and cracked his knuckles.

Johnny followed them till they halted. The barrel organ squeaked. "Tilly-lilly-lon-ton!" the man intoned and jerked the chain.

The bear rose up wearily, shuffled slowly, lurched from side to side. His coat was rubbed and rusty, his powerful forepaws hung against his chest in a begging posture, his eyes were tired like the woman's.

Those big paws, sturdy yet helpless, pulled at Johnny's heart as, years before, the pleading hands of the fisher-coon had pulled. He turned away.

The first event, a farmer's race, was being called. He went to the ropes where Wylie Jones, the starter, was lining up the field. Among the dozen half-bred colts he saw the bound-boy from Slade's Ordinary, his shirt sleeves rolled up to his shoulder, astride a hammer-headed ancient blood horse who stood motionless except for the trembling of his battered knees.

"Go!" cried Wylie Jones, and dropped his handkerchief. The bound-boy's nag got away with the rest under a liberal fusillade of blows. At the turn, however, Johnny saw a cloud of dust, a rolling horse, and the seat of the bound-boy's cowhide breeches sailing through the air.

The morning passed with short races for local horses. Impromptu matches, got up to decide disputes, ended in single combats or massed engagements between the partisans. The constable in his silver chain and badge marshalled his deputies and waited with nice judgment for the moment when it was prudent to intervene.

Toward two o'clock they fell to on their dinners; saddle-bags and hampers were spread on the grass, bottles and jugs passed from hand to hand. Pastry boys in white aprons sold tarts from shallow wooden trays, a fat old free-Negro woman peddled 'lasses candy.

Johnny strolled slowly to and fro, exhibiting himself and basking gratefully in the blaze of his own magnificence. His hands were clasped behind him, his eyes were bent on the ground as though abstracted, overwhelmed by weighty affairs. He noted accurately, however, the respectful glances of many a worthy burgher, and not a few feminine glances which, though not precisely respectful, were even more gratifying. It was a long cry, indeed, from the little back-country tadpole in moccasins to the well-set-up and irreproachably turned-out young gentleman who now paraded the race-course for the edification of the Province. Nor was his elegance specious in the least degree. Its crowning glory lay in the fact that it did no more than represent the actuality. He was received as friend and familiar by the un-assailable few whose lofty position looked up to no man—by Captain Ten-nant, by Wylie Jones, and, especially gratifying on this day of the great race, by Sir Nat.

At this point in his pleasing contemplation of himself, his thoughts shot off abruptly to Peregrine, walking lightly up and down among the pines, cocking his ears and waiting. A swift clutch of insupportable excitement, of chill apprehension, closed on his heart, the hour for the race was almost here. He turned clammy, empty, almost sick. If he did not do something his mind would turn blank, or he would froth and fall down in a fit.

He saw Eve perched on Master Cherry's trap and wandered over.

"Why, sir!" she cried down to him, "you look quite gloomy."

"Fact is, ma'm, I'm nervous about this race."

"Isn't it exciting!" she said without conviction. "But Peregrine will win, won't he?"

"I hope so," he answered listlessly. There was no use trying to tell the things he felt.

"Have some tucker?" Master Cherry mumbled from the corner of a stuffed mouth.

Johnny nibbled at a large fish sandwich mechanically. The bread, the curry and the shredded fish stuck miserably in his throat, went down with hideous gulpings, lay sodden on his chest.

Captain Tennant came up, bristling with excitement and indignation.

"Hello, young Fraser! Where's Sir Nat—with the horse? Good. We must beat these Virginia chaps—by Jove, we must! One of them just had the dashed impudence to offer me five to two against Peregrine!"

"Yes, seh. Virginians certainly are overweening."

"Infernally overweening, sir. I told the young man that I would take nothing but even money and laid him fifteen guineas." He puffed angrily. "Rather a large order on my Collector's pay, but hang me, I won't stand impudence."

At this moment a fat hand clasped Johnny's, a second hand, covered with rings, closed over it.

"Well, suh, young Master Fraser, and how do we fine ou'selves today?"

Mr. Jenney, the pack-horse man, very much frilled and wigged, without, however, great attention either to good taste or cleanliness, clung to Johnny's hand and pressed it to his bosom. His bows included Eve, Captain Tennant, and Master Cherry. He had evidently forgotten the incident of the fur tippet.

"Master Fraser," he explained to the company, "is the son of a ve'y dear frien' of mine, the gallant and cultivated Mr. Fraser, of Little River. Our relationship is peculiarly close, Mrs. Fraser being a Moore, of Wilmington, and my late wife"—he raised his eyes to heaven—"deceased March 9, 1764, having been a Tollifer and related through the Desaussures to the Moores."

"Did Mr. Arrocks come with you?" asked Johnny hurriedly.

"There he stands," said Mr. Jenney, pointing into the crowd, "the salt of the earth, the positive salt of the earth."

Johnny led Mr. Jenney away to where the grim face of Mr. Arrocks cast its saturnine eye on the throngs below. Mr. Arrocks tilted his long beak vertically as a salutation, then tilted it horizontally with a meaning glance to indicate that he desired a private interview. Disengaging his hand from Mr. Jenney's, Johnny stepped aside.

"Who's to ride Dukinfield's horse?" he said in a hoarse stage whisper.

"Mr. Heywood, of Black River."

Mr. Arrocks shook his head lugubriously. In pantomime he poured out a monumental drink, drank it and simulated stupor. He shook his head again and walked away.

So Mr. Heywood, then, had got drunk the night before the race? He hurried to Sir Nat with the news.

"Nat, has Mr. Heywood come?"

Sir Nat shifted the straw in his mouth.

"Yes," he replied without enthusiasm.

"Is he all right?"

"Seedy. Have to do, though. Too late now——" He bit the straw in two and turned to his horse.

"I just saw a fellow I knew; he told me he'd drunk himself stiff last night."

"Yes, yes, I know," Sir Nat shook his head—"too late now."

Johnny strode moodily up and down before the little group who had gathered to watch Peregrine saddled. He bowed his head, the picture of a high-minded sportsman deploring the less admirable qualities of others. And indeed, beneath this pantomime, he was truly outraged. To be picked to ride Peregrine and then get drunk the night before—such sacrilege would bring a judgment from God.

An expectant hush had fallen on the race crowd, their restless movement ceased; they lined up at the track.

Looking quite alert and fit, Heywood appeared on the other side of Peregrine. He took a pull at the girths, stripped off his coat, gave Sir Nat his thin-lipped grin across the saddle.

"Never fear, Nat, I'll bring him home first!" His speech was hearty, confident, but Johnny noticed that his face, around the sharp mouth, was gray.

"Listen!" said Sir Nat. "Should win the first heat. But the second and third heats—" He whispered to him.

Heywood pulled back the sleeves of his yellow silk jacket and nodded impatiently. "Here, groom, a leg up!" The rug was slipped off Peregrine's loins and Heywood vaulted into the light racing saddle. "Groom, hold my iron—not that way, damn you!" He got his feet home in the stirrups, took a light feel of the reins; horse and rider moved off quietly for the starting-post. Sir Nat trudged alongside, softly whistling. Already the scarlet jacket of Mr. Gerrould's jockey could be seen above the heads of the crowd.

Forgetful now of dignity, of earthly pomp and vanity, Johnny trotted behind Peregrine's bay quarters with the three strappers and the old groom. The crowd gave way, closed in behind. They were at the post. It seemed impossible that the event had arrived. He was fighting through the crowd—

he would be too late. He heard an angry voice, "What in the nation!" And another, "Let him through. It's Sir Nat's friend." Then he was on the ropes. He saw a strange gentleman standing with a raised flag; he saw Comus lay back an ear, whirl, come up to the line; he saw Peregrine, steady enough and ready except for a hint of unfathomed apprehension in his eye.

The flag went down with a shout of "Go!" They broke away in a scurry, straightened out side by side down the roaring lane. They disappeared around the turn; the roar of the crowd sank to a busy murmur. Standing on tiptoe, Johnny could just see the scarlet jacket and the yellow moving above the packed heads. Side by side they glided along, like two small colored disks drawn on strings. At the end of the back stretch they vanished.

Now they were coming. A cheer ran down the line with the beat of their hoofs. They passed by, shoulder to shoulder, both horses settled into the long, steady gallop of the four-mile test.

The rest seemed like a dream to Johnny. Horses and riders now glided, two spots in the distance, now drummed past in a shower of turf clods. He heard the people shouting, "Last mile! Peregrine! Go it, Peregrine! Last mile!" He must see! He must see!

He was backing furiously through the press of bodies, he was frantically climbing an over-loaded chaise. A hand reached down and hoisted him.

The two horses, on the back stretch, were level just the same. But as they reached the turn a scarlet arm rose and fell. The chestnut horse jumped forward, made his drive for home. The crowd gave a whispered groan. Then Peregrine strode out as well; he rounded into the stretch with his head along the other's saddle-girth. Johnny saw the bay ears flash forward, the bay neck stretch out. He knew the meaning. The horse was going to make his dash. Sit still, Heywood, sit still! But just then Heywood's whip swung fiercely back, Peregrine swerved, checked his stride, lost half a length, a length, came forward under the whip, made a desperate run, passed the judges a head and neck behind.

Johnny fumbled for his handkerchief. He was going to cry. The beautiful bay horse whom he had ridden so often, the roguish, gallant horse, who knew just when and how to gather himself for one of his tremendous bursts, was beaten. He blew his nose. Below him a little knot of Virginia supporters were throwing their hats aloft and cheering in the heart of the silent throng. The arm which held him to the hub of the chaise tightened. Mr. Teague Battle stared at the huzzaing young bloods.

"I'd give my hide," he said, "to send those young scoundrels home with their tails between their legs."

Here came Peregrine under his sheet, his sweat-blackened neck hanging low. Sir Nat beside him, pale and troubled, was casting anxious glances around.

"Bantam," he said in a low voice, "come down!"

They walked silently back to the clump of pines. Silently the crowd gave way for them.

They watched the poor old groom sponging out Peregrine's nostrils, and crying distractedly into the water bucket.

"Heywood," Sir Nat said gravely, "won't do."

"I know, Nat," Johnny mumbled, "but they's no one else. If only you were light enough. Tell him not to use the whip. O my, O my! The horse was all fixed to run."

Sir Nat withdrew a pine needle from his mouth—"You ride."

The world turned slowly upside down, burst into a million fragments which showered on Johnny's head.

"What!" he heard himself say.

"Boy, bring me those boots. Bantam, sit down."

"But, Nat, I've never ridden a race."

"Know horse—horse knows you. Sit still—that's all—speak to him."

Sir Nat was tugging the boots on Johnny's trembling legs and puffing. Heywood came up, a plaster of mud across his lean jaw.

"Heywood, give Bantam your jacket."

"What!"

"Put this boy up—only chance."

Heywood stripped his jacket and threw it on the ground. "God's teeth!" he said. "You don't expect me to make a good horse out of a bad one, do you?" He walked away.

Now the jacket was on over Johnny's ruffled shirt, now he was hoisted, numb and powerless, into the saddle. By Zooks! He couldn't do it!

But with the familiar feel of the horse between his knees the strength flowed back in him. He took up on the reins. Sir Nat's light hand closed on his thigh.

"Good chap!" he said. "Sit still—speak to him."

He was at the starting post. He heard the crowd's murmur of surprise. A voice cried, "Ride him, youngster!" "Ride him—ride him!" they roared.

The flag went down—he closed his knees and shot away. As the ranks of faces and waving hats flew past, his heart rose up inside him. He took a breath. "Good horse!" he whispered.

Now they were galloping, galloping through the empty back stretch, through the thundering lane, and he was riding, riding, sitting steady in the saddle, keeping an even feeling on the bit. Back stretch and lane, back stretch and lane wheeled by in dizzy procession.

He heard the cry, "Last mile!" The jockey beside him touched the chestnut horse. Comus quickened stride and drew away—half a length, a length, then two. "Ride him! Ride him!" the crowd implored. He chewed on his tongue, sat still.

He trailed the other around the back stretch, squinting his eyes against the flying sods. At the turn the jockey grinned back at him over his shoulder. Above the tumult he heard Sir Nat's voice, "Now!"

He closed his legs, leaned forward for the coming shock. But the bay horse hung back, thinking of the whip. "Peregrine!" he called. "Peregrine!"

An ear twirled, the reins pulled sharply tight, Peregrine reached for his bit. The crowd shot past in a gray mist; the scarlet jacket was coming back to him. He saw it whipping. "Now sit steady!" he muttered.

As they rounded into the homestretch, the saddle beneath him again thrust forward. By Zooks, he didn't know there was such speed!

In one tremendous instant the chestnut horse fell rapidly behind him. He finished going away.

At the first pull Peregrine came in to him and stopped. The crowd was running down the track, swarming around him. Hats, sticks, greatcoats were in the air. "That's a-ridin', boy! That's a-ridin'!" "Do it again now, son!" "Carolina wins!"

Sir Nat fought through the press. Johnny slipped off weakly into his arms. A hundred hands shook his, reached for him, patted him as they made their way back to the little clump of trees.

"Listen, Bantam!" Sir Nat jerked a thumb toward Comus. "Won't be beat so easy next time. Start racin' third mile, or you won't see him again." He gazed at Peregrine's heavy flanks. "Hold him together," he said; "tired."

Again in the mist and tumult of a dream, Johnny was off the score beside the chestnut. He hugged the rail and waited, sick and anxious, for Peregrine now was not galloping so strong. They made two rounds together, the other horse just a neck and head behind. Then from the corner of his eye he saw the jockey raise his whip. He closed his legs and drew away.

He was galloping into the fourth mile now amid the shrieks of Bedlam. "Carolina! Carolina! Peregrine!" The cursed fools! Couldn't they see the horse was fading fast, his head nodding, his weight all on the bit?

On the next turn he heard the whip behind; the chestnut muzzle crept up to his knee. He shoved his horse along as fast as he dared, but again the whip came down; the chestnut muzzle stayed there.

Cursing and whipping like a madman, the scarlet jockey drew up on the turn, hung knee to knee, passed him by. A hundred yards to go and no more running in his beaten horse, though the chestnut was just ahead and, whip as the rider might, could not draw away. Johnny took up on the reins. "Go it, good horse!" he shouted thickly. He closed his numb legs; the horse's head came up; he felt his hocks come under; with a last uncertain burst, he drew up to the chestnut, fell back, crawled up, hung forever, it seemed, in a black roaring cavern, then edged an inch ahead.

Peregrine pulled up, stumbling; stood there, legs outspread, muzzle hanging low. Johnny leaned forward and laid his face on the drooping neck. Then the crowd was on them. He was pulled from the saddle, he was rocking aloft on a dozen shoulders. A thousand faces turned up to him, shouted. Men danced, leaped, threw arms about each other, reached up frantic hands. Sir Nat's pink face was rocking above the crowd as well.

They drifted slowly together, were hoisted together to the seat of a chaise. The people cheered and cheered again, then fell silent. "Speech! Speech!" they cried. Sir Nat, quite crimson, cleared his throat, touched Johnny's shoulder.

"Good chap!"

"Huzzah!" they howled.

He pointed a stubby finger to where the old groom, laughing, crying, stumbling over his Hessian boots, was leading Peregrine away.

"Good horse!" he said.

THE HORSE RACE

*Cursing and whipping like a madman, the scarlet jockey drew up on the turn, hung knee to knee, passed him by*

# CHAPTER XXII

For some weeks after the race Johnny lived on the glory of achievement, on distinction. When he went down the street strangers gazed at him and spoke, shopkeepers nodded affably, little boys stared. After a time, however, no strangers turned their heads, curious and deferential; the little boys continued their game of tipcat as he passed; shopkeepers were cordial, but no more so than before the great event. The great event, it seemed, and he himself had been forgotten. Ah, well, he told himself, what could a man who knew life expect? He was too old and wise to put faith in fleeting human applause. He stalked abroad, a shade disconsolate perhaps, but chiefly the natural philosopher, meditating in resignation on the transiency of human affairs.

Then spring came; a mournful spring. The words seemed contradictory. Always till now, spring with warm winds and stirring life had made him want to snort and paw like the bull-calf in the lane and frolic like the rabbits

199

in the dusk. Now he was a man, or nearly so, and spring was not the same. Not only had life proved indifferent, the satisfaction of triumph ephemeral, men forgetful of his great deed. That was bad enough. He had, however, strength of mind to meet it. But he had no strength of mind to meet a far vaster adversity—an adversity, elusive, intangible, and therefore invincible. Everywhere, close around him, in distant provinces, on sea and mountain, he seemed to hear the sullen marching of events. Yet those events, however formidable, were still unborn and fragile. If one voice should speak the word, those senseless gathering shadows would shatter into atoms and leave the Carolina sky as brilliant as before.

The word was not spoken. With every moment, the doom still nebulous, invisible, gained strength and potency, he felt, against the hour of its birth.

Looking on spring, he seemed to himself wan and old. Why should Spring make her gallant effort every year, knowing full well that Autumn, inexorable Autumn, soon would follow? Why should the bull pine push his new green shoots aloft, the dogwood spread her silver to the moon, when so soon every blossom must wither, every leaf must die? He watched the greening trees and pastures morosely and not without a gloomy relish. No one else, he told himself, looked on them as he did. He stood, bowed with years, with sadness and wisdom—he stood alone. Other men viewed the future with indifference or with childish confidence. Dr. Clapton had faith in the wisdom of the King, Captain Tennant in the power of the British Navy, while some, like Wylie Jones and Mr. Battle, seemed to rush fiercely to meet events with open eyes and open arms. The rest were stolidly indifferent, holding no views beyond the next day's dinner.

Sir Nat's opinion, if by no means profound, was at least as sensible as any.

"Nonsense!" he said. "No row between gentlemen sportsmen. Fight Mounseers, other odd chaps. Good job, too."

With such remarks as these and pink, untroubled face, Sir Nat busied himself about his place, boxing up his meagre effects for his trip to England. He held an auction of his horses, at which Peregrine was not put up.

When Johnny spoke of it Sir Nat mumbled uncomfortably, "Give him to you—present." It was only by pointing out that at Squire Fraser's Little

River farm Peregrine would have but indifferent care and no chance to race
that Sir Nat was dissuaded, and Peregrine sold to Wylie Jones by private
treaty. Sir Nat, however, insisted on opening up a packing-case and fishing
out a silver mounted hunting-crop. "Belonged to my governor," he said,
putting it into Johnny's hands.

The case was nailed up again and with the rest of Sir Nat's luggage put
on board the Bristol brigantine which, having lain careened a month on the
beach while her bottom was cleaning, was now at her dock and ready to
sail.

The night before she was to leave a quiet party gathered at Hornblower's
—Wylie Jones, Captain Tennant, Teague Battle and Mr. Hewes. Far from
talking politics or entering on a dispute, each gentleman of the oddly contrasted group contributed his best to the occasion, conscious, perhaps, how
slight the chance that they would ever sit down together again. Different as
they then were, they seemed to find common ground in reminiscences of
boyhoods more different still. The captain told of his first attempt to ride to
hounds on a New Forest pony, and received their laughter with a pleased if
somewhat puzzled bow. Teague Battle told of his father firing at the Indians through the loopholes while he and his mother filled their mouths
with milk and squirted it between the cracks to douse the blazing arrows.
Wylie Jones had a polished anecdote involving fags and champagne at
Eton, and Joseph Hewes, a grim tale of smuggled rum and Dr. Wither-
spoon at Nassau Hall.

"Have you no story of your youth, Johnny?" Wylie Jones asked with his
smile. "Or does not your memory run back so far?"

"No, seh," said Johnny, blushing. "Things are always mighty quiet along
the Little River."

"Tell 'em about the time you knocked young Cherry's nose," Sir Nat
urged earnestly.

"Oh, I couldn't, Nat. That was a fool kind of thing."

But they all turned toward him importunately. "Go on, Johnny." "Let's
have it, boy." "Don't funk, young Fraser." The back of his neck grew hot
and rigid.

"Why, I was on his boat," he stammered, "swimming—and along he came and more or less cussed me. And then after some little chat he hit me and I hit him and he fell down."

Wylie Jones eyed him sternly. "You are a deplorable raconteur. Tell us what really happened, Nat."

Sir Nat jerked a thumb toward Johnny.

"Bantam used to swim with dockside boys——"

"Not very exclusive of you, my dear young friend," said Wylie Jones, wagging a reproachful finger.

"Let be, Wylie," Sir Nat went on; "always played with stable lads myself. Anyhow, Bantam and dockside boys swimmin' off young Cherry's sloop. Along comes Cherry. Ragamuffins dive overboard—Bantam stands ground —gives Cherry lip—throws water on Cherry's bottom. Cherry makes for him—Bantam takes two knocks to square accounts, then starts millin' on his own." Sir Nat illustrated Johnny's attack with professional skill. He finished with one tremendous swing. Gazing gravely around the circle, he told off the damages on his fingers. "Cherry—two black eyes—bloody nose—loose tooth. Flat on back—sound asleep." He closed his round little eyes, then opened them very wide and grinned delightedly.

"Bravo, Johnny!" cried Captain Tennant. "I can't stick these third-rate gentlemen. Here or at home, they are bad 'uns wherever you find 'em." He swelled with the importance of the pronouncement.

"All our back-country boys is like Fraser, seh," observed Teague Battle, bestowing a brief but searching glance of endorsement on Johnny. "They start slow and they finish strong."

"The first of these characteristics," said Mr. Hewes, "can be observed in Teague's practice of the law."

"Like all back-country boys," said Wylie Jones, "Teague thinks that any effort on his part could only serve to spoil what already stands as nature's perfect work."

To Johnny's relief the talk had shifted away from him. They fell to rough, good-natured banter, the banter of affection, like the frolic of young bears— with Wylie Jones deftly slipping in and out of the conversation and Captain

Tennant nodding his approval in the manner of one who does not comprehend the jokes but accords them full recognition as the jokes of gentlemen.

Toward midnight the party broke up. With a jerking handshake and a
blunt "God bless you!" for Nat, the captain left them. The others walked
down to the dock and up the narrow gangplank. They crowded into Nat's
tiny cabin, tried his little bunk in turn, sat in a row on its edge, assuming
postures of seasickness for his benefit.

"Sick nothin'," said Sir Nat. "Can't be. Look here." He pointed beneath
the bunk to a phalanx of bottles.

The others left at last. Sir Nat and Johnny were alone, alone with nothing
to say.

"Good-bye, Nat," Johnny murmured, suddenly wretched and inarticulate.

" 'Bye, old chap. Write me. Don't go in for writin', but send you a letter."

"Yes, do. I'll look for it."

"When I join regiment," Sir Nat went on, "have a look round—see if
there's a place for you. Good idea—what?"

"Oh, I don't know, Nat. I'd like the horses fine, but I don't reckon I'd like
to fight. It don't seem as though there was any sense to it."

Sir Nat's brow clouded. "Good God—don't talk as if your heart wasn't in
right place. 'Course it is. Knocked Cherry. Won race."

"I know, but—it would be different to fight against somebody you never
saw before."

Sir Nat brought out a bottle from under the bunk—his face cleared.
"That's all right," he said. "Got to show Mounseers and Spanish Johnnies
their place—what? Port?"

They drank a solemn glass together and shook hands.

Now Johnny was on the dock beneath the stars; Sir Nat's dim figure
waved to him from the rail. Like the horse race, Sir Nat's farewell, an event
stupendous, long awaited, seemed, once here, a mere hallucination.

Who could believe, for instance, that months, years, eternity, perhaps,
would roll by Hornblower's tap-room and Sir Nat not be seen there? Johnny
waved again, then walked up the dark lane.

The week that followed showed unmistakably that Sir Nat had really gone. Each evening Johnny dropped in at Hornblower's as though there might still be a chance of finding him at his favorite table. The fact of his departure was, however, unescapable and in the end Johnny not only became reconciled to it but clung to it, used it as an argument to prove to himself that war with England could not occur. Else how could Sir Nat have left him so casually, so cheerfully, he asked himself, to join the British Army?

Walking from the tavern one evening, he heard the sound of galloping far up the Norfolk road. Some drunken reveller riding wildly home. The beating hoofs drew nearer, came on down the street. Drunk or sober, the man knew how to ride. He stood in his stirrups behind the tired horse's nodding head. He swung the corner in a cloud of starlit dust, pulled up at Teague Battle's door. Johnny watched him hurry stiffly to the steps. He heard the knocker roughly hammering. A light flared up in the window. He longed to find out more, but he knew too much to ask the business of a man like Mr. Battle.

He walked slowly up the street, overwhelmed with sadness and foreboding. With those galloping hoofs, events seemed to gallop as well. As he neared the drowsy little parsonage nestling in its garden, he heard behind him the distant drumming of a fresh horse galloping away.

A tocsin was beating in his troubled dreams. Louder and louder it beat. Its iron clangor swelled insupportably, burst open wide the dark dome in which he lay. He stared at the gray ceiling in the gray half-dawn. Outside the town-crier's bell was clanging frantically.

"Oyez! Oyez! Oyez! Good folk!" the voice croaked. "News from the North, news, news!"

Johnny went to the window. At the corner the crier stopped and held up his link. Windows were thrown open by dames in wrappers. Householders hurrying out in night-caps and great-coats formed a group around the palsied figure. Johnny saw the gleam of white paper in the lean hand and caught snatches of the crier's words.

"This day the militia . . . British troops . . . two hundred killed and wounded . . . Lexington . . . Let every province send aid . . . Speed the message . . ."

"War!" said a man in an awestruck whisper.

"Damnation!" cried another. "Who's scared of the bloody beef-eaters!"

From a shaded porch Johnny heard a desperate woman's voice, "I'll not believe it. Oh, my poor children!"

The crier shouldered his link indifferently and marched away.

## CHAPTER XXIII

THE MONTHS of May and June in Edenton were months of suspense, of utter inactivity, when men lived not for action but for despatches. Every private advice from the North was read aloud at Hornblower's. Expresses rode in to Teague Battle's and rode away again. After each, news items in Teague Battle's handwriting were posted on the tavern wall and read with much discussion as to how much Mr. Battle chose to post, how much to conceal. Between these various sources, the picture grew—a picture of New England militia mustering, marching on Boston, hemming the British within the limits of the town; a picture of fresh British troops disembarking, of fresh militia hurrying in support until two armies faced each other. Tension at Edenton, growing with the news of each re-enforcement, at last broke out in action.

A quiet night was shattered by the sound of Terry's drinking place emptying itself into the street in a torrent of smashing glass and swinging blows. Shouts of "Turn out, Americans! Turn out!" and the sound of many running feet rang through the lanes. The worthy burghers locked their doors, the constable locked his. Late into the night they listened anxiously to the skirmishing of Edenton shipwrights and British seamen.

Next day the matter was not mentioned, the battered heads were hid from sight. But a coaster which was to sail within the week for New York found a dozen Tories anxiously bidding against each other for cabin-room.

The gate of Master Cherry's plantation was barred, Master Cherry's sloop was hauled out of water and stripped down, Master Cherry's father, a proud, solitary, beaten-looking man, and the raddled harridan he called his wife, drove to the dock by night with endless carts of luggage. Huzzah! thought Johnny to himself, the fat boy was about to leave. Eve, so dazzled by Cherry's vulgar pomp, would now soon learn his own true worth and quieter elegance.

The next afternoon he walked up to the captain's to see how Eve was taking the news. The lower hall was littered with bandboxes and portmanteaux, above stairs papers rustled, feet thumped Hoddin, bearing a travelling box, came down.

"Hello, Hoddin!" said Johnny in astonishment. "You all aren't leaving, are you?"

"Ho, no, sir," Hoddin said, setting down the box and standing very straight. "The Keptin is only just sending Miss Heve off on the packet, till matters shakes down 'ere a bit, as you might say, sir."

"Oh," said Johnny, dumbfounded and crestfallen, "on account of that cursed tavern fight, I reckon."

"Why—yes and no, sir. In course the Keptin is hopposed to the presence of ladies where there is hany unpleasantness habout, but w'ot I says is: 'W'ot a pity we 'aven't the old company 'ere.' We should 'ave the 'ole Province in order in no time at all, sir."

Johnny grinned. "But, Hoddin, they's a hundred and twenty thousand people in this Province."

"Quite so, sir," said Hoddin woodenly, "but the company musters an

'undred and ten." He dismissed the subject. "Shall I announce you to Miss
Heve, sir?"

In a moment Eve came down, threaded her way drearily through the
luggage in the hall, dropped him a mournful curtsey from the door.

"You're leaving," said Johnny, stupidly enough.

"Yes. Papa insists. Isn't it silly of him?" She answered without conviction.

"Where you bound? England?"

"Oh, no," she laughed uneasily, "I take the packet to New York, where
Papa has friends."

"I certainly hope you'll come back soon."

"That depends," she said coolly, "on how your countrymen carry themselves—or on how soon his Majesty chooses to bring them to terms."

"The folks here will be all right if the King will only see them justly
used."

"Americans are fine ones to talk of justice, when they shoot British troops
and beat poor innocent British seamen."

"Well, the provincials only ask justice. What right have the British got
messin' with the folks in Boston?"

"I only wish Papa's old regiment was here!" she broke in hotly. "Your
friends would get more justice than they want."

"I reckon you've never seen our boys shoot."

"I've seen them parade!" She laughed derisively. "They looked like a set
of stranded hop-pickers!"

"All right!" cried Johnny, with a savage grin, "you do the paradin' and
we'll do the shootin', and let's see who wins!"

For answer she sank into a chair and burst into tears. "Oh, dear!" she
cried. "What shall I do? Everyone hates us here."

Johnny was on one knee beside her. He paused to note that the honeysuckle screened them from the street, then took her hand.

"Look hyer, Eve. I didn't go to say all that. I just got mad. I like the
English best of all, honestly I do. They know how to do things and how to
dress and how to act the gentleman. That's the truth. I don't hold with these
fellows here that are stirring up a fuss. The most part of them is no 'count.

And the fellows at the head I don't like neither. Teague Battle is just looking for a fight, whether anybody wants to fight or not. And Wylie Jones, he's so slick, he'll let somebody else do the work and come out on top himself. I declare I'm like you. I don't know what to do neither. Nat's gone, and now you're going, and it looks like everybody in the world was fixing to fight each other, and there's no sense to it."

"Oh—I don't know." She wiped her eyes and looked at him pleadingly. "I suppose you're just saying that to make amends."

"No, I'm not." He still held her hand. "You know I think more of your father and Dr. Clapton than of anybody else."

She pouted through her tears. "And is that all?"

"Why, no," he floundered, "I think so much of you that I wouldn't fight against the British, not if you were to offer me a captain's commission right now."

She smiled. "You compliment me. But what if you were offered a British commission?"

Now it was his turn to feel miserable. He released her hand. "I couldn't," he muttered laboriously. "I don't reckon I could. A man can't fight against his folks."

"I shouldn't have said that," she broke in. She looked at him tenderly again. "Now *you* must forgive *me*, Johnny." She held out a hand.

Johnny took it between his own. She drew toward him, pliant, slightly swaying. With a hurried glance behind him, he bent down and kissed her parted lips. Her hand stole round his neck. They seemed to swim together in a whirling pool.

Hoddin coughed decorously in the hall. They sprang apart. Johnny saw her breast rise and fall unsteadily; on his own forehead he felt a big vein pumping. He shook her gravely by the hand.

"Good-bye," he said, "and take care of yourself."

"I shan't need to," she answered airily, already quite herself again. "Master Cherry is to be on board." She laughed, turned swiftly tender, her eyes, her hands clung to him. "Good-bye, Johnny," she whispered and ran in the house.

Walking away from the captain's, Johnny fanned himself uneasily with his hat; his face was a furnace, his head a whirligig. What in the nation—! He hadn't meant to get messed up like that. And yet it was wonderful. She was a wonderful girl. Did she expect to marry him now? Did he expect to marry her? And if he didn't marry her, would the captain call him no gentleman? Well, what ought he to have done? And how in the nation could a man tell what to do when a girl acted that way. Anyhow, he certainly felt very much the young gentleman now. Maybe more hot and flustered than he ought to be, but a good deal of a man just the same. And, however matters stood, she was sailing tomorrow. If she had been staying on, he reflected for his consolation, he would be more flustered still. He clapped his hat on at an angle and strode into Hornblower's.

"Hornblower!" he cried in a hearty, ringing voice. "A sherry flip!"

"Very good, sir," said Mr. Hornblower. "Our nautical friend," he continued, industriously whipping up the bowl of milk, "has been by here looking for you. Have you seen him?"

"Captain Flood? No." Johnny reflected uneasily. That must mean a letter from home, and a letter from home in these troubled days was not likely to bear good tidings.

The sherry flip, intended to be sipped elegantly after the manner of a man of the world, a conqueror of hearts, was swallowed in hasty gulps. Johnny started in search of Captain Flood.

He was not at the dock nor was he amid the ruins of Terry's Ordinary. In the main harbor, however, where bales of Tory carpets and crated Tory pictures were being stowed aboard the coasting packet, Johnny caught the familiar glint of whiskers. Puffing his pipe at a short distance from the gang of loafers who, silent and saturnine, watched the steady procession of fleeing Tories' effects, the captain enumerated each article as it was carried past.

"'Hogany sofy for front hall—reclinin' chair for old gentleman—'broidery frame for young lady—two dozen best Oporto wine—— Hello, bucko!" he called. "This is like old times for me—used to be purser *and* supercargo on the 'Clyde Cahoon' of New Bern, and this is the way I'd do—when the

ship was takin' on cargo I'd holler out ever'thing that come aboard—holler
it out an' write it down. Then when she unloaded, if anything was missin',
I'd cross it off, so that made all square." He took a pull at his pipe. "I sometimes wish," he said, "that I'd 'a' went in for to be a merchant—figures an' all
such comes so easy to me."

"Yes, seh, that's so," said Johnny absently. "They told me you were looking for me."

"And so I was. I figured you'd come along here sooner or later to see these
English-lovers' duffle stowed on board. Here——"

Johnny hurriedly opened the letter which the captain held out.

> "Little River,
> "8 April, 1775.

"My dear Son:—

"I take advantage of a passing Freighter to send you these Instructions which I beg you will observe with the utmost particularity.
Affairs in this part of the Province are in by no means so satisfactory a
State as I wou'd have them. There is some Unrest and much Vaunting
and Vaporing among a Certain Few who are naturally so inclined, and
who have ever been, as they are now, a Reproach to the Province and a
Menace to our Happy and Peaceable Condition. I have no notion,
however, that matters will proceed beyond the sphere of Oratory. For
even were these bombastical Gentry inclined to follow Words and
Deeds the state of the Province would preclude the possibility. We
have few musquets, little powder and shot, no soldiery trained to meet
an European style of army and no ships whatever fit to contest the
Mastery of the Sea, especially against a nation who has ever found it
her Native Element. I therefore have no uneasiness for ourselves on
Little River. But as I do not clearly gather from your last what posture
affairs may be in at Edenton, I send you the following Instructions for
your Guidance.

"As long as matters remain unchanged you should continue your
Schooling, endeavoring at the same time to divest your mind of Apprehension and bringing every Faculty to bear upon your Duties, Latin in
especial. Should, however, British authority be defied, as has been the

case at Boston, I charge you immediately to repair to Mr. Wylie Jones at Halifax, whence we shall carry you home. You are to employ your own judgment but by no means to delay over long, for in such humours of the Body Politic, no man can predict how far the Democratical Rebels will carry their infatuation. You will be well off, however, with Mr. Jones as he, I am sorry to say, appears to hold a high place in their Councils.

"I shall expect an acknowledgment under the hand of Captain Flood.

"I trust this finds you, as it leaves your Mother and myself, enjoying as good Health and Spirits as might be expected under the present Circumstances.

"Your aff'nate father,

"John Fraser."

Johnny's heart sank. Somehow his father's well ordered reasons why active revolt was impossible seemed, more than anything which yet had happened, to lend revolt reality. Catastrophe was closing in.

The captain nudged him. "See that earthen jar?" he whispered. "She's sealed like she was full of Malaga grapes, but the way those chaps totes her looks more like plate to me." He smoked again. "Things is quiet here, bucko —mighty quiet. Now in the back country they wouldn't let these Tories haul off their duffle quite so easy."

"Do you mean they'd plunder them?" Johnny paused. "Hasn't a man a right to his opinion?"

" 'Course he has. But what I say is this: Let the Tories keep their opinion and let us keep their plate. It don't look good to have gold sovereigns and silver teapots and all such carried out of the Province just as a matter of opinion."

"That's no way to fight," said Johnny, "to steal a man's teapot."

The captain took his pipe from his mouth and mused. "They's lots of ways to fight, bucko, and different folks tries different ways to start with, but they all end the same. They do whatever in the nation they can do to hit the other fellow. And what I says is this: If that's the way you're going to end, why, that's the way you might as well begin. That's logic, ain't it?"

"It may be logic," said Johnny bluntly, "and it may be what they'd do in the back country, but it's not the way people act here, thank God."

"When I was up the river," the captain answered reflectively, "there was talk that the man, Boone, had seen Indian war parties with Englishmen leading them." The captain spat and grinned. "Now, bucko, if you turn loose the Indians against a back country man and his family, you're liable to make him mad enough," he spat again, "to steal your spoons." His eye lighted up. "There's another yarn I heard at Halifax. They said that a express had just come for Wylie Jones that the Americans had whipped the British at Boston again, an' whipped 'em good."

"Oh, I don't reckon that can be so. Militia can't stand up against British troops—they lack the schooling."

"Well, you ask Teague Battle and see if it ain't so. A express passed me, ridin' down the river."

Johnny pocketed the letter and walked away. The captain's whiskers and little monkey figure were hateful; there he sat, counting the luggage of the Tory refugees, as mirthful, as indifferent to the hurrying clouds of doom, to the poignant meaning of those pitiful crates and bundles, as the meanest blackguard loafer of the dockside. How could Johnny ever have thought the captain, with his chatter and tawdry sea finery, a figure of adventure? If, as he used to dream, but as now seemed most unlikely, there was such a thing as high adventure, if life held any third alternative to dull routine and senseless butchery, assuredly the captain was the last person in the world to embody it. Nor had Johnny ever met a man who did—Sir Nat with a quicker intellect, perhaps; Teague Battle with a little less hardness and restraint. Perhaps this Daniel Boone might be the one. He shook his head wearily. He didn't know how things ought to be, but as they were, there was no sense to them. He wandered irresolutely toward the rectory.

Mr. Battle, far from irresolute, came walking with a paper in his hand. His face was grimly radiant; he walked with unbelievable swiftness. Johnny screwed up his courage to ask him the news, but Mr. Battle, suddenly conscious, thrust the paper in his pocket, gave Johnny the merest nod and hurried by.

Evening was falling, supper was ready, yet the look in Mr. Battle's face had taken away what little appetite survived the talk with Captain Flood. Something was afoot. Something was astir, he could not tell what. While he still puzzled the question he turned back toward the waterfront, hurried up the little hill and knocked softly on Captain Tennant's door. As he waited, his mind, which had cleared somewhat while he walked, flew into fragments. What a fool he was, he was saying one moment; what warning could he give Captain Tennant? He could only say that he had seen Teague Battle go by with a queer look on his face. The Captain would laugh him out of the house. Teague Battle had probably won a case at court—merely that. What would happen to him, he was saying the next moment, if Teague Battle saw him on Captain Tennant's porch? If the war was really starting, he might be hung as a spy or as a traitor, hung for having tried to give warning to the Collector of the Port. He withdrew behind the honeysuckle. Give warning? What kind of warning could he give?

Hoddin was peering at him through a side pane of the door—the face vanished. The door was unlocked. Inside, the house was dark except for two candles in the disordered hall. The shutters must all be bolted. He hadn't noticed from outside. He should have—a spy always noticed things like that.

"Good evening, Hoddin. Are Miss Eve and the Captain at home?"

"The Keptin is at 'ome, sir, but Miss Heve is gorn."

"What—on board the packet?"

"Yes, sir."

"I expect Miss Eve would be better off here until she sails."

"Ho, sir, I thought you'd noticed. The packet 'as left her dock and dropped anchor in the sound."

Notice. By Zooks, he never noticed anything! He was no use at all. Here came the captain, and what in the nation should he say?

"Ah, there, young Fraser," said the captain in a tone alert and full of gusto.

"Why, Captain, seh," he stammered, "I saw Mr. Teague Battle with a curious look on his face and I heard rumors about a big fight around Boston, and I just thought maybe I'd better come here and tell you about it."

The captain grasped his hand. "Good of you, Fraser, and quite right, too,

egad. As a matter of fact, the King still has a few friends here and I learned
of the affair quite as soon as our friend Battle. It seems our troops attacked
the rebels on a hill called Bunker, or something of that sort. The triumph of
the Provincials springs from the fact that it was not till the third British
charge that they ran away. At all events the skirmish has so inflamed the
martial ardor of your fellow countrymen here that they talk of attacking me
and Hoddin."

"By Zooks, seh! They wouldn't do that, would they?"

"I can't say, I'm sure." The captain replied composedly. "Curious chaps,
Americans! Wild Indian sort of johnnies. Of course, I sent Eve aboard and
ordered the packet to drop down stream out of rifle shot."

"But what about you, seh? It's near about dark now. I could get a boat
and row you out to the packet."

"Good of you," the captain turned very red. "But I shouldn't quite care to
quit my post in that fashion."

"Well, seh, I'd certainly like to do anything I could."

"I'm immensely obliged, my dear fellow, immensely. But you had best
keep quite clear of me for the present. If you are seen about here and it
were supposed you were trying to assist me, one can't say what might not
happen." He waved a baffled hand. "By Jove, sir, I've lived all over the
world and I must say I've never seen an odder lot than these people of
yours. However," he turned a furious glance at a shuttered window as if he
would survey the town, "before the Crown forces get done with them
they'll be far less odd, never fear! And now, my boy," he held out his hand,
"really you must not stay. Good night and God bless you! Hoddin, show the
gentleman out."

Amid the darkness and the litter of bags and boxes in the hall, Johnny
thought he noticed a brilliant scarlet coat which he had never seen the
captain wear. He did not pause, however. Hoddin was waiting punctiliously
to perform his part in the ceremony.

That night Johnny saw from the rectory windows a flame against the sky.
He turned numb with fright and anger. The scoundrels were setting fire to
Captain Tennant's home—it could be nothing else. Without hat or coat he

ran down the street. At its end, between Hornblower's and the docks, a bonfire blazed in the middle of the road, figures weird and wild danced round it: "Bunker Hill!" they shouted. "Huzza! Huzza!" They crouched on all fours, drank from the bungs of rum kegs and shouted again. They tore off palings and threw them on the blaze. Militiamen tossed cockaded hats aloft, fired their rifles in air, drilled each other with drunken mock solemnity, snored, indifferent, beneath the trees. A twist of the firelight showed Teague Battle withdrawn between two houses. Whatever Mr. Battle might say or do, thought Johnny, he himself must hold back no longer. He slipped away among the shadowy trees and houses and came up to Mr. Battle's side.

The fire-lit face held neither its accustomed iron resolution nor cool salty humor. It was deeply graven with lines of sadness.

"Hello, son," he nodded slowly. "I reckon you've come to see the bonfire."

"I saw the light from the rectory," Johnny replied evasively.

"They've had a battle near Boston." Mr. Battle smiled without mirth. "And I suppose this is the way we're bound to act. But when the shouting's done, that's when the work begins."

He gazed at Johnny intently. "And that's when the Province will find out the men that believe in her. I hope you'll be among them."

A strip of palings hurled on the fire crashed and crackled up in flame.

"Our militia," said Mr. Battle, "have lost near half their officers who would not join our cause. That's why they're wilder tonight than common."

"I hope, seh, they don't intend harm to Captain Tennant."

Teague Battle eyed him. "I declare, I believe you're half a Troy." He smiled at Johnny's mounting color and laid an arm on his shoulder. "But never mind, son, it's no crime to stick by your friends." He patted him humorously. "Especially when there's a lady in the case. Don't you fret, though," he went on, "I've just come from the captain. He wouldn't leave tonight like I advised so I gave him till noon tomorrow, as that seemed to please him better, though I certainly wish he'd clear out now before the crowd gets rough. I declare," he added, "I can't make these ignorant British out. He's got to leave and he knows it and if he left tonight, it would be

better for him and make things a heap easier for me." He sighed. "But it
ain't any use in the world to talk about British sense. If they had any, we
wouldn't have come to this——" He pointed to the bonfire.

"I reckon, seh," said Johnny guardedly, "the Captain thought it would
look like he was running away."

"God above!" said Mr. Battle, "of course it'll look like he's running away.
But to run away is just exactly what he has got to do. If he stays, it won't
help his side. He'll be taken prisoner and we can use him for exchange.
Well, then, the sensible thing and the best thing for the interest of his
Majesty, the King of Great Britain and Ireland, an' so forth, is fo' Captain
Tennant to run away. And the captain admits it. So when we had got that
far in our chat I naturally thought everything was settled. When a man
decides he must clear out he generally clears out the best way he can. And I
ordered him a boat and a guard. But no, sir, the captain is determined to
run away in some special tomfool English manner."

Mr. Battle eyed him with exasperation.

"If that old pouter pigeon had any wits, I could do something with him,
and if he were scared, I could do something with him, but when you've got
a nit-wit that's scared of nothing in the world," he looked at Johnny judicially, "well, then, my bright young Tory, what have you got, tell me that?"
He walked away. "Hyer, you!" Johnny heard him call, "stave in this keg.
These men have had enough."

"Who are you to give orders?" said a surly voice.

"That's a fair question," said Mr. Battle quietly. "I'm placed in charge of
this district by the Continental Congress."

"I'll fight the British," said the militiaman thickly, "but I'll take no orders
from that what-do-you-call-it!"

Mr. Battle laughed. "Yes, and you'll beat the British, too, I reckon, but if
you won't take orders, you'll have to beat me first." He stood face to face
with the big country boy, quite good natured, but watchful. The boy hesitated, made an awkward salute, and slunk away.

## CHAPTER XXIV

BY ELEVEN o'clock the next morning all of Edenton and many people from the country round were gathered in front of Captain Tennant's house or along the street which led down to the dock. They buzzed and murmured, moved restlessly about, joked the militia boys who, grinning self-consciously, leaned on their muskets, with no more than cockade and powder horn to mark them from civilians. Down by the docks another knot of people showed where the jolly-boat from the packet waited to receive the captain. There Teague Battle, towering above the crowd, glanced now and again up to the captain's house and looked at his watch.

"The Englishman better shake a leg," a man said. "Mr. Battle only gave him till noon."

"Why he give him till anything beats me," another answered. "We've got him—why don't we keep him?"

"It wouldn't do," a third broke in. "I'm no English lover myself, but there's plenty among us that is and it won't do to provoke 'em."

"Maybe you're no Tory," said the first suspiciously, "but you're mighty tender of the English."

"Aye, he is that!" a woman cried. "The dirty butchers that killed our boys in Massachusetts Bay and would kill them here if they but had the means!"

The man attacked shifted uneasily. "I'd fight 'em if they came to North Carolina, but let the New Englanders take care of theirselves."

Captain Flood thrust into the group. "New Englanders is mean, sir, and their country is the desert of God's deserted work, but bung me if I wouldn't go back there again for a crack at one of these hyer stuck-up, bull-dosin' Redcoats!"

The others murmured applause. An old farmer eagerly elbowed his way into the circle. "And so would I!" he cried in a shaking voice. "They flogged my boy in the Indian wars until he died," he raised an impotently quivering stick, "the Bloody Backs!"

The crowd fell silent, stared at the trembling old farmer. "The Bloody Backs—the Bloody Backs!" He stopped; but still he trembled.

Now it was ten minutes to the hour, all eyes were on the captain's door. It swung open with deliberation. There was a dull glow of color in the depths of the hall, then a flash of brilliant scarlet as Captain Tennant stepped into the light of the noonday sun. Sturdy, composed, unhurried, he stood on the top step in the full uniform of an officer of the line. His pipe-clayed cross-belts, his high, white gaiters gleamed; his buttons, his buckles, his varnished shoes twinkled in the light; his cocked hat was clapped confidently on his immaculately powdered wig; he gripped his malacca stick decisively. Behind him Hoddin, uniformed as well, locked the door, dropped the big key in his cartouche box. Looking straight ahead, Captain Tennant marched smartly down the steps—one, two, three, four. Now he was on the street, marching toward the crowd, Hoddin, stiff and sturdy, three paces in his rear. One—two—three—four—their shining boots struck the ground together, their shining gaitered legs moved like scissors, the captain's sword on its hook, the fringes of his epaulets, the cartouche box by Hoddin's side, swung smartly in time.

Astonished, half admiring, the crowd fell away. The two solitary figures, brilliant, perfect, indifferent, passed them by. But as they reached the old farmer, he raised again his quivering stick—"The Bloody Backs!" he cried.

With the cracked note of despairing hate, the charm of their splendor broke. "The Bloody Backs, the Bloody Backs!" The murmur ran beside them, gathered force until, as the two bright figures reached the landing-stage, it seemed to close above them, envelop them in a steady malignant roar.

Johnny had run down the hill behind the people's straining shoulders and now strove to fight his way to the landing-stage. Whatever happened he would say good-bye to the captain like a man; let them do what they would—the cowards, to jeer the captain—eight hundred against one! He shoved and pushed. Now he was in the center and almost clear. The captain had halted by the jolly-boat and faced the crowd. He opened his mouth as if to speak. They howled the louder—an oyster shell skimmed through the air. A hulking 'prentice lad near Johnny picked a dead herring from the sand and threw it. It struck against the captain's scarlet breast. The crowd burst into a triumphant guffaw.

Doubling his fists, Johnny ran for the 'prentice—the dirty low-lived coward! He drew back to smash the coarse face. A slim, strong hand seized his wrist, pulled him deftly into the crowd, held him there.

"Not so fast, my young friend," said Wylie Jones' voice. "Let us pause and reflect."

"Let me go!" he cried, wrenching his arms.

"Never!" said Mr. Jones with a light laugh. "I do you a service."

Oblivious of this piece of by-play, the crowd had closed round them again. The 'prentice lad was gone. Through the mist of angry tears Johnny saw Captain Tennant draw a cambric handkerchief from his sleeve, brush his coat meticulously. Replacing the handkerchief, he turned to Mr. Battle, made him a salute, perfectly correct, perfectly distant and formal, pointed Hoddin into the jolly-boat and descended after him. The boat pushed off with alacrity, rowed hurriedly for the channel. A few stray rocks and oyster shells kicked spurts of water around her. Captain Tennant, sitting rigid in the stern, did not turn his head.

CAPTAIN TENNANT

*Sturdy, composed, unhurried, he stood on the top step in the full uniform of an officer of the line. Behind him Hoddin, uniformed as well, locked the door*

The crowd broke up about Johnny; Wylie Jones released him. He whirled about, furious.

"What do you mean, seh, by interfering with my business?"

"You would not ask that," said Mr. Jones with unexpected seriousness, "if you knew as much as I."

"I thought you were a gentleman."

"A purely relative term," said Mr. Jones with the suspicion of a smile.

"And hyer you stand and see a gentleman and a friend of yours mobbed, and grab me when I try to help him."

"Perhaps I am more attached to your interest than to his—you must consider that."

"I don't consider anything but what I told you."

"My boy, will you talk like a man, or will you play the peevish child?"

For a moment Johnny looked away, unappeased, followed the jolly-boat as she drew alongside the packet.

"Well, what is it?" he muttered.

"It is this," said Mr. Jones. "Affairs are graver than you imagine. The colonies are now engaged in no mere tax riot—we, some of us, have taken steps from which there is no turning back. We are about to put all to the touch. The struggle will be desperate, the feeling bitter, and action such as you just now intended might sow the seeds of ruin for yourself and your family."

"I don't care what they do to me. I'll never stand by and see a gentleman mobbed, and I never thought you would neither."

Mr. Jones smiled, though he flushed as well. "I confess I do not enjoy the experience. Lesser affairs, however, must give place to greater. However ideal the principles of a political movement, in practice the mob must be allowed self-expression. I agree with you that the recent incident was deplorable, but we cannot allow a dead herring to obstruct the independence of these colonies." He looked at Johnny with the complacence which accompanied his epigrams.

Johnny's eyes opened wide. "What!" he said. "Independence?"

The look of complacence vanished. "You are too literal, my friend. The

figure of speech is the epigrammatist's chief medium. I referred, of course, to
independence within our constitutional sphere. Teague, my boy!" he cried.
"A word with you!" he hurried after Mr. Battle toward the tavern.

Perching his iron spectacles on his nose, Dr. Clapton read the letter
which Squire Fraser had written Johnny. He tapped the pages reflectively
with the tip of his quilled pen.

"The sense of these instructions, my son," he said, "is admirable—
although, perhaps, I could have wished that your respected father attrib-
uted the probability of peace more to his Gracious Majesty's attachment to
the interest of his subjects, and less to those subjects' lack of means to
conduct a war. I, too, am confident of peace, but I rest my belief on arguments more creditable to human nature, and therefore," he smiled serenely,
"more convincing. Indeed, the absence of military engines of destruction
has by no means always in history proved an obstacle to conflict. Instances
where this has proven true are numerous, notably the siege of Carthage by
Matho. Likewise, at Syracuse——" Dr. Clapton's eye wandered, fell on the
letter, and slowly came to bear again on Johnny's face. "But now, as to the
problem at hand: in the serious prospect of unrest, you should not, I think,
delay here longer. The question then arises: How serious such prospect may
be. Little accustomed to practical affairs, I confess I incline to apply for an
answer to those who are. Would it not be well to put the case to Mr. Jones,
say—or to Mr. Battle?"

"I don't want to ask them, seh," said Johnny. "Mr. Jones interfered with
my business this morning, and Mr. Battle is in all kinds of secret plots with
Mr. Jones and other people. He's at the back of all this trouble"—he paused
unhappily—"I can't bear the idea of fighting and mobbing and robbing and
all such. I don't want to be under obligation to men like that."

"Perhaps, then," said Dr. Clapton kindly, "you will leave the matter for
the moment in my hands."

He rose and paced the floor, first slowly then faster, till his quick little
steps were moving almost at a trot. He halted, looked out the window to the

street where people still hummed, gathered, argued, where chance militia-men lounged by, muskets trailing, hats askew.

"My trust is in God," he murmured, "and under God's providence, in his Majesty, the King. With faith and patience we shall see all set to rights." His face cleared, grew faintly rosy, soft, serene. "See those people," he said. "Where can you find hate or cruelty in their faces? Some may be foolish, some easily led, but you may search far, my boy, before you find the marks of wickedness."

Johnny went to Dr. Clapton's side, almost prepared to see with him an unguessed merit in the low scoundrels. As he looked out the window, how-ever, they seemed no different from the fierce mob who had dogged Captain Tennant to the dock, who had let him go uninjured only because he was cool and they were not quite ready. Their faces were calm now, but that was only because they had things their own way. Let them be crossed— they would bare their teeth and bay like wolves again. Johnny felt worn, world-wise as he stood there beside the poor, innocent Dr. Clapton and saw people as they were. The Doctor, however, beamed and even pointed. "Among the children of God," he said, "brother cannot fight brother."

Taking his plain hat and long blue cloak, he left the house. Still at the window, Johnny watched him trotting down the street, sprinkling greetings, kind and gently confident, along the way. The people responded, but some seemed singularly awkward, ill at ease, and once Johnny caught a sour grimace and a stabbing thumb jerked at Dr. Clapton's back.

By evening all was settled. Most of the Province, Dr. Clapton had learned, was in a turmoil. There had been no violence as yet, but Mr. Battle's secret dispatches told him that the Royal Governor at Cape Fear was ready at any moment to flee for his life on board an English frigate. Mr. Battle did not look for violence in the Edenton district until the British attacked. Tories, however, were numerous, and if they attempted action, they would be put down. And when British troops came, as they doubtless would, they were prepared to fight them to the last.

"It pains me mightily, Doctor, to tell you this," Mr. Battle had said, "for I declare, sir, I have only respect and affection for your cloth and for your private character, but we who lead this movement are wholly convinced of the justice of our cause—and," he added dryly, "we are too conscious of our position to propose to be the prime movers of an *unsuccessful* rising against British authority."

So there was nothing more then to be done except what the Doctor, agitated and pitiably distressed, had undertaken. He had seen Wylie Jones, whose barge was to carry him up the river on the morrow, and easily exacted an amused promise to carry Johnny Fraser with him.

"I think, my boy," said Dr. Clapton as they sat in the candlelit study after supper, "that this arrangement, whatever your private sentiments, most exactly carries out the wishes of your father. As to my own wishes," he paused and wiped his spectacles, "I hardly care to mention them, for they seem to grow more fantastical each moment. My wishes," he went on, "had been that you might finish your studies undisturbed, that with your scholarship, your gentle birth and training and your mind, so much more adept than my own in practical affairs, you might become one of those rare and valuable persons who direct the actual course of public policy and at the same time lead men's thoughts." He nodded his little head at Johnny as though encouraging the infant Hercules to great deeds.

"I know, seh," said Johnny. "I don't know whether I'd ever have amounted to much," he added, not quite sincerely, "and I know I never would have cut any kind of figure in Latin, but I surely did aim to amount to something. I surely did."

"Of course you did, my boy, and till this afternoon— Till this afternoon I still hoped that nothing more than an interruption promised in the achievement of this prospect. Now I feel grave uncertainty."

He stared into the cold fireplace as though he sought the warmth of happier days.

"I—I'm mighty sorry, seh," said Johnny, seeking helplessly for a word that would bring comfort. "I'll try to keep on with my studies by myself."

Dr. Clapton roused himself and smiled.

"Continue with your Virgil and your Plutarch. If you wish it, I shall try to help by letter."

"Yes, seh. Thank you."

"As for me," Dr. Clapton went on in a low voice, "I shall remain in my parish while there is a soul who desires my ministrations." He drew his silk handkerchief across his eyes. "It seems sometimes as though the whole impending future could be but an hallucination which will vanish at the touch of loving kindness. The touch of loving kindness," he murmured. " 'Tis all we need—so little and yet so much." He laid down his spectacles, looked at Johnny with delicate radiance. "And you shall see, my dear son; the King will speak a word to his children here."

# CHAPTER XXV

For a night and a day Johnny had sat, huddled and wretched, in the cockpit of Wylie Jones' barge. She was double manned; every hour one black crew relieved the other at the oars. Their songs grew faint and weary as they sweated at the thwarts. Beside Johnny, Mr. Wylie Jones and Mr. Battle talked enigmatically together through the night, dozed toward morning, roused themselves, read despatches, wrote letters, silently showed papers to each other with a meaning glance.

More than ever darkly foreboding, the long ranks of cypress floated by. It was not from them, however, that Johnny drew his heaviness of heart, it was rather from a picture in his mind, a picture ever receding yet ever clear, of Doctor Clapton's little blue-cloaked figure on the dock, waving farewell —waving—waving—and smiling with desperate gallantry. The boat could row, days could go on forever, but the blue-cloaked figure would never wholly fall behind.

As the big clearings and great houses came in sight Johnny felt a ray of cheer. They were nearing Halifax, whose frigid elegance was warmed for him by thoughts of the day when, coming up from Edenton, a homesick little boy, he had met his mother there. She would not come to meet him now, in these troubled times, but Wylie Jones' place still remained an outpost of his home.

When with a last strong pull and a swelling chanty they glided up to Wylie Jones' private landing, Johnny leaped eagerly, almost happily ashore.

Surprisingly, the fields, the elms, the tall white house seemed just the same. What he had expected in this feudal domain of a leader of revolt he did not know. An army camped on the sloping lawns? Dead Tories swinging from limbs? Hardly that—he smiled. But it did seem odd—it seemed uncanny, almost menacing, to drive up the avenue to the seat of evil designs, of plotted violence, and find only careless, lazy summer peace. Burgwyn was there on the steps to meet them, composed, majestic as before. Young Mose, full-grown, pert and polished, took Johnny's bag, laid out his clothes in the room "Parnassus." But when, changed to fresh linen and his broadcloth suit, Johnny descended for supper, menace again had reared its head. Wylie Jones and Mr. Battle, in the drawing room, talked deeply with a short dark man, glanced up, fell silent as Johnny came through the wide door.

"You know this gentleman?" said Wylie Jones. "No, hardly. Mr. Paul—my friend, Mr. Johnny Fraser, of Little River, sir."

Mr. Paul, in a fine brown coat, too long and fitting rather ill, stood up and bowed with somewhat laborious precision.

"Honored, sir," he remarked brusquely, and sat down again.

The faint burr of his speech held echoes, echoes perhaps of Squire Fraser's Highland tongue. It must be merely that; Johnny looked more closely at Mr. Paul. But the face also, saturnine, grim, aggressive, was reminiscent. Yet the man was a stranger. In the narrow society of the province Johnny had never so much as heard his name.

"Now as to fighting, gentlemen," said Mr. Paul, turning to the other two.

It's on the sea they'll trouble ye. Look here." Unceremoniously, he dumped small piles of snuff at intervals on an embroidered table cover. "That's Boston," he said—"Philadelphia—Charleston—Antigua—"

"One moment, I beg," murmured Wylie Jones, glancing toward Johnny, "our young friend here in not of unmixed sentiments."

"What!" said Teague Battle. "A back-country boy and won't stick by his folks!"

"I don't know what I am." Johnny said as stoutly as he could manage. "My father is a Highland man."

Mr. Paul flashed him a look, brown-eyed, quick, searching, and, coming from such a face, incredibly warm and luminous. The glance just touched Johnny and was gone. Mr. Paul sat silent and gnarled as before.

"And his mother," Wylie Jones remarked, "is a Moore, of Wilmington. Come, Teague, be reasonable. You see the young man's difficulty."

"I see his difficulty, seh," Teague answered. He turned to Johnny not unkindly, but with rugged bluntness. "It's a difficulty, though, my son, that I advise you not to be too long in solving. We need every man," he went on earnestly, "but, Johnny boy, I hope you'll think I'm a friend of yours when I say I'd rather see you come out for the wrong side than to squirm and straddle betwixt the two."

"That's all very well, Teague, and has a gallant ring, but if Johnny turned Tory what price would you give for his father's place?"

"They won't touch it, Wylie," said Mr. Battle, "they sha'n't touch it. I'm for fighting the Tories fair—not robbing them."

"And so we should, Teague, were all of us of an heroic mould. We are not all, however, I fear, disciples of Cincinnatus, as are you."

"Well, enough of us are so to make the others follow. You must believe that, Wylie. If I didn't believe that," he cried, "I'd never have raised a finger in this cause!"

Wylie Jones shot him a look of affectionate amusement, seemed about to speak, checked himself, turned preternaturally grave.

"Well said, Teague!" He placed a hand a trifle theatrically on Mr. Battle's shoulder. "Ten men like you, my friend, and we shall do it!"

Mr. Paul seemed moved to emulation by this pantomime. He sprang to his feet, held out a hand each to Mr. Jones and Mr. Battle.

"And as for me," he said, "a cause whose principles are so scared shall ever command my devotion and my services."

He withdrew his hands, short, square and calloused, clenched them tightly, thrust them in his pockets.

"Now i' the matter o' ships——You must just put your mind on ships——" he threw a hard look at Johnny. "We'll do no harm to talk o' ships before this young man, whatever side he's on. And if I'm to leave tomorrow, we must use our time. We'll need plenty o' ships and that means officers and seamen and gunners."

"Already, my dear sir," Wylie Jones replied, "every province is commissioning privateers in numbers."

At this moment Burgwyn announced supper from the doorway. His words, however, were unheard, for Mr. Paul, his face twisted with unutterable scorn, was speaking bitterly.

"Privateers! Skulking buzzards! All for prize money and a whole skin!"

The others slowly threaded their way among the gilded chairs toward the dining-room. Mr. Paul, however, stumping straight ahead, speaking with low, tight-lipped emphasis, pushed the chairs from his path with a thrust of his foot.

"Ye'll gain nothing by privateers, do ye mind, and ye'll lose much. The object of a war is not to annoy the enemy, but to annihilate him. Your lousy privateers will capture a few stray merchantmen, pocket the booty, and leave ye to fight the men of war which their raids have brought into these waters." He pushed the last chair vehemently aside, strode on through the hall and library, leaving the others to follow.

"And another thing, hark'ee! When ye then go to recruit your navy, ye'll find nobody to enlist—and why? Because your seamen are a'ready all a privateerin' where the pay is big and the danger sma'."

He sat down at the table and thumped it. "My sword is at the call o' liberty and human rights and a' that, but, friends, I'll tell ye plain I'm no' the fool to serve a set o' ninnies that think to beat England wi' privateers!"

"Well, seh," Mr. Battle interposed, "that sounds fair enough. As you know, Mr. Hewes is already with the Congress in Philadelphia, and our letters which you bear will assure you access to those in charge of naval affairs."

Mr. Paul appeared somewhat appeased, but not wholly so.

"Very kind of ye, gentlemen, it is. But if it's access tae ninnies ye're giving me, ye'd best not hope for too much."

"I would not restrict the freedom of any man's opinions," remarked Wylie Jones coldly, "but may I suggest, sir, that you do not so qualify the honorable members of the Congress until you have made their acquaintance."

Mr. Paul's tough, grim face broke into an engaging smile. "I'm o'er hasty, sir," he said. "Dinna take it amiss." He still smiled, but his eye was bright and fiery—"And we must have ships!"

"Well spoken, sir," said Mr. Jones. "We are at one. I will add to my letter whatever I think can aid you. You will find your obstacles, however, not in the ignorance of the Congress at large but in the selfish arrogance of the New England members. Their leaders are as greedy of power in the Congress as their followers are of profit in the war. They will be loath to listen to the proposals of a man who does not spring from their sacred, if sterile, soil. They hold the men from the South in pious contempt. Little better, then, can be hoped for by a man——"

"By a man," broke in Mr. Paul, "from the sea as well as of it."

"Bravo! Well put!" said Mr. Jones. "A glass with you, sir!"

"Well, gentlemen, while you're about to drink," said Mr. Battle, "hyer's a toast you can't complain of," he reached forward his big hand, clinked glasses with each of them, "Ships and Officers!"

Mr. Paul's face glowed again. "No heel-taps," he said and threw the glassful down his throat.

Johnny studied the three faces drawn close together in the candle light. Teague Battle's, kindly, negligent, yet strong and daring, was the face of a gentleman; and the fine drawn lines of Wylie Jones' face were the lines of a very elegant gentleman indeed. But as for the blue-jawed hard little man who sat between—if he were a gentleman, it was of a sort that Johnny had never seen before.

In their plans, vast, impudent, decisive—in the eager agreement and elation of the three, each so different from the others—the doom which had been slowly creeping on him seemed to Johnny to take a swift stride toward reality. "Ships . . . gunners . . . seamen"—the words were ominous. He heard the creak of tackle, saw the lofty canvas tremble. He saw the flash and smoke-cloud of the broadside and heard the rumble of the guns. He saw the beaten hulk, charred black from stem to stern, except for a thin red trickle down her side. He reached a cold hand for his glass of wine. What ailed him? Other men were not like this. Others planned fiercely, keenly, for the fight, or, at the worst, stumped stolidly along their ways, humped an imperturbable shoulder against impending fate. He alone was frightened, fluttered by events—he of all people—he, who had spent his youth in dreams of high adventure, had woven fire-lit pictures of grim mountain enterprise, of charging legions, now cowered before the very language of his dreams. Destined to be a leader of the Province, puffed up with pride and self-conceit in the soft years of peace, here at the proof he shrank even from following where others led. He had never been aught but a secret craven, an empty egoist, after all. He set down his glass—the wine was bitter. Sitting with eyes downcast, he waited till at length he felt it warm him, give him heart. "Ships . . . gunners . . . seamen"—they were speaking again. These men designed the very things his father wrote could not be done. His father, the infallible, was not likely to be wrong. These three, then, and others like them, must have lost their senses. He could not leave the Grove too quickly; he could not too quickly gain the safety of his home, his mother's slender arms, his father's firm intelligence.

"I expect, Mr. Jones, seh," he said, "that my folks will send for me tomorrow. I'm afeared I impose on your hospitality."

"Oh, my dear fellow," Mr. Jones replied in some concern. "Please do not say that. It is I who should apologise. We make you ill at ease with our talk here—something, I vow, I never thought to do to a gentleman in my home. But Mr. Paul leaves tomorrow and we are under necessity to seize the moments that remain."

"I know, seh," said Johnny wretchedly. "I reckon it can't be helped."

"There is much now that can't be helped," said Mr. Jones gravely, "and I only hope that on both sides, men, whatever their convictions, will bear themselves toward each other as gentlemen should." He bowed quite seriously to Johnny. "And, as, may I add, sir, do you."

"I don't know," said Johnny, "I was near about ready to fight you, seh, when that scoundrel threw a fish at Captain Tennant."

Wylie Jones smiled with vast entertainment at Johnny's earnest face. "There will always be distinctions," he said, "between young gentlemen and older gentlemen, but each, let us hope, have merits of their own. Now as to your plans. Your father has sent no word, but I know your anxiety and would therefore propose to lend you a horse tomorrow for the journey. You can send him back at your convenience."

"Thank you, seh, but I couldn't do that. I don't know how I'd get him back."

"In that case," replied Mr. Jones, "it will give me pleasure to feel that the horse is in the hands of one whom I still hope I can call a friend, and who, I know, is well able both to care for horses and to ride them."

"I don't know, seh——"

"Take the horse, boy," Teague Battle broke in. "We'll soon have expresses riding in that part of the country that can bring him back."

"Well, then," said Johnny, "I expect I'd better do that, thank you, seh."

Soon after supper Johnny went to bed. He lay restless for an hour beneath the lace canopy. Through the night he dozed uneasily and woke again to hear the steady murmur of the three men's voices in the library below. A deep sleep overtook him just before dawn.

The sun was high before he roused himself and dressed. Descending the broad stairs, he saw silhouetted in the open door the figures of Mr. Paul and Wylie Jones.

"And now, farewell," Mr. Jones was saying. He held out a long, slim purse, "and accept this, I beg."

"I'll take no money," the other answered roughly, then paused. "Ye've but one thing, sir, that ye can give me." He spoke softly.

"And what is that, pray?"

"Your name."

"Good Gad, sir, you surprise me!"

"In a' my life, ye're the first to treat me like a gentleman. Give me your name, sir. I'll not shame it."

Mr. Jones withdrew the purse and took the stranger's hand.

"I am complimented, sir—overcome. As to the name, take it, my friend, and welcome. It is not without honor in this country; but I believe that you will confer far more honor on it than it can possibly confer on you." He put his other hand on the stranger's. "So good-bye, Mr. Jones!" He laughed to cover his embarrassment and turned away.

Johnny, who had stopped uncertainly on the landing, now came down the stairs.

"Oh, there you are, Johnny! You slept late. Your horse is ready when you like—and Mr. Paul is leaving now."

Johnny looked through the door at the retreating figure. In the light of day he saw that the ill-fitting brown coat was a former coat of Wylie Jones' . . . Here was mystery enough. Wylie Jones was not in the custom of entertaining men who wore cast-off clothes. He looked again, more closely. Beneath the coat he saw, in a flash of recollection, the bristling terrier back of the dockside loafer he had seen at Edenton.

## CHAPTER XXVI

THE BORROWED horse was a horse to make time on, there was no doubt of that. He trotted on by the hour as smooth and steady as a spinning wheel. It was still broad daylight when Johnny reached the forest of tall pines and came in sight of Blue's Crossing: Here, too, as at Wylie Jones', things were still the same. The slip-shod, casual hamlet was unchanged. The spectacled German chairmaker wove a rush bottom before his door; in the smithy, the hammer thumped on hot metal, rang on the anvil; two horses switched flies and nudged each other at the store.

"Vell, vell," the little German said, "you iss back home yet. Dot's good." He shook his head profoundly. "Bad times ist gekommen, no?"

The blacksmith came to his door. "Hi, brother, what's the news from down yonder? They chased out the Collector? Good. The dirty——"

"Hold on!" said Johnny. "He's a friend of mine!"

"Why, dang me!" said the smith, "if you ain't come back here full o' notions!"

234

Johnny gathered his reins and rode on.

Ahead of him a horse was trotting. Another countryman to look down on his clothes, his manner, his thoughts! Johnny pulled up; he wished to meet no one else till he got home.

It was all very well for his father and Dr. Clapton to talk about his birth and schooling fitting him to be a leader of the Province. Maybe birth and schooling could do that in his father's time. The fact was, however, that the only thought these people gave his birth was to wonder, now and then, if he would ever be half as good a man as the old Squire. And as for schooling— he had felt their good-natured contempt the first time he had come back from Edenton; they looked on learning as something fantastic, decadent, emasculating. Let a man be able to fight, ride, speak the truth, he needed no more to fit him for all eventualities of life. Anything more, in fact, could only weaken him. Johnny had felt their unspoken comment on him long ago, felt it with chagrin and surprise, but with complaisance unshaken. The loss was the back-country's, not his. But now he was not in shape to withstand it altogether; he had already had a little too much isolation. Let the figure on the road jog out of sight. If he drew up to it, the chances were that he would get only another blunt greeting, another appraising glance like the blacksmith's.

As he watched it, however, a light wind blew out the dark red folds of a woman's cloak. Ah, that was different. It could not be his mother. Perhaps one of the blacksmith's girls. They were over-bold, but he was now mature and competent. He hurried on.

Around a turn through the forest the Fearnaught colt, slender and fawn-like, stood pastern-deep in a ford, nuzzled the dark water delicately. Sally Merrillee, her cloak thrown back, stretched her arm forward to give him rein. His own horse made no sound on the soft road. He was able to watch her and to hear her sing in a low monotone, admonishing the colt by beating time on his shoulder.

"Drink, young colt, and stop yo' foolin'!
Recollect yo' raisin' an' yo' schoolin'!"

He did not wish to speak, and yet he must. If she turned and saw him watching her he would feel foolish.

"Hello, Sally," he said.

She looked up, surprised and angry.

"You Johnny! What's the idea to sneak up that way—you might have scared this horse."

It was too much—everybody was down on him.

"I didn't sneak up," he answered lifelessly. "I just came along."

She looked at him closely.

"I know, I know. I'm glad to see you. How you been?" Her face took on some concern. "You appear kind of peaked."

"I expect I do. I've been workin' hard. I've been studyin' hard and they's been big doin's down on the coast. I reckon you've heard."

"Yes," she said, "I bet it was fun."

"More fun to hear tell about than to be in, I expect."

She raised the horse's head from the water. Johnny walked his horse beside hers down the road. Again Sally looked at him.

"I don't believe they know how to feed a person right, down yonder. It don't look like you had yo' hea'th the way you ought to."

Johnny's heart warmed; he grinned good-naturedly.

"They fed me fine."

She rode on in silence, pulled an oak branch, swung it at the flies.

"Well, then," she said, "something on yo' mind?"

To this he did not answer. A half-mile more and he would be at home.

"I don't aim to meddle with yo' affairs," she said with an effort, "but I declare I hate to see anyone so peaked."

He felt the glow of her shy, sturdy friendliness.

"I'm all right, Sally." He added, "Thank you."

"Don't thank me," she said, "for common manners."

Half hidden by the broad bright sycamore leaves, the log and plaster house came in sight. A film of smoke idled through the warm evening air. Immemorial and stoutly built, it seemed a strong defense which waited through good fortune and ill, ready to give him comfort, refuge.

"Won't you step in?" he said to Sally after the manner of the country.

"I must be getting home."

'I'd better go along with you, I expect."

"I'm obliged to you, but yo' folks is waitin' fo' you."

The ceremonial requirements were fulfilled. "Good night, Sally!" He raised his hat. "I'm glad I saw you."

"Good night, Johnny! Come over and visit."

Johnny watched her trot away. Her cloak was linsey woolsey, her dress was callimanco, but she surely sat a horse to beat anything in Edenton. If Sir Nat could see her he'd have to change some of his notions about the back country.

Johnny turned down the lane. Another moment and he was sliding from his horse amid the murmur of his father, Scipio, and Sofa, and the delighted clapping of his mother's hands.

"I have to reach up now," she laughed, releasing him.

"Ye got my letter, then," his father said. "I'm well pleased that ye're come."

"Whoa, now, you ho'se!" said Scipio, timidly reaching for the reins. "Don' you cock yo' eye at me!"

His mother followed Johnny upstairs.

"You're home," she murmured, incredulous, "and I never want you to leave it again! Even your father," she laughed, "has been fretting this time. It almost did me good to see him! Let me help you." She brought out a fresh stock and his brush and comb from the saddle-bags. She flushed shyly. "You've a silly mother."

The supper table was hidden under mounds of veal-loaf, pickled pig's feet, jams, greens, and crowned with a huge stone jug of persimmon beer. Sofa revolved unceasingly in her orbit, bore in fresh plates of biscuit and spoon bread. Scenting a heavy surplus from this profligate magnificence, Scipio waited expectantly on a kitchen chair.

"Eat your fill, lad, and we will talk later," his father said. He himself munched steadily, his beard rising and falling with slow power, like a ground swell of the sea, his big fists guarding his plate like flanking strongholds.

"There's much tae be said," he continued, "but frae the Highlander and the Indian, not tae mention the old Greeks, I've learned tae ask no questions of a man until ye've fed him."

"Why should you bother him at all?" his mother said. "He's come safe home and we shall all be happy together. What more would you have?" She shook her head at her husband. "I never saw a man yet that would let well enough alone."

"If letting well enough alone is a virtue, my lass, ye should reserve your admiration for the ostrich."

They moved out on the porch. John Fraser, his kilt pulled back, his hands on his bare knees, leaned forward, stared into the dusk. On a low rocker beside Johnny, Mrs. Fraser slipped her hand in his. In the presence of the danger which Squire Fraser seemed to see gathering with the night, they drew close like children, as they had sometimes done before.

"Ye've had uneasy times, I've no doubt," his father said.

"Yes, seh. The crowd chased out Captain Tennant and near-about mobbed him."

"Did they now? I'd not heard that."

"It was only three days ago and I came away with Mr. Wylie Jones the next morning. Dr. Clapton thought it best, and I did, too."

"Ye did well. Political humors are like the fever: ye may check them at the very first, and it's a pity the government did not see fit tae do so. But if ye're too late for that ye must just let the disease run its course. In a few months these same randy-dandy lads that are breathing brimstone will be slinkin' away, rackin' their addled brains tae find out what on airth possessed them."

"Yes, seh. That's so, but some of 'em is makin' mighty big plans. Mr. Battle was at Wylie Jones' and there was another man named Paul—his talk was more or less like a Scotchman—and the three of them were laying schemes about ships and all to fight the English."

"Paul? I never heard of such a name in the Province. Do ye know him?"

"No, seh, but I saw him hangin' around the dock when I was in Edenton."

"What was his ship, then?"

"He wouldn't say, and I reckon he didn't have any."

His father's deep chuckle shook the dusk. "That's a fine tale tae scare the

King o' England. Cock-fightin' Wylie Jones and Teague Battle, a back-country lawyer, and an unknown sea-vagabond named Paul,—who if he be a Scot can be naught but a Lawland Scot—a mere chance sailor out of employ,—these three worthies design tae destroy the British Navy!" He laughed aloud. "*Quos Deus vult perdere*—eh, lad?"

"I don't know what your Latin means," said Mrs. Fraser, "but Wylie Jones has a heap of sense."

"Ye're still blind tae his faults, I see, Caroline—and all because the young popinjay asked ye for a minuet four years since. As for the Latin, Johnny, tell your mother what it means."

"It means," said Johnny proudly, "that those whom the God would destroy he first drives mad."

His mother withdrew her hand. "Oh, and does it! Well, I think it mightily ill-natured of you to say such a thing about a pleasant young man who has entertained you and lent you a horse."

"But, Mother, I didn't say it. I just told you what Father said."

"Well, when your father says anything like that I don't care to be told."

"But, Mother," he pleaded, "you asked."

"Hoots toots, lad!" broke in his father. "Ye might as well save your breath. She'll hear no ill of that young whipper-snapper since the minuet, and we must just make up our minds tae it."

Johnny giggled. His father in admitting him to a share in teasing his mother had exalted him to maturity and fellowship.

"You're horrid—both of you!" she cried. "You must be proud of me indeed if you think me so little charming that I must be grateful all my life to a man who dances with me."

"Noo, then, lass, dinna blame the lad. He only did as I tauld him; and beside," John Fraser added anxiously, "ye might just put him out o' conceit with his Latin, which would be no sma' thing tae answer for after a' the trouble we've been tae tae teach it him, not tae mention the expense!"

"Well, I hope I do put him out of conceit with it," she answered, unappeased, "if he's to use it against me."

"Why, Mother, I didn't aim to use it against you—I told you——"

"Be silent, boy!" his father broke in. "Caroline, ye should be ashamed to distress the lad; and as for what I said, are ye grown so witless, then, that ye cannot see that unless ye were the sort that can draw all kinds of men, wise and foolish alike, after ye when ye have the mind, I'd be the last man in the world tae make sport o' your admirers? It gives me sma' pleasure tae tell ye this, for well I ken it but ministers tae your vanity. But I will not have discord here among us the first evening the lad is home—nor any other evening, for the matter o' that." He slapped a hand on his bare knee. "And as for your vanity, 'tis something, I'm glad tae say, you'll be answerable for tae your Maker and not tae me!"

She laughed. "Your compliments, sir, are not like to turn my head, what with their reluctance and their reservations."

"The Frasers," he said, "were never ones for compliments, but what they say they mean!"

"And more, too, I always hope—or is that my vanity?"

"Hoots, lass, ye'll not be startin' tae wrangle again!"

She turned serious. "No, John, I reckon I'm silly. I should not have been so quick to take offense. Perhaps I am too anxious to have you and Johnny think well of me."

"It's an admirable fault," John Fraser answered imperturbably, "and one that need cause ye no uneasiness—eh, Johnny?"

"Why, John," she cried, "you're a courtier! I never thought a Fraser would be so ready with a pretty speech."

"Little ye ken the Frasers, then. They're no courtiers, but it's due tae good judgment and not tae slow wits." He lit his pipe composedly and smoked.

Johnny leaned back, relieved, contented. A July copper moon broke through the trees, banished darkness, touched the strong house and the enfolding leaves with a radiance, faint, delicate, yet warm. It fell on the hand-rived boards beneath his feet, on the twelve-inch logs above his head, on his father's square, undaunted face, on his mother, slim, tender, passionate and brave. Fireflies winked in the currant bushes; a tree-toad pitched his thin, high note; an owl slipped by on padded wings. He sat relaxed, breathing slow. Here, in field, in house, and in the two beside him, was abiding peace and strength. Here was refuge.

# CHAPTER XXVII

THE SUMMER passed quietly enough; the peace of the long, warm Carolina days enfolded Johnny Fraser, enfolded the fields, the forest, the hamlet, and seemed to enfold the people of the Province as well. Perhaps the fever of which his father spoke had reached its climax; perhaps men of North Carolina and the other provinces now rested passive in the languor of convalescence. Only one piece of news reached them through the soft, unending days and that was favorable; a petition, moderate, well-reasoned, fair, respectful, had been sent by the Continental Congress to the King. It seemed as though the moment for which Dr. Clapton confidently waited was now at hand. The King had heard the voice of his people. He had but to answer, to speak the word. Clouds would vanish.

Johnny spent the days on the farm. Riding the colt, with Grizzly Gray trotting sedately at his heels, he drove the cows to pasture. He laid off a piece of ground for clearing, astonishing the field-hands by his mathematical skill. He drove the ox team to the mill with sacks of corn; fished for perch in the mill-pond while the mill wheel grumbled, drove home at dusk with sacks of flour. In the evenings he kept up his reading of Plutarch's Lives. Freed from Dr. Clapton's microscopic eye, he read his Latin like a gentleman, taking it easy, skipping over the more difficult passages but getting the general sense quite well enough for a young man of parts. His father could not wholly conceal his delighted amazement at the sight of his son browsing through a classic with the casual easy glance he would bestow on a copy of the Cape Fear *Mercury*. How long this agreeable state of his father's mind would continue, Johnny did not dare to ask. He had, however, forebodings of the day when he would be called upon for an exact rendering of the passage he was reading.

Sometimes after supper he rode over to the Merrillees'. Joe had become a big-knuckled man, whose powerful frame had outgrown his fat and somewhat truculent face. While hardly cordial, he no longer sought quarrels, but rested after his long day's work on the place, his hands hanging down in what might or might not be a posture of sombre reflection. With Joe big enough to work, the Merrillee place had taken on some semblance of good order. Even Mrs. Merrillee, peering through the twilight at well-filled barns and mended fences, could not resist a wintry smile.

"Joe aims to make the place pay like it should," she said, "and he will, too! He don't favor his Paw."

"Hush, Mother," said Sally, but there was no need, for Mr. Merrillee, inside at his desk, read and wrote, oblivious; alone of that household, he seemed more disturbed and more disturbing than in the days of Johnny's youth. He read the Athenian orators, he composed addresses to his fellow-citizens and waited eagerly and in vain for their appearance in the Cape Fear *Mercury*. When he did join them on the porch it was to talk of the Palladium of Liberty, the Brotherhood of Man, the New Utopia. His fluttering enthusiasm, his gentle and elegant rhetoric were almost pitiful.

"Don't you fret so, Father," Sally said. "I don't reckon they's goin' to be a fight with England now——"

"And if they is," her mother broke in, "they'll be enough to do to lick the English, let alone bothering heads about Utopias and such!"

"No!" he cried, pacing nervously along the porch, "you are both quite wrong, my dears—quite wrong!" He cleared his throat. "If a spark of the primal virtue with which our first forebears in their perfect state of nature were endowed survives in us, this, my friends, is but the lull before the storm. We shall rise, strike off the fetters, reclaim our long lost heritage, form a new state where every law is just, every man free!"

A few months before when matters looked grave such words might have disquieted Johnny. But now that the actual crisis was past, that the colonies, quiet again, only waited for the word from the King which would set all to rights, he felt merely embarrassed at this last and most futile flare-up of a charming old gentleman's incompetent career. He breathed freer when the slim, stooped figure passed in through the door and plied once again the scratching quill.

"It's lucky we have you, Joe," Mrs. Merrillee said. "With this war business on his mind he'll never settle down now." She turned to Johnny. "He's not looked at the stock in a month."

"He's all right," said Joe gruffly. "Knows more than all of us put together. Night." He stumped upstairs to his chamber beneath the eaves.

"Well, if he does," Mrs. Merrillee muttered, "tell me what it's worth to him or to us."

"You shouldn't say that, Mother."

"Oh!" she cried harshly. "It's easy for you to stick up for your Paw, but it's a sight different for me." She fell silent. Her worn shoes shifted listlessly, her worn hands crooked over her sharp knees.

"I was a pretty girl when I married him," she went on in a bitter whisper.

"Mother—don't."

"I will. Yes, sir," she said. "I was pretty—and I come from a good country family where things was nice but plain, and when James Merrillee came along with all his learnin' and his clothes and courted me, I thought it was something fine. That was in 'forty-five. And what's it been ever since? Dreams—and foolishness. Big ideas and big schemes, and nothin' but putterin' round and loafin' to back 'em. Who kept things together and kept 'em goin'? Me. I've driven ox-teams, I've squared logs, I've beat the slaves—I've got in the crops, and done all the woman's work besides. And what's the upshot? To the end of time folks'll say what a pity James Merrillee married a woman that wasn't up to him. And that's what my children say now." She rose up, gaunt and weary. "I expect that cream's set." She walked down to the spring-house. Sally ran to overtake her. In the starlight Johnny saw her hand slide round the meagre stooping shoulders.

He sat alone on the porch, unhappy and uncertain. Inside the pen scratched on. He caught a glimpse of Mr. Merrillee's thin, fine-drawn face glowing with strange fantastic passion as he wrote. By the hitching rail the colt chucked his bit, switched softly at a moth. Joe's boots clumped on the floor above. Down near the spring he heard the broken murmur of Sally and her mother. Ought he not to mount the colt and ride away?

The two came back from the spring-house. He heard Mrs. Merrillee's worn, slip-shod feet move toward the kitchen, mount the step. The kitchen door slammed to.

"Are you there, Sally?"

"Yes."

"I reckon I better be leaving."

"Don't go."

"I don't want to go. I want to stay."

She sat down. He stood above her. "I feel sorry for you."

She looked off into the night. He sat beside her. "When folks at home don't get along together it makes it hard."

"I don't mind."

"It's wearing, though. And you're not yet grown hardly."

"I don't mind. But what frets me is that when I think so much of both of them they can't see any good in each other."

"That's a fact. It's mighty curious how that can be."

"I reckon," she was speaking to herself, "it's because they were in love once."

To a statement so unreasonable he had no reply. But he must speak.

"I believe when folks are really in love, though, they always stay in love. It looks like that ought to be the way."

"I don't know. I've never been in love."

"Well, I never have, neither. But if I was, that's the way I would be in love."

Her voice brightened. "I don't believe you'll ever be in love at all. Not in any way."

He was outraged. "How can you talk so? How do you know?"

"I don't know. That's what I think."

"But what makes you think it?"

"I don't know."

He was not displeased. She thought him reserved, not easily moved.

"Oh, I reckon I'll fall in love soon enough, one of these days. When I'm done my studies and have a little money of my own."

"Right there's one of my reasons."

"How's that?"

"You figure things out so. You finish schooling, you make some money. Then you fall in love. I don't believe people fall in love that way."

"But my Lord, Sally, they's no harm in figuring when a man's not in love. It's not like figuring after he is in love."

"No, I reckon not. If you can stop."

"Well, I expect you never can tell what it's going to be like. Maybe when it comes to it you will do more figuring than me."

"I don't know. I haven't even figured that much. But I reckon women generally figure more about it than men. They'd better."

"I don't see why they need. Not if the man loves them and is a sure-enough man."

"Not if—that's true. But that's what a woman's got to figure."

He felt the complexities growing too much for him.

"Well, anyway, it's a mighty interesting thing to talk about. Now my folks, they have little fusses, but it makes no difference. Sometimes it looks like they started them for fun." He checked himself. Was it not disloyal to discuss his parents with anyone? But it was exciting. There was something in it both daring and intimate.

"I know," she was saying. "I noticed. Joe and I used to be the same."

The comparison did not please him.

"When I'm in love I want no fusses at all." He looked at her firmly. "If it can't be that way," he was stern, "I don't want it."

"You want a lot." She looked at him a little sadly. "And maybe you'll get it some day. But will you give a lot to get it?"

"Why, yes," he answered easily. "Of course."

It was a pleasant time. Beside the genial warmth of summer and of his home, a curious unreasoning radiance stole into him. For no cause and with no object it filled him with a soft, trance-like elation, and touched the world around him with the soft and tender beauty of a trance. The pines had never seemed so kindly, gravely, brooding; streams had never woven shadows so amber, so profound; no clouds had ever raised such dazzling coronets to catch the sun. Why that should be he did not know—unless, perhaps, escape from dangers left behind had made him silly. At all events he was happy, and if he were silly—why, he had always been so, more or less, and had all kinds of silly notions. Fortunately his dreamy, secret cheer, so unwarrantably at variance with the darkness of the future, not to mention the general sinfulness of man, escaped his father's eye. His mother, however, seemed now and then to glance at him curiously.

But before the fall days turned cool, a messenger arrived who changed things, destroyed peace. A parched, scant-haired, little man, he looked as he drove up in his rickety freighter's wagon too undistinguished to change anything, still less destroy it. He shifted his quid and held out two letters for Johnny.

"Flood sent 'em. Two bob to pay."

One was plainly from Dr. Clapton, the other bore the uncertain scrawl of Sir Nathaniel Dukinfield. As Johnny tore open the seal he heard the freighter-man speaking around the corner of his tobacco cud.

"Thanks, my lady, I'll not tarry; but if you had any beer handy, now——"

Johnny opened the letter.

"Fifth Royal Dragoons.
Carlisle Castle, England.
28 July 1775

"Dear Bantam well old chap here we are a soldierin! Topping fel-
lowes the Fifth wine suppers no end can't ride though bad hands. Do
come over, can get you cornet's commission £700. Make your govnor
put up the screw.

"Write me a letter Bantam do,

"Your fast friend,

"Nat.

"O I near forgot. Chap from the Horse Guards here last week. What
about a War with the Colonies I says. Infurnel damn nonsense says
he. So that's all right. N."

By Zooks—good old Nat was the same as ever! He should have written
him—he must write him at once. Johnny opened the letter from Dr.
Clapton.

"St. Paul's Rectory.
Edenton.
20th October, 1775.

"My dear Johnny:—

"I send you this to inquire how you do and what progress you make
in Plutarch's Lives. The Latin itself presents no difficulties and I am
confident that by taking a certain amount of pains you shall master it
completely. I would also have you pause frequently to reflect upon the
Context, particularly when reading the Lives of such ancients as Cato
the Younger, Cincinnatus and The Gracchi. It is among such that you
will find examples of the Patriot, the Philosopher and the Man of
Publick Affairs such as, my dear young Friend, I am confident you are,
in a small sphere, destined to become. By no means lacking in natural
parts, you need only due attention to the chief Examples of Antique
Times in order to realize the hopes of your Respected Parents and of
your well-wishers among whom I think I may number myself as first.

"I make no doubt that you have perused the Address to The King
presented by the Continental Congress. The Congress itself is, of

course, quite irregular, but I am bound to say that the address is admirable in Spirit and accurately reflects the Sentiments of all gentlemen of Good Judgment, Good Temper, and Substance with whom I have conversed. I rejoice that more violent councils in that Body did not prevail, for I now have no doubts whatever that His Majesty will answer the Petition in a manner so gracious, so temperate and so just as to make further agitation appear despicable in the sight of all Right-minded Persons of whatever Party. It will then be time to talk of your returning here to complete your studies and when that Favorable Moment arrives you may rest assured that it will bring Infinite Gratification to

"Your Old Devoted and Firm Friend,<br>"Hugh Clapton."

The freighter-man wiped his mouth with the back of his wrist.

"Thank 'ee—servant, ma'm!" the horses started—"Whoa!" He pulled up, looked at Squire Fraser. "I near-about forgot to tell you the news, Mister. They's just come in a ship from England with word that the King has declared we was all rebels."

"What!" said John Fraser. "Ye're surely mistaken, my friend! The Congress sent him a petition only three months since."

"That's right, Mister, but they say he wouldn't look at it. He says we're rebels and had better look out for ourselves—that's what they tell." The freighter spat reflectively over the wheel. "I never had nothin' against him myself, but if that's the way he feels I reckon we can look out for ourselves. —Come on, hosses!" The slabsided team creaked out of sight.

"John," said Mrs. Fraser, "he can't be right, can he?"

"I've nae doubt he is," John Fraser answered heavily, "these freighter-lads get the news straight as a rule."

"But, Dadder, I never thought the King would act like that."

"Nor I, my lad, tae tell ye the truth. So far the British have made nothing but blunders. They were easy when they should ha' been hard, and now, when a few soft words would do nae harm, they're hard as iron. It'll make no difference i' the outcome, but it's a pity."

He sat down on the edge of the porch, planted his hands on his bare knees and gazed at the freighter-wagon's dust.

But Johnny was not listening. He heard his mother's sharp voice, "They're liable to make a mistake if they try to force North Carolina!" He heard his father rumbling on, but his mind had turned numb, lay stunned by the long-expected but now incredible blow. A war? It could not be. Here in his hand he held the pledges of happiness and peace—Doctor Clapton's learned view and Sir Nat's word straight from an officer in London. And yet he knew it must be so. There was more authority in that stolidly spitting freighter than in all the letters that were ever penned. He knew in his heart that it was so—by Zooks, he had known it six months ago. But he had fooled himself, consoled himself. He had fled away from the portents at Edenton, fortified his spirit in the false security of home. The portents now had found him here; here by the square strong house, the sturdy trees; here with father and mother by his side. Where else could he go? He repeated the question, pondered it as if there were an answer. Suddenly in the midst of his dazed and unhappy musings he felt that he must speak to Sally Merrillee.

Sitting in the evening shadows of the porch, she ran the spinning wheel. Her foot worked the treadle evenly, her left hand pulled down the carded wool from the distaff, her right hand fed it in a thin stream to the whirring flys.

"I can't stop till I finish this spindle," she said, "but you alight and we can talk just the same."

Tying up the colt, Johnny sat on the porch and watched her rhythmic movement. Quick, sure, graceful, her figure in the blue-gray camlet gown swayed gently, half lost in the blue-gray shadows of the porch. Lulled by the rhythm of her spinning, her gray eyes gazed out through the mist of wheel-spokes as though into a far country. She was more mysterious than he had ever imagined, Johnny thought—more mysterious. It seemed strange that not so long ago he had regarded her merely as a brisk, nice-looking, friendly girl, and not long before that as a particularly indefensible nuisance—so strange, indeed, that he had been glad enough to dismiss such pictures of her from his mind and, soon after, to deny that they had ever existed there. Now, as she sat spinning, her dark hair shadowing her eyes, her face, not sad, not happy, merely gazing content at some hidden scene and touched in turn by its reflected loveliness, she might almost be a goddess, gray-eyed Athene or Clotho who patiently spun the thread of life which others measured and cut. It might be possible to do something, Johnny reflected, in the way of a quatrain after the manner of Mr. Pope. But let that be deferred. For the moment he was happy to sit and watch the spinning wheel and her.

"What's on your mind?" she said. "You don't usually sit so still."

He started—yes—what was on his mind? He had almost forgot. Caught up in the revolving wheel, enmeshed by her gentle endless motion, he had almost forgot.

The wheel slowed down, his mind emerged from the web to meet the picture of the heavy-chewing freighter and his news.

"We got some bad news this evening!" he said.

"None of you all sick, I hope?"

"No—but a freighter came by and said the King had declared we were all rebels and had better look out for ourselves."

"I suppose that is bad news, although I don't know much about such things."

She unhooked the reel from the spindle and looked up at him with a smile of friendly amusement. "It looks to me like you were in a push to carry bad news over here, though."

"I didn't come to carry the news. I came to talk."

She laughed. "Well, you've not done what you came for, then. I never saw you so quiet."

"This news about the war just makes me sick!" he broke out. "Down there at Edenton I felt it coming and here I felt it coming!" He paused. "I dread it—and it looks like everybody else wanted it but me. There must be something ails me. On the coast all the folks were getting ready to fight—the one side saying what they intended doing against the English and the Tories saying what the English were going to do to the rebels. And all I felt was a lump in my chest like the green sickness. I reckon there must be something wrong with me."

"I don't know much about politics," she said, "back here in the country and with all the work, I don't get much chance to study 'em. Father's got a lot of ideas but he gets 'em all from Greek books." Her eyes shot straight into his. "But I don't reckon you're a coward. You're just different. I always did notice that."

"I'm glad you think I'm not scared," he said. "I haven't talked like this to anybody else. They wouldn't understand. It's made me feel mighty lonely, though. Sometimes I'd notice them looking at me kind of curious. It's taken a weight off my mind to talk to you." He fell silent.

"They's bad times coming," he went on, "mighty bad. I declare I don't know what I'll do."

"Don't you fret," she said gently, "when the time comes you'll do right, I reckon."

He put his hand in hers. "It makes me want to do right when you talk like that. You are the only real friend I've got."

She laughed. "That's your own fault then. You could have all the friends you wanted."

"I don't want others."

She made no answer. He said no more. She withdrew her hand and folded it with the other in her lap. She broke the silence.

"From a boy who's lived among those folks at Edenton, that's a compliment." He did not speak. And she felt she must go on. "Especially after the way I always used to plague you."

"I never think of that." He was magnanimous. "You seem so different."

Now she laughed. "I reckon you'll remember, if I ever start it again."

It was late when he unhitched the colt. As he drew up the girths, the colt's head, the ears pricked in reproachful inquiry, turned toward him; the soft muzzle stole up his side, gave a little thrust, then rested for an instant underneath his arm. He pressed against it. "Colt——Colt," he whispered.

The night was cold and clear, but he did not hurry. Swaying to the colt's light walk, the reins swinging against the slender neck, he drifted away into another world, a shadowy world, more fragile, lovelier, more intimate, yet more elusive. Transfigured beneath the stars, the sombre slumbering pines, the fields of broom straw, shining with frosted dew, the dark silent streams and mist-enfolded cypresses now held a beauty shy, but live, intense, and eager, which from its unsuspected fastnesses hailed him as comrade as he passed.

SALLY MERRILLEE AND JOHNNY

*"I'm glad you think I'm not scared," he said. "I haven't talked like this to anybody else"*

## CHAPTER XXVIII

CRISP NOVEMBER, following hard on the King's Proclamation, stirred the Province to life. There was a bustle of drilling among the militia, a creaking of guarded wagon-trains of smuggled arms and powder, a redoubled galloping of messengers, a sense of danger, of pleasurable expectation. In taprooms, men whispered, huzzahed, boasted, threatened, spat, traced old campaigns on sanded floors, made dire prophecies, rubbed gleeful hands. Small boys paraded lanes with petty dust and tumult. Lick-chop crones wagged brooding heads, forecast who would be the first to die.

In county towns Committees of Safety, abrupt and active, laid plans, scrutinized, passed sentences. Two words of Tory nonsense were enough to clap a man in jail.

The English were also busy. The governor still hung about the coast and schemed. The rumor spread that men o' war and transports would soon be off Cape Fear, that when they came the Highland emigrants in the center of the Province would rise, march to the sea and join them.

253

"The poor lads," said Squire Fraser, "had their fill o' rebellion when they turned out for Charlie in 'forty-five and I'm no thinkin' they'll make that mistake again. If they asked it," he added, "my advice tae them would be the same as that I gave the old Cherokee some years since: tae bide quiet and if there's tae be fightin', tae leave it tae them that have some interest i' the matter. But yon Scots, kennin' naught but Gaelic, are no likely tae hear any advice but what their leaders give them. And as tae the leaders"—he humped a dour shoulder—"it would not be the first time a chieftain has been willing tae buy a knighthood and a pension frae the British at the price o' a few hundred dead clansmen."

The first spit of snow fell, marked by scanty, ironic cheer, Christmas came. The country folk met in the freezing meeting house, sang Christmas hymns with tongue in cheek and a slant-wise glance which sought to fathom what side the neighbor next to them might be on.

On a frosty, gray morning the militia were called out for duty. They mustered at Blue's Crossing—some, sickly green and sweating, some boastful, martial, the most part moodily drunk. The company fell in. The blacksmith's wife presented to the ensign a flag worked by the women of the neighborhood. On a white ground the figure of a militiaman was depicted, liberally covered with bright red wounds. His hands were on his breast, his eyes were raised to heaven. From his mouth proceeded the words, "Posterity, for thee I bleed!" The ensign saluted, the captain of the company bowed and made a short speech of thanks adorned with halting catch phrases: "Defy our oppressors—strike off our fetters—the palladium of liberty." The men raised caps on rifle muzzles and gave a perfunctory cheer. They shouldered arms, swung into an uneven column, trailed away to the south. "Huzzah!" shouted the crowd; the women cried.

A week later a company from the northern counties came down the road and went into camp in the Merrillees' pasture field. They pitched a few patched and unstable tents, knocked together some rough shelters of pine boughs, huddled forlornly in these or in the Merrillees' tobacco barns and corn cribs. Their commanding officer, Captain Poscob, an orator and crossroads storekeeper, elected to lead the company on the strength of a patriotic harangue, billetted himself and his two lieutenants in the Merrillees' home. His appearance, superficially imposing, did not, however, bear minute inspection. Behind the impressive façade of his countenance, his head sloped away to insignificance, and even the façade itself was fundamentally disappointing. His lofty brow carried no conviction of intelligence; his large jaw suggested only weakness; it was as if the architect of Captain Poscob had attempted a magnificence out of all proportion to the materials at hand.

He devoted himself to conversation on the exalted purposes of the conflict and to the indefatigable consumption of Jamaica rum. His chief interest in the affairs of his company lay in reimbursing himself out of the pay of such enlisted men as had been his creditors in civilian life. Erecting a shed at the end of the straggling company street, he conducted a small business in dry groceries and liquors on a cash basis.

His first lieutenant was an immaculate, polished and well-turned-out buck of uncertain age, and of uncertain eye. His wit, while not profound, was adroit and easy, his manner irreproachable. His glance, quick, intimate and smiling, would pass as the glance of youth except for faintly weary shadows round the mouth which hinted that he might have seen too much of life and seen it too soon. He amused himself vastly with bon-mots of a simple type at the expense of the second lieutenant, a shy, well-bred youth, fresh from the College of William and Mary and none too happy in his present associations. All three officers had been at pains to procure from Norfolk good uniforms of blue, turned back with scarlet, which shone in brilliant contrast to the buck and homespun of the ranks.

The ranks themselves soon showed that, however deficient in all other arts of war, they were already capable of living off a country. Some vague loyalty in them spared the Merrillees' plantation, but every night took its toll of chickens, geese and pigs from the other farms of the settlement. All day the rifles and the fowling-pieces of the Sons of Liberty bombarded the wild turkeys and rabbits in the branches. The evening saw them playing endless games of hazard and drinking.

There was now small satisfaction for Johnny in visits to the Merrillee place. In the big fire-lit front room Mr. Merrillee and Captain Poscob talked warmly of freedom. The fluttering old gentleman exchanged select quotations from Demosthenes for the florid is somewhat ungrammatical pronouncements of the captain. Sally, flanked by the two younger officers, formed an exasperating tableau before the hearth. Animated and responsive, she appeared to be stimulated to deplorable coquetry alike by the infantile advances of little Ensign Rolly and by the sophisticated, bantering, and subtly dangerous manner of Lieutenant Faushay. No place was left for Johnny except along the wall beside the stolid Joe. From the back room came the grim, vindictive click and clatter of Mrs. Merrillee's loom.

Sally might better be helping her mother than frolicking with two militia officers—one a mere babe, the other easy and elegant enough, but to Johnny's experienced eye clearly not one of the right sort. That was the worst part of having lived only in the country—a girl like Sally never had a chance to measure men. Otherwise she would quickly laugh young Rolly out of countenance and preserve toward Faushay a demeanor sufficiently guarded to imply well-founded suspicions. But however inexperienced in estimating the opposite sex, Sally seemed surprisingly and disturbingly adroit in pleasing them. Rolly, immature, soft of head and heart, would no doubt hang about any skirt, but Faushay, as Johnny put it to himself, had been there before—been there often and far. His careless flattering impudence masked the unsleeping calculation of the campaigner. Why such a citizen of the world should think it worth while to stalk a back-country girl was more than Johnny could surmise. But as he watched her from his seat in the shadows, it dawned on him that Sally, turning to Faushay with quick wit and quick smile, her glance now kindly, now derisive, had quite enough charm for any man, whether he were sophisticated or no, and—Johnny added with a surprisingly bitter twist of his mouth—whether he were honorable or no.

What most exasperated him were the occasional words she threw him over shoulder. At times she seemed to treat him like a faithful retainer, a pensioner long since outgrown all usefulness; at others she made him out the worthy youth whose attachment she viewed as a well meant compliment, not without its inconveniences. By Zooks, he wanted to stalk out of the door! But that would never do. He would hear them laughing behind his back before he left the porch. He racked his brains for a superior, worldly-wise, corroding phrase. Unconscious of his sardonic eye, they talked.

"I wish I'd seen Norfolk, Mr. Faushay," Sally was saying, "especially in its heyday," she sighed heavily, "when you lived there."

"The heyday of Norfolk, ma'm," Mr. Faushay replied, "would be the day you set foot in it—eh, Rolly?"

"Yes, sir, it would," Lieutenant Rolly replied with profound conviction, "and you ought to see Williamsburg where I attended the college. If this cursed war hadn't just come along," he brooded, "I'd have loved mighty well to invite you up there for the college exercises."

"But if it hadn't come," she laughed, "you wouldn't have known me, sir!"

"Indeed he would that!" broke in Faushay. "When a man's smitten like Rolly here, his love can accomplish anything."

Rolly grinned and blushed at Sally's laughter. She turned to Faushay.

"You speak glibly enough for Lieutenant Rolly, but what about yourself, sir?"

"I lack the talent for romance—my devotion performs no miracles. I offer merely all that is humanly possible, including several matters which are highly improbable——"

"For example?"

He flashed her a brazen look. "As, for example, that I shall remain constant."

"You not romantic?" She raised her eyebrows—"You talk of greater miracles than Mr. Rolly."

"Should it be shown, sir," Mr. Merrillee was saying, "that the British have incited the Indians to a general war upon us, you will, my dear sir, find that this crime shall prove the Katharsis of the drama which now unfolds before us, wherein by pity and terror men's souls are purged of baseness, purified for the sacred mission on which we are now embarked."

"Yes, sir," said Captain Poscob. "If the British turn loose the Redskins, I assure you, sir, that the flag of this yer state will be gloriously unfurled, never to be sheathed until it bears us aloft in triumph over the prostrated bodies of our tyrannic foe!"

Mr. Merrillee's look of fine Quixotic folly met the glance, pompous, gross and meaningless, of Captain Poscob. They raised their mugs of toddy.

Life, the world, and particularly this roomful of people with their affected cleverness of youth or their affected wisdom of age, struck Johnny as unbelievably flat. The silence of poor stupid Joe was more tolerable by far than the pretentious imbecilities of the older men or the pinch-beck repartee of Sally and her militia friends. He tilted his chair to the ground and rose.

"Good night to you, miss," he was employing his very best manner. "Gentlemen, your servant!" With a sweep of his cocked hat to the breast of his broadcloth coat he was out the door.

In the light of a cold keen sickle moon he saw the bare, stripped trees, the frozen ground, the staring, dejected coat of the colt at the hitching rail. He wrapped the muffler around his throat and blew a breath of air. Inside it had been hot enough to smother a man; it was enough to make a man sick to come out from that room into this nipping night. He would not be surprised if it made him ill. It might be a small illness, but on the other hand many people had been carried off, cut down in their prime by causes far more trivial. He tucked the muffler around his chest, strode recklessly down the steps—well, what of it! There was no sense to life—a man like himself could see that with half an eye.

"Johnny!" Sally called from the porch.

He turned, stood still while his heart missed a beat, then gave three, close together. But before he answered he was quite himself, or rather quite the disillusioned and ironic taster of the lees of life, again.

"Well?" he said.

"Why—you went off so sudden. I never said good-night!"

Her voice was disturbed. He wanted to reach up his hands to hers. To stand there forever hand in hand. But no, by Zooks! Was he a sappy booby to be melted by a single belated word? He gave a short laugh.

"Good night to you, ma'm," he said with frigid elegance. Immediately he had suspicions that he was playing the fool. But he could not stop. From now on he seemed to sit, an unwilling, a disapproving, yet a hopelessly fascinated spectator of the idiotic and discreditable drama which he himself proceeded to enact.

"I don't know why you should take it amiss," said Sally, "it wasn't meant that way."

"Take it amiss! Why, I should take nothing that you do amiss, ma'm!"

"I came out here to say good-night friendly," she retorted with some fire, "and——"

"And I said good-night politely, I hope——"

"And if you don't feel friendly," she went on, "I don't see why you put yourself out to come."

"As to that, I sha'n't do so soon again."

"Well, then," she flashed, "we're all suited."

"Not," he went on, disregarding the thrust, "after what I've seen these last few nights."

"What have you seen?"

"I've seen the way you frolic with those two soldiers."

She bridled. "They're both very pleasant gentlemen. I'm mighty sensible of their politeness to me."

"Their politeness! Rolly's just a weanling that has no better sense——"

"You compliment me!"

"And Faushay," he rushed blindly on, "he's just amusing himself with you. He's seen life, that man has. You don't know these smooth town-bred men like I do. He's just going to make a monkey of you and then laugh."

"Well, anyhow, I've had my warning," she answered humbly enough. Aha! She was not too far gone to take advice—"I can see what a fool he might make of me——" Johnny smiled complacently—"by what a fool he has made of you!"

The door closed sharply behind her. He stood stunned, alone. Mounting the colt with an oath of Captain Flood's, he started galloping.

# CHAPTER XXIX

IN THE month that followed Johnny kept home. There was wood to haul and corn to grind during the short winter days. At night before the fire his mother hackled flax or spun yarn, his father, pipe in mouth, cut shoe pegs or, true to his ancient rearing, knitted a stocking with slow exactitude. Johnny himself spent the long evenings reading Horace and The Lives, glancing frequently from the pages to indulge in highly philosophical and disinterested reflections. Indeed he was surprised to find how pregnant the classic authors were with meaning, and with meaning particularly applicable to himself. Hardly a word which did not illustrate either the inconstancy and lightness of woman or the fortitude with which the man of upright life, confident in his own integrity, fronted adversity, misfortune, and the indifference or malignity of those whom, let it be said without rancor, nature had denied the power of appreciation. At long intervals, however, his cool detachment was overwhelmed by hot blasts of anger as he recalled the last scene with Sally Merrillee. Worse still were the moments when ironic fate vouchsafed him fleeting but unforgettable glimpses of his own imbecility. Such moments were too rare, however, to carry conviction. He managed to brush their implications aside and maintain his attitude of stern, Homeric steadfastness.

In early March the militia company marched South as other companies had done before. With the departure of the Protectors of the Oppressed, peace and order once more held sway. The swamps were silent, domestic fowls were given their liberty. Repose, however, did not extend itself to Johnny. He found that all the questions of the virtuous man's unshakeable independence, of woman's place in the scheme of things, which had been so decisively answered while the militia officers were at the Merrillees', seemed to reopen themselves now that they were gone. The logic of the situation was not clear although he invented plausible reasons why he should reconsider his position. What really determined him, however, were the quite simple, unaffected pictures of Sally which came into his mind. Mere glimpses—a turn of the head, a way of raising a hand to her hair—they were enough to make him want to see her, and see her soon.

Riding up through a cold, lemon-colored sunset he saw the litter of the departed military—ashes, bare patches, barrel-staves, assorted junk and, here and there, a gruesome fragment unpleasantly reminiscent of the recent high mortality among Squire Fraser's pigs. But let him forget, Johnny told himself, the unsavory odors and the unsavory memories of the ill-conditioned band, and particularly of the two lieutenants. It was the part both of wisdom and of dignity to ignore the past; to make his visit merely casual and friendly.

Unfortunately while he was still tying up the colt, his heart began pounding, and when Sally herself opened the door to his knock and gave him a smile, even though a sly, almost malicious smile, his throat, closing automatically, utterly obstructed the well-turned speech which had been prepared by his mind. He was obliged to content himself with a bow.

Inside the house Mr. Merrillee nodded by the fire, disconsolate no doubt at the loss of the political philosopher, Captain Poscob.

His face, so fine-cut, its skin so white, transparent, showed like a delicate decadent cameo against the dark, ruddy battens of the wall. His hand reached out and fluttered among the fluttering papers on his desk. The gust of air died with the closing of the door.

"I bid you good evening and welcome," said Mr. Merrillee in vague courtly tones.

"Good evening, seh," said Johnny.

Mrs. Merrillee did not look up. Her sallow cheeks, tanned, as they seemed, by the acid of her life, were drawn taut over the high cheek bones, her head was bent to the coarse unyielding drugget on which she sewed.

"How you, Mrs. Merrillee?" said Johnny. "Where's Joe?"

She punched the needle through the stuff.

"Joe's gone."

"What?"

She made no answer. Her head with its twist of sparse, limp hair dropped lower. She bit the thread off sharply and turned the drugget over.

"He hung around," Sally explained, "a couple of days after the militia left. But he was uneasy. Then he took the colt and put out after them. Joe has the idea there's going to be a battle."

"Is that a fact?" muttered Johnny. "I didn't know Joe was much for soldiering."

"He wa'n't," said Mrs. Merrillee, "till he saw how little work and how much stealin' there was to it."

"That's not so, Mother—it was the talk of a fight that fetched him."

Mr. Merrillee's light, wavering eye brightened fervidly.

"Joe's is the ardor of youthful Perseus. He goes to strike a blow against the oppressive monster."

Mrs. Merrillee's long glance of scorn rested on her husband's unconscious face. She gathered her work and tramped from the room.

Mr. Merrillee's gaze, uncertain, yet fiery and exalted, remained fixed on the embers. Johnny sat down more at loss than ever for something to say. You could count on Joe, he told himself, to do the irritating thing. Despite himself, however, he was stirred by the event, envious too. He himself, the man of important ideas, of glittering prospects, of beckoning dreams, stayed tamely at home while Joe, stolid, almost loutish, turned out the true adventurer. As he thought of Joe, perhaps now bivouacking near the enemy beneath the frosty stars, or even, perhaps, on picquet within sight of their camp fires, he felt the tug of admiration and excitement.

"It's near about a month since I've seen you," said Sally. She favored him with a hardy, small girl's grin. "Have you been mad at me all that time?"

"Me?" he said, lofty and detached. "I haven't been mad. I just figured that if you felt the way you talked about me I better not come around."

"You might have kept an eye on those two officers, though," she answered brazenly, "to see they didn't wrong me. Where's your sense of duty?"

He rose to the occasion, "Oh, I figured they weren't serious enough to be dangerous."

"Your manners are no better than they were the last time I saw you," she reflected, though not ill-pleased, "but you've got more sense."

"Maybe that's because my head is now my guide and not my heart." He pulled down his stock complacently—by Zooks, he was doing well!

He glanced at Mr. Merrillee. The elderly gentleman had fallen asleep, his long, narrow head rested on his long, slim hand, his face in repose was more than ever like a cameo.

"I got too easy upset, I reckon, Sally," Johnny said in a low voice. "I expect it's the war—you remember that time we talked about it?"

"Yes," she said, "I remember. But you oughtn't to get mad at me."

"I was mad at those militia jackanapes—and maybe a little mad," he added, "at how soft you were with them."

"You can't be hard," she said quietly, "with men that are going off to a fight."

"You think that's what every man ought to be doing, I expect."

"Oh! I don't know," she whispered unhappily, "Joe's gone too, now."

"I expect he'll make a fine soldier," Johnny said without enthusiasm. "He was always a good one to fight."

She was not satisfied.

"You don't know Joe," she answered stoutly. "You don't understand him.

He can't talk and be smart like you can, but he's a powerful listener and he does a heap of thinking." Her eye lit up with a maternal glow. "I knew two months past that Joe would do it—nobody else did, but I noticed him listening to Father and reading whatever newspapers came, and thinking. Why, even in the fall when he claimed he was going jack-fishing, he was just walking up and down in the woods by himself." She shot him a glance, deep, warm and sad. "You don't know Joe," she said.

Her gaze, still resting on him, thrilled him, troubled and humbled him.

"That's so, I reckon," he said, almost sincerely, "I expect Joe's worth three of me. While I've been shufflin' and worryin', Joe's made up his mind."

"Well," she said, "you aim to do right, too, I know that."

She was fair, friendly, even kind. But it was easy to see where her heart lay. If he came to her to say that he had enlisted, how would she look at him, what would she say? He pictured such a scene—dramatic, touching.

And after all, why not enlist? There would be a thrill to it, and popular acclaim as well as Sally's. He had argued the merits of the question now for half a year and gotten nowhere, for his pains. The war had come—war-time was a time for action, not for thinking. A leering, despicable thought stole through his mind: there was small chance anyhow, it whispered, of the militia doing heavy fighting.

"If things keep on," he said experimentally, "I reckon I'll come around to joining the army too."

She said nothing. But the look he had pictured to himself was there.

They may have sat for an hour when, with sounds of miniature ruin, a charred log plunged downward into flames. Mr. Merrillee opened his eyes.

"As I was saying," he remarked in his manner of mild and cheerful elegance, "like Theseus and the Minotaur." His eye clouded, his face fell. "Joe is gone," his long hands fluttered ever so slightly on the knees of his worn nankeen breeches. He stood up and turned to Johnny with his courtly half-smile, "and I am proud. May I offer you a glass of toddy? We have nothing else, I fear. No?" He held out his hand with a finished gesture— "Well, then, if you must leave—good-night."

Sally followed Johnny out on the porch.

"Good-night," she said, "I'm glad you're come again." She put her hand in his. Its touch, so sure, so strong, so tranquil, shamed him into something like a man. He drew a breath; he would hang back no longer, he would play his part and if there must be fighting, he would fight with the best of them. Her hand relaxed without haste, without lingering. It withdrew, leaving an aftermath of tenderness and softness which engulfed him, closed his throat, pounded against his temples.

"Good-night," he muttered. Turning uncertainly, he stumbled toward the hitching-rail.

# CHAPTER XXX

IT WAS long past the supper hour and Squire Fraser had not come home. Johnny and his mother had finished; the table was clear; they drew close to the fire against the winter night. Chance snow-flakes diving down the chimney, vanished with a hiss.

Outside the slow hoof-beats of Grampus crunched on the frozen ground, passed by to the barn.

"Well—there he is at last," said Mrs. Fraser. "He's mighty late, though."

"Maybe he had to wait for the wagon-bolt," said Johnny. "The smith's been busy this last month."

"That smith ought to 'tend to his old customers first instead of making guns for militiamen that most likely won't ever pay. He'd rather make guns for nothing than earn a living shoeing horses."

"That smith," said Johnny with judicial gloom, "is naturally possessed about guns. He told me he'd make a copy of a Deckardt rifle so close that

266

God himself couldn't tell the difference. Not," he added in an uneasy whisper, "if you was to shoot 'em at Him."

"That smith'll come to no good to talk like that about God."

"He'll come to no good to be making guns for folks to kill each other with."

His mother's glance, searching, rested on his face. Defeated, it fell to the floor.

"Well," she said, "people will always fight, I expect, and it can't be helped —but it can be helped to talk that way about God."

Squire Fraser's feet stamped on the porch. He clicked open the door, strode stiffly into the firelight, a muffled mountain of greatcoat and woollen tippets. Mrs. Fraser unwound the tippets from his ruddy nose and ears. Heaving himself out of his greatcoat, he sat down, chafed his cold and bristling knees in gloomy silence.

"Couldn't you get the wagon-bolt then, John?"

"Aye, it's i' the barn."

"He kept you long enough. You must be starved."

She went into the kitchen. Johnny heard the rattle of dishes and Sofa's voice: "Now, Mis' Car'line, don' you fuss yo'self up. I'll 'tend to the vittles."

"But, Sofa, I like to."

She came back with a bowl of mush and a slice of cornpone. John Fraser ate, drank a smoking mug of rum and water, sat as before.

"Was it a good bolt, then, Dadder?" Johnny ventured, knowing how mechanical imperfections preyed upon his father's mind.

"Aye, lad—a good bolt."

There was nothing more, then, to be said, nothing more for his mother and himself to do except to sit silent, giving way, as they always had, to his father's mood.

"I stayed," he said at last, "tae hear the news. There's been a fight down by Cape Fear."

"A fight!" his mother cried. The awe and fear which hushed her voice could not quite muffle its defiant ring. "A fight by Cape Fear! Are you sure, John? That's home."

"Sure. A man passed by that was in it. He'd had his head laid open." Squire Fraser indulged in a grim half smile. "I saw the wound and it fair made me homesick."

"Was it so bad then, John? Poor man!"

"O—aye—but 'twasna that. The wound," he went on, almost with relish, "was made by a Highland Claymore—and the Claymore, ye ken, doesna make sma' wounds!"

"So the Scots have risen, then?"

"Aye, fifteen hundred o' them. They were marching tae join the British on the coast."

"Who beat, Dadder?"

"The militia. It was rifles against swords, I tell ye."

"But what happened, John? Were any of my folks in it?"

"I dinna ken any names o' the Americans, lass, except that Lillington and Dick Caswell were leading them."

Mrs. Fraser glanced up, frightened but defiant. "Well, if Dick Caswell was in it," she said, "my folks were!"

"Dadder," said Johnny against his will. "What happened?"

"Well, when the Scots got near tae Wilmington, they came tae a sort of burn ca'd Moore's Creek."

"It's named for my granddad," said Mrs. Fraser.

"The Americans had got ahead o' the Tories and held the bridge. The Highlanders attacked them just at dawn. Under cover of the dark the Americans had torn up the planks o' the bridge, but a hundred clansmen managed tae wade across. They raised the cry, 'King George and Broadswords!' and the wounded man said ye could ha' heard it tae Cape Hatteras. Then they rushed the Americans, thinking tae surprise them. But it seems the militia were ready, for once, and cut them tae pieces wi' rifle fire. It was over in half an hour."

"I wonder if many of our people were killed," said Mrs. Fraser.

"The man said not many."

"They couldn't figure to kill the militia with swords if the militia had rifles, could they, Dadder?"

"My son, ye've never seen a Highland charge as I have. In the 'forty-five the best regiments in England threw down their muskets and ran like rabbits before it." He knocked out his pipe and leaned back in his chair.

Johnny felt sorry for the poor Tories and Highlanders rushing against the deadly, cracking line, yet as he pictured the close-locked ranks of North Carolinians sweeping their enemies away with gusts of fire, he felt a stir of strange and savage joy. The war was on, by Zooks! The first attackers of the Province had been cut to pieces, but more would follow. Close up the ranks, then! That was the word! Have done with qualms and arguments, shut your mouth, join the colors, show the world what North Carolina boys were made of!

His heart, too long a waverer, burned with the steady fire that lighted his mother's eyes and Sally Merrillee's. Rigid, trancelike, he stared in the fire; in its weaving flames he saw the rawboned, hurrying columns wheel into line. "The war's come," he muttered, his eyes still fixed on the glowing embers, "and I reckon I'd better go."

Minutes passed, they sat silent, motionless; it was as if his words had cast a spell.

"Caroline," his father spoke laboriously, "ye might just leave us. I've somewhat tae say tae the lad."

Without a look behind her, his mother lit a rush light and climbed the narrow stair. Again they sat silent. His mother's light footfalls sounded overhead, a damp log sizzled, the wind whined in a crevice.

"Culloden——" the word was like a sigh. "Dae ye remember when ye were a little tyke, how ye were always after me tae tell ye of Culloden?"

"But you never did, Dadder."

"No, for it's something I've been trying to forget these thirty years." John Fraser drew his heavy legs under him and leaned forward. "But now," he said, "I'll tell ye o' Culloden." He slowly shifted first one foot then the other. "And when I'm through ye'll understand the reason."

He settled heavily in his seat, curled a ponderous hand on each knee and gazed in the embers.

"For twa long hours that day we lay in our ranks on the moor, just lay there and pressed our faces in the heather while the British round-shot ploughed us through and through."

Closing his eyes, he drew a heavy breath then opened them again. "I can still see the bloody Highland bodies spinning through the air." He paused again, his breath came quick and sharp.

"At last we could bear no more. There were no orders, but suddenly the Highland line, three thousand strong, rose taegether and charged. All down across the moor I could see their broadswords swinging. Their blue bonnets were bobbing, their kilts were swirling. We hit their line wi' the Highland cry and smashed it. The Claymores were rising and falling on English backs like scythes of the harvesters—up—down." He raised his hand to the measure of the stroke. It wavered and fell to his side.

"Then came the trap. Back of the line we broke we met a second. The first rank were kneeling and twa ranks stood behind. Before we could come tae grips, they fired their volleys. Our men withered like flowers in the blast, withered away. There were none left—only a handful—we fell back up the hill. At the top I looked behind me. There, all across the English front, were white patches lying in close spots and heaps on the moor—the legs and thighs of the clansmen; the lads had gone down still charging, their kilts had fallen forward and left them bare. Every white spot showed where lay a Fraser, or a MacLean, or a Cameron, or an Appin Stewart."

He stared straight ahead through the fire into the burning heart of the by-gone tragedy.

"So that was the end, boy. The end of the fight but the beginning of the butchery. They chased us and they harried us through the glens, they killed our men wherever they found them, and drove our cattle and our women, too. The Highlands were a waste when they were done and have been ever since. I did not stop myself tae see the finish of the ruin. I learned of a French brig that lay off the coast and ran for my life. But on my way I saw enough of smoking cots and stripped dead bodies tae wake me up sweating until I die."

His father turned his steady, deep-set eyes on him. "Ye've said just now, ye'd join the rising in the Provinces. Well, son, ye're a man now and must do as ye've a mind, but before ye make your choice, I'd have ye know both sides. There's no glory to war except i' the silly dreams of children or the false memories of old men. It's bloody, and no good comes of it. And as for rebellion, if rebels against Great Britain could ever succeed, we should have; we were united, we were fighters a' and at our head we had our lawful King. We'd beaten the English a dozen times and chased them clean tae London; but still they sent fresh troops against us. We lost." He glanced again in the fire, then leaned toward Johnny. "What chance then have these provinces wi' a dozen different nationalities within their borders, wi' thousands honestly loyal tae King George and tens of thousands indifferent, or cannily waiting tae see which way the cat will jump, wi' no arms, no ammunition, no ships, no training, and wi' the Indians on one flank, the British Navy on the other? I tell ye, lad, the business is fantastical. And if against all reason it should succeed what have ye got? What have ye got at the price o' a' that blood and misery? Ye've merely traded a government of tinsel fops for a government of fustian demagogues!"

"But Dadder, you can't say that of Mr. Washington, or Mr. Laurens, or even Wylie Jones!"

"They are gentlemen, I grant, and they are leading now, but bide a while, my son. The people, having been told that they are free and equal, will never stop till they have driven from office every man wi' a clean shirt tae his back," John Fraser smiled grimly and touched Johnny's arm. "That's if ye win; and if ye lose, have ye thought of that? It may mean that your mother and I have lost our boy for less than nothing, and it will surely mean that we'll be driven frae the country." He drew a long, judicial breath. "I've lost one home through rebelling against the British rule," he said, "and nae doubt, I could endure tae lose another! But what of your mother, lad? Her roots are here; it might be over hard for her tae be set a wandering with naught but an old outworn man like me tae care for her." John Fraser hugged his arms across his chest. "I still look like an oak, I know," he shook his head. "But I'm afeared that if I'm thrown into the world, I'll no be the man tae light as cat-like on my feet as I used tae thirty years ago. 'Tis not myself that frets me, mind ye," he added hastily. He lowered his voice. "But I'd have no hardship come tae Caroline."

John Fraser lit his pipe and smoked it to the heel. "I would not speak o' my fears for your mother," he said with difficulty, "if it was tae urge ye tae do wrong. But underneath the bombast, war's naught but a cockfight and I dinna see how God's blessing can rest on it."

"But what can I do, Dadder?" Johnny Fraser said. "I can't stay on like this."

"I've thought of that," his father said, "and ye can just help me as I'll soon show ye. I lost all I had in the 'forty-five," he went on in a confidential whisper, "but I've managed to save a bit since then. I've a nest-egg for your mother in case I should be called before she"—he looked down at his big wrinkled hands—"which I hope I shall."

"Well, then. The question is: what am I to do wi' these savings? They'll not be safe here. There will be raiders, bandits, tax-gatherers and confiscations; the banks and commercial houses will fail, the very land itself will lie waste and lacking purchasers. But I thought that if ye could just go tae England for me, I'd give ye a letter tae a couple——"

"Go to England!" Johnny tried to focus on his father's deliberate, well-considered speech. He caught phrases, "Friends o' mine——" "MacKellor and Tavish——" "London——" "In the exporting way——" But at the first magic words his mind had drifted afar. He saw tall knights in armor, grenadiers, ruffed yeomen of the guard; he saw a royal levee, all stars and garters, perukes and diamond buckles; he saw the close-built streets of long stone palaces and overarching gable ends down whose quaint windings swarmed men and merchandise of all the world.

And in the background of his shifting dreams lay all of England—like a tapestry—her downs, her moors, her fens, her forests, her ship-thronged harbors, her cleanly, bustling market towns. He saw her fat-tailed flocks, her sleek red herds, her black plough lands, her stone-fenced pastures. He saw rotund and mild-eyed Clydesdales with huge shining rumps and tufted pasterns strain into their brass-bound collars, while ruddy lads in smock and leather gaiter cheered them on. He saw the thatch, the white-washed walls of cottages where decent wrinkled dames were knitting and fresh-faced children ate curds from scoured bowls. The land he saw, the land he pictured in his glowing thoughts was rich and stalwart, well ordered, lovely, perfect.

"My plan for ye is this," his father was saying. "There's a French barque ready now tae sail from Edenton. She's slow, I fear, but on that account the passage will be cheap and, beside, it will give me long enough tae send a letter by the Norfolk packet tae tell Tavish ye're on your way. There'll be no time tae lose—neutral ships are scarce; ye must not miss the barque." He stared in the fire. "That's if ye think well o' what I've just said."

Johnny Fraser's heart swelled with relief, with thankfulness, with golden expectations. Escape was offered. And escape so honorable, so useful, so necessary, so clear a duty to his parents that no honest man need be ashamed to seize it.

"Yes, seh," he said, "I hadn't thought of all those things. I reckon I better do what you say."

## CHAPTER XXXI

THE DAY was given over to preparations for Johnny's voyage—preparations hurried, exciting, of stupendous import. His mother overhauled shirts, stocks; brushed, pressed, folded, packed his clothing in the horse-hide travelling box. His father wrote letters of introduction, made out bills of exchange, covered sheets of paper with colossal calculations in his careful hand, brought out clinking little sacks of pistoles and half-jos from an iron-bound chest; he cut down his own huge pigskin money belt to fit young Johnny, oiled and tested a case of pistols and presented them in grave silence to his son. Sofa packed boxes of salt beef and fine-ground corn, as if her young master were embarking on a voyage of polar exploration. Scipio, supplied with a tin of Captain Tennant's special boot-paste, closeted himself for the afternoon with Johnny's boots and shoes. He bore them triumphantly into the big room before supper. Spread out with a flourish for inspection, their dull and sticky surfaces showed that Scipio depended upon a maximum of paste and a minimum of elbow power for his effects.

"Yes, suh, Misteh Johnneh, suh!" he exclaimed, beaming on the doleful row with ineffable satisfaction. "Dey ain't a servant in de Province can th'ow dust on Scipio when it come to put de high shine on brogans, an' wha's mo', de ain't des shine fo' dis week, de's shine to las'. Time you get wher' you gwine, dem boots'll still be a-shinin'." He breathed professionally on a slipper and rubbed it against the seat of his breeches. "Yes, suh," he said, "I reckon de quality folks on big ship 'low you got a servant at home da's a natchel bo'n high shiner!"

"All right, Scipio. Where's the rest of the paste?"

"I done used de mos' part—an' den 'long come de white shote an' et de balance. He lyin' under de fence now, swelled up an' moanin' scandalous. I'm surprised you ain't heard him."

Confound the Negro!—his special paste! But looking into Scipio's face, so incompetent, so proudly affectionate, Johnny could only say:

"My land, Scipio, you ought to give him some salt—that blacking's liable to kill him!"

"Oh, I ain't studyin' 'bout de blackin', Misteh Johnneh, but I declare I'd be easier in my mind if dat shote ain't done et de lid off'n de box."

Scipio reflected, seeking to draw a moral precept from the incident. "Dat shote," he said, "too ambitious fo' his own good." He shuffled out.

Supper, the last Johnny should eat at home for months, perhaps years, afforded no pleasure. He was oppressed with weariness and the haunting conviction that despite their efforts they had overlooked some detail of his equipment, probably the most essential detail of all.

At the end Johnny was glad enough to say, "Well, I reckon I'll take the colt and go up to the Merrillees'."

He saw his father grin and start to speak. He saw his mother check him with a sign, and thanked her in his heart. What with the war and going away and thoughts of Sally, to say nothing of the loss of his English blacking, he was in no mood for his father's heavy-handed mirth.

A quick turn in the weather had given the evening the warmth of false spring. Riding up to the Merrillee house, he made out Sally's silhouette against the fire-lit kitchen door. She was hanging up dish-cloths on the back porch. Somehow the business of hanging dish-cloths did not strike him as prosaic; perhaps because the silhouette was strong and graceful, such as he imagined the silhouette of one of the lesser Greek divinities might be. Tying the colt, he walked to the back of the house and stood looking up at her.

"Hello, Sally,—it's Johnny."

"Yes," she said, "I knew the colt. How you?"

"Oh, I'm all right. I've got some news."

She laughed. "My land! This is a great winter for news!" She turned serious. "I expect it's something about the war."

"Yes," he said uneasily. "I reckon you heard tell about the fight at Moore's Creek."

"Dad heard it this morning. He's in there now, writing a letter to *The Mercury*. The war isn't good for Dad. He gets himself so excited. Was that your news—about Moore's Creek?"

"No—about me."

She laughed again. "Oh—big news!"

"I didn't mean it that way. I just wanted to tell you."

"Go on," she said warmly. "I 'spect I know what it is, though. With the war and all, I knew you couldn't stay here forever."

"No," he admitted guardedly, "I—I'm going to England."

"What!"

"To England—Dadder wants me to."

"But we're fighting the English! I don't reckon I understand."

"Why, it's this way," he explained laboriously, "Dadder's got some property and some business that he wants me to attend to."

For a time she did not answer. She hung the last dish-cloth and stood looking down at him. He strove to read her glance through the darkness.

"Is that your news?" Her voice was quiet but incredulous.

"Yes—that's news enough, ain't it? Folks don't go to England every day."

To this she made no reply.

"You see," he went on defensively, "Dadder's mighty anxious for me to get all his affairs in good fix before it's too late. If he don't get what he's saved put away safe pretty quick he might lose it in the war. Anything might happen, and there's no one else to do that for him but me. I hate to leave, Sally—honest—I declare I do—and miss the chance to see you for I don't know how long. It won't be long, though—the war will soon be over. But it looks like it was the right thing for me to do. A man ought to take care of his folks—that's what I think—don't you?"

"I wasn't thinking about you." Her voice was small and cold. He could see that she looked out over his head over the fields to the dark, distant forest. "I was thinking about Joe. We've not heard from Joe since the fight."

"I expect Joe was in it," he said uncomfortably. "If there was a fight, Joe would be."

"That's what he went for."

"I hope he's all right," said Johnny, putting some tenderness into his tone. "It would be a shame if anything happened to Joe!"

"A shame!" She startled him with her bitter laugh. "You don't know what a shame it would be. Joe's never had any learning, he's never had any chance. He's lived in the sticks and grown up like a clod-hopper. But he's got a mind of his own. He don't need Greek and Latin to figure what's right—and when he's figured it he goes and does it! But you—you've got schooling and fine clothes and all such, but when it comes to standing on your own feet, you shift and you shuffle; and now when you can't shift any more you go away. Joe," she said proudly, "don't need any sorrow from you!"

"Why, Sally," he muttered, flustered, aghast, and angry, "you needn't take on so. Joe's your brother and you naturally think what he does is right. But I've got my father's affairs." His self-confidence was returning. "I've got my business to attend to, and I'm going to attend to it. A woman don't understand about such things."

She shook her head. "I understand about you, I reckon. The last time you were here you talked of enlisting. I thought you meant it—maybe you did. But I expect it was because you didn't see any way out of it, and figured you'd play the hero!

"But now," she went on, "as soon as there is a way out—you're gone!" She raised a hand in a stabbing gesture of finality.

"So you think I'm a coward, then?" He drew himself up with an air of frigid dignity.

"I don't think anything"—her voice broke—"and I don't care anything!"

She turned swiftly away and shut the door in his face.

A hot, surging wave of anger and mortification engulfed him. White and choking, he stared at the shut door.

God's teeth! To think that any woman could talk to him like that! To think that any woman was such an obstinate fool! To think that he could have grown sentimental about her! He shrugged his shoulders, twisted his lips. Well, there was one good thing about the business: it showed Sally Merrillee to him as she was.

He clapped on his hat. It would be a cold day when he got fooled again.

## CHAPTER XXXII

JOHNNY FRASER, journeying from Blue's Crossing to Slade's Ordinary on the Roanoke, had enough reasons to feel depressed. His mind held pictures of his father's inarticulate farewell, of his mother's face, sad, distracted and shaded, he could not help thinking, by an unhappiness not due to the parting alone; it held pictures of Sofa, all majesty forgotten, weeping convulsively, patting his head, of Grizzly Gray sniffing his travelling box with foreboding and lugubrious sniffs. Through all the rest flashed the outrageous and unforgivable scene with Sally Merrillee.

But, as he travelled on, elation, defying laws of reason, welled up in his heart. After all, those things, sorrowful, no doubt, were past, and here he was, travelling in grandeur, as the independent gentleman of means—travelling in what was, to all effects, his chaise, with Scipio, to all effects, his servant beside him, with his box strapped on the running-gear behind, his pistols under the seat, his money-belt around his waist.

To complete his self-esteem, he passed many farmers and settlers on the road who looked at him not perhaps with deference—one could hardly expect that in the back country—but with a certain flattering curiosity. They might perhaps assume broad amusement, but he knew that in their hearts they could not escape a touch of awe at the radiant vision of a young gentleman travelling turned out in proper style. As the numbers of these secret admirers continued to increase, Johnny wondered what occasion brought them on the road—oh, yes—he had near about forgot: this was election day. These worthy back-country free-holders were riding in to the crossroad hamlets to elect the Provincial Congress. He frowned; an election, particularly an election which signified the triumph of freedom, would mean an unusually disturbing night at Slade's Ordinary. He grew apprehensive and uneasy. Nor, as he approached the place, did the portents which he saw relieve his mind. Several broken stone bottles and a cracked demijohn lay beside the road. A riderless horse passed them, his saddle under his belly. In the shelter of a pine grove two loose horses seemed to graze. On approaching Johnny saw that their bridle reins had been made fast by some considerate fellow-citizen to the ankles of their prostrate owners. He touched up Grampus, in disgust. The thing for him to do was to get a boat out of Slade's as fast as ever he could.

The long street was filled from end to end with the dingy crowd and their ill-kempt, sorrowful horses. Here three callow youths played pitch and toss with loud gusts of filthy language. There two old men hugged each other, raised cracked voices in song. A woman with a child tugged at the coat skirts of a man who swayed against a hitching-post. He struck her with the back of his hand.

In front of the Ordinary stood the polling booth. There the crowd was thickest. The last votes were being cast amid a bedlam of fighting, drunken cheering, and oratory. Mounted on tubs and barrels, half a dozen patriots bellowed praise of freedom to rings of glassy-eyed and inarticulately roaring auditors.

Leaving the chaise in the inn stable with Scipio, whose spirits had been noticeably quelled by the formidable spectacle of the white folks' political machinery in operation, Johnny walked out to the street. A ruddy, decent-looking farmer had just come up to the polling-booth. The crowd surrounded him.

"Merrick—who you votin' fo'?" they shouted.

"I don't have to tell," he answered bluntly.

"I know!" a voice cried. "Merrick's for Gentleman Jones, the lousy aristocrat!"

A hand fell on the farmer's shoulder. "We're all for Sam Leech here, Merrick. You don't vote!"

"Huzzah for Sam!" they cheered. "The people's Friend! The Plain Folks' Pardner!"

A dozen hands seized the farmer, hustled him from the booth.

"I'll have my rights!" he said, struggling.

A huge man towered over him. "You got no complaint, Merrick. We're lettin' you off easy. The others that tried to vote aristocrat all went in the river."

"That's right!" a philosopher observed thickly. "You leave us alone, Merrick, and we'll leave you alone!"

The crowd laughed, cheered again, closed around him and bore him from the booth.

"Merrick's all right," a bystander remarked to Johnny complacently, "but if it was Granger now, they'd bust his scalp open."

Johnny walked off in haughty silence; he must find a boat and get away.

Some skiffs lay hauled up on the beach and beside the crazy landing-stage a long dugout canoe swayed in the current. Johnny walked out on the pier and looked down into it. That petty-auger, with its paddles, poles and small mast amidships, would do to make the trip to Edenton. He looked about for the owner. On shore white teeth and eyeballs moved slowly in the black shadow of a shed. Captain Flood's deck-hand crept into the sunset light, padded through the dust, over the loose planks, and came to a halt with a sidewise glance and a pull at his forehead.

"Where's Captain Flood?" said Johnny.

"De captain gone away, suh."

"Where?"

"He gone in de gunboat business."

"Privateering?"

"Yassuh."

"Have you run away?"

"No, suh. He taken de big boat. Ah run dis lil' pettyauger like he tol' me."

"Where's your ticket?"

The Negro fumbled in his dungarees, produced a crumpled paper. "To the Publique," Johnny read. "The Barer my black man Lonny is ordered by me to run the pettiauger on the Roanoke and toe collec the moneys I allus charge therefore. Capn Ready Flood."

"All right," said Johnny, "what time do you leave?"

"'Mos' any time. Das when I mos'ly leaves."

"Well, I want to go to Edenton right off. Go up to Slade's stable and carry down my boxes."

From the main street came cheers, jeers, sounds of fighting. The Negro, Johnny's box swinging easily on his shoulder, stole out of a quiet back lane, moving swiftly. Trotting behind him, Scipio chattered orders and advice over the case of pistols which he clasped to his bosom. The box and case of pistols and Johnny's greatcoat were stowed amidships. Balancing a long paddle in one hand, the Negro dropped into the stern and held the boat steady for Johnny.

"Good-bye, Scipio," said Johnny. He reached up from his seat in the bow and threw a shilling on the dock at Scipio's feet. Scipio, however, did not stoop to pick it up. His lips trembled, he beat his two hands softly together.

"I thank you, Mist' Johnneh. I most sho'ly does, but I ain't so busy 'bout de shillin', no suh. It's dis yer travellin' like you is: das what's on my mind."

"Oh, that's all right, Scipio. Don't you fret. I'll take care of myself."

"You talk mighty big, Mist' Johnneh, but it ain't right for young white gentleman to go a travellin' without a servant." He made a protesting gesture of emphasis. "I's always taken care you, Mist' Johnneh. I ought to go along wher' you gwine."

"I'd love to have you with me, Scipio, mighty well, and that's a fact, but I'd feel easier in my mind to know you're going to be at home to look after my mother and the place."

"Yes, suh," said Scipio disconsolately, "I 'spect it's fo' de bes', but des you remember, Mist' Johnneh, dat I's raised you and I's 'sponsible fo' you."

Johnny held up his hand. Scipio's hand, limp and leathery, slid awkwardly into his.

"De Lo'd bless you, Mist' Johnneh"—again he beat his hands together, then hung them at his sides.

The Negro in the stern gave a stroke with his paddle; the dugout canoe slid out into the evening mist which hung on the stream, faintly glowing in the last sunset light. The misty river path stretched away between the banks of dark cypresses. Above, the twilight sky was faint translucent green. Johnny looked behind him. On the landing-stage the figure of Scipio, seen dimly through the haze, waved silently, unceasingly, like some absurd and touching marionette.

Now they were coasting down the stream. The waving figure, the last familiar picture of his home, was left behind. The mist around him chilled him to the marrow and seemed to creep into his heart. The black water, strong-flowing, silent, inexorable, which carried him away, became in his mind a stream of dark fate, a flood of loneliness.

Let him turn and paddle back to Scipio, to Grampus and the chaise. Who could see what lay ahead? And the night was closing in.

Just then, from up the river, from Slade's landing, now falling so swiftly behind, came a roar, faint but still malign and bestial, of the drunken election crowd. It was hardly more than a whisper, but a whisper hoarse and sinister which gave decision to Johnny Fraser.

"Turn back?" he asked himself. "Turn back to a country where such men claimed to rule?" He leaned forward in the bows. Let the Negro paddle, let the stream flow: he was for England.

Next afternoon they came to the mouth of the Roanoke. The tawny river water paled, melted into the bleak gray waters of the Sound. A sodden gray sky pressed down on them. On beach and sand pit, old pines swayed in the wind, raised trembling branches in a gesture of despair. The deck-hand hoisted a little sail. They cut through the choppy shallow sea, laid their course for where the court house of Edenton showed dead white against weathered roofs and naked trees.

Heavily, listlessly, bumping through the chop, the boat threw wisps of brackish water across Johnny Fraser's mouth.

# CHAPTER XXXIII

Hornblower's tavern was sad and deserted, no patrons rattled dice boxes or clinked glasses at the tap-room tables, no pewter shone against the tap-room wall. But at the sound of Johnny's footsteps on the sanded floor, Hornblower himself appeared at the door of the bar, smiled, rubbed his fat clean hands on his green baize apron with the same deferential gusto. He may perhaps have seemed less rosy, less rotund, his greeting may perhaps have been less full-flavored, but he came forward briskly enough.

"Well! bless my soul and body, young Mr. Fraser, it does me good to see you, sir." He bowed again. "You desire supper, sir, I make no doubt."

"Yes," said Johnny, "and a chamber. The servant will carry up my boxes later." He dropped into a chair. "I'm cold and tired. Bring me what you like."

Waiting for his supper, Johnny listened to the bustling sounds of cooking

which now could be heard in the kitchen and wondered why Hornblower
did not return. It had always been Hornblower's custom to entertain the
waiting guests with news of the district. Johnny Fraser had looked forward
to learning from him the state of affairs at Edenton. Even more than the
matter of Hornblower's discourse, he had looked forward to its manner, to
Hornblower's discreet and delicate respect. After the election scene at
Slade's, it would be a solace to talk to Hornblower, to be again in the
presence of a man who realized his own position, knew his place, accepted
it cheerfully and recognized a gentleman when he saw one. Still Hornblower did not appear. Johnny's disappointment gave way to annoyance.
Was he a mere chance bag-man to be thus set down unceremoniously and
left to his own devices?

He listened to the kitchen noises again; the busy footfalls between
kitchen fireplace and serving-table were the footfalls of Hornblower himself. Hornblower, who in the days of his glory presided, a benevolent
despot, over the bevy of serving-maids and bus-boys, poor Hornblower, now
cooked the meals himself and doubtless made up the beds and scrubbed the
floors as well. Stuffing his hands in his waistcoat pockets, Johnny mused on
the fallen estate of this good man.

"Coming directly, sir!" Hornblower called out in an anxious tone as
though he guessed Johnny's impatience. He soon appeared with a large
dish of mackerel and greens. "I must ask your pardon, young sir," he said,
placing it on the table, "for serving you with an iron plate. But the fact is,
sir, we have no pewter left in the house."

"I noticed there was none on the wall," said Johnny. "I hope you have not
been obliged to sell it, Hornblower."

"No, sir, thank you, not quite that, though I should doubtless have been
better off than what I am now. The fact is, sir, the Committee of Safety took
it all to be run into bullets." Mr. Hornblower raised an unhappy glance to
the wainscot. "They came for it three months ago, sir. I recollect it was a
Thursday, just three days after it had all been freshly burnished."

"Yes, I remember," said Johnny. "You always used to keep it looking
mighty nice."

"Indeed, I tried to, sir. My class of trade," he added proudly, "would not be satisfied with less. That is what I told the soldiers when they came. 'It is not the money loss, my boys,' I said, 'but you must understand that my patrons are quite unaccustomed to eat off iron.' " Mr. Hornblower drew himself up proudly to exemplify his demeanor on the dramatic occasion.

"And what did they say?" Johnny asked.

"I am sorry to have to tell you, sir," said Mr. Hornblower earnestly, "that they were quite unfeeling, quite ill-bred. 'You ought to have spoke sooner, old fellow,' the Corporal said. 'We never would have undertook this war if we'd know'd how it was going to put your patrons out,' and with that he handed me a grubby-looking receipt, and marched off. But bless me!" cried Mr. Hornblower, contritely, "I forgot your drink. What are your commands, sir? We still have our cellar, I am happy to say. Fayal? Very good, sir."

He brought the bottle, showed it to Johnny ceremoniously, carefully wiped the neck and drew the cork. With his napkin on his arm, he stationed himself a few paces away. As he ate and drank, Johnny stole glances at the face which, turned considerately aside, presided over his meal. Hornblower was growing old. "Sit down, Hornblower," he said; "you look tired."

"Thank you very much, sir," Hornblower replied, "but I should not care to do that, thanking you just the same. Some other gentleman might come in,—not many do so now, it is true—but if he did it might give the place a bad character with him to see me seated while you supped. As you know, my gentlemen are most particular about such matters, sir. Yes, indeed," Mr. Hornblower went on reflectively, "business is not what it used to be, not at all, sir. The Committee has forbid race-meetings, routs and frolics of all sorts, so that we lose a good deal of custom in that way. But what I most deplore is the loss of our regular patrons—the gentlemen who, if I may say so, gave the tone to the place. They are nearly all gone: Captain Tennant, of course, left while you were still here, I believe, sir; Mr. Hewes remains in the Congress at Philadelphia. Mr. Jones busies himself in public affairs and comes here seldom, though I half expect him shortly on account of some business with the French Barque. Major Battle, of course, is gone—"

"*Major* Battle?" said Johnny.

"Yes, sir. He accepted a commission in the militia some time ago. I have no doubt he was in the affair at Moore's Creek. He always struck me as an eager gentleman and most keen for the business."

Supper finished, Johnny Fraser put on his greatcoat and went in search of the French Barque. He had small desire to stumble about the dark, half-deserted dockside on this cold November night, but the barque might sail at any moment now. He must take his passage on her at once. There was no time to lose. The streets were empty, the town seemed dead, no citizens passed by with lanterns, scarcely a strip of candlelight showed behind barred shutters. He listened in vain for cheerful voices, buzzing in idle chatter or raised in song.

Inside a barred house a child cried. Far off a sentry called his rounds. Dark, sullenly gnawing at dock and pier, the waters of the harbor no longer reflected the high riding-lights of many ships at anchor, the broad floods of golden lamplight from carved windows of masters' cabins, the cheery side-lights which used to lace the bay with narrow wavering patterns of red and green. All was blackness save where, alongside the stone dock, the French Barque's binnacle showed a feeble, hooded gleam.

As Johnny Fraser came up to the gang-plank, a sharp voice challenged him:

"'Allo! What you want, eh?"

"Is this the 'Hirondelle'?" he said.

"*Mais oui.*"

"I want to speak to the captain."

A little toy man in pointed mustaches and goatee peered over the side, flashed a lantern in Johnny's face.

"Ah!" he murmured, with a gratifying change of tone. "*Un monsieur!*"

He beckoned Johnny to come aboard, trotted rapidly across the deck, knocked at the captain's door and cocked a theatrical ear, for all the world like a particularly clever little dog.

In the cabin beneath a hanging lamp sat a short-haired, ruddy chunk of a man. His shirt sleeves were rolled back, he wrote laboriously with his right hand and patted his left reflectively on his long sealskin waistcoat.

"Monsieur desires?" he said with a blunt yet lively glance.

"I aim to take passage to London, seh," said Johnny, with a bow. "Fraser is my name, seh."

The captain pointed a finger at the center of his sealskin waistcoat. "Lautrec," he announced briefly. "Be seated, sir, if you please. Pierre!" cried Captain Lautrec, in a voice which made the papers on the table tremble. "Cognac!"

A young French boy, large-eyed, pasty-faced and thin-shanked, brought in a brown bottle and placed it before the captain. Filling two small tumblers, the captain bowed to Johnny with curt geniality and hurled his glassful down his throat.

He fell at once to business. The passage money would be sixteen guineas; weather favoring, they would put him ashore at Tillbury Dock; he could see his cabin in the morning; his luggage should be on board by noon as they expected to sail next evening.

Johnny sipped the thick, fiery liquid with grateful shudders, nodded his head in sage endorsement. At the end of half an hour all was settled. He threw the golden coins on the table, shook the captain warmly by the hand and marched ashore, thoroughly aglow, his body fortified against the cold night wind, his spirit against all machinations of a hostile world.

Breakfasting in the tap-room the next morning, Johnny Fraser heard the sound of rapid carriage wheels. A yellow travelling coach drew up before the door. The Negro postillion climbed stiffly down, stuck his whip in his padded off-side boot, stretched his cramped back, opened the coach door. Wylie Jones, wan and dishevelled, stepped into the wan light of the winter sun, came up the path. The postillion followed with his travelling escritoire and valise.

"Ah, Fraser," exclaimed Mr. Jones as he entered the room. "This is indeed a pleasure," he added lifelessly.

The Negro helped him out of his surtout. "May I join you? Thanks. What do you here? Oh, your pardon. One does not ask that question nowadays, I believe. I suppose you have heard the results of the election."

"No, seh," said Johnny, with a sour grin, "but I saw them voting at Slade's landing when I came through."

"Ah, and an edifying show it was, I have no doubt." He waved a graceful, deprecating hand. "From what news I have, I fear it was the same story everywhere. The gentlemen who have been the heart and soul of the Revolution, who have devoted their substance and their distinguished minds to the cause, were everywhere defeated, by fair means or foul,—principally the latter,—and a set of ignorant and dangerous demagogues have been put in their place."

"Hornblower!" he called out impatiently. "Bread and tea!"

"The new Provincial Congress," Mr. Jones went on, "has been elected for the purpose of writing a Constitution of the State of North Carolina. As matters stand, half the new members cannot sign their names."

The tea arrived; he sipped it and made a slight grimace. "It would seem obvious that a man cannot likely write a Constitution who cannot write at all. I am touched by the masses' faith in a protecting Providence." He broke a crust of bread and nibbled it. "I should doubtless be far happier where I, too, able to believe in an Omnipotent Being who could be implicitly relied upon to rectify every imbecility committed by those who worship Him."

"I'm mighty sorry you got beat, seh." Johnny Fraser could find nothing better than that to say. His proffered consolation had an unhappy effect on Mr. Jones. He relapsed into silence, brooded over his cup of tea. His breakfast finished, he called for a church-warden pipe and smoked.

"Your people are well?" he inquired languidly. "My duty to Mistress Fraser; embrace your father for me when next you see him." He laughed.

"Thank you, seh," said Johnny uncomfortably, "but I reckon that will be some time."

"So?"

"I'm bound for England."

"Indeed," said Mr. Jones, unimpressed. "I used to hear England well spoken of. But do not expect too much. Not in these times. The Englishman is intolerant of the Colonial who opposes him and contemptuous of the Colonial who supports him."

"I hope to find friends, seh, in the firm I am to engage with, MacKellor and Tavish. My father knows them."

"Ah, the importing house."

"Yes, seh. Is they anything I can do fo' you, seh?" Johnny answered with admirable *savoir faire*.

"Why, yes." Mr. Jones gave him a cool grin. "Persuade them to make shipments of arms to the Continental Congress, in unlimited amounts and on unlimited credit."

"Oh, I couldn't do that, seh. I aim to keep clear of any such trouble till I can settle my Dadder's affairs."

"Surely," said Mr. Jones, "you might try. Merely as a delicate attention to me. You would be quite safe. 'MacKellor and Tavish'—the very names are a guarantee against the success of a credit transaction. No? My dear fellow, you are no man of the world. You should learn the uses of promises which cannot be fulfilled."

Johnny eyed Mr. Jones askance. How much of this was banter, how much stamped the man?

"You do not take me, eh? I puzzle you? Well, you are not the first. I am too clever for my own interest, perhaps. Whatever my beliefs, I cannot bear the heavy-footed speech of solid worth. A pity. A shade more dullness would have won me the election. But I left the honest burghers floundering among my epigrams."

His smile was bitter, twisted and sincere.

"And yet I cannot change. I, too, must play my own peculiar antics like all my simian blood-brothers."

Distressed, at loss, Johnny could only venture:

"The election at Slade's, seh, wasn't fair. I think if it had been you'd have been returned."

"I doubt it," said Mr. Jones moodily. "The movement has gone too far." He rose, dusted his waistcoat with his lace handkerchief.

"Future historians," he said, "will divide my life into two epochs: the first devoted to starting a Revolution, the second"—he favored Johnny with an ironical smile—"to stopping it."

With the whole day before him, Johnny Fraser's thoughts turned to a duty which he had till now declined to face. He must call on Dr. Clapton. It seemed odd, discreditable, to shrink from this meeting. The picture of the little figure in the blue cloak waving and smiling gallantly was still in his mind as vivid as ever. The outlines of that parting silhouette had grown no less sharp, no less poignant. Their very sharpness was, indeed, the cause of his reluctance. How could he bring himself to meet the sight of that tender spirit, its fluttering, low-voiced beliefs now turned to mockery by strident, harsh events? What could he say to a man so jeered at by inexorable facts? And yet to leave without a word was unthinkable.

"Hornblower, where's my greatcoat?" he called. "If anybody calls for me," he added importantly, "I'm going up to the Rectory."

"Very good, sir," said Mr. Hornblower. He made no further comment.

But as Johnny Fraser walked from the room, he felt that Hornblower's eyes were following him with an expression of polite interrogation and surprise.

No shopkeepers kneaded ingratiating hands at doorways, no basket-laden customers leaned over counters as Johnny passed by. The street was lonely and deserted except for a red-nosed boy, lugging a string of onions, who called his wares without conviction, and a high-wheeled ox-cart, silvered with fish scales, tied to a tree, whose scrubby ox licked the bark avidly, his tongue, broad, oily, smoothly flopping, like a paint brush. Hauled by two men and a woman, a wagon-load of cordwood creaked by. Johnny stared; he had never seen a man between the shafts before, and as for a woman—he looked away. Then he must look again; their shoulders were raised like straining withers, their sullen heads hung low, like the heads of oxen.

Johnny Fraser turned off by the churchyard. It, too, had fallen into some decay. Weeds grew in the unraked gravel paths, dead magnolia leaves littered the old, heraldic tombstones; he felt the stirring of vague, dark premonitions and hurried on.

The windows of the rectory appeared blank and cold, like the eyes of the dead; lintels bore the marks of fire and smoke, the front door was cracked from top to bottom. He knocked on it, absurdly.

"Dr. Clapton! Dr. Clapton!" he called. There was, of course, no answer. He pushed against the door. It gave with a groan.

Inside was only a dark, charred ruin of shelves, and the odor of burnt leather and wet ashes. In a corner where long ago had stood a mound of books piled up by Dr. Clapton's system now lay a heap of ashes and stray leaves. A leaf, half-burned, was at Johnny's feet. He picked it up, carried it to the light as if he would find there some message from the old owner of that once warm and friendly room. And, indeed, the sheet he held was inscribed in Dr. Clapton's delicate hand, "The Sminthiad," he read, "or the Cosmopolis of Smiths."

> "Shew, then, O Clio, heaven's immortal plan,
> Whereby Basil, the Macedonian——"

The paper fell from his hand, his under lip trembled like a little boy's. So The Work, too, was destroyed? They might have spared him that. A black mist of rage and grief enveloped him, he dropped on his knees amongst the dust and ashes and gathered up the few stray leaves.

As he walked back down the street distractedly, a grubby, jewelled hand arrested him. He heard the voice of Mr. Jenney, the pack-horse man.

"Master Fraser, suh. An' how do we fine ourselves to-day?"

Johnny did not deign to turn his head, but he could not escape the glitter of Mr. Jenney's new-bought finery, the shoddy plum-colored coat, the cheap, green satin waistcoat, the large imitation diamonds of his stock buckle.

"I certainly do trust, suh," Mr. Jenney went on, "that your distinguished father keeps his hea'th." He kept pace with Johnny, his hand clung to Johnny's arm with a damp embrace. "And as for me, suh, I can't complain, I'm doing mighty well in every way. Look at these yer clothes," he smoothered his iridescent paunch. "A man can't buy these clothes for nothing. I

reckon you've heard about me." He paused to give an opportunity for inquiry of which Johnny did not avail himself. "I'm under contract, suh," he
continued impressively, "to supply the entire gallant militia of this yer Province with salt beef. I may say, suh, that I embrace the chance to render
patriotic service to the Province, which, though a South Carolinian born,
suh, I shall ever regard as my foster-mother."

"I thought you were a Tory," said Johnny coldly.

Mr. Jenney's grasp on Johnny's arm tightened. "Hush," he whispered.
"Affairs are in a very different posture now, suh. In Charleston, Major
Moultrie, Mr. Pinckney, Mr. Laurens, and in fact all the leading families
have declared for the Colonies." He placed an interrogatory finger against
Johnny's bosom. "With all his kith and kin thus committed to the cause, is
Cassoway G. Jenney a man to hang back? Suh," he added with subdued
ferocity, "were it not for our long standing and mutually creditable in-
timacy I should most sho'ly resent your imputation."

They had by now reached the lane which led from Terry's waterfront
ordinary up to the street. Here some twenty men had gathered on the
cobbled roadway. There was not an honest fact amongst them, thought
Johnny, recognizing perhaps a dozen dockside loafers, smugglers, barroom
hangers-on of the old days, now blossomed forth in cheap magnificence
which rivalled Mr. Jenney's.

"The boys," Mr. Jenney explained, "gather here to get the election news."

Johnny was about to extricate himself from Mr. Jenney's embrace and
pass by on the other side of the street, when one of the group called out to
him.

"Hey, mister, what you got in your hand?" A shambling, old-young man
in a soiled tan greatcoat and silver-buckled hat followed his question with
an impudent grin.

Mechanically Johnny glanced down at the sheaf of leaves. —"Shew, then,
O Clio, heaven's immortal plan," he read. His throat grew hard and tight.
Shaking off Mr. Jenney, he strode up to the man.

"Where's Dr. Clapton?" he said. The words sounded harsh, dry, unlike his
own.

"He left in a hurry."

"Who burnt his books?"

The man grinned back at the circle of his friends, jerked a thumb at Johnny's face. "Thinks he's the King of England," he explained. He turned to Johnny. "Well, young poke-snout, what if you knew?"

"I——" said Johnny in a strangling voice, "I'd smash the man that did it."

"Smash me, then," said the other, and pushed him in the face with a greasy hand.

Then they were swinging fiercely toe to toe. The other gave ground, Johnny followed up, a knee jerked up and hit him in the stomach. He turned sick and numb. So that was the game, then. He steadied himself, rushed at the grinning face. A blow behind struck him on the head. He was falling through dizzy chaos. Now he lay on the cobbles; a heavy boot swung against his ribs.

"Let be, my friends," cried Mr. Jenney's voice; Mr. Jenney's hands were under his armpits, lifting him.

"He's had enough my brave boys," he added in an ingratiating tone. "Come with me, suh," he whispered to Johnny, "I'll take care of you."

He supported Johnny down the lane, the others followed, called out obscenities at Johnny in low malignant tones. As they passed Terry's Ordinary, a drooping figure in a tan coat was being carried through the door. "I know where you're bound," Mr. Jenney went on, soothingly, "and I'm gwine to put you safe on boa'd, where you can stay until you sail. I'll have your boxes brought down to you. Don't you fret, suh," he added complacently. "They all know Cassoway G. Jenney hyer now, and they ain't a man of 'em dare touch you."

He led Johnny along the stone dock, up the gangplank of the French Barque and deposited him on a coil of rope before the astonished eyes of the little French sailors.

"Take care of this gentleman," he admonished them with pompous gravity. He dropped a hand on Johnny's shoulder.

"Thanks," said Johnny thickly.

Mr. Jenney seized him by the hand. "Not a word, suh, I beg. Whatever our principles, us gentlemen must stick together."

Going ashore, he led his glowering satellites up the lane.

Late next day they sailed. With his bruised face and cut lip, Johnny did not wish to appear on deck, lest some of his recent adversaries should be among the little crowd which lined the quay. Still less did he care to meet the proprietary and intimate glances of Mr. Jenney.

The thought of that tawdry, absurd, pretentious figure filled him with disgust. And when he pictured himself, solicitously escorted from the land of his birth under the protection of this same intolerable Mr. Jenney, now, it would seem, a leader of the rag-tag and bob-tail democracy as well as a battener off the misfortunes of the Province, when this humiliating scene came back to Johnny's mind, his bruised face burned with shame, he hardly dared look out his little port-hole.

At last he heard French orders on the deck above. He heard men hauling on the braces, heard the flop of a cast-off hawser on the dock, the groan of timbers against a pile. The cabin floor tilted ever so slightly beneath his feet. He looked up from his bunk. Across the thick glass of his port-hole, a lattice of bare trees and the distant courthouse cupola slipped slowly by.

They were off, by Zooks! And a good job, too. But as they cleared the harbor, Johnny Fraser stood up, stepped to the port. Ahead lay the tawny waters of the sound; astern, he saw a streak of sandy beach; above it, the close ranks of immemorial pines; pines, tall, true, shaggy, gently whispering like those which joined protecting branches over the old clay plastered house where he was born. He cast himself, face down, on his bunk and pressed his eyes against the musty counterpane.

Three weeks of sea; three weeks of dirt and damp, of hearty salted winds, of creaking sheets and pattering reef-points, three weeks of swaying through grave imperturbable expanse. They raised the cliffs, white, sturdy, turf-crowned, of England. The cliffs of England! What a world lay in the staunch yet magic word! A world of hope, of gold-encrusted legends, of dimly sensed but potent heritage, of dreams that seemed like memories, of memories like dreams. The cliffs of England! Johnny Fraser, leaning taut against the rail, strained eyes for every glimpse of the buttressed, long, chalk wall and licked the salt cake from his lips to keep them steady.

JOHNNY'S DEFEAT AT THE DOCK

*He supported Johnny down the lane, the others followed, called out obscenities at Johhny in*
*low malignant tones*

They stood in until he could make out sheep grazing on the downs above and tiny figures hauling nets on the shining beach below. All day they ran along the coast, the many sails of channel traffic to starboard and on their lee the fields, the woods, the hedge-flanked roads, the brown-roofed white-walled towns, the faintly chiming spires of old England.

Toward afternoon they doubled a fore-land and ran before the wind. The coast grew dim, but the seaways were filled with many sails of luggers, hoys, trawlers, tall merchant ships.

Now the water turned yellow, low shores closed in on either hand, they passed a channel buoy. Stooping gently to the helm, the ship was brought up in the wind. A pilot, in a leather hat and blue pea jacket, incredibly unmoved by the momentous occasion, climbed stolidly up the side and took the wheel. The yards were squared, he stood on up the stream. The river narrowed, turned South. Above the low-lying banks, Johnny Fraser made out the masts and rigging of innumerable ships, evenly spaced like soldiers on parade. The pilot spun the wheel, they changed their course. The banks receded; slowly, one by one, the British Fleet at anchor came in view. Their upper works shone a brilliant blue against the darkening sky, their great brown hulls swung sullenly at the cables, their gunports stared straight ahead like stupid and vindictive eyes. As they drew abreast, he saw the crimson muzzles and black throats of the guns. On the nearest ship a captain in white breeches and blue coat, pacing his gilded stern-walk, stopped and brought his glass to bear on a barge rowing smartly by, its long pennant trailing out behind. When the barge drew alongside the flagship white-coated side boys manned the companionway and with stately long-drawn notes the bosun's whistle piped the side.

Westward, up the river, the sun was sinking in a low-hung pall of smoke. Johnny Fraser's heart jumped. There lay the smoke of London; he would sleep tonight in London; he could almost hear the roar and rumble of the town.

They cleared the last ship of the line and stood in for low sprawling docks. Behind them, now faint, now clear, a hundred ships' bells sounded eight.

Ahead a wherry hailed them, "Hirondelle Ahoy!" The wherryman stopped rowing, a small, sandy-haired man in a black cloak stood up in the bows and ran his sharp glance down the French Barque's rail. He stopped at Johnny and gazed kindly but keenly into his face.

"You're Fraser," he announced decisively, "and I'm Tavish." He nodded brusquely, shook hands with himself and flashed a smile. "Welcome to England," he said.

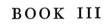

BOOK III

## CHAPTER XXXIV

O F ALL the anti-climaxes which had attended Johnny Fraser's initia-
tion into London's smart society none had forecast its character with
such dreary certitude, or so far in advance, as had the final try-on of his new
lute-string suit. Ordered in a moment of elation early in the season when
Johnny's conquest of the town had seemed less improbable to him than ever
since, the suit had dragged its wretched embryonic life through months of
fittings, its progress never swift and often totally arrested to make way,
Johnny suspected, for the orders of more distinguished patrons. Now that
April was almost here, the season almost ended, and now, above all, that
Johnny Fraser had lost zest for the smart world and in consequence had
acquired active disgust for the suit intended to impress it, a card had come
announcing that Mr. Tilley begged most respectfully to advise him of the
suit's completion. To add the final touch to the distasteful episode the post
which had brought Mr. Tilley's card had brought Johnny a letter from Sir

301

Nat which seemed to reduce him and his fine airs and his lute-string suit to infinitesimal proportions. Yet so good-hearted, so honest and friendly was its intention that Johnny could hardly let it leave his hand. It lay now in his waistcoat pocket as he walked down Villiers Street to Mr. Tilley's shop.

The shop itself, as all London knew, was so pre-eminent that it could afford to be unpretentious. Two ancient windows, their small panes all askew, flanked the green door which bore a neat brass plate inscribed with the single, solemn word: "Tilley." Johnny entered with a sigh.

The inside of the shop was panelled white, a worn blue drugget carpet covered the floor. On one wall hung a long mirror in a Chinese lattice frame, across the other stretched a row of gorgeous finished costumes, looking for all the world like a company of Piccadilly Beaux formed up and panoplied for social conquest. The illusion was complete, thought Johnny with an ironic smile; the iridescent figures lacked all real substance; symbolic of their owners, they existed only in two dimensions, mere gaudy silhouettes of fashion.

While Johnny was enjoying these sagacious and witty reflections, the blue baize curtains at the rear parted, the suave and solicitous young gentleman employed by Mr. Tilley for the sole purpose, apparently, of discussing with Mr. Tilley's patrons the state of the weather and of their health, stood before him smoothing down the pocket flaps of his tight black mohair coat with an air of elegant complaisance touched with self-deprecation. His small pale face, which just fell short of aristocracy, lit up in facile welcome.

"Good day, sir, and how have you been?"

"Oh, I'm all right," Johnny grinned. "But it looks as if the weather had gone into a decline."

"Quite so, sir," the other answered in a mystified tone. He touched a bellpull by the curtain. "We are quite ready for you, sir. Your suit will be up directly. Pray take this chair."

Hugging one knee, Johnny gazed out the window at the dripping street. The young man's soothing murmur was in his ear, but he answered only with a perfunctory nod. He was thinking again of the letter in his pocket. He knew the scrawling words, each one of them, by heart and every time he recalled them he felt a flush on his face, an ache deep down within him. Yet he must read the letter again. He drew it out and spread it on his knee. With a discreet and slightly injured cough the young man withdrew. Johnny held the letter to the light.

"Carlisle, England, April 20, 1778

"Dear Bantam.

"You will be surprised at the news I have to give you I have quitted the Regiment. There was talk of sending us to America and I said Americans were downright Sportsmen and I w'd be damned if I fought 'em and they said they were a sett of low Shopkeepers and one thing led to another and to make a long story short the Col. made me resign only I resigned first. He was fewrious, and w'd not give me leave to sell so I have lost my Comm" and my Money too. Otherwise w'd come to see you which I wish you w'd do if ever you intend for this part of the country. Write me Bantam do

"Your fast friend Nat.

"P. S. You don't know anyone who wants a top weight hunter do you a blood horse by Castor bright chestnut and very bold and flippent.
"P. S. He roars a bit galloping but it doesn't stopp him."

He read the uneven scrawl over again then twice more. With an effort he raised his eyes and gazed out the window; after all, why should he sit there staring forever at a letter which only seemed to cheapen everything he had conceived himself to be; which destroyed at a stroke everything for which he had labored the past two years. He ran them over in his mind. First, as a junior clerk in MacKellor and Tavish's he had spent months writing bills for tierces of Malaga grapes, for sacks of Tyneside coals, for pipes of canary; copying sea-letters, muster rolls, and bills of lading—writing insurance in a cobwebbed room where clerks talked ponderously of bottomry and respondentia; then, later, promoted to a small desk of his own, he inscribed in neat, flowing hand letters of credit and bills of exchange for masters and mates who sat before him rotating their hats in their hands and shifting uncomfortably in their broadcloth shore-suits.

He smiled with tender reminiscence. England was then new and wonderful, his own position as a junior clerk in a well-established old firm nothing short of distinguished. And beside mastering business practice without great effort and with no small credit to himself, he had been pleasantly conscious of becoming week by week more of a knowing young Londoner. There had been suppers at Shoreditch at the house of Mr. Tavish and dinners in the Mile End Road at Mr. MacKellor's; he and other junior clerks had witnessed the illuminations at Vauxhall condescendingly, had vouchsafed approval to Mr. Garrick from the balcony of Covent Garden and had enjoyed many quiet and several noisy dinners at their favorite coffee house, the Cat and Fiddle.

He stared disconsolately out the window at the black and dripping cobblestones of Villiers street. That first year had been full of gusto, of hope and promise. The life in MacKellor and Tavish's and out of it had been vastly inspiring and had, in his own esteem, added new perfection to him as a man of the world. There were, indeed, moments when, writing a bill of lading for supplies to Lord Howe's Army at New York or reading a news letter which told how General Washington fleeing across New Jersey had turned and struck at Trenton, he felt, if not uneasy or ashamed, at least less distinguished than he could have wished. But then came another dinner at the Cat and Fiddle.

With the second autumn his life had changed. Eve and Captain Tennant, arriving in London from Halifax, took a small house in Bird Cage Walk. He could still feel vividly the thrill which her first note of invitation had given him, could recall each detail of his first visit. Again he saw himself before the neat buff-plastered little house with its dark blue shutters, its white stone steps and wrought iron hand rails. He remembered pausing for a moment, smoothing down his stock ruffle and wishing that he could smooth down his fluttering heart as well. Mounting the steps, he scraped the London mud off his French leather slippers and pulled the shining brass handle of the bell.

Liveried and powdered, Hoddin swung back the door and permitted himself a quickly mastered smile of recognition.

"Fraser!" cried Captain Tennant from the drawing-room. "Egad, sir, an uncommon pleasure!"

He shook hands with Johnny in the doorway, placed Johnny's hand beneath his own blue velvet sleeve and led him into the room.

Candles, reflected by a hundred pendant prisms, shone in two candelabra, dark portraits and closed curtains showed dimly in the furthest light. Standing before a grate of coals in a low-cut gown of green satin, Eve Tennant smiled. "And now, sir," the Captain said, "tell me what do you do here? Eve, sit there. Fraser, this chair."

Johnny Fraser remembered with what alacrity he launched on his narrative. No one could deny that it was distinctly creditable to have achieved a private desk at MacKellor and Tavish's within the space of fifteen months. Yet as he described his career to these two, its distinction seemed to suffer a subtle diminution. Captain Tennant nodded vaguely and without enthusiasm as though to suggest that commercial life might possibly be well enough in its way, but that it lay outside his ken and was therefore in all probability dubious, while Eve, far from being impressed, seemed to view his clerkship with baffled amusement as she would the hair-brained escapades of young bucks who drove public hackney carriages or, for their own peculiar entertainment, mingled with the lower orders disguised as costers. Johnny's voice trailed away rather lamely.

"Yes, seh, we do business with 'most every country in the world," he ended.

"Ah," said the Captain with a blank stare.

After supper the Captain had left the two of them to themselves in the drawing room. From the sofa Eve, smoothing her satin skirts, raised her eye to Johnny with a warm arch smile.

"Well," she said, as if this was the first moment of their meeting, "how have you been, sir?" She withdrew her skirts to make a place beside her and smiled again. She was older, riper, more striking and, for better or worse, Johnny had told himself, more assured, more competent than ever. "The last time we met," she went on, as Johnny took the seat beside her, "we quarreled——"

"And made it up, ma'm."

"I wonder. You have not written."

"That's a fact, Eve, but I didn't know where you were."

"Quite so. That relieved you of responsibility."

Johnny Fraser paused, at loss. By Zooks, the low-grade repartee of junior clerks had unfitted him for a delicate crisis like the present. He must move about in the smart world and brush up again.

"You don't think me sincere, then?"

"I do, when you neglect me."

"I don't think you suffer much from neglect," he said bluntly, "with Master Cherry to escort you out of Edenton and a thousand young British officers waitin' fo' you wherever you landed. What's become of Master Cherry?" he asked, well pleased to find a different subject even though it were only the ridiculous fat boy.

"Master Cherry? Oh! he has joined a marching regiment."

"That ought to take some of the pork-fat off his ribs."

"He is looking very well," she answered coldly.

"You've seen him then; where'bouts is he?"

Now it was her turn to be somewhat confused. "He is stationed at Woolwich, I believe."

Etiquette was thrown aside, he scoffed openly in the manner of a small boy.

"You believe? Why, my Lord, Eve, you know!"

But here he had gone too far.

"I suppose you think that I should break off all my friendships, on the chance that I might some day receive a letter from you."

Damnation! They were back on the same ground.

"Eve, I did write, I tell you. I expect you didn't ever get the most of my letters." He had passed on quickly lest she should call for an enumeration. "Anyhow, now that I know where you are I'll write or come to see you as often as you'll let me."

He could see her soft figure turning languidly beneath the satin gown. Her eyes, dark and provocative, dwelt on his. She leaned forward, touched him with her fan. The slender sticks of ivory seemed charged with fire.

WITH EVE IN LONDON

*"Well," she said as if this was the first moment of their meeting, "how have you been, sir?"*

"Indeed!" she gave a low-voiced laugh. "Well, we shall see."

She shrugged a white shoulder and turned idly away. It was now Johnny Fraser who leaned forward. He whispered protestations into her averted ear. In the face of her continued indifference, his language grew almost poetical, especially when describing his own loneliness in London, waiting, he implied, for her to come. He drew the picture with authentic pathos; she did not move, but her eyes grew softer. At this most unpropitious moment, Captain Tennant's step was heard on the stair.

"Hush!" She laid a warning hand on his. With a swift movement she gave him a glimpse of parted lips and warm brown eyes, close to his own. Captain Tennant's footfalls were descending; Johnny Fraser just had time to spring up giddily and take his post by the grate before the curtains parted.

As far as constant attendance on the house in Bird Cage Walk was concerned, Johnny Fraser had been as good as his word. He played backgammon with the Captain patiently enough and learned loo and ombre from Eve. He decided to act on her suggestion that, in preparation for the coming winter, a few lessons in the minuet at Signor Angelo's would be as well; otherwise, she hinted, he might find too late that there was some difference between the dancing of North Carolina and that of London. She also mentioned that a certain stock tie, vastly puffed and ruffled, which had been the sensation of Edenton and even caused no little favorable comment among the junior clerks at MacKellor and Tavish's, was no longer being worn. Her meaning was of course not literal; he had seen precisely the same sort of stock among the gentlemen who matched horses on Hampstead Heath and, indeed, at the very moment when Eve announced that stocks of this particular design were not being worn, he had his on. When she used the phrase she evidently had in mind some other class of persons, a class so dazzling, so indisputably authoritative, that beside them the sportsmen on Hampstead Heath and Johnny Fraser himself sank to nonentity. From other remarks of Eve and from her expectant attitude, Johnny Fraser gathered that this class, absent from London during the summer, was now about to return, that their arrival, with their wives, their children, their dowagers, their mistresses, their private chaplains, their lackeys, footmen, flunkeys, French horns, knifeboys, their pomatum, peruques and patches, would signalize the opening of the London Season, a phenomenon which Johnny Fraser's provincial wits had been too dull to recognize the winter before, but which, he was given to understand, operated each January in the twinkling of an eye to transform London from an ant-hill of laboring insects to a giddy Olympus of butterflies.

And sure enough, no sooner had the first frost fallen on tiles and cobbled roadways than there was a great shaking of dust cloths from the windows of Green Park and Piccadilly, a great scouring of knobs and marble doorsteps by red-armed slaveys, a great clattering of pots in areas; then, well-caked with country mud, the coronetted carriages rolled up to the curb. Footmen laid their blunderbusses beneath the boxes, climbed down, opened carriage doors; the ladies and the gentlemen on whose somewhat tired-looking shoulders rested the responsibility of transforming London, entered their town houses.

The house in Bird Cage Walk seemed to vibrate to the rattle of every carriage-wheel. Eve continued to talk about The Season, but her manner was nervous and at times a little sharp. Once, laying aside his hat in the hallway, Johnny Fraser heard her voice, angry and tearful, and the Captain's blunt reply.

"Egad, I'll not stand nagging! I tell you I'm doing the best I can for you, my girl!"

At last came a radiant day when an immensely tall and immensely powdered footman left Lady Southport's cards at Captain Tennant's door. Other footmen, still taller, still more powdered, rang the bell. Within a fortnight, the mirror above the drawing-room mantel was fringed with cartes de visite and invitations to drums and routs.

"I reckon I won't see much of you from now on," Johnny had said disconsolately.

"Indeed you shall. We shall take you with us; they are always amused, Papa says, to meet someone different to the ordinary. A young American gentleman——" she laughed. "You may be the sensation of the season."

"I don't know whether I'll know how to act," he had muttered uneasily. His self-confidence had been shaken by the mere preliminaries, so portentous and grave, of the coming campaign.

"Just be yourself. They will think it delightful." She reflected. "Perhaps you might say," she had added with an effort to be casual, "that you are here as your father's agent; I mean you might say merely that."

"Why? What's the matter with MacKellor and Tavish? That's a mighty good house, isn't it?"

"I'm sure it is, but no one goes in for city merchants here; perhaps they might not understand. It's quite different to America, you know. However, do as you like."

"No, I'm much obliged for the hint. I'll do what you say."

As the season progressed, his interest in the house of MacKellor and Tavish had suffered abatement. Perhaps it was the late hours, perhaps the quantities of negus; perhaps it was his ill-starred play at whist which sent him to his desk each morning a little more jaded, a little more bored, a little more conscious of the other junior clerks' mediocrity. The junior clerks, on their side, had also changed their attitude toward him since his elevation to the hierarchy of Mayfair. Their bearing toward him was marked by a certain envious contempt; he was, they had discovered, a macaroni, a fashionable swell, and that in itself was well enough. "But what, then," they seemed to ask, "was he doing in the offices of a city merchant?" Despite his present loftier status, Johnny Fraser half regretted the easy vulgarity of the suppers at the Cat and Fiddle; among his more brilliant new associations, he had, were he to acknowledge it, found nothing to replace them. Still it was too early to judge; one did not gain Mayfair in a month; he must keep on, become established in the circle which was his by rights.

That must have been in February. The winter now had passed, early spring was here and he was no nearer achieving success in the world of fashion. Far from becoming the sensation of the season, he seemed to have lost ground. The first interest which, as a strange American, he had excited, waned with the season's waning glory. The second thoughts which the beau monde gave him, if, indeed, they gave him any thoughts at all, were unfavorable. They looked down on his accent, his impulsive manner; they divined his commercial pursuits, classed him coldly as a "cit." Oblivious of his dreams of England, of his difficult loyalty to the King, they showed for him the dull, contemptuous dislike they felt for all Americans.

He, on his part, having come to know society, more than suspected that its seal was not authoritative. Though never quite admitted as an intimate of the elegants, he was close enough to observe them, to catch beneath their suave veneer the half-veiled, stabbing looks, the soft-spoken, venomed words which passed between them. He heard great ladies whisper filthy stories or, in moments of furious unrestraint, curse their servants with hard-bitten bursts of filthy language; he saw pomaded bucks and so-called maidens pass secret glances not greatly different from the glances of mulatto trulls and seamen in a certain alleyway of Edenton. Just as London rouge, cologne and powder covered bodies not over frequently washed, he told himself, so the bright enameled London manner covered fierce spitefulness and petty joyless license.

April was here, dull summer about to fall on the town. Well, he was just as glad. He would sink back into the obscurity of the city.

"Quite ready, sir," the young man's smooth voice said.

Johnny thrust Sir Nat's letter in his pocket and followed the slender impeccable figure through the curtains to a dressing-room.

He had no more than changed to the breeches of his new suit than his door was opened by the fitter, a stout, stoop-shouldered, exhausted looking little man, who knelt down before him and remained for several moments surveying the breeches in an attitude of adoration.

"Indeed, sir," he breathed at last, "I feel very happy about these breeches." He removed a pin which had been held ready in his mouth and stuck it among the others on his waistcoat to indicate that further alteration was unthinkable.

"And now, shall we try the coat and waistcoat, sir?" He scrambled up and held the garments out.

A step sounded in the passageway outside. A door handle clicked from the adjoining dressing-room, a high-pitched voice cried, "Ged's Life! Send me Tilley. I'll see none but Tilley."

A look of profound anxiety crossed the fitter's face.

"One moment, sir, I beg," he muttered. "Perhaps you would care to view yourself, sir, in the pier glass out front." He vanished.

As Johnny walked to the front of the shop the young man in the mohair coat rushed past, vastly preoccupied. He heard another "Ged's Life!" followed by hushed whispers in the rear, and then the august and mighty footfalls of Mr. Tilley, himself, descending from his office above stairs.

Johnny smiled. He recognized the high-pitched voice as that of young Lord Twitterhurst, a noble simpleton, who, if not quite as wealthy as believed, was at least wealthy enough and simple enough to be held by social London in the highest esteem. A few months ago Johnny would not have suffered himself to be thrust aside in favor of another patron of any birth whatsoever. He would have played the young buck, stood on his rights, made a scene. But now, perhaps because of Sir Nat's letter, he did not seem to care. Even if he did reduce the proud Tilley to humble deference, what would he gain thereby? That was not the sort of pride he needed. The game, of which the present moment was a part, was not worth the candle. Resigning himself to a wait, he surveyed his dark maroon lute-string in the glass. The effect was really splendid. His slim, strong figure displayed its perfect fit most gracefully. Its deep red color harmonized with a face from which two years in London had not quite removed the North Carolina tan and contrasted to advantage with the deep blue of his eyes. His brown hair, unpowdered and tied back in a simple club, was probably as thick, as dark, as warmly tinted as that of any man in London. What would he not have given a few years back to see himself in Tilley's mirror thus arrayed. Now, his achievement of a perfect suit of clothes possessed the one irremediable defect of arriving a shade too late. He recalled his first suit of homespun coat and calfskin breeches which he had worn away to Edenton. In spite of homesickness and foreboding, how proud he had been of those crude products of his mother's loving toil. Later on at Edenton the suit had been hidden away in favor of garments more technically correct and even they, as his knowledge grew, had been regarded as mere interludes in his progress toward a splendid London habit. Well, here it was at last, and here was he inside it. But except for the bare physical fact he seemed to have nothing else to show for all his pains. Sitting down in a chair, he stared at the gorgeous, dejected figure in the glass. That was the question; what had he to show? When Eve and Captain Tennant had first introduced him to society, he had been frightened but dazzled, fascinated and profoundly impressed by the glittering pageant. But as the winter passed he had come to learn by slow degrees, though hardly daring to confess his secret to himself, that the ritual of drums, assemblies, unending games of lansquenet and unending passages of modish conversation which Mayfair followed, was tedious and, for him at least, onerous and depressing out of all proportion to its intrinsic levity. Still, he had been convinced, that the process of becoming a smart young London beau, disappointing though it might be as a source of pleasure, remained at least a solemn duty; that there was some profound if indefinable advantage in becoming identified with this world; that the people who composed it were vastly important and that association with them would confer added importance on him.

Now that last and most far-fetched of his illusions had vanished like the rest. Still he must play the farce out to the end of the season. Not many weeks remained. To retire now would appear a confession of defeat and little as his presence was noted by Mayfair, his absence would, no doubt, be the subject of triumphant jibes. It might not be too difficult. He could gain a certain amusement independently of others, could go through the posturings with the rest, remaining the while withdrawn in himself, a sage and a penetrating observer. Besides there was another compensation.

Eve, who had at first produced him with something like triumph, or at least with high hopes, had on reading the unmistakable signs of his social failure, found ways, too subtle for any specific exception to be taken, to dissociate herself from it, to disclaim before the others responsibility for him. On the other hand her intimacy with Cherry had grown. Johnny laid it to the imminent departure of Cherry's regiment for the American war. He looked forward with gloomy satisfaction to the day when the troops embarked. But now it seemed that he need hardly wait till then. She had of late seemed less preoccupied with Cherry, more cordial and unaffected toward him. She, too, perhaps, saw through the unmeaning masquerade. At all events she seemed now to feel that the two of them had more in common. She was open, cheerful, more like the girls of North Carolina, and she took a good deal of pains, Johnny guessed, to make sure that he was asked to the same houses as herself. As a member of Lady Southport's party, he was to take Eve that evening, for instance, to the last ball of the season at the Pantheon in Oxford Road. The lute-string suit was ready for the occasion, and he himself, encased in its smooth radiance, would be perfect yet lightly contemptuous of his perfection.

"Quite ready now, sir," the fitter said. Johnny Fraser started, smiled and sprang up almost with alacrity.

## CHAPTER XXXV

PICCADILLY was ablaze with streaming flambeaux held high by footmen who swayed on the perches of a hundred coaches. Passing and repassing, their light shot incessant beams into the depths of Lady Southport's great town carriage and illuminated the ample brocaded bosom and jaded yet determined face of Lady Southport, who sat facing Johnny. They showed the warm red lips of Eve, beside which the third lady of the party, a certain Honorable Agatha Foljambe, distinguished chiefly for her pedigree, appeared more colorless than ever. Sharing the seat with Johnny, sat Captain Tennant, very stiff, meticulously turned out, and radiating cautious satisfaction at the prospect of appearing in such exclusive company. Beyond him young Lord Twitterhurst rested his receding chin on his malacca stick and greeted all remarks impartially with high-pitched, foolish laughter. The carriage stopped with a jerk, crept forward, stopped again; the wheels grated on the curb, the door flew open. The footmen forced a passage for

314

the distinguished party through swaying sedan chairs, through sober, plodding citizens and insolently staring macaronis. They paused in the buzzing
ante-room while the ladies removed their clogs and gave them into the footmen's charge. Another moment and they were in the colonaded lobby of the
Pantheon. While Johnny Fraser still blinked in the blaze of a thousand
candles, one flunkey whisked Eve away, another bore off his own hat, cloak
and stick. Bereft, he stared ahead at the vast rotunda where, to the solemn
strains of horn and viol, plumed head-dresses and powdered periwigs were
already nodding in the first quadrille. The inexorable flunkies passed him on
to the ballroom. Seeking cover behind a column, he studied the assemblage.
The quadrille continued with a sweeping of brocaded skirts and quilted
petticoats, a pointing of diamond buckled toes, with genteel inclinations of
satin coats and measured posturings of silk-stockinged calves. Among the
columns which circumscribed the room, new arrivals circulated, formed
knots, laughed, kissed hands, curtsied, made compliments, grimaced politely and moved on. In a farther ante-room, the iron-faced dowagers were
already entrenching for a night of whist; nearby, three flamboyant Irish
gentlemen had preempted a punch bowl and now with the most affecting
cordiality offered what little remained of its contents to every lady who
passed. Beside the column next to Johnny, a group of ruddy country Members in coats as ancient and hereditary as their untitled names, talked doggedly of blister rust, of winter wheat, of stud hounds. Their well-pondered,
homely chat touched Johnny with a sense of loneliness. Those fellows were
more like people in North Carolina; it was talk that you could bite your
teeth on. But just then Eve's green satin dress appeared among the crowd.

"Oh, there you are," she said, "I thought you had deserted me."

"No, ma'm," he replied, "I never repeat myself."

"I vow," she cried, "if you have not at least the impudence of a London
wit!"

Lady Southport and the others joined them. The music had stopped.
Marshalling her party, she advanced across the polished floor. Now perukes
and powdered head-dresses nodded, lorgnettes and perspective glasses were

brought into play. Lady Southport bridled complacently; all was well; their party was observed.

On the farther side between two columns, at a table reserved for them, Italian waiters, discreetly ecstatic, bowed low, adjusted chairs solicitously, proffered negus and wafers.

Studiously oblivious of whatever sensation their arrival was causing, they chatted among themselves, inclined their heads, leaned forward, laughed.

"Has your la'yship been to the play this week at Covent Garden?" Lord Twitterhurst was saying. "What? No? Ged smite me, ma'm, if they have not built a barricado before the stage since Darey Sparks' last frolic. Mounst'ous iron spikes, I vow."

"Ah," said Lady Southport, "Sir Darey was the young rakehell who carried Mrs. Wilder off from the play."

"The same, ma'm, and I was there the night it happened. Ged's life, I shall never forget it! It was the third act of 'Julius Cæsar,' and the fair Wilder as Calpurnia was looking uncommon fetching in a mob cap and quilted petticoat. Some sparkish wags and I were in the pit, enjoying ourselves immoderately, when presto! Darey leaps upon the stage, seizes the Wilder, and out through the wings before you could say, 'Ged's life!' " He gave his high laugh. "And there we sat, Ged love me, without our heroine."

"His intentions," said Lady Southport, "were more obvious than honorable, I suppose."

Captain Tennant tapped his stick on the floor. "An epigram!" he chuckled. "Good, Egad! Good! An epigram!" But Lady Southport was by no means complimented.

"You call that an epigram, sir? You have lived too long in the Provinces."

"Honorable intentions!" cried the young baronet. "Why, ma'm, the Wilder is naught but an actress, while Darey is as well-bred as any man in England, and no fool, neither." He drew himself up with dignity. "I mean to say, there was never a question of honorable intentions."

"Now, Captain," said Lady Southport calmly, "you may cry epigram."

Eve Tennant, turning in her chair, smiled back at Johnny. "Lord Twitterhurst," she said, "in one word has given us the character of the times." She glanced at the young nobleman with a mocking inclination of her head.

"Ha!" he said. "Ged love me! Have I so?" He giggled uncertainly. "Capital! Ha! ha!"

Lady Southport was in one of her rare moods of animation. Her broad, grim face was rigid under its white enamel, but her small eyes blazed malignantly, her constricted bosom heaved, her wrinkled dewlap swung. A sudden thought almost made Johnny laugh out loud. He pictured Lady Southport meeting his mother. He saw the mean and pompous old beldame attempt to patronize his mother in her plain camlet gown. He saw his mother's mouth and eyes, so boyish, innocent and frank, yet so deadly in their acumen. By Zooks! Two words of his mother's would send the great, fat, painted harridan trundling, baffled and disconcerted, on her way.

"And so," Lady Southport was saying, "she began by keeping a coachman, and now the coachman"—she glanced over her shoulder at the Honorable Agatha—"and now their position is reversed." Her enamel cracked in an evil smile.

Eve was turning again to speak to him.

"Edenton," she whispered, "is a long way from here."

"Yes," he said, "it's a long way from London in some things."

"I know. Sometimes I think I am tiring of London."

"I got tired of London some time back."

"I have no doubt, but you are more acute than I."

"Or maybe less popular," he answered with a grin.

They talked together in confidential whispers. Eve had never seemed so warmly friendly, so free from affectation. She seemed to Johnny to stand out, unrivalled, in this wilderness of snobs. Why had she never been quite like this before? He expanded, broke down his reserve, and, gazing into her comprehending eyes, poured out with just a light touch of self-pity the story of his isolation. Withdrawn behind the column, he took no note of the passing scene until the music ceased. Then glancing across the floor, he saw a figure in a scarlet uniform rise abruptly and hurry from its table. A moment later Master Cherry, bursting from his gold and scarlet uniform, was peering at them. With creakings of the waistcoat he bent and kissed Eve's hand. "Oh, good evening, Hal," Eve said listlessly. "You know Lady Southport and the rest." Master Cherry bobbed his small round head to the company. He popped his little eyes and stuck out a skin-tight glove at Johnny, "How do, Fraser. Coffee, Eve?" and crooked his stubby arm.

"Oh," said Eve with reluctance, "I was just talking with Mr. Fraser here. Perhaps he will join us?"

"Quite," said Master Cherry, turning his fat back on Johnny. "You are irresistible, seh," said Johnny coldly. "But I must decline."

The music sounded. And still Johnny was alone.

Again alone he remained; Master Cherry had brought with him a retinue of young subalterns from his regiment, rather dubious and avid-looking youths who hung about him, flattered him disdainfully and bared their teeth in sardonic grins behind his fat back. There was nothing specious, however, in the attention which they devoted to Eve. Johnny Fraser, forgotten, could only console himself by observing that the same oblivion seemed about to overtake Master Cherry. He drank many glasses of negus with the Captain and was presented by him to many ladies who, he was given to understand, had been monstrous belles and toasts of the town in their day, but who now appeared intent only upon obtaining partners for daughters that had obviously no prospects of equalling their mothers' successes. To these young ladies, plain, awkward, ungracious, Johnny accorded only perfunctory attention; indeed, it required studied efforts to achieve this much, to conceal the baffled and impotent rage in his heart. Arriving as the titulary escort of a charmer, he had been swiftly relegated to a position lower than that of the flunkies at the door. The keen-eyed dowagers had seen his fall and now swooped on him as their lawful prey; he was to be forthwith consigned to the limbo where cast-off youths maintained a joyless semblance of revelry with misfit maidens. By Zooks, he never would accept such fate. He sought out Eve; the next dance but three, she said; he waited.

They danced in silence; he did his best and it was by no means bad. While not affecting the extravagances of the Mounseers, his dancing was altogether less wooden than that of the solemn Britons around him. Eve, too, had brought back grace and lightness from the colonies; they were a perfect couple.

"You do dance well," she murmured at the end.

"But not often, it appears."

"Oh!" she cried, "you are jealous. You should not be."

"Why not?"

"Their regiment may get orders for America at any time. One cannot be cruel." She leaned forward with something tender yet something hard in her eyes. "Were you wearing the King's colors," she said, "I should dance with you most of all."

"If you're looking for uniforms," he said, "you should have stayed in America. There's plenty there, I hear; all kinds—Brandenburg, Saxon, Hessian; they've got fine uniforms in those regiments."

"You are merely rude," she said disdainfully. "You have lived too long as a hero among junior clerks. You——" She checked herself, placed a hand on his arm. "No, no," she said, "you must not, and I must not either. Why do we always quarrel so? I said more than I meant. I only meant that I would have the fashionable world appreciate you, and if you continue a mohair in time of war, I fear they will not do so."

"Continue a what?"

"Oh, I should not have said that; it is what the soldiers call the civilians."

Across the floor, Johnny Fraser saw Master Cherry and his entourage, laughing together and staring at him. "I wish," he said with earnestness, "that some soldier would call me that to my face."

She gave him an admiring smile. "I should never again speak to one who did," she said. "Will you dance the next with me?"

The ball broke up; the Pantheon disgorged the smart assemblage into Oxford Road, where hackney carriages locked wheels and cursed each other, where sedan chairs shouldered through the press; where vociferous link boys spilled grease on ladies' capuchins, cockaded footmen escorted tottering duchesses in clogs, porters bellowed: "Chair! chair!" and chair-men, well stupefied with gin, came stumbling from the public house; where dirty-nosed ragamuffins opened chair doors and were kicked by chairmen; where chairmen were pelted from behind by dirty-nosed ragamuffins; where, in a word, the rag-tag of the town contended with incredible tumult for possession of the elegant, until the last magnifico, yawning in the last sedan chair, had bobbed and lurched out of sight down the ill-lit, muddy highway; and where Johnny Fraser, still thrilling to the lingering farewell pressure of Eve Tennant's hand, marched with a becoming degree of swagger toward his lodgings in the Strand, more pleased with life and himself than for some time past.

"Good night," she had said. "Pray come to see me Thursday evening"— her warmest glance—"I shall look for you then."

# CHAPTER XXXVI

DURING THE year and more which Johnny Fraser had served as junior clerk in the house of MacKellor and Tavish, Export Merchants, Threadneedle Street, Cheapside, London, he had formed more or less the habit of strolling down King William Lane each evening after hours to sit on a wooden wall near London Bridge and watch the traffic, hear the sounds and smell the smells of London river. Nearly always something of import was stirring on that oily stream or among the huddled, crazy houses and walks which bordered it. Barges fouled each other with bursts of astounding language, skiffs stole softly among dark shadows, blunt fishing-smacks heaved their odorous, white-bellied cargoes ashore. Hackney carriages, post-chaises, farmers' wains, the Dover night coach rattled and rumbled over the cobbles and across the bridge. At dusk, stout citizens from counting-houses, wigged lawyers from the Inns of Court hurried along the bridge's footway, homeward bound.

Once it was dark, interest was greater still. Every light on shore and stream held mystery. Bedizened, intriguing ladies swung by in sedan chairs; pomaded bucks were now astir, and by the same token the scarlet waistcoats of Bow Street runners showed furtively in alleyways. On some nights, Johnny Fraser heard a warning whistle and saw the dockside wastrels and water-rats scatter for cover as a man-o'-war's guard-boat with a press crew aboard dropped down stream. But even on uneventful evenings Johnny liked to sit there, if only to watch the battlements of the Tower and the distant spars and topmasts by London Docks fade with the day.

The scene was always pleasant and never more so than on this April evening when the oil-streaked stream, the tumbled roofs and perilously leaning balconies were veiled and gilded by the twilight haze of summer's first faint intimation.

He had ceased to frequent the riverside during the past London season, when nearly every evening was given over to sartorial preparations for the expected conquests of the night. The season now was over, the conquests unachieved; he was glad to rest here again, to watch the homely heart of London perform its twilight transformation from grotesque to magical, and most of all on this particular evening, to fill in the hour before he could with propriety pay his call on Eve.

He hoped not so much to reproach her for having made him a stalking horse for Cherry, as that some happier explanation of her strategy would come from the meeting, some explanation which would restore his self-esteem and, more important, would allow him again to look on her as standing out in inspiring contrast against the dreary background of social London.

The darkness fell; the points of light on water, pier, tiled roof and spire died. The golden city vanished before his eyes as in his dreams golden England had vanished long ago.

Swinging a casual ladder, the lamp-boy made his rounds. The watch, an ancient, feeble hand, passed by with staves and lanterns. He felt the night mist rising from the river. It was time for him to move.

But Eve was not at home. Captain Tennant met him in the drawing-room.

"Eve is gone out."

"Gone out?"

"With young Cherry."

"Cherry! But his regiment sailed last night."

"Ah, no doubt. He was transferred to the staff at the Horse Guards the other day."

The Captain cleared his throat uneasily.

"Not a bad sort, Cherry." His voice held a note almost of appeal. "I believe he has prospects now. Eve tells me something has been done about his father's marriage."

"Is that so, seh?" said Johnny, vaguely wondering what could be done about a marriage at so late a date.

"Yes, I understand the Marquis of Cheyne, his uncle, is to make Cherry his heir. I am sorry Eve is not at home," he added. His voice was almost apologetic and faintly weary.

"But perhaps you would care to walk over to Brooks's with me. Parliament may soon adjourn. You might enjoy the opportunity to see some of our principal public characters before they are gone down from London."

Walking beside the Captain up St. James Street, Johnny Fraser mused on fate's weakness for the ironic. As with the lute-string suit, again it must have its jest. Brooks's club was the goal of every smart young man in town. In his walks he had often passed its drawn blinds respectfully and envied the élite who were privileged to step with such careless jauntiness through its pilastered door. Now he was to be a guest—five minutes after learning that Eve to whose friendship he had clung as the one thing genuine in fashion's weary masquerade, that Eve and her friendship had used him as a decoy in the game of catching Cherry. Not that he cared for Eve, although, indeed, he might have—but it struck his pride. Here was the Georgian portal of the club. He pulled down his waistcoat. Damn the girl. He swung his stick. Damn the girl. Was he not about to see the cream of England?

They were on the immaculate marble steps. A servant bowed to Captain Tennant from the vestibule.

Upstairs the long, green-panelled main room of Brooks's Club was crowded yet silent, the members, many clad in dark linen gaming coats, their sleeve ruffles protected by leather cuffs, clustered motionless around the great pharo table in the centre or faced each other like pairs of duellists at the écarté tables along the wall. Candles in thick silver candlesticks shed a theatrical light on the impassive faces; above the rigid groups tall white pilasters and narrow, gilded moldings rose, faded into the dimmer whiteness of the arched ceiling.

There was something profoundly ritualistic in the scene. At Edenton the casual, good-natured games of hazard and 'spoil five' had always been marked by noisy gusto, laughter, broad repartee, ironic cheers; spectators, leaning over the players' shoulders, offered a humorous running commentary on the game. Here all was different. Even those who were not engaged in play appeared to feel the deference due the celebration of the rites—they read their papers in corners, smoked quietly, spoke in low tones; the murmur of their conversation and of the gamblers' hushed syllables was shot through only by the clink of golden coins in the great silver tank of the pharo table.

"Hello!" said Captain Tennant. "There's Oddom." Taking Johnny's arm, he marched across the room to a settee where a man, very like himself, but older, duller looking, more choleric, was reading the "Standard."

"Good evening, Colonel," said Captain Tennant. To this salutation, Colonel Oddom made no reply whatever for the space of a minute. He then emitted a tortured grunt without raising his eyes from the paper. With admirable pertinacity, Captain Tennant continued to stand before him.

"You are not in the House tonight, sir," he finally observed.

The Colonel raised his small eyes with the look of a boar driven to bay. "Sit down," he burst out. "No," he went on in answer to the Captain's question, "paired."

"I suppose the House will rise at any moment now," Captain Tennant ventured.

"Should do, directly," the Colonel conceded, and plunged again into his newspaper.

"Coffee, young Fraser?" inquired Captain Tennant; he beckoned to one of the discreet servants in black satin knee-breeches who prowled silently about the room.

Sipping his coffee, Johnny stared at the scene before him—a scene so unchanging that it seemed as though the actors must have been condemned in some incredibly remote past to sit forever immobile in the toils of their obsession; it seemed as though the group around the clinking coins and the silver tank must be the centre of the universe, the one indestructible reality beside which casual figures passing through the room appeared mere ephemeral butterflies. And yet again their rigidly controlled intensity, devoted to an end so artificial, so far removed from life, made Johnny Fraser half suspect that the central group possessed no actuality at all, that it was a pure hypothesis, a man-made illusion, that the very waiters, preoccupied in their menial tasks, were more real, more significant.

Near Johnny Fraser's chair, a hollow-eyed young man stood looking out the window on St. James Street. A second hollow-eyed young man rose from the pharo table and joined him.

"Done play?"

"Yes, altogether done, I fancy."

"What, can't you raise the wind?"

"Not another penny; tried everything. I'm simply buried under a mound of stamped paper and post obits. Expect I shall have to live on the continent, what?"

"Oh, I say, never say die; I'll give you a letter to Thompson."

"Who's he?"

"He's an old putt who takes care of the King's Friends in Parliament. I daresay he'll see you out of debt."

"Ah! And what do I do?"

"You shut your eyes and your mouth and do what Thompson says. Do you care for the idea?"

"Good Gad!" cried the other. "You don't expect a man to be squeamish when he owes ten thousand guineas, do you?"

"Ah!" said the first young gentleman in an understanding tone. He continued to stare out the window. "There goes Belinda in her chair."

"To Lady Southport's, I make no doubt," replied the other. "The little strumpet. Did you hear——"

They whispered together, broke into an unctuous laugh and moved off down the room.

Wondering whether Captain Tennant had heard them, Johnny stole a covert glance at him; it was evident that he had not. But something in his face arrested Johnny; it showed a trace of disappointment, a trace almost too nebulous to be perceived by anyone, or perhaps to be felt by Captain Tennant himself. Johnny Fraser had long been aware that Captain Tennant regarded his membership in Brooks's as the most important single factor in his life. Brooks's was the quintessence of London, and London itself the quintessence of the universe. All through the winter the Captain had continually referred to Brooks's, to what was going on at Brooks's, to what was being rumored at Brooks's, to what he had said to a fellow at Brooks's; yet as the Captain sat there before Johnny's eyes, it became increasingly evident that his membership in Brooks's was purely an honorary distinction. It was hard for Johnny, accustomed to the Captain's supremacy at Edenton, to see him in this new perspective. The look of disappointment on Captain Tennant's unconscious face had, however, given Johnny an unhappy moment of detachment in which he saw that Captain Tennant's position at Brooks's was an illusion which imposed on no one else and had almost ceased to deceive the Captain himself; that in point of fact the Captain had apparently but one acquaintance in the club and that this acquaintance regarded him with unconcealed hostility. Perhaps Brooks's merely found the Captain lacking in sufficient attributes of rank, wealth, distinction to compensate for a certain general tediousness of manner; perhaps, with the fatuity of the unimaginative expert, the Captain had talked over-long and over-often on American affairs. More likely than either, he had merely committed the offense of remaining for too many years of his life absent from London and had returned to find himself classed as démodé, a subtle stigma which, once incurred, is from its very subtlety incapable of erasure.

As if conscious that he was not establishing his position at Brooks's in Johnny's sight, Captain Tennant roused himself for a new attempt against Colonel Oddom.

"I have introduced my young friend here, sir," he said, "because as an American——"

The Colonel's newspaper barricade came down with a slap.

"An American? A cursed rebel?"

"No, sir," replied Captain Tennant stiffly and with conscious pride. "A loyal subject of his Majesty."

Colonel Oddom was by no means appeased by this intelligence. "A loyal subject? Egad, why shouldn't he be? There's no merit, sir, in common gratitude!"

Captain Tennant turned very red. "You'd find more merit, sir, did you know conditions there as well as I."

"I fancy," the Colonel replied, "that in Parliament we know far more of the conditions than does any single individual." He gave his paper an impatient shake. "If the so-called American loyalists had a spark of principle or courage about them, they would have ended this rebellion months ago; but they seemed to expect the English to do their fighting for them." He shot an angry glance at Johnny.

Johnny Fraser's heart stopped beating, froze. It beat again, a small vein drummed against his temple. "And the English expect the Indians and Germans to do *their* fighting for *them*."

The Colonel's eyes protruded. "Quite good enough for rebels, too, young man."

Now his heart was burning with a steady rage. He took a breath and made his stiff lips grin. He relaxed into the drawling impudence of his native dialect.

"Well, old gentleman, the Germans weren't good enough for 'em at Trenton, I reckon."

The Colonel turned angrily to Captain Tennant. "By God, Tennant, a fine type of loyalist you've brought into this club, I must say. Since when has Brooks's been open to every enemy of the King?"

"Since when, sir," retorted the Captain, bristling, "have you become so squeamish? You hear Charles Fox say harsher things every night in this room."

"Quite so," the Colonel drew himself up magnificently, "but damme, sir, he's an Englishman." He retired behind his newspaper to signify that the interview was ended.

Johnny Fraser was on his feet. He would bid good-night to the Captain and retire from the club. Just then he heard many footfalls on the marble stairs and a burst of talk and laughter from the open door; the Captain stood up beside him.

"There's Fox now," he said.

In the midst of the Parliamentary group which entered with such scant respect for the sanctity of the gaming tables, there stood, all glowing eyes, warm laughter, and quick gesture, a stout but delicate young man. Yet as he drew slowly nearer with many cordial nods and easy greetings, Johnny Fraser saw that this gentleman was in fact far older than he first appeared. The eyes, the vivid mouth were shadowed by delicate but innumerable lines. Many around him and around the gaming table, by means of cosmetics and the beautifier's art, had managed to keep the semblance of a youthful mask over a spirit long since dead; but here was a man whose radiance leaped out and fairly mocked the unmistakable etching of his face. Nor was that etching the work of time alone; vices, follies, desperate excesses had left their faint yet ineradicable record; and yet the face was noble, lofty, pure. As with those who pass through the smallpox, it seemed as though this man had been exposed to corruption, had suffered corruption, until nature had conferred on him perpetual immunity, asking for her bounty only that its price should be recorded in the scars.

"Clever chap—Fox," Captain Tennant whispered in Johnny's ear. "Pity he's on the wrong side, what?"

To a remark so vastly inadequate, Johnny could only incline his head perfunctorily, nor had he, indeed, the time to do more, for Mr. Fox, by now close upon him, caught his eye and nodded. There was something magnetic in the nod, something of youthful eagerness, of ancient kindly wisdom, some affectionate hint that their meeting was but the renewal of a perpetual friendship.

"Your servant, seh," said Johnny politely.

At the sound of Johnny's accent, Mr. Fox smiled, held out his hand. "You are an American—I hear," he said and laughed.

"But a loyalist American," interposed Captain Tennant.

Mr. Fox looked at Johnny a little sadly. "My sympathies, sir, are with the American loyalists." His eye brightened. "Although the Revolutionaries claim my admiration. However," he went on lightly, "I shall not attempt to convert you; your American Tory is as staunch from principle, I am persuaded, as our Parliamentary Tory is so from self-interest."

"I'm liable to be converted some day," Johnny replied with a dry grin. "By the way some Tory gentlemen talk about my people——"

"Oh! but, my dear sir," Mr. Fox cried with mock earnestness, "you must be prepared for that. Our English Toryism owes its very existence to lack of imagination. The English Tory," he went on, "arrives at his position by manfully turning his back on sentiment and natural feeling, both products of the imagination, and by following a philosophical system, perfectly logical in every element save its premises. He renounces comprehension of his fellow-man for the sake of a fallacious conclusion in the realms of abstract political thought. Allow me to illustrate."

While Mr. Fox was talking he had sat down and motioned Johnny to a place beside him; the group which had followed him into the club drew up chairs, players left the gaming tables and stood behind them, listening. For a moment Johnny was embarrassed by his conspicuous position beside the great man; nor was he reassured by the actions of Captain Tennant, who seized the moment to explain in loud whispers to those about him.

"Young American—excellent family—in London on important business— most particular friend of mine."

"In a word," Mr. Fox was saying, "the Tory theory of government is so simple that even the Tories themselves can understand it," he smiled. "It is merely the consequence of that theory which escapes them. The duty of the Parliament, they say, is to carry out, not the wishes of the people, but the wishes of the King. I do not believe the American loyalists understand that this is the issue to which their brethren the English Tories are committed. They still imagine that the government of England is the safest guarantee of individual liberty, that it is constitutional and represents the people. It is for this reason," Mr. Fox went on, after a pause, "that I said just now that the American loyalists have my sympathy; not so much because they stand to lose their homes, their lands, their possessions, but because they stand to lose them for devotion to constitutional monarchy—a principle of British government which has, at the moment, no existence in fact; they are martyrs to a cause which lacks validity; nor does the misfortune springing from their misconception end with their own sufferings. They have actually, if unwittingly, thrown their weight against the body of men who are fighting autocracy, corruption and oppression in our government here."

He laid a hand on Johnny's knee. "My friend, I do not regard the present calamity as a struggle between a parent country and her revolted colonies. I regard it as a struggle on both sides of the water between autocracy and freedom, a struggle which has already, of course, divided the people of your country and which will assuredly divide the people of this, divide them with increasing decisiveness as the issue at stake is more distinctly perceived."

"Maybe the government here," said Johnny, "is not as good as the American loyalists think it is, but it's better than an American Revolutionary mob."

"I am sure it is," replied Mr. Fox cordially. "Any government is better than any mob. The mob, however, dissolves; but you cannot dissolve Franklin and Jefferson and Washington." His eye caught fire. "Were you to hang all three at Newgate tomorrow, they would still exist."

"Charles," a listener observed with a laugh, "you and this young gentleman should change places."

"Not I!" cried Mr. Fox. He looked at Johnny with a touch of affectionate sadness. "I would gladly change my youth for his, I confess. But as things stand now, I would not change my place with any man alive."

The ring of gamblers and political henchmen received Mr. Fox's honest pronouncement with grins of sceptical admiration.

"Well, Charles," said one, by way of winding up the conversation appropriately, "what shall we drink?"

A bowl of claret punch was brought. They took snuff and fell to. Talk became general, commonplace, but Mr. Fox remained the centre of the busy murmur. Now he was being asked to decide a question of handicap weights at Newmarket, now the value of a half-bred hunter at Melton

Mowbray; a speculator wished an opinion on the future of consols, a bank-
rupt desired Mr. Fox to contribute, from the vast store of his own experience, a few hints on money-lenders; asked to record a wager, Mr. Fox called
for a servant to bring him the ponderous betting book of the club.

Before he could make the entry, a commotion in the hallway and the flash
of a dirty yellow face plunging downward to the clubroom floor brought
them all to their feet. The man, an ancient gutter vagabond, with tattered
hair and clothing, twitched, rolled over, lay face up on the thick green
carpet.

"Simms!" a member cried, "what's this?"

"Sorry, my lord," the liveried doorman answered in a flustered voice.
"Should never have happened, I know, sir." He pressed his plump hands
together in exquisite mortification.

"Well, what did happen, Simms?"

"I couldn't say, sir, except that this old chap must have took a spell, just
as he was passing by. First thing I know, sir, he comes tumbling up the
stairs."

The members crowded round. "He's had a fit!" cried one.

"He's drunk!"

"He's dead!"

"Nonsense!"

"He *is* dead, I tell you!"

"Damme, do you mean to say I don't know a dead man when I see one?"

"I'll lay you fifty guineas even he's dead."

"Taken. Let Charles enter it; he has the book."

In common with the others, Johnny turned his eyes toward Mr. Fox. But
Charles Fox had laid the betting book aside and amid the clamor of—"Let
some one enter it!" "Who'll take ten guineas more?" "I will." "Thirty, he's
alive!" "That makes a hundred at evens"—he walked to the door and stood
looking down at the parched, unshaven face, the rigid hands, the shapeless
rags and shapeless body.

"Simms," he said in a low voice, "do you run to Number Seven, to Doctor
Joliffe's. My compliments and ask him to attend here at once."

His words, however, had been overheard.

"Oh, I say, Fox!" a member shouted. "That's not fair, you know. I'd never have bet even if I'd known Joliffe was to be called. Look here, you fellows." He turned to the rest protestingly. "Fox has sent for Joliffe."

"Damned unsporting of you, Charles, I must say."

"Not at all," said a third; "that's all part of the bet. If he's dead, Joliffe can't save him."

"That's all very well for you, St. Claire, you stand to win a hundred if Joliffe pulls him through."

They argued over the odds, sat down at last with their glasses of punch to wait for Joliffe. A few made unskillful efforts to determine their chances of winning. They felt the man's stringy wrist to see if a pulse still fluttered; one held a silver button before his tortured mouth in hopes that it might cloud indubitably over. The vagabond, however, obstinately withheld all information. They took snuff and sipped their glasses impatiently.

A bustling little step was heard on the landing, a round and bustling little man burst into the room.

"Servant, gentlemen!" He bowed till the seals on his waistcoat clinked together, then knelt down by the man.

"Well, Joliffe?"

The doctor rose with maddening deliberation. "Dead."

"By God, George!" a loud voice shouted, "you owe me fifty guineas!"

## CHAPTER XXXVII

THE LETTER which lay on Johnny Fraser's desk at MacKellor and Tavish's bore signs of distant travel, and the stamp of Edenton. The elegant, flowing superscripture was in Wylie Jones' hand. Johnny Fraser opened it. Enclosed in the letter itself lay a letter of credit.

"Edenton, 10 March, 1778.

"To Mr. Arthur Baring, Merchant.
        London.
"Sir:—

"The design of this is to desire you to furnish and pay to the bearer hereof, Mr. John Fraser Jr., Gentleman, the value of two hundred pounds at one or more times as he shall have occasion and as he shall require the same of you; for which take his receipt or bill of exchange on me. And this, my letter of credit with mine of advice by the post,

333

will be your sufficient warrant.

"I am sir,

"Your obedient servant,
"Wylie Jones."

Why in the nation, said Johnny to himself, should Wylie Jones be sending him two hundred pounds? He read the letter:

"Edenton, 10 March, 1778.

"My dear young friend,

"You will doubtless be surprised to hear from me and no less so to learn the object with which I now write you. Let me first recall to your mind a certain Mr. Paul whom you met at this house some two years since and who has since done me the honour to take my name and himself the honour to serve this country as a Captain in the Continental Navy. Captain Jones has a Mother, Mrs. Jeannie Paul, who lives near the hamlet of Carsethorn in the County of Kirkcudbright in Scotland and for whose welfare he has often expressed solicitude. Having on several occasions despatched remittances to his Mother for the purpose of relieving her possible want, without receiving any intelligence whatever of their arrival, Captain Paul did, at our last meeting, confide to me a sum of money which he prayed I would use my offices to see delivered safe into his Mother's hands. As you may imagine, a business of this character requires no small address and circumspection, for the British government persists in regarding Captain Jones as a pirate and a fugitive from justice. It is therefore inadvisable if not impracticable to transmit these moneys through the customary channels and it is particularly pressing to place them in her hands before the 10th of May for reasons which Captain Jones has not seen proper to disclose but importance of w'ch, he has emphasized in the strongest possible manner. In these circumstances my thoughts turned to you, not because I conceive that I have placed you under any obligations, but because, though of the other party, you share with me the view that the asperities of civil conflict should be softened wherever such amenity does not affect the progress of the war. I send you the enclosed letter of credit trusting to your own judgment and discretion as to the means by which the sum represented may be conveyed into the hands of the worthy woman above mentioned. Should you not care to undertake the business, you have only to return the enclosed letter of credit to the agent to whom it is directed without any apprehension of ill-will on my part. In any case, you should destroy this letter as soon as you are fully possessed of its contents. It has, of course, not been sent you through the post but by the hand of a confidential agent. It can not, therefore, bring you under suspicion of the authorities.

"Of affairs in this country, in which I assume you still feel some small interest, I can only say that they are in better posture than I had hoped. The earlier triumph of incompetence having proved disappointing in its results, those who in the first flush of democratical exhuberence believed that ignorance was the sole indispensible requisite for public office have so far receded as to permit our principal citizens to share in the councils of the State. In consequence much progress toward orderly government has been made and in especial the public treasury has been protected from knavery, thieving and jobbery. Which last reminds me that I had the pleasure of seeing your former acquaintance, Jenney, drummed out of camp by the first North Carolina Brigade.

"By recent advices from the Back Country I learn that your parents remain in good health. Our friend Hewes labors unceasingly in Congress to the detriment of his health while Teague Battle like a petrel rides the storm. This I believe is all the news I have to give you. I can only add my compliments and of course my thanks for any action you may take in the matter upon which I write you and repeat that if you are disposed to act it must be before the 10th of May.

"I am, sir, your obedient servant, and well wisher,

"Wylie Jones."

Johnny Fraser folded the letter cautiously and thrust it in his pocket. His heart was stirring, his mind, long drugged by office routine and empty social intercourse, was forming bright pictures. He must strap on his pigskin money-belt, must prime his pistols, must take the road for Scotland. He hurried to the dingy inner office where the active, sandy-haired little Mr.

Tavish concocted daring commercial enterprises and Mr. MacKellor, sad-eyed and ponderous, vetoed them.

"Tae be sure ye may have two weeks' leave," said Mr. Tavish. "Ye've done your work well. Barring mayhap the last six months," he added with a grin.

"It'll be wi'out pay, ye'll understand," said Mr. MacKellor, "and it's tae be hoped ye'll come back cured of vain social ambition."

The day passed in a whirl; he turned his desk over to another clerk; he drew the money across Mr. Baring's counter; at the Bull Inn he booked an outside seat on the Chester coach. Back in his lodgings, he burned Wylie Jones' letter, snapped the triggers of his pistols, filled his money-belt, packed his portmanteau. Three hours remained before the coach would leave. There was nothing more to be done. Yes, one thing. Before he left he would like to talk with Eve. What he would say he did not know. He had not seen her since the night at the Pantheon ball, and there was, as far as his feelings toward her went, no reason for seeing her now. But the season was almost over; when he returned she might be gone. Simply to drop out of her life without a word might seem as though on discovering that he was being made a stalking-horse for Cherry he had quit her in a childish pet, or worse still, as a defeated rival. He set out for the West End.

In the drawing-room of Bird Cage Walk he inspected the furniture minutely, he glanced through the pages of "Clarissa Harlowe," a popular and elegant work by Mr. Richardson; he stood at the window and followed a hoarse-voiced fish-wife out of sight. The room was stuffy, London was stuffy. By nightfall he would be rolling through open country. Open country. He drew a breath.

"Heavens!" cried Eve from the doorway.

He started. By Zooks, he had near about forgotten her.

"Why, you have your old Edenton coat on!"

Johnny looked down at the sober brown broadcloth with dignity. "This is my travelling suit," he announced.

"What! do you intend a voyage, then?"

"I aim to go to Scotland," he said.

"Oh!" she answered indifferently. "If you intend for Scotland, then I daresay you are well dressed enough."

"I thought I'd come to say good-bye," he said with some irritation.

She dropped her eyes. "You will be missed."

"I hardly reckon so; you seem to have got on without me well enough of late."

"I have made so many friends," she murmured.

"That you can afford to lose a few, I suppose."

"Oh, no!" She was earnest. "One cannot have too many friends if one is to succeed in London."

"I reckon I shall never succeed, then. I don't seem to get along in this town," he added wearily; "that's the reason I counted so much on you. When I first heard you had come to London my heart jumped."

She brightened. "Did it?"

"Yes. I said to myself, 'Hyer's somebody that knows how to be friends the way people in North Carolina are friends.'"

"Oh," she replied listlessly, "you find a difference?"

"Yes ma'm, I do. Back home they take a man fo' what he is."

They were seated now; he rose from his chair and stood before her with his hands in his pockets in the easy North Carolina manner. "You think I'm jealous, I reckon; but I'm not. If you preferred these officers and noblemen because you thought more of 'em than you did of me, I wouldn't have a word to say. And that is what I thought it was at first. I thought those fellows must be better men than me; I'd always looked up to the English, anyhow."

She laughed briefly not quite pleasantly. "What do you attempt, Johnny, to lecture me or to publish your own merits? You can't do both together."

"I only wonder sometimes what are your real feelings toward me."

"Most men," she said disdainfully, "who knew women's real feelings would lose interest in them."

"That's no answer. It's like all the talk I've heard this winter; it sounds smart, but it don't mean anything."

"Whereas your conversation," she flashed, "has a clear enough meaning. The wonder is that you have the ill-grace to trouble me with it."

"I don't want to pick a quarrel. I only want to know the truth."

"You wish me to declare my feelings toward you without your declaring yours toward me. You are cautious."

He flushed.

"Do not be angry," she hurried on, "I did only tease you." She gave him her warmest glance. "I like you as much as ever, Johnny."

He shook his head. "I'm mighty sorry to hear you say that."

"What!" she cried, "is there no pleasing you?"

"It means, I reckon, you've thrown me over just as part of the game."

"As for my having thrown you over—that is silly, if only because you have not been mine to throw. As for the game—it is a game we all play; surely you are old enough to know that." She swept her hand around the room. "How long do you suppose we can keep this house on papa's half-pay? We go to Wells next month for the summer. Perhaps we can manage another season in town; after that, if nothing turns up, it will mean a villa at Broadstairs or some second-rate continental watering-place." Her mouth was smiling, determined, but her eyes weary and a little sad. "You see, I think enough of you to be frank, franker than I have ever been to anyone before, and perhaps," she laughed lightly, "than I shall ever be again."

"Eve!" he cried out in distress, "you mustn't talk like that." He took her hand. "I'm only just your friend, maybe not that, and I'm not a jealous friend. I wouldn't care if you used me as you have if it was to help get a man you cared for."

"My dear," she said, half laughing, half tender, "you touch me, indeed you do. But I have 'got' no one as yet. And perhaps," she added, "when I do I shall grow to care for him some day."

"You? Cherry!" he gave a short laugh.

She froze.

"You should learn better balance, sir. As you are, in counsel you always go too far, while in war and love hardly far enough."

He turned red at her thrust.

"Why should I trouble to go far with this crowd of London belles? You are all the same. You are nothing to me and I'm not what you all are looking for. It's a game, just as you said, and I'm too sick of it to want to play it even if I could."

She did not resent this.

"You will never belong to London, I know, and that is not the worst that can be said of a man neither. I know that also." She gave him a bright, hard smile. "But on the other hand, I do belong to London and to the game which you despise. Perhaps that has always been the trouble between us; we belong to different worlds."

"I wish I could do something, Eve," he murmured unhappily. "What can I do?"

She stood up. "You can wish me joy and say good-bye. I have only made you unhappy and you have sometimes——troubled me."

"I'm sorry, Eve, forgive me! I've been rude and bothersome, I know."

She laughed without mirth. "Not that, I did not mean that. Tell me," she hurried on, "what do you do in Scotland?"

"I aim to pay a visit to Sir Nat," he said absently.

"Indeed; pray pay him my compliments."

"Eve!" he cried out. "Eve!" But her mask was on.

"Hush!" she whispered with a half smile. "What would poor Hoddin think? And now again, adieu." She held out her hand unmistakably. As Johnny took it, she raised her face to him with a flash of impudence. "Kiss me." He kissed her lightly, his lips were cold, his eyes blinded by unhappy mists. "Some day," she cried, "you will perhaps be able to tell your friends back home that you have kissed a Marchioness."

The cobbled courtyard of the Bull Inn was in an easy-going turmoil; above the heads of porters, waiters, green-aproned boots and agitated travellers, the old coach loomed like a ponderous caravel on troubled seas. The scarred and battered horses hung their heads, the rat-faced post boys tossed off final pots of porter and winked at chambermaids in upper casements. Over the edge of the huge basket, slung behind, peered a bailiff, two felons in clinking irons and a sailor with a patch on his eye.

The guard stored Johnny's portmanteau in the boot and held the little ladder while Johnny mounted the outside seat. The seat already held a recruiting officer and a parson, both heavily fortified with liquor against the rigors of the journey. On Johnny's heels followed a perfectly square and stolid West Country farmer who wrapped an aromatic horse-blanket three times around his legs, then sat down on Johnny with crushing impact and went to sleep.

The post boys mounted, the inside passengers rustled their feet in the straw and peeped out anxiously. At the cracking of whips, the horses leaned wearily into their collars, the wheels rattled slowly on the cobbles, rumbled through the archway of the courtyard.

Borne majestically aloft, Johnny surveyed in turn the roaring traffic of the Strand, the smart traps and carriages of Piccadilly, the vans and country carts of Oxford Street. Dusk was falling as they turned up the Edgeware Road; candles shone in cottage windows as they came to Finchley Common; behind them, Johnny heard the guard cock the hammer of his blunderbuss.

Now they were in deserted country; all was blackness except for the two coach lamps by the dashboard whose light wavered on the horses' rumps, the bobbing backs of the post boys and crept with the coach along the grass-fringed road. Johnny Fraser muffled his chin in his woollen tippet and dozed.

# CHAPTER XXXVIII

FIVE DAYS later, Johnny Fraser, sitting stiff and cold beside the driver of a canvas-covered travelling wagon, crunched along the sandy post road to White Haven. To the left the Irish sea lay hushed beneath a mist, to the right brown cliffs pressed their shoulders into low, wet clouds, ahead, through the mist and twilight, Johnny Fraser felt rather than saw a crowded harbor and a close-built sandstone town.

Now their wheels and hoof-beats echoed in the solid sober streets.

"Hellaw, Wullie," a bystander hailed the driver in the border tongue. With a clinking of trace chains, they pulled up at the Black Lion where the tapster was just lighting the lamps which flanked the door. Throwing his reins across the wheelers' backs, the driver dismounted, walked heavily round to the tailgate and proceeded impartially to haul out five creels of fish, two wool-sacks and three old country women. Johnny Fraser proffered him a sixpenny tip; he took it without remark, carried it to the door light, inspected it minutely, then touched his hat in gratitude. The tapster, possessed of Johnny's portmanteau, was beckoning him with quiet insistence to enter the inn. Within an hour Johnny had made his supper of plaice and beer and crawled wearily into his bed in a chamber above the street.

He was still tired from the long journey when he woke at dawn next morning, but he could not rest while the two hundred pounds weighted the money-belt around his waist. He made inquiries of the tapster for a boat-man to take him to Carsethorn; the tapster warmly recommended a per-sonal friend and hurried off in the direction of the docks. As Johnny finished his tea and porridge, he was confronted by a member of a species common to all the harbors of the world, part fisherman, part boatman, part dockside loafer and in addition, a man who might be depended on, provided the profits were great and the risks small, for any odd job in the smuggling way. He touched his woollen cap to Johnny but with no hint of deference.

"Ye want a boat? I've a boat. Carsethorn? Seven bob; we should be startin' noo." He trudged off without a glance behind him. Ten minutes later Johnny was sailing over the waters of the Solway Firth in a particu-larly evil smelling skiff.

Such was Johnny's weariness, such the disreputable seafaring man's calm air of foreordination, that almost before Johnny knew it, it was late after-noon and they were sailing back again. Gulls were sheering, ships were standing out to sea; behind the cliff-flanked sandstone town rose long green hills and back of them the summits of the fells, a distant, tumbling mass of silver gray. Best of all, the money-belt was light; he had made his inquiries circumspectly in Carsethorn village. He had started out on foot and come to the whitewashed cottage on the great estate, then he had waited till an honest-looking young boy came by. The money, done in a package, was given to the lad and, while he received instructions, a bright new shilling was held beneath his nose. Peering between two bushes, Johnny Fraser had seen the boy leave the money on the flagstone, knock and run away. A woman's drawn, sad face appeared at the door; she picked up the package, weighed it in her hand, then despite her years, shouted with extraordinary vigor at the fleeing youngster. Leaving the shilling in a bit of paper, Johnny had hurried down the lane.

THE MOTHER OF JOHN PAUL JONES

*A woman's drawn, sad face appeared at the door; she picked up the package, weighed it in
her hand, then despite her years, shouted with extraordinary vigor at the fleeing youngster*

In a word the job was done and well done; there was not a chance in a hundred that his connection with the American privateer, or pirate, if that were the word, would ever be discovered; and, now that it was safely over, he felt great satisfaction in the episode. First, the journey by coach and wagon across England, fully armed, burdened with gold and a strange secret, and pressing onward to arrive, as he had only just managed to do, before that mysterious tenth of May. What would guards, coachmen, fellow travellers have said had they known that the quiet young gentleman beside them was linked with Paul Jones, the American sea-raider? And then at last to stand hidden, unbeknown, and see his service to the strong-faced old Scotch dame brought to its fruition—there was pleasure enough in that for anyone. There was pleasure, too, however secret and unconfessed, in having served that sour, rude son of hers who had sent the British scurrying. Well, the business was over now and very little of interest seemed to lie ahead of him; he would go to Stirling and see Sir Nat. But the nearer that meeting drew, the less favor it seemed to hold.

Instead of going to the Black Lion, he turned right handed down the street by which they had entered the night before and followed it till he was once again on the road which lay between the cliffs and the sea. Climbing down over a narrow strip of sod, he found a sheltered spot and stretched out on the sand and gravel. Below him sparse beach grass arched in the wind, further down, wet pebbles shone and drained away in the clutches of each receding wave. Out to sea he saw three ships under full press of canvas, hurrying, no doubt, to make port before night fell; their topsails showed black yet faintly translucent against the setting sun. That sun, so soon to leave him in darkness, was just now high in heaven above America, and he, himself, if he could fly along its burning track, would speed from where he sat in the gorse, across the waves to the sombre coast of North Carolina; and then, he told himself, it would be easy to fly on, up the river, over the whispering dark-green tops, till, in the well-known clearing, he saw the old clay-plastered house and saw his mother wave to him, laugh and cry beside the ancient sycamore. Down by the ford another figure waved, the colt beneath her drank the shadowy waters, her dark red cloak bellied in the April breeze, her brown hair blew across her brown, upraised face, her arm showing slim in the blue camlet gown, lifted in a gesture of salutation.

Johnny Fraser came to himself; his cheeks were hot, his hands were cold. By Zooks, he thought he had outgrown foolish notions! This was the first that had ever come to him since the day he landed in England. Perhaps he had been too much tired by his journey; he would rest a few days here before he went on to Carlisle. But after Carlisle, what then—what lay ahead? He had been cheered for a few days by the small adventure which had just been concluded; that was behind him now and there was nothing much to do but to sit on the beach and ask himself what lay before. He threw a pebble into the vast, indifferent sea. The world, to put it bluntly, was turning out a failure. It had not been hard to leave America, slip-shod, easy-going, broadly ironic, uncouth. He had felt only relief at his escape from her shirt-tailed patriots and shambling military. But in those days the dream of England beckoned him, led him on. Where now was that dream? So lost that he could hardly reconstruct it in his mind. Its pictures were almost blotted out by scenes of London, where life, beneath its brilliant thin enamel, was savage, corrupt, coldly contemptuous of all the world. There was something a little sickening in the barbarism of the grandees, there was something profoundly angering in their dull pride. He threw a pebble with all his might. By Zooks, at home where he came from a lot of those high-toned Londoners couldn't pass for well-bred with anybody. He dusted the sand off his stockings and started for town.

His dreams that night in the chamber above the street were troubled. Perhaps the damp room and the clammy sheets made him imagine in his restless sleep that he was swimming, swimming a great river; behind him a musket cracked, a bullet kicked a jet of water in his face. He looked back; redcoats were running up and down the shore and stopping to take aim at him. Now they were firing volleys, the bullets hummed, the water churned and curdled. He swam with all his might against the clinging current; then from the farther bank he heard a roar; the race track crowds were cheering him. "Come on, Carolina! Carolina wins!" He buried his head in the water, swam desperately for the sound. Now he could see them on the bank, the raw-boned countrymen, the shipwrights, the sailors, the Negroes, the tall mountain men; they waded into the shallows for him, stretched out imploring hands, "Come on, Carolina!" He swam again. The bullets were falling short, he dared to look behind; a twinkle of brass among the redcoats caused his heart to sink. It shone steady for an instant, a great curling ball of smoke shot out, the cannon's blunt reverberation followed, rocked his head, awoke him wet and shuddering.

A ruddy light played on the ceiling, sea boots rang on the flags below; musketry rattled down by the docks, across the street a door creaked open.

"God save us!" cried a flustered householder, "what is this?"

Right under Johnny's window a pistol cocked, a Southern voice drawled, "Shut that do'!" The door slammed hurriedly.

All down his back, Johnny Fraser felt the hackles rise, he was tugging at his boots and cursing them; he was running down the stairs, thrusting his pistols in his greatcoat pockets. The tapster, white and weeping, met him at the bottom.

"Oh, God, oh, God, sir, the Americans!"

Johnny brushed him aside and opened the front door cautiously. "Hi, brother," he whispered to the muffled figure with the cutlass. "Don't shoot, I aim to join you."

"Come out hyer," the seaman answered after a pause, "an' keep yo' han's high. An' if you try any flimflams," he added earnestly, "I'll lay yo' guts open."

The seaman took the pistols from Johnny's pockets. He fired one at a nightcap which leaned out a window down the street. The nightcap shot back out of sight; the sailor returned the empty pistol. "Hyer, Sonny, you take that."

The sky reddened till the stone cornices above them seemed streaked with fire. The sailor shifted impatiently and blew on his knuckles.

"Wher' you from?"

"From North Carolina—Little River."

"Who do you know ther'?"

"Why, Doctor Clapton and Teague Battle and Wylie Jones."

The sailor grunted.

"What's the idea in coming ashore?" Johnny was emboldened to ask. "You all don't aim to conquer England, do you?"

"No, seh," the man admitted modestly, "just to burn the shipping, that's all. Listen!"

A patrol of seamen came running up the street. "All done!" New England voices shouted, "Boat-crews away!" The seaman and Johnny joined them; together they ran for the beach. The town was up and after them; cobblestones rained out of alleyways, a fowling piece was fired at them from a roof; Johnny heard the shot spatter on a wall above his head. They reached the beach where other patrols were running. Ahead of them, in the green sickly dawn the ship's boats lay hauled up under guard. Johnny threw his weight against a stern and shoved; he felt her move, slide down, float free; wet to the waist, he tumbled over the stern; oars rattled in the rowlocks; the men gave way. By the light of the blazing shipping he saw crowds forming on the beach; their muskets flashed, bullets kicked spurts of water, just as in the dream. Indeed, it seemed more than likely that the dream was still going on.

"Easy all!" the boatswain cried, "the Captain's not off yet." They lay on their oars till the Captain's longboat overtook them; a hearty voice roared at them from its stern.

"Give way, ye lousy bastards, they'll be after ye wi' their cannon next!"

"We were waiting for you, sir," the boatswain called.

"Give way, I tell ye!" the answer came, " 'tis no time for etiquette."

Ten minutes later they were alongside the ship and scrambling up the ladder to the deck, where barefoot men were running like mad, hoisting the ship's boats inboard, hauling on mainsheets, squaring yards away.

"Here you, prisoner!" said the gruff and whiskered master-at-arms. "Under hatches!" He collared Johnny and led him aft. The light in the sky illumined the quarterdeck where the Captain, legs apart, facing the stern, shouted an order to the after-guard. As the master-at-arms propelled him down the companionway, Johnny Fraser recalled without the least surprise that the back of the Captain on the quarterdeck was the bristling, terrier back of Mr. Paul.

# CHAPTER XXXIX

AFTER A night in the brig, close to the foul, thickly gurgling bilge water, Johnny Fraser answered the summons of the master-at-arms and was haled on deck, blinking, hungry and dejected. His hair, untied, hung about his white face, his nightshirt stuck out ludicrously beneath his great coat, his boot tops flopped about his heels. The master-at-arms knocked on the Captain's door, opened it and thrust Johnny inside. The man in the blue gold-braided uniform who sat at a table drinking a large bowl of tea was, beneath his surprising elegance, the grim-faced, stocky man of Edenton and Halifax. He looked up brusquely; his stare deepened; incredulous, he rubbed his chin. "I'll call ye, Smithers," he said to the master-at-arms, "when ye're wanted."

As soon as they were alone he leaned back in his chair and whistled between his teeth. "Well, my friend," he said, "have ye ever seen me before?"

"Yes, seh," said Johnny. "I saw you at Halifax and—at Edenton."

The Captain nodded. "Ah!" he said with a faint grin. "In those days it was you that had the fine clothes, eh, lad?"

"And I'd had 'em now, seh," said Johnny boldly, "if I hadn't left 'em to join yo' boat-crew."

"And why did ye do that?"

Johnny paused. Why indeed?

"I don't know, seh. I heard a fellow talking like the folks at home."

"Aye," said the Captain, nodding again, "and what do ye intend?"

"I intend to do whatever the other boys hyer do."

"You mean ye'd like to join the ship's company?"

"Yes, seh. I reckon that's what I do mean."

"Ye'll do your duty?"

"Yes, seh."

"Are ye a keen lad for a fight?"

"I don't know, seh," said Johnny truthfully. "But it looks like I am."

The other laughed. "Aweel, ye're no braggart. I'll just give ye a try. But stay; what were ye up to in White Haven? Are ye in business there?"

"No, seh. I'm in business in London. I got a letter from Mr. Wylie Jones about some money for a lady near Carsethorn in Kirkcudbright."

Captain Jones leaned forward, fixed Johnny with his deep eyes, drummed on the table. "And did ye deliver it?"

"Yesterday, two hundred pounds."

"Ye saw her, then?"

"Yes, seh. I hid in the bushes and watched a boy I'd hired deliver it. She came to the door."

"And was she well, could ye see?"

"Yes, seh. She looked well and when she hollered after the boy her voice was mighty strong."

The Captain smiled, looked out the cabin windows along the wake which led from Scotland. "Ah," he said after many moments, "she was aye a great one tae shout." He rose brusquely from the table. "There's nothing I can say tae ye," his grip closed on Johnny's hand, "but whatever I can do for ye I will." He grinned. "And if it's a chance to fight ye're wishin' for, I think there's no man in the world can be of greater service. But listen—not a

word to the lads on board here of what ye've just said; the half of them are
New Englanders and always looking for a grievance; they'd say I'd made a
favorite of ye if they knew what lay between us. Master-at-arms!" he cried.

The door opened, the master-at-arms saluted. "Sling this man's hammock
on the main deck and have him entered on the muster roll as a gunner's
mate. He's to help the Gunner in charge of small arms." He turned to
Johnny. "If ye know anything of use, young man," he said severely, "it
should be how tae clean a musket."

A line of bare-legged seamen on hands and knees holy-stoned the upper
deck; the last of the hammocks, lashed in long thin rolls, were being carried
up from below and stowed in the netting along the sides. Down the companionway, the main deck, a vast low-roofed cavern which stretched clear
from stem to stern, was now lighted by brilliant squares of green sunlight
from open gunports; to port and starboard the two long rows of guns
creaked in their heavy lashings at the deck's low lift and fall. In the open
space between the batteries the Gunner and the ship's carpenter had set up
their work benches. There was something incongruous in the two ancient
leather-aproned figures methodically plying their trades among the grim
breeches of the guns. The Gunner blew the steel dust from a flat file and
squinted at Johnny's makeshift costume over his iron spectacles.

"Waal, Nightshirt," he said, "what d' ye know?"

While Johnny attempted to formulate an answer to this question, the
Gunner wiped the file reflectively on the seat of his dungarees, pointed it at
Johnny and turned to the master-at-arms. "That's what we get for gunner's
mates, these here days." The file waggled accusingly at Johnny's bosom.

"I can test a rifle sight," said Johnny firmly.

The file was slowly lowered to the bench. "Waal, durn me!" the gunner
cried. "If ye're lyin' I'll soon find ye out. They'll pipe all hands to breakfast
now and after that ye'll draw some proper dunnage from Slops, and after
that," he hopped up, brisk as a bird, and slammed his tool box shut, "I'll see
what God durned stuff ye're made of."

The day passed quickly. On the main deck, the cutlasses, pistols and
muskets used by the raiding party were overhauled, then stored in the
armory, abaft the cable tiers below. Under the Gunner's eyes Johnny

cleaned barrels, drew charges, oiled locks, turned the grindstone while another Gunner's mate put an edge on the cutlasses. The salt air blew through
the open port, the green light wavered above his head. Around him were
the high cheekbones, the thin sardonic mouths, the keen eyes, the brown,
grim, kindly faces of Americans. He kept an ear cocked for their talk, for
the clipped Yankee speech, for the heavy, full-rounded speech of Penn-
sylvanians, for the soft, singing language of the South. He had never been so
happy. By Zooks, it was almost good to hear the New Englanders!

Toward evening he felt the ship come up in the wind, he saw a strip of
green shore out the porthole and a landing-party putting off from the side.

"Nightshirt," said the Gunner, "if you was to sling your hammock by that
port, ye'd rest a sight easier."

Johnny flushed and fell to work again. An hour later they were under way
again. That night the Gunner slung Johnny's hammock for him outside his
own little cubby-hole down in the hold beside the cable tier.

The next thing Johnny knew, the boatswain's whistle was screaming in
his ear, the boatswain's voice was roaring, "What d' ye say, sailors? Rise and
shine! Lash and carry! Out or down there, you lubbers!" Johnny tumbled to
the loose planking, lashed his hammock like the rest and carried it on deck.
A pale sun was rising; over the side a low mist slipped by; muffled to their
bleary eyes, the morning watch climbed down from the tops and lined up
for hot tea at the galley door. He curled his bare toes on the dew-soaked
deck, stretched, rubbed his empty belly; he was cold and hungry, but somehow, by Zooks, he felt mighty good.

He passed the morning at the Gunner's work-bench, ate his dinner of
plum-duff and molasses with the other gunner's mates on the open deck,
squatting comfortably in the lee of the hammock nettings.

That afternoon, as he was setting a flint in a gun-lock, suddenly from quarterdeck the boatswain's whistle piped wildly, a stream of orders rang
through the speaking trumpet, a hundred feet were running. The mates
beside him hurled their tools in the chest and hove it down below. They
knocked the legs off the work-bench, hove it through a gun-port over the
side.

"What is it?" said Johnny.

"Clear for action!" they shouted. Johnny ran after the Gunner, who was skipping down the companionway.

"What are my orders, seh?" he shouted.

The Gunner turned and peered at him intently. "You go with that man there," he pointed, "and keep the magazine blankets wet." He disappeared down the hatch, but his voice trailed back to Johnny. "And if they ain't drippin' when I find ye, God durn me, you'll swing!"

"Come on, boy!" the gunner's mate cried. The two dived down the hatch into the dark hole. By the dim light of a battle-lantern, they saw the Gunner unlock the magazine door.

"Rig blankets!" he jerked out, and skipped aloft, piping, "Armorer, stand by to issue small arms!" With incredible dexterity the gunner's mate lashed the two blankets across the magazine door.

"There's your buckets," he said, as he drew on a pair of felt boots and cut the metal buckle off his belt. "And there's the well to draw the water from." He threw his knife and buckle into the scuppers. "Wet them blankets all acrost the tops and keep wettin' 'em!" He slipped through the magazine door.

Johnny Fraser threw a bucket down the well, hauled on the slimy rope, wet the blanket again and again till the water ran out the bottom. A marine with fixed bayonet dropped down the hatchway and took his post by the magazine. Johnny stopped hauling water and listened; he could hear nothing but the bilge water murmuring in the hold and the sea water lapping along the strakes outside. "Have they begun?" he asked in a low voice. The marine shook his head.

The powder-monkeys came running down; each showed the marine his cartridge-case, then passed it into the magazine. It was filled and passed out to him. One by one the powder-monkeys ran up on deck again. Johnny Fraser fell to on the blankets.

He was pausing to catch his breath in the close, tainted air, when the planks beneath his feet leaped up. Muffled and distant, but stupendous, the first broadside roared. A moment's lull, then by twos and threes, the deep, coughing grunts of single guns.

From then on, the ship never ceased to tremble, the dim battle-lantern never ceased to flicker, the powder-monkeys never ceased to tumble down the hatch, wipe sweat from blackened faces, scramble up again. At last, faint and far above them, the boatswain's whistle sounded a thrilling call.

"Boarders away!" the marine whispered. Listening, they heard the ship's timbers grind and groan against another hull. The light popping of musketry followed.

After many minutes a cheery voice shouted, "Cease action!" down the hatchway. The gunner's mate crawled out between the blankets, pitch black except for two grotesque white rings around his eyes. He triple-locked the door, unlashed the blankets.

"Wet enough, son," he said, as he wrung them out. "Let's get a whiff of air."

On the main deck half-naked gun-crews swabbed out the guns and lashed them fast. Powder-monkeys doused smoking fuses in the match tubs and passed them below. Above deck, the boarding-party, waving pikes and cutlasses and grinning cheerfully, stood guard over a hundred sullen British prisoners. A sprightly American lieutenant, with a prize crew at his heels, dropped into the waist of the captured enemy. Captain Jones walked the quarterdeck with a crestfallen British officer; his eye was aloft; he paused to shout orders to the reefers who hung in the rigging, splicing sheets and stays. The grapnels were cast off; they hoisted sail and stood clear of the prize. Then, for the first time, Johnny noticed four huddled forms and a pool of blood around the foremast.

"God durn ye, Nightshirt!"

He started guiltily, dodged down the hatchway and lent a hand to the other gunner's mates who gathered up the small arms and racked them in the armory.

They ate their supper on the upper deck, fresh-washed but showing dim strains of blood and powder; all 'around, the horizon lay bare of sails or land; they drove before an east wind into the eye of the setting sun. Gazing aloft, they saw the sunlight peep through the shot-holes in the straining canvas, and talked of the action in monosyllables, inadequate, trivial, incoherent. But except for the shot-holes and the bent old sailmaker shrouding a body by the foremast, the fight already seemed as dim and faded as the stains on the deck. Night fell; they hove the hammocks out of the nettings and, squatting beneath a deck lantern, overhauled them where shot and bullets had cut the cordage.

The ship's bell struck eight; its echo hung about them on the following wind; a seaman's harsh, true voice sounded a long "Farewell!"

"Farewell!" they joined in—

> "Farewell and adieu to you, fine Spanish ladies!
> Farewell and adieu, all you ladies of Spain!
> For we've received orders to sail for old England,
> And perhaps we shall never more see you again!"

The third day they raised the coast of France, a stretch of round, green, looming hills, in whose shadow lay the dead white walls and red roofs of Brest. White-coated soldiers climbed the embrasures of the harbor-entrance forts, pointed to the Stars and Stripes, which flew at the masthead above the captured British ensign, wavered, cheered.

They stood up the narrow channel till they were abreast of the town and the dock-fringed basin at its foot. They hove to, the canvas trembled, flapped, the anchor rattled down, the top-men clewed up the sails, lashed the sail-coverings home. On wharf and sea wall tiny figures buzzed and danced about; small boats put out from shore. The deck watch manned the side as the mustachioed port commander came aboard; the ship's company were mustered aft. The gentleman made them a vehement speech in the French language and then, to the insupportable delight of all hands, turned and kissed the Captain on both cheeks.

Going below, Johnny Fraser watched the liberty men overhauling the shore clothes in their ditty-bags and wondered rather disconsolately what was to become of him now. The Captain's boy, a supercilious little jackanapes, peered down the open hatchway and beckoned. Johnny followed him to the cabin.

Captain Jones, still perspiring from the Frenchman's embrace, was pacing up and down. He stopped, tilted complacently on his heels. "Well, lad, I didn't keep ye waitin' long for a fight, did I, now?"

"No, seh, but I didn't see much. I was down in the magazine."

"Aweel, ye can't expect tae be on the quarterdeck the first day ye join a ship, but if ye're not satisfied with the view ye had, just ye stick by me, and the next fight I'll promise ye an eyefull."

"When does the next fight come?" said Johnny.

The Captain laughed. "That's a fair question. Thank God ye're no like these New Englanders, all for prize money and a whole skin! The next fight comes, my lad, as soon as I can get to sea in this ship or any other. If ye'll just bide on board a while I'll have ye put in the midshipman's berth as a gentleman volunteer; and as to pay, ye have a bit of prize money due ye when it comes, which, to judge by the way the Congress uses me, will be the morning after the Day of Judgment. But here's twa louis d'or." Captain Jones held out the coins.

"Thank you, seh," said Johnny, "but I've got a little money left of my own."

"Good!" said the Captain, and thrust the coins back in his own pocket. "That will do for the present, then." He nodded shortly and turned away.

## CHAPTER XL

TEN DAYS of bedlam followed; liberty parties were forever leaving the ship's side with cheering and lewd repartee, and returning at all hours of the night to be hoisted, roaring and bellowing, on board. All day the bumboats hung about the ship, the boatmen cried their wares and dickered for passengers. All night the seamen left on board held carnival below with any casual ladies of sufficient spirit to crawl through a gunport after dark. The officers were ashore, save one lieutenant, who prudently kept his cabin till the convivial tornado had spent its force.

In between alarms and excursions, Johnny found time to write his mother, telling her as best he could what had happened and suggesting ways by which his change of fortune, so abrupt, so irrational and still so incoherent in his own mind, might best be presented to his father. He also wrote a short letter to MacKellor and Tavish in which, with no attempt at explanation, he merely gave his present forwarding address and in language recollected from the pages of "The Young Secretary's Assistant," expressed his regret at the termination of their business association. He debated a letter to Sir Nat, but decided against it; France, newly allied to America by treaty, might soon become the active enemy of England; at all events, letters from France would doubtless be opened by the British Post. Discharged from his regiment, Sir Nat would at best be held under suspicion; it would make his lot no easier to be known as the recipient of a letter from an American in France.

After ten days Johnny could bear the ship no more; aboard there were no rumors or prospects of action; exhausted by their excesses, the men lounged gloomily around the decks and longed for home. Among the fetes and other less formal entertainments tendered him by the rapturous town, Captain Jones, they said, had forgotten them.

"I wish I had a shillin'," said one, "for every mile that fellow's walked the streets of Brest."

"What's he walk for?" another asked.

"Why, so's the folks'll turn and look at him; you can see him any day swaggerin' up and down the Marine Parade."

"He ought to be on board."

"Aboard? He won't come aboard till the last mounseer has stopped buggin' his eyes at him."

"Well, then," concluded Johnny, "I'll go ashore." He signalled to a boatman.

Biting Johnny's shilling with a tooth apparently designed for that purpose, the malevolent-looking bandit stood up in the stern of his bum-boat and fell to sculling languidly.

They drifted away from the ship's high bulging side. The many-colored reflections in the slick harbor water were turning soft in the sunset light. Along the docks, shadows checkered the high, plastered street fronts, but further up, the hillside houses and the green looming hills still shone. Faint bugles sounded from the harbor forts; across the water a bronze carrillon chimed slowly, then fell silent with a long reverberating hum. Rowing on through the twilight breathlessness, they seemed to float on the bronze bell's infinitely protracted sound.

The bow grated on stones. Johnny climbed the granite waterstairs. Beside a dreaming plaza stood the church from which the carrillon had sounded; a church, bizarre, ornate, indecent; a church such as Johnny Fraser had never seen before; its gaudy yellow stone was encrusted with moldings, wreaths, shields, volutes; its niches harbored Papish images; its great cross flaunted brazenly against the sky. Even as he looked, two priests in shovel hats and stealthy cassocks slipped in through the curtained door.

Along the far side of the little plaza, a line of awnings marked the cafés where small white-coated soldiers and little short-jacketed sailors sipped endless glasses and devoted themselves to endless contemplation of the town.

Seating himself at an iron table, Johnny Fraser commanded the long-aproned waiter to bring him a bock; with the bock in his hand he leaned back like the rest and watched the city of Brest, or such fragments of it as cared to cross the sun-warmed plaza, go by. Figures passed slowly along the pavement by ones and twos, a cockaded officer, two black-smocked gawky schoolboys, a crimp, a shifty Levantine. Up the street, white-winged Breton caps nodded before the mercers' stalls, big Breton farmers in flat hats and embroidered monkey-jackets smoked pipes along the curb, moved slowly aside for the teams of percherons which, single file, came clumping and grating down the granite street, tossing their bridle plumes, their plaited manes, their peaked goatskin collars. Beside the overtowering wheels, the carters leaned back on the reins with strange barbaric cries. Nuns, hooded and soberly shrouded, passed two and two; and other women, also in pairs, who, far from shrouded, exposed seductive bosoms and dragged ironical alluring glances along the iron tables. Johnny Fraser blushed and tingled; such matters, he reflected indignantly, should be conducted in secret as they were in Edenton. It was a peculiar country, this France, not to say a deplorable one; not only did the cyprians ply their trade in broad daylight, but the churches, giddily decorated, were open at all hours; at all hours people of all sorts drifted in and out of them as if they were coffee houses. It was, in a word, a country without propriety. He frowned. To put to sea again; to live on hard work, salt air and salt beef, with no thought of the morrow; and, best of all, to feel around him the lanky, hard-bitten men from home—he sipped his bock reflectively; for three years now, these men, he told himself, and men like them, had waged grotesque, mismanaged war, had met with almost nothing but defeat. Yet in the teeth of all the experts they seemed today no nearer overthrow. No nearer? Why, now they talked as if they could not lose. A race incomprehensible to all the world and most of all to themselves, they seemed, beneath their dry irony in action, their drunken insubordination in idleness, to cling to some vague notion of their own peculiar heritage.

He set the empty glass upon the table and cast down his eyes; there was just one thing for him to do—make up for lost time. He gave a bitter smile. Make up for lost time? It was easy said. But do what he might, he could never stand with those who had turned out at the first call, with the fellows like Joe Merrillee. The shaded café, the bright plaza faded, he saw again the surly, inexpressive face, the big impassive hands which he had used to think so loutish. But Joe's thoughts, however inarticulate and circumscribed, had carried him unswervingly to their honorable goal. No wonder Sally Merrillee had flamed out at his condescending praise of Joe, the wonder was that he himself should have been blind to the justice of her scorn. He saw her standing on the porch in her old blue gown and read with new insight, with new humiliation, the meaning in her eyes. Hers was no cheap and easy charge of cowardice nor even, as with more justice it might have been, of a snobbery which never fights for an ill-dressed man against a well-dressed one. Without experience or knowledge, she nevertheless divined in him what it had taken him three years to learn about himself. She saw that he was a man who did not know when he had a cause worth fighting for; he bowed his head.

A murmur from the other tables roused him, "Voila le Bostonné!" Surrounded by a group of chattering French naval officers, and with a lady, by no means sedate, on each arm, Captain Paul Jones was making his royal progress through the town. Immaculate, in blue frock and white breeches, he walked very erect and martial, bowing acknowledgment to the scattered plaudits and salutations from the café tables. The ladies smiled archly and squeezed his hands. It was too late for Johnny to escape. Standing up, he pulled off his woollen sailor cap. Captain Jones stopped.

"M'sieur Fraser!" He pointed out Johnny with a somewhat theatrical gesture. "Un brave gentilhomme volontier de ma frigate!" he announced to his entourage in a French accent bad enough for Johnny to understand.

The officers clicked their heels and bowed rather superciliously to the gentilhomme volontier in wrinkled watchcoat and common seaman's clothes. The ladies, however, smiled with something more than kindness in their eyes.

"Ye've not left the ship, have ye?" said Captain Jones.

"No, seh; I just came ashore for the evening. I hope we're going to sea soon."

"And so we should do, lad, if the low-spirited Commissioners in Paris would use me as a man of honor should be used." He smote the gold buttons on his breast. "What's all these compliments on shore to me?" he asked rhetorically, "when out i' the channel," he swung his arm, "there's fame and glory to be had? But listen!" He disengaged himself from the ladies and, drawing near to Johnny's table, raised his grim, discontented, eager face and whispered in Johnny's ear, "That frigate o' mine's too small. I've plans afoot to get a finer ship, and then," he seized Johnny's arm, "not all the slinkin' detractors in America can rob me of my just reward of glory. Bide here in Brest till I get my new ship." He clapped Johnny on the shoulders. "If ye're for fightin', lad, stick by *me* and your name will be known wherever there's such a thing as fame."

"Yes, seh," said Johnny. "Will it be long before we start?"

"Two months, maybe; she's still to be fitted, this new ship I'm speaking of. Take lodgings in town. I'll see ye from time to time. If ye should run short of funds, I'll make ye an advance. There's no risk," he added, with his dogged grin. "Ye'll be able to pay me a thousand times over in prize money when our next cruise is done. And now, my dears," he hooked a lady on either arm, and moved off down the street.

On the strength of his conversation with Captain Jones, Johnny Fraser took a small chamber in an alleyway devoted to seamen's lodging houses. There was just room between the plastered walls for the curtained, high feather-bed and a single tottering chair. When Madam Legaude, hugebosomed, hairy-faced, filled the doorway demanding her rent in advance, Johnny could find no space for retreat; even the window was barred by an intricate iron railing. After a deep-voiced hurricane of indignation, Madam Legaude turned ferociously maternal, patted Johnny on the head with a flail-like hand, dismissed the room-rent from her mind. She then poured forth a stream of advice for the guidance of young gentlemen temporarily resident in the town of Brest; especially with reference to the girls of the arrondissement; her counsel was not couched in terms of general warning and reprobation, such as Johnny had been accustomed to hear, but was devoted, in a practical way, to the compilation of a list of jeunes filles who were desirable and of others who were otherwise, and to giving, in each case, with astounding particularity, the reasons for the classification. Many of her remarks were lost on Johnny, whose French, gleaned from Dr. Clapton, was hardly suited to the present tenor of the conversation. He managed to thank Madam Legaude gravely and send her downstairs well pleased with the position she occupied in his esteem.

After three weeks' uncomfortable wait, a remittance came from MacKellor and Tavish, together with a letter of grieved surprise, expressed in highly formal language. "That's MacKellor," thought Johnny. And sure enough at the end was a postscript in Mr. Tavish's hand.

"Best luck to you, young Fraser," it read. "The Frasers were always good men for a fight. I send you good wishes as should not, for since the White Haven affair the marine insurance rates are like to be our ruin."

Another month passed and, except for the fact that the French of Corneille and Racine had been supplanted by the French of the Rue Canaille, there was little that Johnny Fraser could show for it. Captain Jones was gone; there was no word from him, nothing but echoes of his triumph at the Court in Paris. Sitting in his little room one evening, Johnny gazed uncomprehendingly at the page of a borrowed book on navigation and wondered whether he would not be better off at home, provided that he could get there. Here he was throwing away the precious moments of the war; at home there was always the army, now watching Philadelphia from the hills of Valley Forge.

It was July; perhaps they had already marched for the summer campaign. By Zooks, he should be with them! He could shoot; he might be of some use there, but here, even if he did find a ship, what use was a rifleman in a battle of thirty-pounder broadsides?

Outside, women squawked and gabbled, children shrieked in the warm night air, weary wooden sabots dragged home from work, a man's voice, rich and fervent, sang a chanson of Languedoc. He felt utterly an alien, solitary, futile, frittering away the priceless, irrevocable days in a strange, incomprehensible land. Well, what else should he expect? Whom else should he blame? It was a law of life, the ancients had discovered long ago, that opportunity, once missed, did not return.

A sturdy footfall sounded on the stair, a blunt fist knocked on his door.

"Entrez," he said mechanically. The door swung back, he sprang to his feet.

"Why, Nat!" he cried. "Good God! Old Nat!" He ran forward, stretching out his arms. "What brought you here?"

For answer the familiar figure in cape coat and riding-boots wrung Johnny's hands in silence for what seemed like many minutes, then mopped his crimson, child-like face with a huge silk handkerchief. Johnny seized him by the arm. "What brought you here, old scoundrel?"

Sir Nat minutely inspected the large horseshoe embroidered on his handkerchief and looked away.

"See you. What?" he said.

"But how did you know where I was?"

"Found out from those Scotch cits you worked for."

"MacKellor and Tavish?"

"Yes; rum chap, MacKellor." He mused.

"You've been in London, then?"

"Went to see what had happened when you didn't turn up."

"My lord, Nat, that was mighty nice of you!"

"Nonsense, enjoyed trip; had plenty money; sold blood horse; did you hear?"

"Why, no!" said Johnny, grinning. "I didn't, but I'm mighty glad."

"Yes," said Sir Nat. "Sold him. Young Marquis—good price, too."

"Did he know he roared, Nat?" asked Johnny with a wink.

"Dessay," said Sir Nat imperturbably. "Said he knew about horses. Dessay he knew that."

Johnny laughed. "Well, bung me, boy," he said, "I'm glad to see you." He turned serious. "But you know you oughtn't to come over here to France now; they's liable to be war between France and England 'most any time."

"Quite right," said Sir Nat. "That's why I came; too late—later."

"But, Nat, you oughtn't to have taken the risk. What gave you the idea?"

"Heard you were nipped in White Haven raid—carried to France—that sort of thing." He shook his head sagely. "Don't trust mounseer johnnies—put you in prison—all sorts of odd games."

"But, Nat, I joined the Americans—we're more or less heroes here now."

"Dammit!" said Sir Nat. "Not my fault. Have a drink." He produced a huge pigskin-covered flask from his pocket. "Stop," he said, "let's make proper toddy."

"Huzzah!" cried Johnny. He rushed to the door. "Madame!" he shouted down the stone stairway, "deux citrons."

"What's that?" asked Sir Nat.

"I asked for lemons."

"See," said Sir Nat. "Odd chaps—always said they were."

By the time Sir Nat had brushed his buckled hat on his sleeve and laid it on the bed with his cape coat neatly folded beside it, the approaching rumble of Madam Legaude was heard on the stair. The door was flung open by a vigorous kick and Madam entered bearing the ingredients for the toddy on a tray.

"Ah," she said with a glance of profound comprehension. "L'ami de votre coeur!" She set the tray on the chair and considered Sir Nat, her arms akimbo. "C'est un galant homme," she announced, and patted Sir Nat on his small round head.

"I say, Bantam," said Sir Nat, looking deeply perturbed, "what's her game, eh?"

"Oh, that's all right, Nat; she does that to everybody!"

"Ah," said Sir Nat dubiously. "Odd idea, though. Fancy goin' about pattin' people's heads. Ha!" He laughed and nodded cordially at Madam Legaude. "Good old Walrus," he said very loudly and distinctly. "Toddy?" He pointed to the tray.

For answer Madam threw up her great hands in horror and with a final glance of blandishment over her huge shoulder, trundled from the room.

As Sir Nat mixed the toddy, Johnny watched his studious puckered face. It was still the face of a small boy, precociously knowing, yet fundamentally innocent. But the three years since the days of Edenton had, it seemed to Johnny, left on the light blue eyes and small quick mouth a new mark, a shadow of incomprehensible frustration, of puzzled despair. It lay so light, however, that Johnny could not be sure; perhaps he mistook merely the weariness of the voyage.

"How you been all this time, Nat?" he said.

"Quite all right, thanks." Sir Nat squinted at the dissolving sugar; he gave Johnny a brief glance. "You're well; rum-looking tack, though." He indicated Johnny's seaman's clothes.

"I know," said Johnny, "but I aim to go to sea again soon."

"What?" said Sir Nat.

"Yes, I—I know I've hung back too long and all that, but now I aim to fight."

"Quite right, too," Sir Nat agreed. "Not at sea, though—no horses, nothing."

"But, Nat, it's the only place they is to fight over here."

"Go home; join cavalry." Sir Nat nodded sage endorsement over the steaming tumbler. "Ride like a Trojan."

"But that takes so long, and I'm afraid the war won't last."

" 'Course it will—last forever." He shook his head.

"I reckon it seems a long time to you, all right, with so many friends on the other side."

"Bad business," Sir Nat admitted, "bein' in the regiment and all that."

"I bet they made it mighty hard for you."

For some moments Sir Nat stirred the toddy without reply.

"Yes," he said in a low voice, "said I was funkin'." With a tug at the lip strap across his waistcoat, he produced his big hunting-case watch and stared at it abstractedly. "Never had that said before."

"Oh, Nat!" cried Johnny. "By God, I'd like to hear a man say that."

"No use, old chap; they don't understand Americans." He polished the watch slowly on his silk handkerchief. "Not clever myself. Couldn't explain."

While Johnny fumbled for the word to say, Sir Nat's quiet voice went on. "See this watch? My governor's regiment gave it him—after Fontenoy." He slipped the watch in his waistcoat pocket. "Funny thing—life. Hello! toddy's right." He passed a glass to Johnny. "Well, Bantam,—North Carolina!"

Johnny raised his glass. "And the best horse ther'!"

"Quite right, old chap—and who rode him?"

## CHAPTER XLI

A WEEK LATER Johnny and Sir Nat were seated at an iron table of the Café Deux Matelots, gazing out over the little plaza and over the long harbor where a squadron of French ships of the line, just in, having taken on stores and ammunition, now lay swinging impatiently at their cables.

"Suppose I should be gettin' back," Sir Nat observed gloomily.

"I'm afraid so, Nat. I hate the idea, but it looks like those ships out there were getting ready for war. I don't reckon you'll mind if England does fight France."

"Shouldn't say that, old chap; nice thing for me, of course. Always did want my whacks at the mounseers. Means I'll hop back into the service, right enough."

"That's fine. I bet you'll show those stuck-up Englishmen a thing or two."

"Shall try to, of course," said Sir Nat modestly. He seemed not altogether satisfied; plunged in thought, his face was strained by reflections of unaccustomed and unmanageable profundity. "Sha'n't like war with France, though," he said; "nice thing for me and all that. But sha'n't like to see the mounseers coming down on old country. Trouble enough with you chaps, what?"

"It certainly is a mess, this war between America and England, and now France too, a sure enough mess."

"Right!" said Sir Nat. "Silly business. Your chaps and our chaps should be together, fightin' mounseers. By jove! What a knock we should give 'em! Heyo, there!" He hailed a passing waiter. "Bock." He held up one finger. "Bock," he repeated, holding a second finger up beside it. "Wonder if he twigged me?" he said, fixing his eyes moodily on the waiter's departing back.

"I reckon so."

"Never be sure. Odd chaps; uncommon odd." A passing team caught his eye. "Look how they put on bridles!" He shook his head morosely. "Every cheek-piece, three holes too short."

The waiter appeared with the bocks. "Hullo! He did twig me," said Sir Nat, burying his nose in the vase-shaped glass. He came up for air. "What would Wylie Jones say," he remarked complacently, "to see me talkin' French?"

Sir Nat, however, did not return to England. Day after day he lingered, sticking close to Johnny's side, saying little, save when some chance word moved him to a labored and inarticulate burst of reminiscence. At one time or another every man, every horse, every hound in the Edenton district was duly considered. It was as if Sir Nat, as the time for separation drew near, felt the compulsion to piece together each least detail of his life there, to establish in his slow mind the picture, perfect, indestructible, of his North Carolina days. Indeed, so lost in memories he became at times that he seemed to be living again the old scenes.

"Pity about that horse," he would say of a horse long since dead; "grand mover, lies on the bit, though." His stubby fingers played delicately in his lap as though he held the reins.

One cloud threatened: The big pigskin flask was emptied. It looked as though they should be reduced to the trivial wines or the deplorable cognac of the French nation.

"Never say die, Bantam," Sir Nat remarked, tapping the empty bottle. "Leave it to me." He descended Madam Legaude's stairs; leaning out the window, Johnny received a knowing wink from the street. He watched the agile, sturdy figure, buttoned tight in his dark green cape-coat, trudge down the alleyway. Johnny's conscience smote him. What was he about, to leave Sir Nat, an utter stranger to the town, without a word of French, to wander about by himself? Night was coming on, the secret police might take him for a spy. He ran down to the street. Sir Nat, however, was out of sight.

To Johnny's great relief, just after dusk the familiar footsteps sounded on the stairs. Hot and somewhat blown, Sir Nat entered and disgorged two bottles of Scotch whiskey from each of his cape-coat pockets. "Now we're safe," he observed.

"That's fine, Nat, but you oughtn't to have done that."

"Why not? Good Scotch—tried it myself."

"I know, but you oughtn't wander round alone; I thought of it afterward; you're liable to be picked up by the Watch."

"Nonsense, they've no notion I'm English."

"What do you do, then, tell them you're an American?"

Sir Nat brought out the glasses and with much crouching and squinting poured out two precisely equal drinks. "Better still," he answered with a touch of pride. "Tell 'em I'm a Frenchman from another part of France.

"Suppose there are other parts of France," Sir Nat went on reflectively, "aren't there, Bantam?"

"Oh, yes, lots of 'em. France is a big country."

Sir Nat eyed his glass morosely. "Pity," he said.

Down by the harbor, up on the hill, the Sunday morning bells boomed and jangled from twenty churches. Their clamor fell at times to a drowsy hum, only to break out again in a burst of high-pitched, nervous dissonance. Perched on the feather-bed, Sir Nat raised a troubled face from his cup of café au lait.

"Too many silly bells." He looked resentfully out the window as though he expected to see the rue Canaille crowded with the strident sound.

"Take a walk," he suggested. "Out of town."

"All right, Nat, but I don't mind the bells; I more or less like 'em."

"Nonsense; not proper—banging about on Sunday!" Sir Nat munched his brioche. "Nothing against one bell, parish church sort of thing—but these chaps"—he swallowed indignantly—"no notion where to stop."

With a loaf of Madam Legaude's bread and two bottles of her beer in their pockets, they trudged down the narrow hillside streets between whose overhanging stone tenements the late morning sun was peering. Grimy childern played "un, deux, trois" for sous under foot, their elders, gaily dressed, paraded the street or, with much ado and chattering, with much adjusting of baskets, wicker flasks and babies, prepared to embark on festive Sunday excursions. At a corner estaminet the aftermath of Saturday night, in the form of two Breton longshoremen and an American petty officer, lay snoring.

"By Zooks!" said Johnny. "I'm surprised to see those fellows together, even if they are asleep. They've had some bad fights between our seamen and the French lately."

"Another last night," Sir Nat said brightly. "Americans cleaned out Café des Marins."

"It that so? How on earth did you find out?"

"Madam."

Johnny laughed. Sir Nat's French consisted in the word "bock"; Madam's English, limited to a few phrases picked up from casual seafaring men, was of far too specialized a meaning for general purposes; yet Sir Nat never let a day pass without at least an hour's earnest discussion in Madam's tiled kitchen. Johnny was not permitted to be present, but every day he could hear the hum of their vehement voices coming up the stairway. Every day Sir Nat returned with a fund of curious information, some of which invariably proved to be correct.

"So they cleaned out the des Marins, did they? I hadn't heard of that."

"Yes. Mounseers under beds, in cellar, up chimney, climbin' trees. Everything. Splendid!"

"I know, Nat, but they ought to put a stop to it; it makes bad feeling."

"Dessay," said Sir Nat complacently. "Any rate Americans chased 'em all on roof."

"That's all right," said Johnny, smiling against his will, "but somebody's going to be hurt before long."

They had reached the outskirts of the town; the street turned into a lane, the lane into a cowpath across a great round hill. They toiled up it and sat down.

"Whew!" said Sir Nat. "Short of work; should have kept on the flat."

"You'll be all right in a minute. It's mighty nice up here, you can see all round!" Johnny gazed down over the jumbled brown-tiled roofs, over the many-masted harbor, over the deep, untroubled sea, the dark green pasture slopes and the distant pattern formed by narrow strips of bright green wheat and purple clover.

"Rotten country, though," Sir Nat observed. "No coverts." He pulled a blade of grass and chewed it dolefully.

Lying back on the turf, Johnny watched the cloud squadrons wheeling slowly through the blue and listened to the bells of far-off, unseen sheep. He lay so long and gazed so fixedly into the vast unfathomed dome that the world beneath him seemed to fade away. The chime of sheep-bells seemed to come from the fleecy flocks of cloud toward which he floated; yet through it all he felt Sir Nat beside him. The world was left behind; they two alone drifted through the thin, clear air, the clear, faint music.

He roused himself. "My land, Natto!" he murmured, "it's mighty nice up here."

"I say, old chap," said Nat, after labored reflection. "I twig you." He pulled the blade of grass from his mouth and observed it critically. "Don't go in for views myself, but I mean to say—last two years bad times for me, that sort of thing. Now," he turned to Johnny with his radiant, child-like smile—"well, I mean, here we are, what?" With an air of solemn complacence, he cocked the blade of grass in the corner of his mouth, pulled his buckled hat down over his eyes and lay down beside Johnny. "Old Bantam!" he muttered.

They lunched off Madam Legaude's bread and beer with a hunk of cheese to go with it. "Nice old thing, the Walrus," said Sir Nat. "Too bad her beer's so weak."

"Yes," said Johnny, "she thinks it's fine, though."

"Thinks I'm fine, too; rum notions, the Walrus, eh? Ha!"

Out to sea, a French squadron maneuvered in the light air, formed line and column, luffed, stood away. The tall white minarets of sails tilted gently in the ocean's swell; the altered canvas now gleamed, now showed darkly shadowed.

"What are those johnnies up to, Bantam?"

"They're having battle practice, I reckon, Nat."

"Ah! Expect I should be gettin' back to England; they've called for volunteers—forty thousand."

"Is that a fact? Where did you hear that?"

Sir Nat waved an authoritative hand. "Madame. What's more," he added, "money's about gone."

Johnny started to speak, but checked himself. Three days before he had seen Nat in conversation with two ragged American seamen, two withered lads whose dead eyes and pasty faces showed that they had just been exchanged from a British prison. On Johnny's approach, Sir Nat had brusquely marched away, but not before Johnny had caught the gleam of a gold coin passing from Sir Nat's short, stubby hand to a hand as parched and yellow as a talon.

"Of course," Johnny said, "if it was just money, they's nothing to that. We could make out on what I have; but I reckon you ought to put out for home."

Sir Nat nodded. "Straight off."

A long silence followed; nothing moved on land or sea except the drifting clouds, the swaying ships, the gulls.

"Hello!" cried Sir Nat. "By Jove!" He was on his feet and marching down the slope. Unnoticed, an old gray horse, in the course of his perfunctory browsing among the stubble and thistles, had rounded the shoulder of the hill. His ribs stared, his sunken back hung like a hammock between gaunt rump and withers; at the sound of Nat's footstep he raised a long sad face

SIR NAT AND THE HORSE

*Johnny watched Sir Nat rub the gray muzzle, run a quick hand down the ewe neck, stand back critically*
*and proceed to a minute and systematic inspection of the antique nag*

and whinnied. Leaning on an elbow, Johnny watched Sir Nat rub the gray muzzle, run a quick hand down the ewe neck, stand back critically and proceed to a minute and systematic inspection of the antique nag. Johnny followed lazily down the hill; Sir Nat, in the posture of a blacksmith, held the patient gray's hind foot in his lap. He raised a flushed and troubled face.

"Shame; feet breaking up." He tapped the cracked hoof with his knuckle and set it down. "Always use tips," he admonished, mopping his face, "on brittle feet." He fixed his eye again on the gray horse. "Bad doer, too; all tucked up." He placed a finger along the cadaverous jaw. "Whoa, horse! Thought so." He nodded reflectively. "Teeth need floatin', feel that." He put Johnny's hand against the jaw. Johnny felt the teeth's sharp edges through the skin. At the pressure the old horse drew back quickly. "See? File 'em down; he'd take on eight stone. Too bad! Poor old fellow!" With a gentle slap on the quarters, he sent the gray horse shuffling down the hill. Chewing a blade of grass reflectively, he watched him out of sight.

For the rest of the afternoon Sir Nat sat silent, deeply preoccupied; toward evening, they walked down the lengthening shadow of the hill, back to the narrow cavernous streets, where premature twilight already gathered. In the Rue Canaille, the door of the maison Legaude, encrusted with ancient dirt and ancient carving, lay before them. Sir Nat's hand closed confidentially on Johnny's arm.

"Tell you what; let's get file, make rope twitch, float that old fellow's teeth; first thing tomorrow, what?"

"But, Nat, where can you get a file for horses' teeth?"

"Madame."

Seated that night at a stone-topped table inside the Café Deux Matelots, Sir Nat and Johnny dallied over the remains of what was tacitly understood to be a farewell supper; a supper whose magnificence was attested by the plate of strawberry pastries and the tall bottle of barsac which remained.

"Good tuck, I call it," said Sir Nat, with a pull at his waistcoat. He glanced complacently round the tables crowded with Sunday merrymakers, perspiring bourgeois, weathered sea captains, stiff, slim officers.

Their chatter filled the low stone-floored room to bursting. "By Jove, what a row!" Sir Nat remarked. "Odd idea of a good time, talkin', laughin', that sort of thing." He eyed the crowd with puzzled curiosity. "Not drunk neither; fancy shoutin' about like that—sober. Wonder what they find to talk of?"

"Oh!" said Johnny. "They mostly just talk about their own small affairs."

"Good God!" said Sir Nat with some concern, "fancy talkin' about one's own affairs, eh, Bantam? See those two officer johnnies," he went on, "been goin' it for an hour. What are they sayin', eh?"

Johnny turned toward the two Frenchmen at the next table. One wore the white, laced uniform of the King's Guards; the other, a nondescript semi-military dress suggestive of a moderately unsuccessful soldier of fortune. Their waxed mustaches bristled as they bent toward each other, talking earnestly. Leaning his hand on his chin, Johnny listened.

"I say," Sir Nat repeated at last, "what are they sayin'?"

"Oh!" said Johnny uneasily, "they're just talking about the army, you know the way officers do." He did not say that the two were discussing the water-front riots between French and American seamen. These riots, stretching over several weeks and culminating in the affair of the Café des Marins, from whose wreckage, it was whispered, both sides had secretly carried away more than one dead body, had changed the attitude of Brest from fantastic adoration of all things American to a hatred equally unreasonable. The conversation of the two Frenchmen was scurrilous and vile. It was further pointed by apparent knowledge of the Colonies on the part of the soldier of fortune. The man was telling lies about America, plausible and most ingeniously defamatory. The scoundrel—the dirty low-bred scoundrel! But it would do no good, but harm, to cause a scene. Moreover, he consoled himself, the man was, no doubt, one of the horde of decayed adventurers who had, in the expectation of high rank and rich booty, flocked from France to offer their services to General Washington, had been courteously received by that gentleman, and then imperturbably shipped home again. Gripping his chin in his hand, he could not resist boldly staring at the two mean, supercilious faces.

The Frenchmen grew conscious of Johnny's glance. They whispered together, bared their teeth, leaned back in their chairs and began to talk in broken English for his benefit.

"So you are just come from America, hein? 'Ow intairesting," the Guardsman said.

The other shrugged disdainfully. "Mais non, they are impossible, the Americain."

"Hullo!" whispered Sir Nat, "those johnnies are tryin' to talk English."

"So," said the Guardsman. "You do not like?"

"Ze Americains!" The other twisted his lips contemptuously. "They are sauvages!"

"Ah," the Guardsman agreed solemnly. "Zat would be very disagréable to you, monsieur."

The other smote his breast. "Moi, I would not remain! They ask to make me majeur général, but no, I do not remain, I say to them, 'I am soldier, man of honneur, not butchaire!' I do not remain!"

"Zey are very cruel, hein?"

"Parbleu! You 'ave not heard of ze scalp?" he grimaced horribly. "Every prisonnier," he ran a graphic finger across his brow, "zey scalp heem."

"I say," said Sir Nat in Johnny's ear, "let's stop their nonsense!"

Johnny laid a hand on his arm. "We can't have another fight between French and Americans just now." Sir Nat gulped. "The best thing is to pay no attention, Nat. Let's talk about something else."

But the loud voice of the French adventurer broke through his words.

"And not onlee prisonnier, but also ze women and babee."

"No, no!" exclaimed the Guardsman in affected surprise.

"Mais oui, in captured town have I seen before ze Quartier Général Americain, thirtee scalp, ze long-'aired scalp of ze women, ze lettle scalp of babee."

Sir Nat was on his feet. Johnny clutched at his coat-skirt; it tore through his fingers as Sir Nat strode to the other table.

"You, johnny," he nodded bluntly at the narrator, "no more lies."

The Frenchman raised his eyebrows. "Ah! you are Americain, ze truth you do not like?"

"No more lies," Sir Nat repeated patiently.

"Go away, Americain," the Guardsman interposed, "we do not talk to you." He thrust a jewelled hand against Sir Nat. In a flash Sir Nat had seized his wrist and bent it back; the three stood motionless. The crowd was forming, muttering.

"You heard me," Sir Nat said steadily. "Mean it."

The other Frenchman rose, leaned close to Sir Nat's face. "You are all babee scalper, you Americain," he drawled. "Get out!" He thrashed his long fingers across Sir Nat's face. The crowd cheered. And still they stood there, while four long white streaks grew slowly on Sir Nat's round pink cheek. Then suddenly the Frenchman's face flicked toward the ceiling; he went backward over his chair. Sir Nat just straightened from the blow in time to block the Guardsman's rush.

The rest was all a haze to Johnny, a mist, now bright, now dark, now bloody, through which Sir Nat and he fought back to back with fists, with bottles, with broken chairs; it might have been hours, it might have been days that they held their ground against the rushes and the crashing plates. Now they were side by side against the wall; an iron chair was in his hand, he saw a sword come out; he swung the chair. The Guardsman dove forward, lay face down, his fingers scrabbled on the bloody stones.

Still they fought on, fought in a black resounding cavern where all was dim, where breath came hard, where there was nothing to be done except stand firm in chaos, lick blood from lips and swing the iron chair.

Then there was nothing left to swing at; the chair dropped from his hand with distant, faint reverberations; his knees were failing, a voice sounded above his head. "That's right, brother, take it easy. Come on, you boys, bring this here Nightshirt some liquor!"

The sting of cognac was in his mouth. He opened his eyes. In the ruined room, some twenty seamen from the frigate stood easing belts and puffing hard. They blew on their knuckles and stared reflectively at the prostrate forms which littered the floor. Some of these crumpled figures tossed feebly; some lay still.

"Wher's Nat?"

"Your gentleman friend? Oh, he's all right, I reckon." The seaman lifted

Johnny up. Grinning a little uncertainly, Sir Nat was seated on a broken table. Two seamen fanned him admiringly with their woollen caps.

"God in the Mountain, boy!" they murmured, "if you ain't a fighter!"

"Yes, seh, a natural born bob-cat!"

Sir Nat's wandering eye came to rest on Johnny's face. "Why, there's Bantam!" he muttered in a tone of puzzled surprise; he tried to rise. With the movement all color drained from his face, left it a tortured mask; he sank to the floor, the sailors bent over him solicitously. "Say, mate, you're hurt!" On unsteady feet Johnny stumbled toward him, knelt down by his side. Sir Nat opened his eyes, the faintest flush showed on his white cheek.

"There's Bantam," he whispered with a sigh of satisfaction. "What happened?" he said.

"Why, Nat, we fought the two Frenchmen, and then all the rest. But where are you hurt?"

"Quite right," Sir Nat's voice went on dreamily; "fought mounseers, Bantam and me; good job too."

"Nat, are you hurt?"

"Dessay, old chap. Fellow—with a knife."

Johnny put his hand in Nat's. "Oh, Nat, I hope you ain't hurt, I don't see any blood!"

"I feel it runin':—inside; 'fraid they've done me in, old chap."

"Somebody get a surgeon!" cried Johnny to the group around him. Two men sprang out.

"Bill, you run uptown, I'll try the ship."

Sir Nat roused at the words. "Don't go; no use." He closed his eyes. The men ran out.

Sir Nat blew softly through his lips. "By Jove," he murmured, "how it runs!"

The color slowly faded from his face, he lay there pale but resting easy and very drowsy.

A ship's bell, seeming to chime from a distant long-forgotten world, struck the hour. Footsteps came to the door. The surgeon! But they passed on again.

Now he seemed faintly troubled; he gently shook his head, laid an uncertain hand on his breast. It touched the watch-guard; his eyes opened instantly, he pulled at the leather. "My governor——" he said. "Fontenoy——"

"Nat!" cried Johnny, "hang on! The surgeon's coming. Why don't he come!" he mumbled distractedly at Sir Nat's faint smile. He started to rise.

"Stay here," Sir Nat clung to his hand, gave his friendly knowing grin; it vanished sharply, he closed his eyes. His face turned wholly white again, then slowly freed from pain, relaxed; he seemed to doze and drift into a dream.

And still no surgeon—only the rhythmic bump of oar-locks over the water and, up the hill, a boy who whistled high and true. Behind, the waiting seamen shifted very softly as if afraid a sound would break the spell.

Now his free hand held a pair of reins. He was on the racecourse at Edenton. "Come on, Carolina!" he whispered. "Carolina wins!" His hand closed on Johnny's; he gave a long faint sigh. "Good horse!" he said; his voice turned clear and ringing, "Good man!" His grip relaxed; a faint flush like a baby's mounted for an instant to the child-like face, hovered, died away. The light blue eyes gave Johnny Fraser one long glance, sober, contented, like a child's.

## CHAPTER XLII

FOR JOHNNY FRASER, the summer was a desolate waste. Interminable, the idle, fruitless days passed without count, without meaning, except for the warm sad evenings when he walked out to the grave of Sir Nathaniel Dukinfield. The graveyard for foreigners lay westward up the river; sloping gently toward the bank, it looked down on the smooth noiseless stream which made a last turn between tall, fantastic willow stumps, before it entered the town and harbor. Sitting on the unkempt grass among the unkempt weeds, he read the legend on the deep brown terra cotta tombstone.

"SIR NATHANIEL DUKINFIELD, BARONET.
1744–1778."

Thrusting softly through the red earth of the grave, the new green shoots of grass were already adding their light touch to the headstone's message of finality. A light touch—yet almost too heavy to be born. Those sparse, fragile tips, thrusting through the clay, weaving their web of roots above the dead, carried more conviction of irrevocable fate than all the mausoleums of antiquity. Indeed, it seemed at times to Johnny as though nothing but the slow growth of the grass could make him believe Sir Nat to be dead; it seemed incredible that a man so simple, so kindly, so without a definite object in life, could die. Historical figures, important personages, earnest strivers, died, of course; it was obvious that for such as they, something should eventually arrive to put an end to their activities. But for Sir Nat, a man who drew his unaffected pleasure from such narrow interests, who wished to accomplish nothing, to influence no one, for such a man death seemed grotesquely out of scale. And what a death! The last of a gallant ancient family killed in a café riot! "Funny thing—life," Sir Nat used to say; and never more senseless, thought Johnny bitterly, than when it brought him to his end.

Yet was it senseless? Or, if senseless, who was he to raise the question? Here lay one who had lived according to his simple creed and when the moment came, had struck his blow. Could that be said of Johnny Fraser? He clasped his hands about his knees and bent his head between them.

No chance for action came. The French fleet had sailed away from Brest before Sir Nat was a fortnight under ground, had fought a drawn battle and returned to spend the summer leisurely refitting. No more was heard from Captain Jones; out by the foreigners' burying ground, the willow leaves turned yellow, fluttered to the stream.

The American frigate lying in the harbor was given to another officer and ordered for home. The faces of American seamen were seen no more along the waterfront; across the harbor their cheerful voices could be heard as they heaved the sea stores on board. Johnny made up his mind to ship aboard her. His heart grew light again.

At this moment Captain Jones, more handsomely turned out than ever, and with a new gold medal on his breast, accosted Johnny in the plaza.

"That's a good riddance," he said after a handshake and a polished bow; he pointed to the frigate. "The most of those lads are nought but privateersmen, the pick of them, like you, will stay wi' me."

"Why, no, seh," said Johnny, "I aim to go home on her."

"What!" cried Captain Jones. "Ye'll not desert me? Come now, friend, don't tell me that." He took Johnny by the arm. "We'll walk and talk a bit."

For an hour they walked on the sea wall; the grim little man striding with quick steps beside Johnny's long ones, touching the sleeve of Johnny's watch coat, painting bright prospects with rude but graphic skill, talking of plunder, duty, glory, stopping, his eye alight, his rough voice bristling, to point a strong square finger out to sea.

"I know, seh," said Johnny uncomfortably. "I'd like mighty well to join the next cruise whenever it comes, but I've waited and waited and nothin' happens." He stopped, looked down at the short commanding figure. His voice fell. "I want to get into this war."

Paul Jones reached up and clapped him on the shoulder, his hard, canny face crinkled, he showed his fine teeth in a winning smile. "I know ye do, my friend, that's why I love ye; and if I'd had my way," his mouth closed like a trap, "by now the two of us would be crowned wi' bays—or seaweed."

"I know," said Johnny. "You can't help it, seh, but I can't wait neither."

For a long moment Paul Jones gazed out over the crowded shipping, down the long narrow harbor, out to the open water; his sturdy legs spread wide, his blunt hand clasped behind his back. He whistled dolefully between his teeth. Rubbing his chin, he turned on Johnny a long look of rough kindliness and smiled again.

"Look ye, young sir," he said, "ye journeyed once to Kirkcudbright to do me, unasked, the greatest favor that any man has, save one. And will ye not just bide here in Brest to do me another?" In the pause which followed, his face turned grave. "Two months—only two! If in two months, a ship for me does not lie in this harbor, fittin' for sea, I'll see ye'll get your wish, I'll send ye home."

"Two months?" said Johnny. "That's a long time to wait."

"It's worth waitin' for. And as for a long time," he gave a twisted grin, "I've waited thirty years."

"I don't know what to say," murmured Johnny uncertainly. "Will the ship be here sure enough, seh?"

"It will. They know me now in Paris," he touched the medal on his breast.

"It's no longer the small fry I talk to; it's the King. Two months and she'll be here." He seized Johnny by the lapels of his coat. "Ye'll not desert me, lad, there's plenty to do that; what I need is a few such as you, wi' their hearts in the right place, to stand by me. They'll be no fightin' till spring at home now and one good seaman off the English coast is worth a hundred soldiers in winter quarters. Ye'll stay, lad, eh? Here's a hand on it." His heavy grip closed on Johnny's hand.

Turning abruptly, he resumed his whistling, cocked his hat over one eye and marched off, very erect and slightly bandy-legged, across the plaza.

And sure enough when the first hard freeze glazed the gutters of the Rue Canaille, a great black hulk was towed up the gray waters of the bay and moored at the naval dockyards.

As Johnny, leaning against a quayside pile, watched her, a mud-streaked chaise galloped to the gate. Muffled in a dark blue surtout, Paul Jones hopped out, stepped down the quay.

"Well, here she is, seh," said Johnny with a touch of elation.

The square jaw shot forward. "Aye, here she is, and what is she? She's not the ship they promised."

"She's mighty big, though."

Captain Jones gave a grating laugh. "Big, aye, big, and what else? An old East Indiaman, rotten to the core!" He smote a fist into his palm. "They dare not give me a proper ship—they dare not! The American commissioners have not the power nor, save for old Franklin, the brains. And the French Marine, knowing the sort of man I am, will never give me a ship that can do more than keep afloat; they have no wish to let the world see me raid the coast of England, single-handed, while the whole French navy lies snugged down in their home ports. And yet," he teetered back and forward, on his wide-spread feet, his face still flushed with anger, but his grim mouth faintly smiling, "and yet, I'll have the laugh o' them, if yon old tub will just bear cannon. We start fitting her tomorrow; I have the shipwrights ready. Do you tell all the Americans in port that wait for me."

"Yes, seh," said Johnny briskly, "I certainly will."

ON THE SEA WALL WITH JOHN PAUL JONES

*For a long moment Paul Jones gazed out over the crowded shipping, down the long narrow harbor, out to the open water. He whistled dolefully between his teeth*

"And stay!" said Captain Jones. "Ye've had commercial trainin' and a very good thing too. I'll make ye clerk of the dock. Wi' a couple of bright lads to help ye, ye'll keep tale o' every stick and bolt that goes into her. Be here at six; I'll show ye." He hurried to the chaise and galloped off.

Matters began to move. Seated among his ledgers in a shanty at the end of the dock, Johnny Fraser, while not content, was happier than before. His life was far from glorious, yet it was farther still from idle. From dawn to dark he counted stores, made entries, kept the shipwrights' time; all day the swarming hulk resounded to the sound of mallets, echoed the rhythmic scratch of saws; great two-wheeled drays unloaded oak and elm timbers on the quay; the master shipwrights swung their compasses on the beams, marked them in chalk with cryptic signs. One by one, yawning heavy-lidded gun ports seemed to grow along the ship's side. And yet they grew so slowly! Spits of snow were falling on Noël wreaths before the last great hole was pierced; then followed two long weeks when all the shipwrights laid off for Christmas cheer and Johnny Fraser had nothing to do but hug the brazier in his shanty, stare at the silent hulk and check his ledgers for the tenth time.

Raw, bitter winter followed, the town seemed empty save for the few chance figures who, muffled and silent as conspirators, stole in straw-filled sabots along snow-dusted streets. Work on the ship was almost congealed, yet somehow her decks were strengthened, a sheer hulk was warped alongside, tackle creaked, great booms swung ponderously, the vessel's masts were stepped.

The first spring wind to melt the icicles brought the white sails of a slim new frigate thirty days from Boston; the purser sought out Johnny's shanty on the quay and, grinning genially, shoved a letter through the window.

"Guess she still loves ye, sonny!"

Johnny looked at the address in his mother's wavering schoolgirl hand. "Yes, seh, old Codfish-Ball!" he shouted. "I reckon she does." Pushing aside a sheepskin-covered ledger, he broke the seal.

"My dear Son,

"Your Letter telling that you had gone to sea with Captn Jones was indeed a great Surprise. I gave your Message to your Father with whatever Words I could summon on your behalf for I feared he would take it ill of you. For a long Space he sat silent, then, 'Well,' he says, 'it's no more than I looked for. The Frasers have ever been in every Fight, and for the most Part on the losing Side.' On hearing these Words, my Mind was much relieved, they being more favorable than could have been expected.

"But as for me, my dear Son, I do not think that we shall lose; I think that we shall win. Here we make great Exertions, near every Man fit to bear Arms, is gone to the Army and we at Home grow Corn and weave Cloth for the Troops. The People hereabouts are fully persuaded Never to Knock Under; Joe Merrillee is a Captn in the Continental Line and Mr. Merrillee went last year to join General Washington in New Jersey, and has not been heard of this long time. Poor Mrs. Merrillee is quite distraught; Sally manages the Place with surprising Address for One so young and Everyone commends her for it. She has had several Offers, I hear, and can quite believe it, for since the War, every Girl of Parts in the County has been besieged; and many have married with less Thought, I fear, than they would bestow upon a new Tippet.

"Your Father keeps his Health, though the poor Man begins a little to show his Years, and I am well, being too busy weaving and sewing Army Cloathes to think of myself. I try, my dearest Son, not to think too much of you, though truth to tell, you are always in my Mind and every Night I pray God send you safe Home again to me. Not that I would have Matters otherwise than as they are. In time of Peace I was ever fearful for your Safety, but now I think myself happy to stand with all the other Women of the Provinces whose Sons serve their Country. And now, my Son, farewell, and God keep you. Write as you may have Opportunity, but your Father bids me caution you to say Nothing in your Letters which might disclose your Commander's designs to the Enemy. Farewell again, my dearest Son, you have ever been my Joy and never more so than now.

"Your loving Mother."

That was a letter to make a man want to do his best, to make him proud of his country and his blood. If only there had not been that line about Sally Merrillee. She was old enough to take care of herself by now, old enough to know her own mind. But what a shame it would be if she threw herself away on some scoundrel who did not appreciate her. It made him almost sick to think of it. He must write his mother at once to let her know how he was. But first perhaps he might send a line to Sally to let her know—to let her know what? To let her know that he was well? What would she care? To let her know that ever and again, at moments swift and unforeseen, before his eyes flashed pictures of her—pictures of her spinning, graceful, patient in her soft blue callimanco gown; riding the colt, her red cloak swaying to the long striding walk—pictures of her which flashed, hovered, vanished mockingly? She would never believe him. Or if she did; again, what would she care? It was impossible to conceive a letter from him to Sally Merrillee which would not be a letter written by a fool. He would write his mother only.

The riggers went aboard in May, they rigged the masts and crossed the yards. Watching their web grow against the blue, Johnny Fraser felt his heart tug at its moorings; by Zooks, the end was now in sight. Below, the roustabouts stowed her cables and her great flat lumps of canvas in the hold, bronze guns were slung aboard, cradled in their carriages, lashed at their ports, kegs of biscuit, of spirits, of shot and powder, butts of water, barrels of salt beef were stored in her hold; the time was almost here.

On the tenth of June her topsails fluttered, she swung out into deep water and dropped anchor. But still delay pursued her.

Ordered on board with the handful of Americans who had worked on her, Johnny Fraser hung over the rail day after day and watched the distant figure of Captain Jones signing on seamen in the plaza. By slow and most unpromising driblets, the crew arrived and slung their hammocks; yellow, shivering lascars, Negroes, Portuguese, dull Breton peasants starved out of their turnip fields, a hundred surly British prisoners and deserters in charge of a none too well pleased detachment of French marines. At last came

some Americans, ninety able seamen with their officers. They were drawn
and sallow from a year in the British hulks out of which they had been
exchanged, but not an eye among them was so listless that it did not light
when they talked of another shot at the Union Jack.

Her crew, if such it could be called, was now made up; the Captain's boat
came alongside, the four hundred offscourings of the earth, mustered aft,
raised an unconvincing cheer for him and for their ship, the "Bonhomme
Richard." Amid unspeakable confusion and a babel of tongues, they somehow managed to weigh anchor, shake out some canvas and stand down the
harbor.

They spent two weary months cruising off the coast of France, training
their motley crew, lying again in port to refit; at last, by August, the worm-
eaten old merchantman and the flotsam and jetsam hands who worked her,
had been brought to such readiness as their wretched natures allowed.
They weighed anchor and with an escort of sloops and frigates stood out to
find the enemy.

# CHAPTER XLIII

WHEN LATE September gales were blowing, they raised the meagre brown, green coasts of Scotland. For a month they had cruised in British waters; a dozen British merchantmen had lowered topsails to them; their orlop deck was crowded with three hundred British prisoners. Quite satisfied with what had been accomplished, the crew of the "Bonhomme Richard" figured out each man's prize money and grumbled in six different languages to be sent home; but every day the home port lay farther from the vessel's course and farther, too, it seemed, from Captain Jones' mind.

To Johnny Fraser, still working on the ship's accounts, spending the weeks at the wardroom table under the lean-faced purser's eye, the future had become a matter of indifference; there was nothing for him in gazing idly over the side while helpless merchantmen hove to and hauled down their colors; and even if it came to fighting, who ever heard of a purser's assistant in a naval battle? Most likely he would be put to passing water or carrying the wounded.

Seated one afternoon among his detested ledgers, he had just copied out an item in duplicate, or was it triplicate? His bored, bemused mind hardly knew; at all events, there it stood in all its futile imbecility:

June 9th, 1779, By 7bbl. best Norwegian turpentine, £7, s.9, d.6.

The Captain's orderly entered, removed his cap, pasted an order on the wardroom wall. Johnny stared at him indifferently; he had long since ceased to look to orders of the day for interest, still less for excitement. Trivial in themselves, they never by any chance had the remotest connection with a purser's assistant, who was, it appeared, a species outside the natural order as far as a ship's company was concerned.

The orderly having stuck the sheet of paper on the wall with two red wafers, turned and, fixing his eyes on the ceiling above Johnny's head, announced in sharp but lifeless tones, "You're in orders, sir." He put on his cap and marched from the room. Johnny stared at the bulkhead through which the man had disappeared.

" 'Seh'?" he said to himself. "Now why did that high-toned scoundrel call me 'Seh'? They ain't a man on the ship has done that except the Negroes." He went to the order board and read the paper:

On board the Bonhomme Richard Sept. 18th 1779
Order No. 99
From this date the following Altered Dispositions of
Small Armed Parties will be observed in Action:
Forecastle——Captain Richard Dale and American Marines
Poop——Colonel Chamillard and French Marines
Foretop——Midshipman Walters and twenty men
Maintop——Lieutenant Fanning and thirty men
Mizzentop——Ensign Crouch and twenty men
Vice-Captains of the tops.
Foretop——Mr. Fraser
Main top——

Johnny Fraser was fumbling under the table. Where in the nation was his hat? There it was—the fine new French cocked hat of naval cut. He clapped it proudly on his spinning head and ran up to the deck. There, all was strangely quiet, orderly, unmoved by the stupendous event. The deck watch lay stretched in the feeble sunlight under the weather bulwarks, the lookout peered stolidly over the foretop's canvas screen; astern, the quartermaster lowered his eyes to the binnacle and touched the great mahogany wheel; on the quarterdeck, the watch-lieutenant paced slowly to and fro on the weather side; alone by the lee rail stood the short, square figure in dark blue just as it had always stood, it seemed, unchanged, immovable, unsleeping, since the first day they had left port. His eyes fixed aloft, he watched minutely how the canvas filled to the blustering, mist-laden wind.

Johnny Fraser gazed at Captain Jones with longing. He would give a hundred pounds to rush up on the quarterdeck, blurt out his thanks and devise, without a moment's delay, grand schemes by which the foretop should be fought. But he had long since learned that however much backclapping, handshaking and convivial laughter there might be to Captain Jones when that commander was seeking to raise a crew on shore, at sea no man so much as spoke to him without authority. Spoke to him? By Zooks, it was worth a man's neck to look at him as Johnny was doing now! He glanced hastily away; he had best let the raw wind cool his burning cheeks until he could compose his mind, then confer in a quiet, steady manner with Midshipman Walters, an ancient, long-nosed seaman, raised temporarily, and much to his own discomfiture, to commissioned rank.

"Fraser!" The little man's great voice boomed up through the wind; the Captain was beckoning him.

"Ye've seen the orders?" Captain Jones asked as Johnny gained the quarterdeck.

"Yes, seh, and I certainly am obliged to you."

"Ye should be," said Captain Jones with a comfortable grin. "I'm over tender, I fear. When a man wishes to risk his life I've never the heart to deny him."

Johnny Fraser laughed, laughed on the quarterdeck where few men dared to smile. "Yes, that's so, but I'm obliged just the same."

"Aweel," said Captain Jones with a friendly jerk of his head toward Johnny, " 'tis no more than your due; ye've stuck by me; ye've done the dirty work and now ye shall have your share of glory."

"I'll try to make out all right, seh," said Johnny modestly, "if we do get in a fight."

"Ye'll make out, I've no doubt; jest ye remember this: to lead men in a fight, the great thing is this—to show them the way yourself and yet to keep your wits and eyes about ye and observe how matters stand." He whistled between his teeth. "It's naught but a question," he added, "of doing two things, neither of them easy, at the same time."

"Yes, seh," said Johnny, "I hope I'll have the chance to try."

Captain Jones leaned over the rail and gazed astern where the vessel's long white wake writhed and heaved across the tumbling seas.

"Nine knots," he observed. "We're logging nine knots toward as fine a chance to fight as ye'll ever wish for, boy."

"Yes, seh," said Johnny without conviction. "That's good. They's been nothing much to this picking up of merchantmen," he added superciliously.

For an instant Captain Jones seemed angry, then he smiled.

"Ye're an arrogant young cock," he observed. "But not so fast. There's more to it perhaps then ye guess. We've made prisoners and we'll exchange them and save just that many Americans from dying in the British hulks."

"Yes, seh," said Johnny more humbly. "I hadn't thought of that."

"Nor of what our raiding has done to the British navy, I dare say. They're scouring the Atlantic for us, which gives us a chance i' the Channel."

"My lord, seh!" Johnny muttered. "Are we bound fo' the Channel?"

"The same." He eyed Johnny keenly. "Have ye enough Scots blood to close your mouth? Well, then, since ye think there's naught to sinking merchantmen, I'll just tell ye what we're up to. We're off to take the Baltic Fleet."

"The Baltic Fleet!" Johnny pursed his lips to whistle. He had heard of that cloud of British merchantmen flanked by British men-of-war.

"Aye. We'll engage their men o' war and leave the convoy to be picked up by the lousy French sloops that are supposed to be our consorts." He drew himself up. "And that's the sort of skipper I am, my gay young fire-eater, so I hope ye're satisfied." He stared complacently into Johnny's awestruck eyes. "They gave me a medal for my last cruise." He gazed out over the sea. "But they'll be put to it to do me proper honor for this." Squaring off to the breeze he whistled gratingly. "Now mind ye. Not a word o' this; these men o' mine would rise against me if they knew where I was fetchin' 'em. Good luck." He nodded brusquely.

As Johnny went down the companionway, the Captain's voice descended after him. "Make the men take aim; it's i' the tops we'll beat 'em." Johnny turned; the ruddy blue-jowled face peered down at him. "I'll be watchin' the foretop for a nice, brisk fire," he favored Johnny with a grin, sardonic, cheerful and inspiring, "as long as there's a man o' ye alive."

On the fifth day they hove to and waited. They lay in a great bay whose circling shore reached round them to the north and ended in a brown, low-lying headland. The wind had fallen to a light air; all round the ship, the soft autumnal sunlight sank deep into the slowly heaving sea; beyond, it glanced and shone from shifting planes of water and, farther still, lay level on the surface of cold shallow green.

The men gathered at the rail and whispered; the coast they saw, the old hands said, was England, Flamborough Head; they knew the "Bonhomme Richard" would not lay to in sight of it without a purpose. There was wagging of whiskered chins amongst the old sea-dogs, rolling of eyes among the Negroes and violent, whispered monkey chatter amongst the Malays and Portuguese.

The two bells marking one o'clock had scarcely died away when the lookout sang out sharply.

"A sail four points off the port quarter!" Silence fell; a young lieutenant with his glass under his arm ran along the gangway overhead and climbed up to the foretop. He had scarcely put his glass to his eye before the quarter-deck hailed him impatiently.

"Weel, Mr. Fanning, what do ye make out?"

"I make out nearly forty sail, sir," the lieutenant answered slowly, "in convoy; their course is South by East."

Johnny Fraser gripped the hammock nettings and peered at the horizon. "The Baltic Fleet!" he whispered to himself.

The boatswain's whistle sounded, the yards were squared away, sails filled, water murmured; the "Bonhomme Richard" stood out to meet the enemy.

By three o'clock the fleet, a long low cloud of canvas, could be seen from the deck where Johnny stood.

Now their own ship had been sighted. Within three minutes forty topsails were let fly, forty main courses fluttered distractedly in the breeze, the Baltic Fleet of merchantmen turned and fled for cover. The leading ship, however, stood on her course, the "Bonhomme Richard" still held hers. Drifting slowly in the light breeze, the two drew together until along the stranger's yellow side they could see the gun-ports of a British man-of-war. Her gilded figurehead shone, her bright blue upper works, fresh-painted, showed clear against the bright green sea. In the soft airs the red ensign at her staff, the pennant at her mast-head, formed graceful, slow-dissolving scrolls of color. Winking points of light across her poop marked where her company of marines paraded. Her new, varnished hull glowed softly in the green reflected light.

On board the "Richard" the boatswain's whistle sounded "Clear for action"; the groups that had been standing by the rail turned and ran for their stations. Fighting his way through the mêlée, Johnny Fraser gained the forecastle and climbed the rat-lines to the top. The foretop crew were at his heels; in quick succession, their faces, keen, leathery, American, popped up above the foretop flooring.

"Stand by to hoist up arms and ammunition!" said Johnny. "Here comes the Captain of the top." Midshipman Walters crawled painfully through the opening; gasping for breath, he wiped his long, thin nose on the back of his wrist.

"You scurvy lime juicers!" he panted, "what the bloody blazes—! Lower away with that rope!" He peered down at the teeming deck. "Ahoy, you below, stand by with them there sandbags!" He turned back to the crew. "Now haul away! Snatch it, you bob-tailed parrots, snatch it!"

The sandbags were hoisted to the top and lashed to form a breastwork; tubs of water, kegs of powder, cases of hand grenades and twenty old French muskets followed. "Now, then, Mister," Walters turned to Johnny, "look at them muskets and see that the flints is right!"

"What if they is?" a tall Vermonter muttered gloomily. "You couldn't hit a man with one of these consarned waffle-irons 'less'n he was to lean his butt against the muzzle."

"Dot's so it iss," a stocky Pennsylvania Dutchman nodded his head with cheerful vigor. "And den efen, by Gott, bullet maybe come out de wrong end." He snapped the lock of his musket disconsolately. "Ach my, for vy ve haven't Deckhardt rifle, eh?"

"Oh, I dun't know," the Vermonter broke in. "Up to Varmount folks dun't set so much by Deckhardts; but there's a feller in Deerfield makes a gun——"

A red haired Georgian turned on the Vermonter. "God in the Mountain, Yankee, talk like you had sense. You know they's nothing to touch a Deckhardt."

"Darned if that ain't so," one said.

"Deckhardts, though," another answered, "ain't what they used to be."

The rest took up the argument. They closed in, disputing earnestly, wagged fingers, clutched each other's sleeves.

Down on the decks, match tubs were being set out behind the batteries, guns run back, tompions drawn, ram-rods, spongers, match sticks unshipped for action. On the forecastle the voice of the sergeant-major of Marines was calling the roll. The butts of their muskets thumped smartly on the deck.

Oblivious of the deck below, the foretop crew grew violent in dispute, they shouted each other down, denied and assented with powerful oaths, shook the despised French muskets in each other's faces.

"Sure she throws to the right—they all do."

"But she bears up her ball—you can draw fine up till sixty."

"But it was only half a charge, I tell ye."

"Yes, sir, a good two hundred yards or I'm an old bitch!"

"Bobcat hell! I bet it was a grey squirrel."

Enthralled by their aimless, incoherent tumult they grudged the second which it took to spit perfunctorily over the side; and as for the British ship, they did not waste a glance on her.

She, however, drew slowly nearer. Johnny could now make out the small blue and white figures of her officers on the quarterdeck. He could hear the faint piping of her bosun's whistle and see the pipe-clayed cross-belts of the British Marines.

The foretop argument having spent its first fury settled down to anecdote and retrospection. Leaning on the muzzles of their muskets, their heads cocked attentively, they rehearsed to each other the merits of all makes of rifles, recalled all known and many fictitious instances of marksmanship, girded themselves up sturdily to cover, re-cover and utterly exhaust the whole grand subject of the rifle.

The bosun's whistle sounded. Reluctantly they took their stations. "By Zooks!" said Johnny, peering under the topsails. "She's nearly on us!" As he watched her, the Britisher came slowly about; the tall, yellow ship filled away, her port-side gun-port lids swung up, the muzzles of her guns peered from her depths. Immediately the "Bonhomme Richard" tacked ship and, paying off before the failing wind, drew slowly closer to her enemy. Below decks, Johnny heard the rumble of the carriages as the "Richard's" guns were run out to starboard.

Slowly, softly, they drifted together. The sunset light was waning but Johnny Fraser could now make out the English gun crews stripping off their singlets and the tall English captain with his blue coat, white breeches, cocked hat, sword and cane, standing by the rail, watching them through his glass, raising his speaking trumpet.

Across the shadowy, still water an English voice hailed them. "What ship is that?"

Captain Jones did not reply. With his eye aloft he turned the wheel himself, seeking some last advantage from the wind; forming a funnel of his hands, he went to the side.

"I can't hear what ye say!" he shouted. He brought his hands down with a chuckle.

For answer, a flame-pierced cloud of smoke burst from the English vessel's side; a dull roar followed, and the thump of round shot against the "Richard's" hull. Splinters leapt spinning through the air, a topsail ripped, a man cried out. Before Johnny could catch his breath, the foremast shuddered with the recoil of the "Richard's" broadside. "Huzzah!" he thought.

"We're after them." He looked triumphantly below. But something had gone wrong; flame leapt from the hatchways; from the started deck seams long lines of smoke curled up in the still air. An endless moment's silence, then deep down in the ship, cries, hoarse, muffled, inarticulate, like the cries of wounded beasts.

Old Walters was beside him; his corded hand trembled on the sandbags. "Good Christ!" he muttered. "Them guns has burst. We're beat before we've started, boy." As he spoke a blackened figure with long red streamers trailing about its knees crawled from a belching hatchway, kicked slowly and lay still. Johnny Fraser looked away, a cold sweat broke out on his brow, crept down to his belly. His throat turned hard, his eyes swam, he felt the slobber running down his chin. By Zooks, he must not faint; he must not! What would his mother say? He rubbed his sleeve across his mouth and took a breath of air. Far off a voice was saying, "Steady, you men, stand by to open fire!" He blinked his eyes, stood up straight. The voice was his.

As they cocked their rifles, a second broadside from the enemy struck them. They fired blindly into the smoke. Before it cleared another broadside followed. Johnny peered down from the top and listened. At last he heard a feeble reply from the few remaining guns.

The two ships closed in. The English salvos began again while the "Richard" could only shiver, helpless, beneath the iron blows.

"Tell 'em to hold their fire," Walters said, "till she gits in range."

The foretop crew crouched down behind their sandbags and watched the British ship appear each time a little nearer through her cloud of broadside smoke.

"Cap'n," said the Georgian in a low voice, "let me have a shot."

"Aye, try it," Walters answered. "But only you, it's too fur yet." The Georgian pressed his lean chin against the stock and fired; the bullet struck half-way down the mast.

"Next time the smoke clears," Johnny said, "she'll be in range."

Walters tugged at his sleeve. "You tell 'em how to shoot, boy, that's out o' my line."

"Fire at their foretop," Johnny said, "and hold about three feet above their heads; lay right dead on 'em, they's no wind now." Another round from the Englishman's main batteries crashed along the "Richard's" littered deck. Then from behind the hovering smoke, the enemy's foretop came slowly into view. "Ready," said Johnny, "take aim, boys. Now let's see something drop. Fire!" The muskets rattled. Except for a few small splinters, the other foretop showed no damage. "My Lord!" thought Johnny, "we missed 'em; curse these muskets!" But now in the English foretop, a red-coated marine rose up slowly, stretched out his arms like a sleeper waking, turned slowly rigid, toppled, plunged to the deck below. "Come on, you boys!" shouted Johnny. "Load! Load! We reached 'em that time!"

From both ships he heard the crackle of small arms now; a spurt of sand flew in his mouth, he spit it out and grinned; he raised his rifle and fired at a figure crouching by the foremast; the man went down.

"You shoot goot," the little Dutchman nodded at him cheerfully over his swiftly sliding ramrod.

"We're bound to clean out their foretop," Johnny answered. "Hold on ther', brother, that's only half a charge." He took a powder-horn and charger from a seaman's hands, filled the charger neatly and poured it down the muzzle. "Take your time!" He crawled on hands and knees behind the crouching ring. "Aim steady at that foretop; we're gwine to burn 'em up!"

Now one thunder cloud enveloped both the ships; the foretop crew were forced to wait and fire at a shrouded flash or through rifts in the smoke; the Englishman, a faster sailer, drew slowly ahead. Shifting to the forward edge of the foretop, they followed her as best they could with their fire. Then she dropped back alongside, hung there just out of reach and pounded the "Richard" to pieces with her heavy guns.

"We ought to grapple," Johnny shouted in Walter's ear, "oughtn't we?"

"Grapple? Aye, but where's our wind?"

The wind indeed had fallen; the "Bonhomme Richard," her deserted decks a ruin, shuddered and wallowed on the oily sea. She answered the British broadsides with a scattered fire from three light guns.

"Whistle for a wind, boys!" Walters roared through the din, "if you want to save your skins. We've got to close with her!" Loading and firing their muskets, the men began to whistle. The only answer to their sailors' prayer was a blast of rifle fire from the enemy. Sand spurted, patches of sacking flew, the little Dutchman, his lips still pursed in a whistle, slid backward across Johnny's legs with a red hole in his forehead.

Unending minutes passed and still she lay becalmed, her big black hulk in splinters, her decks aflame.

"Oh, God," said Johnny, "send us a little breeze. Amen!" Peering over the port-side bags, he saw through a rift in the smoke, the littered deck, deserted except where under the pent house the helmsman still held his post and, beside him, Captain Jones stared up at the flapping topsails with a face to break a man's heart.

While Johnny looked at the smoke-rift it seemed to widen; over the water crept a small breath of air. He looked aloft. By Zooks, the topsails filled! He looked below, the water was slowly curdling along her strakes; she gathered way. The blunt, quick figure at the wheelhouse sprang to the wheel and spun it. The old ship answered, squared away, slid athwart the enemy's bows. The Englishman's bowsprit crackled amongst her rigging; a dozen men sprang up and lashed it fast; another breathless instant, and the two ships hung together, stem to stem.

From decks and tops burst out the frantic rattle of small-arms. Old Walters squinted through a crack between two sandbags.

"We're just athwart their mizzentop," he said. "Let's clear it. When I say 'three,' we'll pop up our heads and give 'em a volley." At the word three, they poured a volley into the mizzentop; pale, smoke-veiled faces withered away before it, but a volley answered them, two men fell backward moaning, they dragged them aside, loaded and fired again.

A ponderous smothered grunt from beneath the enemy's deck made the foretop tremble; the heavy English guns were firing through their own port lids into the "Bonhomme Richard's" side. They could hear the muffled shouting of the British gun-crews and the heavy trundle of the guns as one by one, deep down, close to the waterline, they coughed and smote her—smote her with measured strokes, beat against her sides, against her desperate seamen's brains, like the drumming of a doom—unhurried yet inexorable. Johnny Fraser cast an anxious glance down through the floor of the foretop.

"Never mind that there below," Walters admonished. Stick to their mizzentop!" They fired their volley again; the answering fire was weak and scattering.

"We've got 'em!" Johnny whispered. "Let this red-headed fellow and four more keep 'em down with muskets; we'll give 'em the hand-grenades!" Walters nodded and passed out the grenades; they rose together; two of them went down before they could let fly, the others hurled their iron bombs at the English mizzentop; it vanished in a burst of flame and smoke. They crouched again and waited till it came in view. They saw three solitary figures drop from the far side of the top and scramble down the rat-lines for the deck. The Georgian was loading like mad, his charge was in, the patch and the bullet were at the muzzle, the ram-rod shot them home. Before the last of the three was half way down he raised his rifle. He fired; the man clutched the rat-lines frantically, his head rolled back, his eyes stared fixedly at the sky; slowly his hands relaxed, he fell, slowly tumbling, into the sea. The foretop crew stood up, grinned, stretched themselves, then turned to the white-lipped wounded on the floor.

"We've done a good job," thought Johnny to himself as he tied a black silk handkerchief around a hairy arm. "A mighty good job."

"Come on now, mister," said Walters, "we got to clear her upper decks."

"All right, Cap'n, but we can't see a doggone thing from here."

"See it from their top, though. Come on! The whole passel of ye!" Old Walters swung out over the sandbags and worked his way along the yard-arm to where the English yardarm fouled it.

"That's something I don't like," thought Johnny, as he watched the old man, spry but unhurried, sliding along the foot-lines. He saw him pause in mid air, turn his long-nosed face over his shoulder in a glance of interrogation; slinging his musket on his back, Johnny followed him. He seemed to spend an age swinging alone and naked through dizzy chaos, the roar of guns beneath his feet, the moan of bullets in his ears, his musket flopping against his trembling thighs. Then Walters' hand seized his, he tumbled into the British mizzentop and fell on a heap of British dead. One by one the others followed; they cleared a space among the bodies and opened fire on the deck below them.

THE FIGHT IN THE FORE-TOP

*At the word three, they poured a volley into the missentop; pale, smoke-veiled faces withered
away before it, but a volley answered them*

But now the ship which they had left burst into flame; all down her starboard side a glowing sheet leapt up, ran up the rigging in sputtering lines, gnawed at the topsails. Below them, too, broad flames climbed from the English hatchways; all firing ceased, on both ships scorched, half-naked seamen with water-buckets ran stumbling across the ruined decks. Aloft, the topmen squirmed out on the yards, clapped their jackets around the blazing shrouds. The locked enemies lay silent except for the running feet along the decks and the fire's low malignant hum. The flames on board the Englishman died out at last, but the "Richard's" rotten timbers burned fiercer still. In the ruddy light, a frantic seaman ran to the "Richard's" quarterdeck.

"Quarter! Quarter!" he screamed out brokenly. His arms flew wide as he went down under the butt of Captain Jones' pistol. The English Captain had heard the cry.

"Have you struck?" His voice was proud and sharp. On both ships every man stood fast, turned anxious eyes to the "Richard's" smoke-veiled quarter-rail. The foretop crew crouched against the shrouds, listening. There was no sound except the seething of the flames. Then the little man's great voice came booming through the tops.

"Struck?" A cheerful, terrier grin was in the very tone. "Why, sir, I've not begun to fight!" Silence again. Then high aloft from the "Richard's" cross-trees they heard a sailor's long sardonic laughter. Cheering hoarsely, they stood up on the dead and opened fire. From behind a cloud rose a bloody harvest moon.

It had seemed after that as though the cloud and the bloody moon had settled down on them, enveloped them. Adrift in a sea of smoke—of blood —of fire—they swam, they sank, came up for air, swam on again. They made a bulwark of dead against the English fire, cursing the stiff, unwieldy bodies for their awkwardness. For uncounted ages they crouched among the corpses, winking their deep-sunk, burning eyes, sighting their red-hot muskets at puffs of smoke, at running figures, at desperate straining faces. And ever and again from high aloft, whirling, hanging, dropping from spar to spar, a dead man plunged slowly through their limbo to the pit where lost souls, black and naked, struck at each other with pikes and cutlasses across the hammock nettings.

And now Johnny Fraser, alone in a ruined blazing universe, was treading the airy footways; a heavy sack hung on his shoulder, clung to him, tried to bear him down. Three blank-eyed ghosts reached out hands to him, seized the sack ravenously, clutched him to themselves. Then the four of them were raining down hand-grenades. The deck on which they fell was a blackened waste; great guns, however, still rumbled somewhere below; a feeble light showed in a hatchway. Johnny Fraser waggled his stiff, thick tongue.

"Throw down the hatchway!" he muttered over and over again. It was hard to do; the hatchway bobbed and swam across his eyes; the thing, he told himself, was to catch it at the turn where it always hung before swimming slowly back again. He tried to tell the others, but his tongue had turned rigid, which made him cry. Now their grenades, too, were bursting on the coamings.

A cone of flame shot from the hatchway, shot higher than the tops; it dropped to a steady blaze which showed the deck fresh-strewn with stripped dead bodies. The English mainmast, eaten half through by the gnawing of a single, distant gun, swayed slowly, plunged over the side.

In the silence which followed, a tall, solitary gentleman in blue coat and white knee-breeches appeared on the deck where no one else dared venture. He climbed to the quarterdeck, climbed to the poop. Looking neither right nor left, he reached the great red ensign at the stern. The British flag dropped down.

Old Walters struggled to his feet. He clapped a bloody hand on Johnny's shoulder. "She's struck, boy!" A man among the heap of bodies gave a gurgling cheer; a great red bubble formed around his lips, burst with a tiny smack. "Go fetch a surgeon's mate," said Walters.

"Yes, seh . . . I will . . . yes, seh!" Johnny Fraser's voice trailed off; he felt a warm stream dripping in his palm. The harvest moon dove down at him and struck him to the ground.

## CHAPTER XLIV

Aʟʟ ɴᴇxᴛ day the hollow-eyed survivors worked unceasingly, they cut the sinking "Bonhomme Richard" free, they moved the wounded and what stores they could to the captured English frigate—the "Serapis," a new-built, fifty-four-gun ship of the line, on her first commission.

Lying on a chest in the cabin of the "Serapis," Johnny Fraser turned his face away from the odor of rum and vinegar, from the rows of wounded huddled on the floor and looked out the cabin window. The sun was far down in the west; across its burnished wake lay the silhouette of the "Bonhomme Richard." Her deserted hulk lurched heavily as she drifted slowly astern, the sunlight glinted through her riddled sides, her head was buried under each light swell. He watched her steadily; the sun was sinking and she, too, was going down. Her decks were now awash, still she hung on— seemed to hang on blindly, sullenly, as if she did not know the fight was over. The end was near; a swell washed clear across her; her head went under, her dripping stern swung up, poised high in air, shone in the sunset light. She shot down out of sight so smoothly, the waters closed over her so smoothly, that Johnny Fraser wondered whether he could really have seen her there at all. And yet he must; for among the American seamen on the deck above him he heard a long-drawn whisper, half a groan, half a hushed cheer.

Three days later they dropped anchor in a broad, calm harbor flanked by salt meadows where belted cattle grazed and windmills made their grotesque gestures against the sky; up the harbor lay high-pitched roofs and brick gable-ends in fanciful designs. Round-faced Dutchmen in baggy pantaloons paddled out to them, pulled short pipes from mouths, grunted their admiration and surprise.

That night the Captain sent for Johnny. Nursing his bandaged arm, he climbed unsteadily to the quarterdeck. The light of the binnacle fell on Captain Jones' face and on a paper which he held in his hand. He nodded to Johnny briefly.

"Ye're good at figures, Fraser, so just tell me the answer to this!" He whistled between his teeth. "I've lost near half my men, I've seven hundred prisoners below decks, and I've got to work this ship to France."

"Well, seh," said Johnny with a white smile, "I reckon you can make the prisoners work—you made 'em fight."

"The answer is correct," said Captain Jones. "And that's the last bit of figurin' I'll ask from ye. The wounded are to be put ashore here, and that means you, I see."

"Yes, seh," said Johnny. "I'm sorry I can't be of more he'p."

"Hoots toots!" said Captain Jones brusquely. "Ye helped when ye were wanted, didn't ye? But here's what I sent for ye about. There's a Dutch brig in port makin' ready to sail for America. I've told them to hold a cabin for ye."

The color flowed into Johnny's face. "Home!" he murmured. "Yes, seh, thank you, thank you!"

"No thanks are due me. It's what I promised, and, on land or sea, I never do less than I promise, but, as a' the world knows, I sometimes do more." He drew himself up and gazed with grim arrogance across the star-strewn waters as if they were his own.

"Yes, seh!" said Johnny.

The inadequacy of this reply seemed to bring Captain Jones to himself; his brusque glance fell on Johnny.

"Have ye the money for your passage?"

"No, seh," said Johnny, "not much."

"Aweel," said Captain Jones comfortably, "your friends can just pay your passage on the other side—and now good luck." He held out his hand, then made Johnny a naval salute. "And if anyone home should ask ye, ye can just say for me, that there was a real brisk fire from the foretop."

Logging the Atlantic's long gray miles, Johnny Fraser lay in his clean, narrow bunk and watched uncounted nights and days slip by outside the porthole. The fever in his arm was throbbing through him like the slow, muffled beats of the naval guns; he could not tell how much the white-washed ceiling rocked above him, how much of the rocking was in his brain; the present was a haze, the past a jumble of gun-fire, smoke clouds and slashing boarding parties; and ever, from high aloft, the dead men slowly tumbled through his dreams. Contorted faces peered at him;—faces —faces and ghastly blank, red masks.

The drumming died away, he seemed to drift far from the battle into a grateful lazy bay, a bay of mists and shadows and of fragmentary memories. He saw tall pines and the nodding heads of horses galloping; he heard the murmur of a taproom crowd, he heard the forest wind and the Negroes singing. Out of the distant recollections and vague sounds, sharper pictures flashed; he saw his father's great beard and the angry whiskers of Captain Flood; again the light died in Sir Nat's blue eyes, again he felt his handclasp of farewell; now a spinning wheel was softly humming; in her dark blue callimanco gown, Sally Merrillee swayed ever so gently to the rhythm, raised her small brown hand to the snowy distaff. He clung to the picture, but it too faded, only the humming of the wheel remained; it deepened, softened, passed above his head; again he heard the murmur of the pines. He opened his eyes.

Outside his porthole the sun had sunk down in a yellow flame; high up against its brilliance swayed the black and ragged tops of pine trees; he stumbled to his feet, pressed his face against the thick round glass. Through the blue dusk, the courthouse tower rose, hearth fires glowed in clustered chimney throats; shadowed and dim, the silvery, shingled roofs seemed folded in for the night.

"Ach!" said the round little Dutch steward behind him, "bad fellow! You get up?" He steadied Johnny to the berth. "That makes you better, eh? We come to your Edenton."

"Just open that porthole, Hans. I want to smell the air."

Leaning on Hans' shoulder, Johnny Fraser walked up the familiar lane. The sun had sunk; he stumbled over the worn cobblestones; a sentry challenged them; his rifle shone in the light of a doorway lantern. Johnny pulled his passport from his pocket and handed it over.

"John Fraser, Esq.," the sentry read. "Acting vice-captain of the foretop —by order, John Paul Jones."

"Yes, sir!" He presented arms.

He knocked on the door of Hornblower's tavern. "Coming, sir, coming!" cried Mr. Hornblower's voice. Mr. Hornblower opened the door, peered at him politely, but without recognition.

"Hornblower, don't you know me? It's Johnny Fraser."

Hornblower's soft, smooth hand closed over Johnny's. "Why, bless my soul and body, sir! But you look ill; and your arm in a sling; and your clothing, sir! If I may say so——" He eyed Johnny's worn watch-coat and sea-boots with concern. "But come in, sir. I do hope matters are quite all right."

"Thanks, Hornblower."

The whiskered face of Captain Flood peeped under Mr. Hornblower's arms; he squinted his little eyes and stared, incredulous.

"How you, Captain?" Johnny said.

"Bucko!" the Captain shouted. "Bucko, or I'm a——! Well, bung my ——!" His wiry hands seized Johnny and drew him to the center of the room. "Bucko!" he muttered, "and togged out in reg'lar sea-slops. Boy, what give you the notion for to go an' disguise yourself?"

"I've been on a ship," said Johnny, "several of them."

"What ships?" asked Captain Flood suspiciously. "Just name 'em over."

"One moment," said Mr. Hornblower. "Have this chair, sir, and what is your order?"

"I reckon I'd like a glass of port."

"Very good—and this person?" Mr. Hornblower eyed Hans coldly.

"Schnapps!" interposed Hans, unimpressed.

"We have rum," said Mr. Hornblower in his most stately manner, "and you may take a seat at the table in the corner."

"What ship?" repeated Captain Flood. "And don't you make up no tales, Bucko, because I know 'em all." Before Johnny could answer, a glass of port was in his hand, he sipped it slowly.

"Well, seh," he said, "they was only two—the 'Ranger' and the 'Bonhomme Richard.' That's where I got this." He pointed to his arm.

Captain Flood did not reply, he turned on Johnny a glance of stupefaction; twice he moistened his lips as if to speak and twice he swallowed. He raised his claw-like hand and beckoned Hornblower. "Friend," he whispered, "what do you most generally consider the highest rated liquor in your spirit room?"

"Well, Captain," said Mr. Hornblower, "we have some Creme Yvette, fifty-six."

"Well, Bucko and me," said Captain Flood, "is a-goin' to drink that very same."

"I can't drink much," said Johnny, "thank you, Cap'n; I just got out of bed."

"You don't need to, son," answered Captain Flood earnestly, "and any time you say the word, Hornblower and me'll tuck you in. Only"—he raised beseeching eyes to Johnny—"give us the yarn about that fight. A packet just brought in the news last week."

Three men who had been seated at the back of the room now rose and came toward them; their dark blue frock coats faced with dark red showed them to be officers of the Continental Line. The candlelight shone on their gold buttons, on their belt buckles, their tasseled sword hilts; one wearing the red sash of a field officer stopped before Johnny; the two younger men stood behind him, smiling.

"I beg your pardon, sir," he said, "but we could not avoid overhearing the conversation which has just passed. My aides and I desire to present our compliments to one who has taken part in so glorious a victory. Pray do not rise." He stretched out a hand. Captain Flood was on his feet.

"Friends," he said with an expansive gesture, "draw up your chairs." He pointed to the long slim bottle which Mr. Hornblower had placed on the table. "And join us. This Bucko, here," he added as they took their seats, "aims to spin a yarn about the fight. You're welcome to hear. Only remember, whatever sea-larnin' he's got," the Captain glanced proudly up to the tall men around him. "I larned it him. Tell 'em what happened, son."

"Well," said Johnny, embarrassed to be thus exhibited, "we came together until we were about as close as from here to the waterfront, and then both ships tacked and fired. Most of our main-deck guns blew up and then we stood on the same course, side by side."

"Hold on!" the Captain cried. "Who had the weather gauge?"

"The weather gauge? I declare I don't now. I never noticed."

"Never noticed! Why, God in the Mountain, boy, in a sea fight the weather gauge is the whole thing; that's what the weather gauge is!"

"Well, it wasn't in this fight," said Johnny, somewhat impatiently, "because the wind died, and there we drifted and they pounded us and we had only six guns left out of fifty-four; and there we'd be still, I reckon, if a little wind hadn't come up so that we could run across their bows."

"Ye hauled on the wind, I suppose?" said Captain Flood eagerly.

"I reckon we did, but I don't know; anyhow, we got there."

Captain Flood's stricken eyes dropped to the sanded floor. "He don't know," he mused, "he don't know."

"But, Cap'n," Johnny said, "I know how we did the fightin' part, all right." He told of the battle in the tops. The three tall soldiers fixed him with their eyes, sat silent, nodded from time to time emphatically. But Captain Flood was not consoled; an hour later, when he and Mr. Hornblower had escorted Johnny upstairs and put him tenderly to bed, the Captain paused for a moment in the chamber doorway.

"I'll take you up river tomorrow," he said. "But, Bucko, when you get back your hea'th, put your mind on that there battle; it don't look good for a fellow to set up for a hero and turn out a ignerammis."

The street of live oaks, once so proud and metropolitan, looked pitifully shabby beneath the brilliant autumn sky as Johnny Fraser, leaning on Mr. Hornblower's arm, walked uncertainly down to Captain Flood's landing-stage. Weeds grew in the very cart ruts, windows were patched with paper or boarded shut, old filth lay heaped in the gutters, the courthouse oak held tattered notices of men now dead and buried. As they reached the corner of the street of sycamores, Johnny paused. At the end of that desolate, dusty waste, across which slowly crept a solitary ancient, lay the charred ruins of the Rectory.

"I don't suppose you know what has become of Dr. Clapton, Hornblower."

"I was thinking you might ask that, sir," said Hornblower in a tone of conscious rectitude. He drew a neatly folded letter from his waistcoat pocket. "This reached me last winter."

"Antigua, 2 Jan. 1779.

"My dear Hornblower—

"This is to advise you of my present whereabouts in order that you may forward to me a statement of my reckoning with you. The Sum is not, if recollection serves, excessive, nevertheless I regret that the Unfortunate Circumstances under which I was obliged to quit Edenton prevented my discharging this Obligation before.

"But of those Circumstances let us say no more. At first I confess I experienced an inexpressible Pang at the thought that one who (albeit with all due Christian sense of his own Unworthiness) had for twenty years served your Parish to the best of his Powers should be cast out from among you with Contumely and Violence. I have since, however, found Consolation at that Source where alone Consolation is ever to be found; and also in the Reflection that the Acts above referred to were committed by an unhappy Few, blinded for the moment (but for the moment only, as I heartily believe) by Evil Passions. Nor has this comforting Conviction been wanting the Support of many of my old parishioners, including yourself, who wrote, while I was still at New York, in the most kindly sense, deprecating (in some instances even more strongly than I could have wished) the Sad Event which terminated my Ministry, and containing most touching Evidences of affectionate Remembrance.

"I have a small Parish at the end of the Island, a pretty little Church built of coral blocks and a Congregation, for the most part black and in a condition of servitude, but gentle and devoted. Here I shall remain until the Storm which now convulses unhappy America is past and God has seen fit to effect a Reconciliation between his Majesty and his colonial subjects.

"Till then I trust, my dear Hornblower, that you will prosper as much as may be expected and that you will, as befits your Station and Calling, remain aloof from participation in Publick Affairs. And in the meantime rest assured that you and the other Parishioners whose Christian Constancy sent me words of succour in the hours of dark Distress will ever be remembered in the prayers of

"Your former rector and perpetual brother in Christ,

"Hugh Clapton."

"Ah," said Johnny, slowly folding the letter and wishing that he too had followed the Doctor's fortunes. "That's a fine letter, Hornblower."

"Indeed it is, sir," said Hornblower. "A letter, if I may say so, that could only have been written by a gentleman."

They had now reached the landing-stage. Except for a dingy privateer at anchor in the bay and infrequent sounds of labor in the shipyards, the harbor was deserted. Only the mast and swinging sail of the Captain's boat showed above the dock.

From the deck the Captain squinted up his little eyes at Johnny and bristled his beard disapprovingly.

"Bung me," he said, "if you ain't peaked. Negro!" he called. "Pass down that there young gentleman to me."

The Negro deckhand shuffled forward bashfully and stood before Johnny in a loose-jointed attitude of deprecation.

"How you?" said Johnny.

For answer the deckhand explored between the paving bricks with a broad black toe on which he fixed his veiled glance.

"Now then, black boy!"

Still looking at his toe, the Negro stole to Johnny's side, encircled him gently with his strong, limber arms. As smoothly, as precisely as a burden-bearing elephant, he gave an easy lift and swung him to the deck below. He straightened up, smiled faintly, padded noiselessly away.

They were creeping round the last bend in the river before Slade's Landing would come in view; Captain Flood, having wound up the story of his privateering, inspected the ornamental figures on his porcelain pipe.

"Yes, seh," he concluded, "no man can say that I ain't served my country. And I'd have been a-servin' of her yet except that latterly they ain't been no money in it, though they're still a-buildin' privateers at Edenton, that's mostly what keeps the town a-goin'."

"I suppose the province is mighty poor, Cap'n."

"Mighty. The gov'ment ought to do somethin' about it. They ought to print more money."

"I thought they had—lots of it."

"Well, so they did—some—but it's the kind of money that the more they print, the less it's worth. What good," he demanded, "is money like that?" He smoked his pipe and revolved the problem. "What this country needs," he observed sententiously, "is a money what the more they turn out of it the *more* it's worth."

"But except for that, the province is in pretty good fix, isn't it, Cap'n?"

"Oh, I suppose so," Captain Flood admitted grudgingly. "Anyhow, the Tories is all cleaned out." His eye brightened. "And there for once the gov'ment done right."

"They arrested them, I hear."

Captain Flood nodded. "Arrested 'em and drafted 'em. They had the right idea, the gov'ment had; if a man won't fight for his country," he eyed Johnny sternly, "the only place for him is in the army. Here's Slade's."

They tied up to the flimsy landing-stage which somehow still maintained itself precariously above the dark, smooth-flowing waters.

"Good-bye, Cap'n," said Johnny. "You've been mighty good to me."

The Captain waved Johnny's hand impatiently aside. "You're in no fix to travel by yourself, Bucko. I aim to see you safe in port." He hopped up on the landing-stage and scuttled over the loose planks. "I'll hire the rig," he called back in his piping voice. "Negro, you stay on board till I get back."

"Ah, ah, suh!" the Negro deckhand whispered from the bows.

The method of hiring a rig was simple. Captain Flood dragged an old chaise from Slade's deserted barn, hitched a flea-bitten iron-faced gray horse to it and shouted:

"Slade, I'm takin' your rig," as he drove by the Ordinary.

Their wheels sifted on the sandy road, Johnny lay back against the moth-eaten cushion, closed his eyes and listened to the grateful sound.

"Slade's more or less down on his luck," Captain Flood commented. "The gov'ment closed up his place for over-charging and his bound-boy run off and joined the army."

"He was a smooth-tongued little scoundrel," Johnny murmured.

"Yes, and the worst of it is, he's got to be a sergeant in the cavalry. But I ain't suprised. In the army, lyin' always carries a man a long ways. It ain't like the navy. I never took no stock in a army."

"But Cap'n, our army seems to be makin' out pretty good."

"Granted, Bucko, granted; but put 'em to fight a navy, now, there'd be a different story." He waggled his whiskers impressively and slapped the reins on the horse's back.

"And even our navy," he went on, "ain't what it would have been if Hewes had held out."

"Held out?"

"Yes. He's dead. Wore hisself down running the navy up there in Philadelphia. I reckon what with fighting the British and all them mean New Englanders it was too much for him."

"He was a mighty hard worker." Johnny mused over the picture in his mind of the long-nosed, shrewd and bustling ship-builder. "I remember how fast he used to walk."

"Too fast," the Captain reflected. "Work was a kind of a failing with him."

Night had long since fallen; just ahead of them the road, a dark, soft gray, crept through the soft blackness; the blackness deepened, dim monumental shapes surrounded them. Above the sifting of the wheels, Johnny Fraser heard the vast, hushed murmur of the pines.

A light glowed in the distance, then two—Blue's Crossing. Their hoof-beats echoed against the shuttered, silent houses and died away again among the fields beyond. Johnny's heart rose up and pounded in his throat. He was almost there. The wheels splashed through shallow water, gritted on gravel, climbed slowly, made a turn. Almost there. Before him shone the firelit windows of his home. Lying in a level path along the lane, their glow reached out to him and bade him welcome. On either hand it touched the dead-white, boldly patterned columns of the two old sycamores and the brown-encrusted trunks of pines.

"Mother!" he shouted, jumping from the chaise. "Dadder!" There was no answer; his heart failed him. Had he lived through warfare and adventure, crossed three thousand miles of ocean, only to find that they were not here to meet him or that something had gone wrong? Stumbling up the hewn wood steps, he looked in the window. The old room was half-filled with a clacking loom. Seated at the treadles, his mother shot the bobbins swiftly, pulled the banging board. The firelight gilded her coiled hair, her earnest, living face, her worn homespun gown. His father sat beside the fire, the massive head bowed, his great beard curled back from his chest; his big square fingers moved delicately, plaiting a candlewick.

The years abroad fell away from Johnny. His mother, the strong old house, the strong old man were unchanged, staunch as ever; he might have left his home only the day before. Not quite unchanged, however; his father did not use to hold his work so near his eyes. Johnny opened the door.

The loom stood still. "Oh!" his mother whispered. "Oh!" and flung her arms about him. "It isn't you!" she murmured. "I know it isn't!" She clapped her hands and laughed unsteadily. "So don't try to make out it is." Like a little girl, she sat down plumply on the weaving-bench and wept.

The great man stood before Johnny, one great hand closed on Johnny's hand, the other on his shoulder; his beard stirred lightly yet profoundly as water is stirred by turmoil in the depths.

"Ye're weel?"

"Yes, seh."

John Fraser's grip relaxed.

"Now, Caroline, dinna grieve, lass; 'tis no the time for that."

Johnny put an arm around his mother.

"Don't you mind Dadder," he said with a laugh; "if you've the idea to cry, go on and do it."

"There it is," Squire Fraser rumbled, "settin' his mother against me the same as ever. It's nae use tae fumble, Caroline," he added resignedly. "Ye never have one." He produced a huge brown silk handkerchief and dropped it in Mrs. Fraser's lap; she wiped her eyes and looked up, smiling; the smile swiftly faded.

"Johnny!" she cried, "what ails your arm?"

"Oh!" he said easily, "we got in a fight with a British boat and my arm got hit." She sprang up, turned white, sat down again.

"What hit ye, lad? A bullet? Draw back your sleeve." His father inspected the long red scar. "Ah—the elbow!" He shook his head. "You're like tae have a stiff arm, I'm afeared. What did I say, Caroline?" he went on with gloomy satisfaction. "I've never known a Fraser yet tae keep out o' a fight and I've never known one that didna get the worst o' it."

"Well, we didn't get the worst of this fight, Dadder—we beat the British."

"Did ye, then?" His father brightened. "But I'll warrant when it was over," he added doggedly, "that every Fraser in it was dead or wounded."

"John," said Mrs. Fraser, "you talk as though you were glad he's hurt."

"I'm glad o' naught but that he's safe home"—John Fraser pulled down Johnny's sleeve gently—"and that he's a Fraser."

"How did you come, son?" his mother asked. "You're too weak to sit a horse."

"I came in a chaise. Oh, my!" he cried remorsefully. "Captain Flood's with me. I thought he was right behind. Captain Flood!" he called.

The Captain, who had waited patiently beside the chaise, hopped through the door. "Servant, ma'm and Squire. I just thought I'd stand by to see the bucko safely berthed."

"You're a real friend, Captain," Mr. Fraser said. "Caroline, fetch the rum;

I'll rouse our Scipio tae put up the horse." Squire Fraser and the Captain went out.

Johnny and his mother sat down, hand in hand. "How are you?" he said after a long silence. "All right?"

"Just fine," she said, "and your father, too. He seems better of late, though his eyes fail him."

"How are the Merrillees? All right?"

"They've had a mighty hard time. First Joe was wounded, then Mr. Merrillee joined the army, though I think he would better have stayed on the place; he was killed at Germantown. I wrote you. Now Joe is sick again; he caught the smallpox."

"I'm sorry," said Johnny mechanically. "How's Sally?"

"Sally's gone."

"Gone?" Inside him his heart was suddenly hushed and still. "Gone?"

"Yes, she went up to New York State to where Joe is, to take care of him; he's too weak to move."

He breathed again. She was not gone for good. Still he would not see her now or soon. He felt that the journey had left him tired and sick.

"Is that bad news for you, son?" she asked.

"Well, yes, I reckon. I don't know."

She put her other hand in his. "I'm sorry—I hope it will come out all right. She's not promised to anyone else; at least, that's what I hear." She smiled at him tenderly. "And I hear near everything."

When Squire Fraser returned with Captain Flood he did not close the door behind him.

"Scipio is here," he said.

Shuffling into the firelight, the old Negro halted, blinked, gathered his flapping coat about him and bowed low.

"Back home safe an' salubrious. An' Ah thanks de Lo'd fo' it, Mist' Johnneh, yesso, das whut Ah does."

He straightened up and eyed Johnny's watchcoat narrowly.

"Whut's dis? All dem fine clo'ses gone? An' de slick leather shoes?" He shook his head lugubriously.

"Anyhow, Scipio," said Johnny, grinning, "I'm back."

"Des like Ah said," Scipio went on with melancholy gusto. "Young white gent'man cain't make out without a 'sperienced servant. Went off dressed so high-tone"—he mused,—"an des look."

The kitchen door swung open. Tall, gaunt and black, Sophonsiba strode to Johnny's side; without speaking, she took his hand and stroked it between her leathery palms. She cast a baleful look at Scipio.

"Clo'ses!"

She looked down at Johnny with a deep, warm glance. "He can come back necked if he de mind, das what my little misto can."

"Dasso," said Scipio grudgingly. "Only it's like whut Ah said."

She drew herself up sternly. "Scipio, you hush; dey ain't a body on dis earth care what you said."

"I'm mighty glad to be home, Sofa," Johnny interposed. "I reckon I'll get fat now." He turned to the dejected Scipio. "How are the horses?" he asked kindly.

"Ain't dey tole you, Mist' Johnneh? De soldier carry 'em off fo' de army."

"What?"

"It's true, lad." John Fraser spoke. "I'd no mind tae tell ye yet. A government requisition."

"Das de word," Scipio's nod was grim. "Das de fine big word. Ah wish Ah knowed 'at word." He laughed shortly. "An' 'at Ah was a gov'ment."

"So they took the colt?" said Johnny slowly.

"Aye. We have an ox now. I'm sorry, son. It's war. That will do, Scipio."

Scipio tugged the wool on his forehead abstractedly. He paused on the threshold and looked back. His face twitched.

"Dat was mos' de gayest colt Ah eveh knowed."

Seated with the smoking toddy-bowl before them, they heard a furious scratching on the door and then a quavering, deep-toned bay. Johnny Fraser started up. "It's Grizzly Gray!" he cried. "He smells my track!"

BOOK IV

# CHAPTER XLV

TRAMPING ON foot to the Merrillees' through the hot August twilight, Johnny Fraser wondered whether the journey was worth while. Here, where the road dropped into a hollow, the gathering damp felt grateful; he slowed up, stopped, sat down among the bunch grass and listened to the senseless, interminable staccato of the frogs.

A year ago today he was aboard the "Bonhomme Richard," harrying English waters. A year ago? It seemed a thousand. It seemed so long that it might never have happened; there was nothing about his life, about him, to remind him of it, nothing except the numb arm hanging stiffly at his side.

November would soon be here; then it would be a year since he had first come home; he still held a vivid picture of that night; of the friendly, glowing windows, of his father before the fire, of his mother at the loom. But the time since then—a thousand years. Half a cripple, he had pottered around the place on jobs too light for able-bodied men, trying by dull

415

methodical labor to make his body so tired by evening that it would sleep despite that blunt ache in his elbow.

By spring the ache was gone. That was enough for him; he had said good-bye to his father and mother, had watched them set themselves for more long days. He had followed the militia on their way for another summer campaign. But everywhere he tried, at every outpost and recruiting station, the answer was the same: "No one-armed men are wanted." The erstwhile hero had slunk home.

Then the summer; Sally was still away with Joe. Confound the fellow, why could he not get well or—anyway, confound him! Her few letters, kindly but distant, had left him no happier than before. Till he could see her there was nothing more to do except one thing. Every day, walking or riding the one old ox which the government had left them, he had gone to the Merrillees' and helped old, broken Mrs. Merrillee to run the place. He had commenced to be a little established again in his own eyes.

Then the bad news had begun to drift in. Charleston besieged—Charleston cut off—Charleston fallen—and with it the whole North Carolina Continental Line and thirty thousand of the best troops in America. The blow was final. But no—by Zooks! Another army marched in from the North; the country rose in arms and stood behind it. Gates, the victor of Saratoga, came down to lead it to victory. And then the news of Camden—the second army wiped out like the first—the North Carolina militia, fighting to the last, gone the way of the North Carolina Line. Drained of men, of horses, harness, wagons, guns, corn, clothing, of everything that goes to make an army, the country's back was to the wall.

Now, in the crisis, what good was he to this land of pines, of long mountain men, of tight-lipped, straight-eyed women—he struck his hand down on the sod—this land of his! He was no more than half a man; he tried to bend his locked elbow on his knee; a sparkling flame shot to his armpit, the elbow would not budge. He let his arm drop with a bitter grin; no more than half a man. Yet why should he complain? What else had he ever been? Did he rate himself a hero or even a man because blind chance had put him to sea on a Continental raider? The man was he who had gone in with open eyes, who through famine, defeat and nakedness had stuck it out or, not permitted to stick it out, now lay safely shrouded, enriching the land which gave him birth.

Let him look at himself as he had been—a youth so large in his own conceit, his silly head so easily turned by specious show, that he could wholly fail to gauge his country's worth just as, blinded by egoism and shabby pride, he had ignored the worth of Sally Merrillee. The country, vast, easy-going, generous Mother, had taken him to herself again, but he was no longer quite fool enough to expect the same of the girl whom, after two years of absence and ten years of imbecility, he was now about to see. A hoot-owl mocked him from the swamp. He rose and trudged on down the road.

But as he walked, the steps which brought him nearer her brought her shining picture closer to his heart; warming within him, it banished desolation, made him glow with what must be, he felt, an almost visible translucence. He strode on through the quiet twilight, radiant and strong. She must not now refuse him; she could not! To harbor jealously against him old follies, long since dead—she was not the one for that! She would see that they had now been shed away, would see him tempered by adventure, knowledge, suffering, a different man, not worthy perhaps, even far from that, but able to know her worth.

It was almost dark. He just made out the lane of cedars and the house. She was there. Her nearness had brought him back his old strength and new powers. He could not fail.

She sat beneath a rushlight inside the open door; the old blue callimanco gown, faded, outgrown, fitted her meagerly. Under her tiny cap her brown hair flowed softly, dimming her face; it curved up at the nape of her neck to droop in a fall of curls. At the sound of his footstep she raised her head. Her face was pale. It was strong and tired. No hint of teasing mirth lurked in her brown eyes; it was hidden or had gone. His heart went out to her. Perhaps she had been waiting for him.

"Who's that?"

"It's Johnny Fraser." His voice was low but eager, ringing.

"Oh!" she said evenly, then added with a touch of formal cordiality. "I'm glad to see you, Johnny. How you?" She reached a hand over the bowl of shelled peas in her lap and took his firmly.

"I'm fine," he said, his spirits a little checked. "How's Joe?"

She was pleased. "Joe's all right again; he's gone to the Headquarters at West Point."

"They ought to make things easier for Joe, now," said Johnny.

"I reckon they will. General Knox said he would. Joe," she added proudly, "is in the artillery now."

"Is that a fact? I expect by this time Joe is high up in the army."

"Joe is a Major and it takes more to be a Major in the artillery than a General anywhere else."

"I reckon that's so." He ventured a grin. "I always did hear the artillery looked down on all the other fellows." She did not respond. At this long awaited moment he had looked for eagerness and warmth. Even old friends would show that. "How you been?" he asked awkwardly.

"Oh, I'm all right. Mother's gone to bed; it appears like she tires easy since father died."

"I know," he murmured. "I'm sorry, mighty sorry. I—I've been comin' over here, kind of helping around the place."

"Yes. Mother told me. I reckon it just about saved her."

She flushed softly in an instant of unguarded tenderness, and at her flush the depths within him stirred, uncontrollable, profound.

"Oh, I was glad——" He began quietly enough. His throat closed. Before him rose a mist through which he swayed toward her, his hands out-stretched, until they fell on the shoulders of her gown, shoulders slim, soft, firm——

The mist was cut through by her upturned gaze, a gaze so unspeakably astounded that it stopped him like a blow. The mist vanished, his hands fell. He stood there, chilled to the marrow, and watched her slow tears of anger or humiliation or whatever it might be she felt at his presumptuous fatuity.

The tears dropped from her cheeks. She raised her hands and pressed them to her eyes.

"I oughtn't to cry," she murmured, "I know I oughtn't." She wept the more.

And why not? Did she not have her pride? Why should it not be broken by this crazy indignity that he had put upon her? He saw it all. What had he ever done but quarrel with her, play with her love, neglect her for years? And now he came back, years too late, even if there had ever been a time, came back a worthless cripple, the ruin of a man, if he had ever been one, and thought that now in his need he could have her for the asking. Small wonder that it struck her down to find how cheap he held her.

And still she cried. And still he stood, silent, numb, tingling with hot and freezing waves of shame. In the name of God, he must speak.

"I'm mighty sorry," he mumbled.

She did not seem to hear. The tears came through her fingers.

"Mighty sorry——" He turned and stumbled down the lane. His lips were moving as he blundered through the dark. "Mighty sorry—mighty sorry," he whispered insanely to himself.

Cold water round his ankles brought him to a halt. He had missed the foot-log at the ford. He climbed up on it, steadying himself and trying to steady his distracted mind. But still a malignant echo, "Mighty sorry," hung about him.

And after all, what more was there to say? Nothing; unless he also wished to remind himself that he was still the fool he had been born. An hour ago when he had crossed that foot-log he was smugly taking stock of the manhood he had attained. And inside the hour he had surpassed himself in imbecility. Surpassed himself! No faint praise that, by Zooks! He laughed aloud and then fell sombre.

But how could even he have expected anything else? It was all obvious, inevitable, now that it was over. No one but he could have assumed that he had merely to walk up to Sally, Sally whom he had patronized, who knew him through and through, and take her in his arms. Why, even he might have guessed that there was less chance for him now than ever. As a country girl she might have been impressed. But she had seen the Continental Army since and learned to gauge the stature of a man.

He was walking slower now, his arm was throbbing as it had last winter.

Wrong about England, wrong about America, wrong about Sally years ago, and now thrice wrong again.

He felt suddenly weary. Was he destined all his life to find out the truth too late?

As he came in sight of the lights of his home he heard footsteps on the road ahead. The footsteps stopped, the man waited for him to overtake him.

"That Johnny Fraser?" It was the blacksmith's voice. "Thought I knew your way of travelling. Sally home?"

"Yes," said Johnny briefly. "What are you doing out this way?"

The blacksmith lowered a long thin burden from his shoulder to the ground.

"Oh," he said, "I come after somethin' I thought I might need."

Johnny made out an earth-stained canvas case.

"Why!" he said, "that looks like a rifle!"

"It is; and the best one I ever made; that's why I hid it."

"You're not goin' to war, are you?" said Johnny. "You're over sixty, man!"

"Sixty-two, but if I ain't too old to make rifles, I reckon I ain't too old to shoot one. Anyhow, that's what Captain Poscob said."

"My Lord, is that old put still hangin' round?"

"He just come in last night, to raise recruits. He says they're tryin' to get 'em together another army down yonder." The blacksmith inclined his rifle to the South. "Well, him and me had a couple of drinks and he got talkin', talkin' powerfully, and the upshot was I told him I'd join his cussed army if he'd give me time to arrange my affairs. Well," he slapped the canvas case, "this here's my affairs."

"I bet that windy scoundrel was drunk," said Johnny. "They won't take a man your age," he added enviously.

"He was sober this morning, son; more than sober; and he said it again. They'll take anybody."

"Anybody?"

"Anybody."

Johnny seized the blacksmith's arm. "Come on," he said, "where is he now?"

Tramping the pine forest's endless miles with his enlistment papers in his pocket, Johnny Fraser's chief thought was whether those enlistment papers

made out in Captain Poscob's gin-palsied hand, would hold good, whether
he would be accepted when he got to Charlotte. So great had been his
doubt on that score, so great his repugnance to another farewell which, like
the last, should lead to nothing, that he had slipped away from home secretly, leaving only a note on the workbench of his mother's loom.

At first the walking had been hard for him; he made but six or seven miles
each day, but now every evening saw him twenty miles nearer the rendez-
vous. The country changed, hardwood groves lay among the pines, the
upland road was stiff, red clay. At night he slept in friendly, lonely cabins
where only women, boys and old men now remained to wring a living from
the encroaching forest. Their thoughts were everywhere the same—no hope
—and no surrender. They were not profound political philosophers, those
solitary hillside people, but what thoughts they had were clear and to the
point. They had seen the mutilated survivors of the British massacre at the
Waxhaws, they had seen the crazed and ravaged prisoners exchanged out of
the British hulks at Charleston. The British would never own that country
while there was a pine tree standing and a man or woman to fire from its
cover.

On the fifteenth day his road turned into another road, wider, rutted by
guns and heavy wagons; ahead of him across cleared fields a log town
straggled along a ridge. The slope seemed crowded with smouldering haystacks. As Johnny climbed the gentle grade, he saw that the smoke was the
smoke of camp fires and the haystacks were rows of weather-beaten huts.
This was the army.

He reached the old rail fence along the road which marked the limits of
the camp. Gaunt men in rags and blankets came to the rails and watched
him pass.

"Ain't he fat?" they said.

"He must have been in the army to get fat like that."

"He ain't in the army; he's got on a pair of pants."

"Them pants is broadcloth, too. Mebbe he's in Congress."

"Huzzah for Congress!" they shouted, "and our eighteen months' back
pay!"

The sentry before the log headquarters was the first man Johnny saw with a whole suit of clothes and they, to judge by their fit, had been loaned for the day by his battalion. His rifle was clean, however, and he brought it to port arms as smartly as a grenadier. He passed Johnny into an orderly room where a long-jawed sergeant was playing solitaire on a wooden table. The sergeant took Johnny's papers without looking at him and made a laborious entry in a book.

"Seen service?" he said indifferently. Johnny proudly presented the passport signed by John Paul Jones. The sergeant made a further entry with equal indifference.

"Orderly!" he called. A raw, downy-faced youth peered in at the door; the sergeant jerked a thumb toward Johnny.

"First battalion, North Carolina." He picked up the greasy deck of cards and resumed his solitaire.

The orderly led Johnny Fraser to a wooden hut at the end of the first regimental street and pushed in the door. "Recruit!" he piped. Stooping his head, Johnny passed through the narrow doorway. By the light of a small fire in the clay-smeared fireplace, he began to make out the objects in the room. A double tier of bunks filled with pine straw ran around the walls. Three men sat on a log before the fire. One, tall, wearing a buckskin shirt, his shaggy hair falling across his high cheek-bones, held above the blaze a pannikin lashed to a stick; the other two, their heads stuck through holes in blankets, were absorbed in rubbing an ear of corn against a canteen-cup with nail holes punched in it to form a grater. Johnny waited. "The orderly told me to come in hyer," he said at last. The smaller of the blanket-clad figures looked up; his pinched face concentrated on Johnny, or rather on his clothing. He nudged the man beside him.

"Hyer's luck," he said, "hyer's the fellow that come up the road."

"Why, so it is," the other said. He scratched his stubble beard and nodded brightly. "Brother," he said to Johnny, "this hyer's Brotherhood Hall; everything any man has in this hut we shares alike." He held up a cup half filled with grated corn.

"Sit you down, son, and you'll get some fire cake."

The tall shaggy man with the pannikin cleared his throat forebodingly. "And on the other hand, Bill," he said, "we get his clothes."

# CHAPTER XLVI

THE MONTH which followed brought no change except that the air turned colder, the nights came sooner, carried a sharper hint of coming winter. Disconsolate, they hugged their fire or stared across the fields of scarlet clay and tawny broom-straw to the cold blue hills beyond. Men so naked, so listless as they, thought Johnny, could not stand much; the first hard freeze would fix them forever where they stood. If that were so, they had not long to wait; December was here.

Up the company street he saw the men gathering by the rail fence to watch a stranger pass. He joined them. A cold white sun foreboded snow, the distant hills looked blue and hard. Hoofs rang on the red, frost-crusted road. In column of fours a troop of dragoons was posting up the valley. By Zooks, they were something like soldiers: nodding plumes curled above their brass helmets, their polished scabbards swung; in the lead, a short, powerful man, in buff and blue, leaned forward on his mud-caked horse and kicked it eagerly along.

As he passed along the old rail fence, he looked at the men's rags and frowned; he looked at their faces and smiled. Pulling up at the whipping-post before headquarters, he swung down, chafed his gloves together smartly, strode in the door.

In all Johnny Fraser's life of adventure there had been no change greater than that between the first month he spent in camp and the month which followed it. The door of headquarters had no sooner closed on the short, broad general in buff and blue than things began to happen. Long wagon trains came rolling from the north, strings of horses on rope halters followed, and a drove of cattle. The crowd along the fence cheered the lowing herd to the last heifer. "Meat!" they shouted and danced grotesquely in their blankets. Rifles were issued, woolen caps, shoes, hunting shirts; they began to look like something, now, when they fell in for drill. Early and late they paraded under arms; they performed the manual by the hour, did foot drill by the month, it seemed, and practice marches by the year.

One night they heard the ring of marching columns on the frozen ground; they woke next morning to see the long straight tent-rows of the Continentals.

"It looks mighty bad," Bill confided to Johnny as he stroked his new-shaved chin. "That Delaware regiment is the one they call the Blue Hen's Chickens."

"That's a curious name," said Johnny.

"The Blue Hen," Bill went on, "bein' the name of a game bird. They tell me they send them boys 'round wherever they's liable to be a fight."

"Well," said Johnny, "I'd as soon be killed fightn' as drillin'."

Bill gazed wistfully down at the herd of stock beyond the horse lines.

"I know," he said, "but after a fellow's et fire-cake for a year, he kind o' despises to have anything come between him and them nice fat steers."

Before Christmas they left the fat beeves behind them and marched away. Standing at ease along the road, Johnny's company taunted the main column with pleasant indecencies as they swung by and disappeared among the rolling hills to the East. Their own force, a thousand strong, wheeled into column and took the straight road to South Carolina. The leather caps of Colonel William Washington's light horse showed at their head; then came the blue coats of Maryland Continentals; then the tan shirts of North Carolina militia; the scarlet facings of the Virginians were in the rear.

At the first halt the blacksmith from Blue's Crossing hobbled back from the leading company. "Look here, son," he said to Johnny, "I joined with the idea that this was to be a shootin' war; if it's to be a walkin' war, I'm goin' home." A big-boned hand fell on the blacksmith's shoulder, the long brown face, stern but fatherly and infinitely worn, of Daniel Morgan, their commander, peered down at him.

"Listen, brother," he said. "I'll make a trade with you. You do all the marching they is to be done and I'll guarantee you get all the shootin' they is to be done." A ghost of a smile just touched his tired mouth and vanished. "You'd better take my offer," he said. "Because you ain't a-goin' home." The blacksmith made an attempt at a salute.

"All right, Captain," he said, and hobbled back to his company.

The blacksmith did not have long to wait; they passed the South Carolina line, turned westerly, and crossing a broad river, camped on a hill. Below them stretched wide meadows, sparsely scattered with pine trees; behind, the distant river circled half around them. They waited while the cavalry patrols clinked off through the forest.

The drums roused them in the chill January dawn; far off to the southward they heard a faint, clear note.

"Them's the Kent bugles," the veterans said. "Here comes the British!" They swallowed their tea and biscuit, put out their fires and fell in. Wheeling into column, the North Carolina brigade marched down to the lower shoulder of the hill. They wheeled again and halted, their long front stretching clear across the slope. Ahead of them a line of buckskin skirmishers in single file moved out, took cover behind scattered trees and lay down in the grass. To their rear, up the hill, stood the straight, stiff ranks of the dark blue Continentals.

Johnny's company, standing at ease in the chill dawn, fingered their rifles and whispered. Their Captain, a veteran of the Carolina Line with a hawklike peak to his high shoulders and sabre-cut across his hawklike face, advanced to the center of the company and held up his hand. The men fell silent; he struggled for utterance, coughed, blew his nose and blushed till his weather-beaten, hollow cheeks turned crimson.

"Well, boys!" he mumbled huskily, "here we are!" He beamed on them with ironic benignity. His voice gained confidence. "They's a river behind us with picquets along the bank to shoot the man that tries to cross it and the British is about to come at us in front. Tarleton is leadin' 'em; he killed all the men that surrendered to him at the Waxhaws——" he paused, the broad scar on his face crinkled in an ugly, friendly grin—"So let every man do his duty!" The men looked at the ground awkwardly and chuckled. The Captain's voice turned sharp. "Two volleys," he said, "and then re-form behind the Continentals." He hesitated, pulled bashfully at his bony fingers. "Boys," he said, "I've fought the British four times and never really whipped 'em. Stick by me!" There was a moment's pause.

"Bill!" said a voice from the rear rank. "The Cap'n means you!" The tension broke in a burst of laughter.

Patches of scarlet glinted through the distant pines. English bugles sounded close at hand, the head of the scarlet column came in view. They marched straight on past the American front, their white breeches flashed rhythmically, their bayonets winked in unison; their precision was unreal, incredible; it was hard for Johnny to think of them as men, their column was a unit, a monstrous toy, red and white and shining, which was being drawn across the scene.

In the cold still air he could hear the words of command passing down their line; the column wheeled together, together their pipe-clayed cross belts flashed in view; their steady-moving legs showed white, then dark, white—dark, in the wan winter sunlight. Behind them Johnny saw two brass cannon gallop to a gentle rise, wheel smartly and unlimber. He saw the green jackets of Tarleton's dragoons.

Now they had come so close that Johnny could make out the epauletted company officers marching in front of the rigid scarlet wall.

"Shoot for the epaulette-men when I give the word!" the Captain called out. "But don't any man fire till I do!"

Ahead of them, the skirmish line, crouching low behind their trees, opened a scattering fire on the enemy. A few gaps showed in the red line, closed up again. The British regiments came on. To right and left the skirmishers ran for cover.

"Ready the North Carolina Brigade!" he heard an officer shout behind them. "Take aim!" the Captain said. Johnny Fraser saw a small toy figure of an epaulette-man through his sights. "Now fire!" A crash and a cloud of smoke enveloped him. Through the haze he saw long, broken fragments of the red line coming on. "Load your pieces, you scoundrels!" the Captain cried. "Now take aim!" Their volley crashed again. The clearing smoke showed scarlet fragments, fragments so close that Johnny could see the faces of the soldiers, pale and haggard as they halted wavering in the blast, or, turning to run, stumbled over the crimson windrows on the ground. The British were stopped; not a man moved forward. Yes, there was one; one little epaulette-man, a slender, pink-faced baby, carrying his big sword as stiffly as on parade, marched steadily up the hill.

Galloping up to the wavering line, a British field officer pointed him out with his gold-laced hat.

"Now then, Seventy-first!" Johnny could hear his voice, "support the little gentleman!"

"Come on, North Carolina!" his Captain shouted. "One more volley!" They fired hastily, broke ranks and fell back under cover of the smoke.

Retreating around the flank of the Continentals, Johnny stopped to look behind him; the red line, newly formed, came on again. He ran his eye along it. The little gentleman was gone.

Below him, to the rear, the hunting shirts were falling in again. He joined them; in column they marched off to the right flank and halted. He saw the British reserves running at the double quick; the blue line and the red were firing at close range; a troop of cavalry passed him, swinging their sabres and cheering.

"Charge!" the word came back; the hunting shirts were running down hill.

They had no bayonets, but they fired from the hip as they hit the British flank, then clubbed their rifles. A red-faced man with staring eyes thrust a long bayonet at Johnny, Johnny cracked the rifle butt against his mouth and felt the bones cave in: still staring at him, the man slid gently down between his knees.

Now his same old arm was bleeding again; the pain, the blood, the smoke, the stench of sweating men were sickening him. He raised his face to the sky for air; above the crowding heads he saw the troop of cavalry, he heard their hoofs and saw their long sabres thrusting and hacking through the mélee. Then suddenly, a forest of hands was raised high in air; down the long line, a thousand British voices called for quarter.

# CHAPTER XLVII

**B**ACK HOME again in the old square house, his arm strapped by a stirrup leather to his side, Johnny Fraser used to wonder how he got there; how he had managed to tramp for uncounted days the long unending forest miles with that aching, dangling thing dragging at his side, until at last, unshaven, gray-faced, he had pushed in the oak door and sat down abruptly with a white smile. "I reckon I'm home for good, now," he had muttered wearily, resting his head against his mother's arm. His father's great hand had fallen lightly on his knee and lain there, lightly trembling.

He sat helpless by the fire during the dark, bleak February days. The pain ebbed slowly from his arm and left it cold and lifeless; not even the patient licking of old Grizzly Gray could warm his fingers. Still he should be well content, he told himself; he had helped to beat the British once on sea and once on land and had come off with his life. A few years ago he would have been happy to lie back and enjoy the admiration due a wounded patriot. But now his restless, straining thoughts were with the Hunting

Shirts who, having struck their blow, retreated northward over frozen roads before the main army of Cornwallis. Each morning he sent Scipio to Blue's Crossing for news. Each sleepless night he tramped the floor, marching in spirit with the hurrying, hard-pressed column.

Little by little the news drifted in. Now the Hunting Shirts had rejoined Greene's Army, now the whole force, still retreating, had gained Virginia, leaving a flooded river as a barrier behind them; now, reinforced, they were marching back again to fight. Then all news ceased.

"You oughtn't to tramp so, son," his mother said. "You'll wear yourself down."

"I can't help it. They's going to be a battle, a big main battle. If we're whipped, we'll never get over it. We're near about played out." He stood still. "It preys on my mind."

She reached up a hand to him from her weaving bench. "I know," she said, "and they's something else preys on it, too." He withdrew his hand awkwardly and fell to tramping again.

March brought a warm day of the first false spring. Wrapped in a patch-work counterpane, Johnny Fraser sat on the sunlit porch. Mocking-birds shook out their feathers and tried a note or two, the hard-eyed chickens searched the sand. Down in the branch a cock-turkey raised his deep-toned, bubbling challenge.

A bent old woman's figure crept up the lane. It was Mrs. Merrillee. Johnny Fraser's hand closed tightly on the arm of his chair.

"Well," she said in her harsh voice, planting herself before him, "looks like they'd fixed you this time."

"Yes'm," Johnny answered with a grin. "It sure looks like they did. I reckon you're come to see my mother."

"Set still," she said. "I come to see you."

She sat down on a joint stool, gazed awkwardly across the fields and woods, cracked her worn fingers. "Winter's about gone out, I expect," she said, "I heard a tree toad."

"Yes, ma'am," Johnny agreed. "I saw the wild geese flying North. How's things out your way?"

"Oh, we makes out to get along," she answered lifelessly.

"How—how's Sally?"

"Middlin'."

"I wish I could help you all out," said Johnny. "It must be mighty hard with Joe in the army—and Mr. Merrillee——"

"Mr. Merrillee!" her sharp voice rent her. "Whatever did Mr. Merrillee do but set in the house writin' Greek and leave me and Joe to get in the crops?" Her voice trembled.

"You oughtn't to talk like that," cried Johnny softly. "He was a mighty brave officer from what I hear."

"Oh, he was brave," she answered bitterly. "But wher' was his sense, tell me that, boy? Else how come him to be killed?" She looked away again into the heart of the dark pine forest. "They was a stone house in the battle," she went on in a toneless murmur, "full of British. It was stout. The only thing to do was to wait for the big guns to come up and bust it down. But James Merrillee, he wouldn't wait; he grabbed a rifle from a soldier and he hollered out some Latin motto and he ran for the house. They was twenty bullets in him before he reached the door." Two great tears rolled down her leathery cheeks. "He was a fool!" she cried out, "a fool! And now—he's gone!" She bent her weary old head between her knees.

"Oh, my, oh, my, I certainly am sorry!" Johnny murmured unhappily.

Mrs. Merrillee straightened up and gazed at him sharply. "Don't you fool with Sally," she said. "That's what I come to say."

She fixed him with her eyes. "What do you intend towards my gal?"

"She knows," he whispered.

"She knows!" Her voice was grim. "She knows! Why would I come here if she knows? She's had no word from you since last she saw you. She's said no word to me but I read her face."

"What? Why I thought—why she cried when I—" his voice trailed off lamely.

"I've not a notion of what passed between you. But whatever it was I reckon yo're a fool." She eyed him with steady scorn.

"They's lots of things that makes a woman cry." She stood up. "And if ever you say what I've told you, I'll have my Joe to kill you." Turning abruptly, she trudged down the lane.

"Mrs. Merrillee!" Johnny called. "Wait! I'll get Scipio to yoke up the ox." She shook her head without a look behind, buried it in her crooked hands and stumbled on.

The sun sank flamingly behind the tattered pines, early dusk was falling, a sharp earth-creeping evening chill stole out from the forest. Still Johnny Fraser sat there, gazing into the cold blue shadows, barred with strips of waning sunlight. Old, forgotten glimpses crowded back to him. He saw the blue-clad figure by the spinning wheel. He saw the red cloak wave above the shining colt. Gray eyes, mocking, friendly, peeped at him over a beaver tippet. Brown hair blew recklessly across a sun-tanned, softly smiling face. A strong, light hand touched his. He felt his warm blood leap to meet it, surge through him, tingle in the finger tips of his numb, helpless arm. His heart grew large and mighty. By Zooks, he told himself, maybe he would amount to something after all.

Squire Fraser came up the road. "Daft," he observed laconically. "Get ye inside. Caroline!" he shouted. "What dae ye mean by letting this oaf sit i' the night air?" He stamped through the door and smacked his great hands together angrily.

Johnny Fraser's mother did not answer. She smiled at Johnny.

"Is there any news at the settlement, Dadder?" asked Johnny, with a grin.

John Fraser pulled up short. "Oh, aye. They've fought the battle." He paused. "The British say they won," he went on slowly. "But the man says they're in full retreat. He says they've left half their strength on the field."

"Did the man know, do you reckon, Dadder?"

"I think he did, son. He was bearing dispatches."

Johnny Fraser reflected. "By Zooks!" he said. "Half their people. They'll never make a showing in the South again."

"Ye're right, lad. I think it means the end—the end of the foolishness."

Johnny laid a hand on his mother's arm. "Hush, Mother. You wouldn't call it foolishness, Dadder, if you had seen the way our troops can fight, and march, and starve."

John Fraser lit his big pipe. "Oh, aye, my lad," he answered slowly. "I have seen troops do all of that in my time. But just ye bide a while. A war," he went on between puffs, "brings out the best o' a man for an hour and the worst o' him for the rest of his life. When the war is over the lads that fought in it will be weary." He laid a kindly hand on Johnny's shoulder. "As well they may be. And that's the time that our radicals and windbags and scoundrels that have been in hiding will come out and take charge i' the name o' Liberty. The men that launched this country on a flood of oratory will be the ones tae scuttle her in a sea of corruption."

"Don't you mind your father," said Mrs. Fraser. Her eyes were bright, her cheeks showed spots of crimson. "He used to say we couldn't win. I reckon he's wrong again."

How soon would he be strong enough to walk? To walk as far as the Merrillees'? Two more days maybe. He practised every hour. And when by evening he was clean played out he sat down on the porch in the last small patch of winter sun, thinking the air would strengthen him.

A tall man in buckskin was swinging up the main road. His long rifle towered above his coonskin cap, his moccasins stole swiftly over the melting ruts, his powder-horn and fringed pouch tapped softly at his side. "Hi, friend!" Johnny Fraser called. "Will you rest a while?"

The man lowered the rifle to the ground and leaned his scrubby chin on the muzzle. "Howdy, brother," he said. "I'd like to, but I can't." He spat professionally into the bushes. "I'm one of Morgan's scouts. The Army's coming." He swung his rifle to his shoulder and strode on.

Down by the ford more coonskin caps appeared. In two long files they climbed the gentle rise. Tall men's knees bent springily to their easy, low-footed strides, their tall black rifle barrels swayed, the silver front sights twinkled high in air. Some wore buck shirts, the rest wore only leggings. Their gaunt, weather-blackened shoulders showed streaks of callous where thongs of pouch and powder-horn had rubbed. They slipped by noiselessly with shy, enigmatic smiles.

Johnny Fraser stood up. His knees had turned to water; he did not know if he could walk down to the road where they were passing. Somehow it might be best simply to sit there on the porch, alone and unobserved, and watch those lean, brown mountain faces climb from the shadows into the light of the sinking sun. He sat down again.

The hoofs of horses splashed and clicked in the water of the ford. He saw the black-plumed helmets of Lee's Dragoons. Their sabres clinked slowly, their beaten horses' heads hung low. But the men themselves, light, wiry, hard-bitten, sat straight in their saddles, smoking and whistling, exchanging succinct indecencies in the rakish manner of the Light Horse. They may have noticed Johnny watching them, for they cocked their helmets over their eyes and began to whistle the Huron March. The shrill staccato passed back through the squadrons and grew in volume till the horses raised their heavy heads and pricked up ears. Long after the dull "clop-clopping" of their hoofs had been lost to hearing over the hill, the piping chorus came back on the still air, high-pitched, assertive, impudent.

The road resounded to the sound of marching boots. Here came the columns. Down to the ford and round the turn short muskets bobbed, sergeants' halberds caught the light, cased standards swayed aloft. The long blue lines of the Maryland Continentals were passing. Their naked feet peeped through their clumping shoes, red clay caked their black gaiters, but their muskets and side-arms shone, their drawn faces were clean-shaven, their queues were freshly powdered. Bent forward beneath their creaking knapsacks, they trudged with a firm, stout step, the marching step of veterans. Like their gait, their faces were dogged and stolid. It was, however, mere professional stolidity which husbanded with patience and unshakeable acumen all activity of mind and body until the moment they should be needed. That moment, as Johnny knew, would see the set faces kindle, the plodding column wheel into line and charge with the long stride of athletes and a high, heart-shivering cheer. But now their endless ranks merely trudged, their musket barrels and cockades nodded heavily, their bayonet scabbards slapped their thighs, their canteens rocked against their buttocks. As they climbed the distant rise they looked, beneath their heavy field equipment, like curious beetles crawling onward in an obscure, inexorable migration.

Four young drummer boys toiled in the rear of the last regiment.

Strapped high on their thin shoulders, their big, deep drums seemed burdens as much too great for their youthfulness as the war itself. But they, too, like the troops, were driven forward by a force still greater than that which pressed them down.

A gap in the marching files showed the General and his officers. Their swaying blue cloaks hung down over their horses. Riding in silence, they ranged the countryside with keen, tired eyes. The General, the same compact Nathaniel Greene who had made them into an army, sat square and solid on his horse. His bridle reins hung in the crook of his elbow, his two big hands held out a map before him. He moved on out of sight without raising his eyes.

On creaking axles a meagre train of ammunition wagons followed. The teamsters, hands in lap, feet cocked up on brakes, lurched high aloft. Drag chains clinked and buckets swung beneath the running-gear. Their spare wheels showed at the tailgates as they passed.

Now the road was filled with linen hunting-shirts, with caps of wool and muskrat and beaver, and with old cocked hats. In uneven, close-locked ranks the militia pounded the frozen clay. Guns of all makes and sizes swayed above their heads: carbines, fowling-pieces, captured Tower muskets, and here and there, over-topping all the rest, the frontier rifle. At their belts swung home-made bayonets of hammered saw-blades or long-handled tomahawks. The legs below the hunting-shirts were clad in linen trousers and sea-boots, in deerskin leggings and moccasins, in the broad-cloth breeches and spun-yarn stockings of a farmer's Sunday best. The motley legs, however, all swung together. The ripple of their movement ran down the line like the back of a serpent crawling. The Regulars had not kept time. Each man of them had used the step best suited to himself. But these Militia seemed to feel the need of rhythm. Perhaps they hoped that its compelling bond would somehow take the place of training, would help, at least, to weld them into one. Perhaps in their long retreat over icy blood-stained roads and their long advance to victory, they had learned that only rhythm could carry them through endless months of marching so far beyond their powers. Even now they seemed to draw their strength, not from themselves, but it. Unseeing, silent, they swept by in the trance of their momentum. On, on they came without end, without pause. The iteration of their footfalls, bluntly pounding all together, mounted in volume, filled the air until the opalescent dome, the fading daylight, seemed to throb. The earth was trembling to their inexorable monotone.

The last sunlight fell across their faces, faces rigid yet composed, with eyes calm, shrewd, sardonic, and mouths bitter and mocking yet touched with childish eagerness. They bore the stamp of weary patience, these endless files of marchers, beneath which lurked a hint of careless impudence and harsh, dry mirth. Old men swung by with dreaming eyes of infants; young boys with close, tight mouths of certitude. With hard self-reliance, with incredibly fantastic dreams, they seemed to move toward some assured, uncomprehended destiny.

Just as the sun sank down the column ended, the last ranks passed, wound up the hill and disappeared from sight. Still the rhythm of their marching floated back through the twilight with a soft, insistent, sifting sound.

On padding moccasins the rear guard stole through the dusk. The white-ringed coon tails of their caps swung behind, their rifle barrels swung above, as they, too, climbed the hill.

A solitary figure followed them, a tall, half-naked mountain man. His lean tawny breast, his beaded leggings, his cheek bones shone through the shadows. He moved without a sound.

Johnny Fraser was stumbling down the lane. But before he reached the road, the man passed by and strode on up the rise. He stopped, forlorn in the shadows. This army that for years had marched without him was now at last perhaps his own. He should have stood up as they passed and raised a cheer. He should have been in time to greet this man. With straining eyes he followed him up the hill, he saw him pause on the crest and look behind. Perhaps the man could see him. He raised his stiff arm in the Indian salutation. A faint halloo, thin, sharp and high, came back on the wind. The distant figure lifted a long black rifle against the sunset sky.

Fic
Boy    Boyd, James

DRUMS

Date Due

|  |  |  |  |
|---|---|---|---|
|  |  |  |  |
|  |  |  |  |
|  |  |  |  |
|  |  |  |  |
|  |  |  |  |
|  |  |  |  |
|  |  |  |  |
|  |  |  |  |
|  |  |  |  |
|  |  |  |  |
|  |  |  |  |